About the Author

PETER CORRIS was born in Stanwell, Victoria, in 1942. He has worked as a lecturer and researcher in history, as well as a freelance writer and journalist, specialising in sports writing. The author of eleven novels about Sydney-based private eye Cliff Hardy, he has also written six other thrillers, a social history of prizefighting in Australia, quiz books, and radio and television scripts. *The Gulliver Fortune* is his first historical novel.

THE GULLIVER FORTUNE

Peter Corris

BANTAM BOOKS
SYDNEY • AUCKLAND • TORONTO • NEW YORK • LONDON

THE GULLIVER FORTUNE

A BANTAM BOOK

Printing History

First published 1989

This edition published 1990

Copyright© Peter Corris 1989

All rights reserved. No part of this publication may be stored in a retrieval system, or transmitted in any form or by any means, electronic, mechanical, photocopying or otherwise, without the prior permission of the publishers.

National Library of Australia
Cataloguing-in-Publication entry
    Corris, Peter 1942-
    The Gulliver Fortune
    ISBN 1 86359 005 6.
    I. Title.
A823'3

Bantam Books are published in Australia by Transworld Publishers (Australia) Pty Limited, 15-25 Helles Avenue, Moorebank NSW 2170 and in New Zealand by Transworld Publishers (NZ) Limited, Cnr Moselle and Waipareira Avenues, Henderson, Auckland.

Cover illustration by Mike Worrall
Cover design by Lizard-esque

Printed by Australian Print Group, Maryborough, Vic.

*For Robert and Elizabeth Corris
and Robert and Beatrice Kennedy
—my immigrant grandparents*

Acknowledgments

The author wishes to thank two men whose names he does not know—the visitor who told him the story of the emigrant family with thirteen members and the art expert who explained the difference between an unknown and a lost masterpiece.

Thanks also to Heather Falkner and to Lisa Baker, Ghersey Downie, Geoffrey Dutton, Michael Fitzjames, Daphne Gollan, Matthew Kelly, Jacqueline Kent, Stephen Scheding, Rafael Viscarra.

Contents

Prologue: The Cromwells & The Gullivers	1
Jack, Stephen, Georgia	25
Carl, Mikhail	117
Susannah, Margot	181
Edward, Juan	235
Leo, Kobi	291
'Harwich Seascape'	349
Epilogue	399

PROLOGUE
The Cromwells
&
The Gullivers

Tunbridge Wells, October 1835

John Gulliver, champion of all England, stared at his opponent through the curtain of blood and sweat that dripped from his lacerated forehead. *Gettin' too old for this game, I am,* he thought. *But surely the bastard can't come up for another round, can he?* The timekeeper shouted the dread word and Gulliver saw 'Jewboy' Jack Elias lever himself from his second's knee. The two men met in the centre of the roped square where the grass had been scraped away by their feet and the earth turned to mud by the water the seconds splashed over their bodies and their sweat and blood, shed in more than two hours' savage fighting.

Gulliver lashed out a right which Elias evaded. He was smaller and quicker than Gulliver. He crashed his left into the champion's ribs and felt the shock run up his arms. *Christ, the man's got bones like an ox,* Elias thought.

They stood and swapped punches for ten minutes, Elias landing more cleanly, but tiring as he fought to stay clear of Gulliver's arms. If the champion got him in a hug it would be the end of him. Gulliver, too, was tired. It was time to go down for a rest but the manoeuvre had to be done skilfully. If he fell without Elias landing a punch to cause the fall, he could lose on a foul. If he let the Jew land too heavily, he might never get up.

Elias' long left had no sting in it but it landed squarely on Gulliver's nose and brought blood.

"Claret!" came the shout from the members of the Fancy pushing and shoving at the ringside. Half of them were drunk and all were uneasy about their money. The fight could go either way. As he slid to the ground, John Gulliver's eyes swept across the crowd and he saw his brother, Tom, steal a watchchain from the brocaded vest of the youngest son of the Duke of Buckinghamshire.

Tom Gulliver, 'Tom the Gypsy' as he was known for his swarthy looks and devious ways, slipped through the crowd to his brother's corner. He squeezed out the vinegar-soaked sponge and handed it to his brother's second.

"Damn your eyes, Tom," Gulliver groaned. "I saw you lift that ticker. What in hell's bloody name am I goin' to do with 'ee?"

Tom the Gypsy grinned. "You'll take care 'a me, Jack, lad. You always have."

When time was called Gulliver strode to the centre of the ring. He brushed aside Elias' left lead and crashed a heavy right to the smaller man's jaw. Elias reeled back, milling, his hands instinctively flicking jabs into the air in front of him.

Gulliver walked through the punches as if they were fleabites. He smashed Elias' left ear to pulp with a deadly hook and his next punch, an uppercut, delivered from a crouch and with the full weight of his uncoiling body behind it, lifted him from his feet and dumped him senseless onto the muddy earth. John Gulliver was still the champion of England, and Tom the Gypsy was still his brother.

The brothers met later in the Dog & Bear, a sporting tavern, as was their custom after one of John Gulliver's fights.

The champion drained his second pint of ale. "I'm quittin' the ring, Tom."

"Wise," Tom the Gypsy said. He wiped beer froth from his face and confirmed his brother's impression that some of his swarthiness was due to dirt. Tom rubbed the now-dirty hand down his vest. "The Jewboy almost had you."

"And the runners'll have *you* one day. Mark my words."

"Not I. And what would it matter if they did catch me and turn me off? I've no one in the world but you. I'm not the marrying sort like yourself, Jack."

John Gulliver, married for twenty years with a large brood, the exact number of whom he was never quite positive about, smiled and laid a golden guinea on the bench. "See that you don't marry, Tom, for the poor woman'd lead a dog's life from the day she said yes."

"She'd have some fun though, along the way."

John looked at his brother indulgently. Tom had stolen and lied from the moment he could move his fingers and tongue. His only talent was painting and even that had got him into trouble, with his scandalous caricatures of prominent persons and copying of Old Masters, complete with signature. But he was never solemn and was no hypocrite. Tom cheered him up, and sobersides John loved him for it. He slid the guinea across. "Aye, Tom me lad, happen she would."

London, June 1986

Montague Cromwell gently applied the brakes and his Jaguar stopped a few centimetres short of the brick wall at the end of his garage. He was proud of never having touched the wall. He got out of the car, set the thief-proof device and unlocked the door that would admit him directly to his house. The house was in Chelsea and worth a lot of money, more every day. He took another look back at the car and remembered the time when his Jaguar, not this one, an earlier model, had touched the wall with some force. His son Ben had been the driver.

Montague Cromwell sighed. *Will he do it?* he thought. *Will I be able to get the young bugger to do something useful?* He went down the passage past the kitchen and dining room and one of the guest rooms to his den. He needed a drink and a cigarette. He never smoked in his car and he could hardly drink while driving through the London evening traffic, although God knew he often felt like it. He was five feet ten inches tall and bulky; his prosperity was displayed by his waistline. In his well-cut lightweight suit he looked solid rather than fat. He liked food and drink and money; he didn't always like his son.

"Hullo, Dad," Ben Cromwell said as his father came through the door. "Get you a whisky?"

"Thanks," the elder Cromwell said, although he didn't see why he should have to thank anyone for pouring him his own whisky. "You shouldn't be drinking."

Ben poured a large measure into a stemmed glass and added a few drops of water. He drank from his own glass before passing his father's drink across. Ben was an inch taller than his father; he shared certain movements and expressions with him, but there the similarity ended. He was slim with thick dark hair. His father's hair was a thin, grey thatch and his skin was pale and blotchy. Ben had favoured his mother; he had an olive complexion and dark eyes. He was wearing faded jeans, espadrilles and an old, collarless business shirt. The back of the shirt's long tail was tucked in but the front was hanging out over the jeans like an apron. There were dirty marks on it which indicated that Ben had used it to wipe his hands.

"You've got that a bit wrong, Dad," Ben said. "I can't drink beer or sweet things. Scotch's all right. Cheers."

Montague Cromwell grunted; he sank into a leather armchair and drank. Ben leaned against the small teak-veneered bar. His father looked at him, thinking that he appeared to have aged considerably since he graduated with first-class honours in History from London University. A proud day for his mother. She'd come over from France for the occasion, the first time Montague had seen her since their divorce ten years before. Then Ben had gone to Sandhurst, full of hope and promise. He'd had an outstanding first year before being diagnosed as mildly diabetic. End of Sandhurst, end of promise.

Since then Ben had taken enthusiastically to drink. He started and quickly abandoned a PhD thesis. He secured work as a private tutor but had difficulty turning up in time for the lessons and keeping his hands off various things he found lying around in the affluent houses. Montague believed Ben for a time when he told him he was dabbling in the antique market. He arranged the sale of a few items and they made money. Then Montague got a scare: a snuffbox Ben claimed to have bought in the Portobello Road was recognized by its owner—the father of one of Ben's pupils. Restitution cost Montague money and Ben had lost that tutoring post and several others. Ben Cromwell was twenty-five and looked thirty.

"Got a job for you," Montague said. He repressed his

irritation at being given his whisky in a stemmed glass. He liked it from the squat Swedish glasses he'd paid a fortune for. But he didn't want to get off on the wrong foot. "Interesting job. Up your street. Good money and there could be a bit of travel in it."

Ben grinned and finished his drink, his third in an hour. "What's in it for you?"

"Jesus, Ben! Is it quite impossible for you to be a bit pleasant?" Montague tossed off his whisky, heaved himself out of the chair and got another drink in a Swedish glass.

Whisky affected Ben Cromwell in erratic ways, which was one of the reasons he liked it. Under its influence his mood could change abruptly, without warning; he found the changes interesting. Just now, aggression gave way to a rare surge of affection for his shrewd, energetic, successful father. "Sorry, Dad. Didn't mean to be a shit."

"The diabetes troubling you?"

"No, not a bit. The quack's trying to control it by diet for the moment. It'll be a matter of taking some pills at the worst." Mention of diabetes sometimes dropped Ben into a bitter mood where he felt the army's rejection like a leg iron, but not now. The whisky helped. "A job. What sort of a job?"

"Research."

Ben groaned. "I thought you mentioned money. There's no money in research. What sort of research?"

Montague found this response very hopeful. Ben often communicated in grunts and shakings of the head recently. For him to follow a reaction with a question was very positive. He offered his cigarettes to Ben, who refused. He'd given up smoking when he'd entered Sandhurst and lost the urge. "Tell you what I'll do," Montague said, lighting up. "I'll take you out for a meal and tell you about it. You'll be interested, I guarantee."

Ben recognised what he called 'the selling note' in his father's voice, one of the things that had made him a successful art dealer, among other things. He nodded. "Okay."

"Ring up Jerry. Ask her along. My treat."

* * *

The Soho restaurant was Monty Cromwell's discovery. That was how he was known there, as Monty. It was Italian but without the corny checked tablecloths and Chianti bottles. The cooking was southern provincial.

"The real thing," Monty said, twirling pasta.

"It's great," Jerry Gallagher said and Monty, mellowed by the food and wine, beamed. He's been alarmed when Ben had first spoken of Jerry and wondered if his son had gone queer under pressure. ('Gay' was a word he'd had difficulty taking into his fluid and progressive vocabulary.) But Jerry had turned out to be a small, plump redheaded female. Montague found her very acceptable, never more so than now as she pressed Ben to let his father tell his story.

"Might spoil a good meal," Ben said. He'd enjoyed the food and the feeling of virtue derived from eating his pasta with plain sauce and limiting his bread and wine intake.

"Ignore him, Montague." Jerry tapped her plate with her fork. "Just talk. I'll stick my fork into him if he interrupts."

"Can we have a brandy when we finish?" Ben said. "I'm not allowed sweets, you see."

"One," Jerry said. "Go on, Montague."

"It starts with a man named John Gulliver," Montague Cromwell said. "He was . . ."

"Heavyweight champion of England. Bare knuckle." Ben sipped some wine. "Early nineteenth century."

"Right." Montague had known that his son would recognise the name. It was part of his strategy that he should. "Gulliver beat all comers for a few years, retired with the title and made a fortune in coal and on the turf, as they said in those days."

"Racing?" Jerry said.

Montague chewed hastily. "Mmm. He was MP for somewhere."

"Bristol," Ben said.

Montague swallowed. "Mmm, well, they bought the seats then, didn't they? Not so different now. Anyway, Gulliver did very well for himself. Left a fortune, but it had to be divided up amongst a heap of kids. A dozen or more. He'd married twice."

"Terrible," Ben said. "This isn't your way of breaking the news of your upcoming nuptials and my disinheritance, is it Dad?" He turned to Jerry. "The only reason I let the old bastard take me out to dinner is that I want to stay in his good books so I can come into the lolly."

"Ben!" Jerry protested.

"What?" Ben said. "Speaking the truth."

Jerry was accustomed to riding the waves of Ben's moods. She found him infuriating when the alcohol level reached a certain mark, but charming and fun up to that point. Sometimes she could divert him from his trip down the dark, destructive track. "I know you hate your father, like all normal boys," she said. "I was reacting to your saying 'upcoming'. Ugh."

Montague was off in a private world, not listening to the banter. "Don't be a fool, Ben," he said. "Marriage is something to do once and once only. And, as you very well know, I plan to spend all I make. You're welcome to any that's left."

"Don't let him sidetrack you," Jerry said. "He's a master at that."

Montague used the interruption to get some wine down. He'd have liked a cigarette but he knew both Ben and Jerry would protest. "John Gulliver had a brother named Tom. Tom the Gypsy they called him."

Ben frowned. "I thought I knew all the fighting families from that time. The Belchers and Cribbs and so on. I never heard of Tom the Gypsy."

"Shows you don't know everything." Jerry speared some salad and nodded to Montague to go on.

"Seems this Tom the Gypsy was a painter and a good-for-nothing. He didn't make any money at painting or anything else. Probably touched his brother for money a hundred times a year if I know painters. But I gather they were usually on good terms. Tom surprised everybody when he got married, but I don't suppose anyone was surprised when he named his son after his prosperous brother."

The Gulliver Fortune

"Sounds like old John had enough kids to have a few Johns of his own," Ben said.

"There was one, but he died. Tom did the right thing at the right time. John Gulliver died in 1863, but not before Tom showed him the baby. Result was, John left his infant nephew something in his will."

"Got it," Ben said. "A painting. This is where you come in."

"That's right." Montague, cleaning his plate with bread, was gratified to see that Jerry had hung on his every word. She was a pleasant-looking rather than beautiful young woman; her eyes were large and grey and her hair was a rich auburn. She wore quite a lot of makeup because her skin wasn't perfect. She had good teeth and full lips which were slightly parted now as she listened. *Wouldn't make a bad model*, Montague thought. He knew several painters who could do a good job of a nude study. *Might make a thoughtful wedding present, cheap too*.

Ben signalled for the waiter. "I'll have a brandy," he said. "Dad?"

"Tartufo," Montague said.

"What about you, love?"

"I'll stick with the wine," Jerry said. "Coffee later. And I want to hear about the painting."

Ben scoffed. "An unknown Constable, no doubt."

Montague's head jerked up angrily. Asserting himself, he took out a cigarette and lit it. "If you knew anything about my business, Ben, if you'd ever shown any interest at all, you'd know how ignorant a remark that is."

The brandy came and Ben accepted it gratefully. The drink reminded him that his father was paying. "Okay, sorry. Go on."

"As it happens, the painting is a Turner. But an unknown Turner wouldn't be worth much. This is a *known* Turner. Ruskin mentions it in a letter. There are a couple of detailed contemporary descriptions of it. There's even a photograph."

"I've seen some Turners," Jerry said. "They're great. He did millions of drawings, didn't he?"

Montague nodded and blew the smoke away from

her. "More's the pity. Kept the prices down and he gave most of them to the nation anyway. This is an oil painting. 'Harwich Seascape', it's called. It's a beauty."

Ben sipped brandy and stifled a yawn. "Worth a bit even then, I guess. Lucky Tom the Gypsy. I assume he flogged it and drank the proceeds?"

Montague put out his cigarette and took a large spoonful of ice cream. He slurped a little as he spoke. "Tom never saw it. He was hanged for counterfeiting. The story is that his execution helped speed John Gulliver to the grave. Anyway, one thing and another, bloody useless lawyers and a big, interfering family and the bequest to the nephew and, incidentally, to his heirs, it never saw the light of day."

"You mean the painting was lost?" Ben said, hoping to speed the narrative along.

"Not really. It's been hanging in a box room in a lawyer's office in Portsmouth all this time. Plenty of evidence of that. No one knew a damn thing about art, took no notice."

"No one noticed a *Turner?*" Jerry said. "For a hundred years?"

Montague nodded. "Room was a sort of closet, I gather. Scarcely any light. No traffic. Now here's the crux of it. The building was up for demolition and the lawyers had to move. They cleaned up the office and they found the old will. It was a codicil to Gulliver's main will, actually. *And* they found the painting. Some young spark who knew a thing or two got into the act and they started contacting today's Gullivers."

"Of whom there must be quite a few," Jerry said.

"Right. Sure you won't try some of this?" Montague pushed the ice cream across the table.

"Come on, Dad," Ben said. "You've got us in. Get on with it."

Montague finished the dessert quickly and wiped his mouth. "Lots of Gullivers around. All hate each other's insides and they all made the same mistake when the lawyers approached them."

"I bet I know," Ben said. "They all claim descent from old John."

"Right." Montague smiled. "They all produced iron-clad evidence of their direct descent from John Gulliver, MP etc. Tom the Gypsy? Never heard of him."

Ben's interests at university had been military and social history. Montague Cromwell was distantly related to the Great Protector and Ben had been fascinated by genealogy and its application to history—'the rise of the Gentry', analyses of the interests of the members of the Long Parliament, Sir Lewis Namier's work on the eighteenth-century parliamentary families. His aborted doctoral thesis had been a study of the interconnection between military and sporting families. Still acutely disappointed because of his rejection by the army, he'd been in no state to tackle the project and the mechanics of detailed research soon wearied him but he retained the interest. "What about John II," he said. "The son of Tom. What happened to him?"

"No one knows," Montague said.

Jerry finished her wine. "The missing heir."

"Heirs by now, probably," Ben said. "Well, it's hard to say. There could be none or a hundred. It's been a while. Does the will leave the picture to John II and his issue?"

Montague nodded. "Legitimate issue, from memory. John Gulliver apparently was somewhat straitlaced. I have a fancy he took to religion in his declining years."

"Interesting," Ben said.

"I hoped you'd think so."

"What's your involvement, Montague?" Jerry said.

"I can be the agent for the sale of the painting if I can locate an heir to authorise a sale. Lawyer chap I knew fixed it up for me. I've got the inside track."

"Your favourite position." Ben licked the edge of his glass. "What if there's ten of them?"

"I think that's unlikely."

Ben recognised the note in his father's voice. It had been there when Montague had told him about the divorce and when he'd lectured him about his small infringements—Ben's adolescent pilfering of money and cigarettes, for example. Montague's message had always been the same—do what you want to do, but don't get caught. He knew that his father was presenting a version of the story for Jerry's benefit, using her as a sounding board, testing the story for credibility. The reality would come later and would be very different.

"Yes," Jerry persisted. "But what if?"

Montague rested his soft chin, threatening to double, on the heel of his hand. His elbow was on the table. "Turner's painting, 'Landscape at Folkestone', sold for more than seven million pounds," he said softly. Jerry had to lean forward to catch the words. "This one's better and there's inflation to consider. If there's ten descendants of John Gulliver the Younger, they're all millionaires, without a shadow of a doubt."

London, June 1986

Ben and Jerry lay in, on and wrapped around by the sheets. It was a warm night; they were sweaty, still perhaps a little drunk, happy and satisfied. Jerry pushed aside the two pillows she'd used to lift her to the angle she liked for intercourse.

"It's very generous of your father," she said drowsily. "Don't you think?"

"I'll say." Ben's right arm was around Jerry's shoulders; he eased it clear and stared up at a damp patch on the ceiling. He liked Jerry and had a vague sense that their relationship kept him somehow honest. But that was an attitude he was finding increasingly difficult to value. "You mustn't expect too much of him, love. Generosity isn't on the fake coat of arms he cooked up for himself."

Jerry giggled. "What is?"

Ben swallowed with a dry throat. "I forget. It should be 'Seize the main chance'."

"I wish someone'd offer me a hundred quid a day and expenses," Jerry said. She worked in a bookshop in Regent Street, where she read more books than she sold. Jerry had a passionate love of American literature and sent a stream of her own short stories across the Atlantic to American magazines, which rejected them. She dreamed of living in Massachusetts, lunching in Manhattan and contributing to the *New Yorker*.

"It's a short-term contract," Ben said. "The solicitors've only given Dad a few months to sew up the deal, remember."

"Why?"

"A very conservative firm, apparently. Sticklers for propriety. They want all the heirs traced. But they really want to get shot of the matter. Not their sort of thing at all."

"How many months, then?"

"He didn't say."

"You're going to do it, aren't you?"

"Yes. Sure."

"I'll help. It'll be fun—working in the archives and all that. I might get some material for a story."

Ben laughed. The sound, coming suddenly in the darkness, seemed almost cruel to Jerry and she drew away from him a little.

"What?"

"You don't think I'm going to do all the hack work myself, do you? London's crawling with people who'll do that sort of thing for a few pounds a day. I'll hunt up a good one and we can have a good time on the difference. Go to Spain maybe."

"Ben, that's not fair to Montague."

Ben wanted a drink and almost felt like getting up to have one. "What's fair in this bloody world?" he said bitterly. "Is what happened to me fair?"

"No," Jerry said, "it isn't. But . . ."

"Dad's too bloody smug sometimes. Okay, he caught me out about lost paintings. I should've had the wit to see that. But he doesn't know how thick on the ground historical researchers are. Now that the academic game's closed up, they're all over the place. He'll get value for money so it's all right."

"I suppose."

Ben groaned. "I'd better get up and do a bloody sugar test. Won't be a tick." He walked naked from the bedroom to where his overnight bag lay on the living room floor. He took out his glucometer, testing strips and finger pricker, went to the kitchen and set the machine up. It was about the size of a small transistor radio and when a reagent strip smeared with blood was inserted it gave a blood sugar reading. Ben pricked his finger, smeared the strip, pressed a button and waited for the reading. He had sixty seconds, which counted down on a small screen, to wait before the result. Plenty of time to open the fridge and pour a glass of cold white wine.

Jerry could smell the wine on his breath when he got back to bed. "How was the test?"

"Five. That's okay." He was lying; the test result was a reading of 9—not so okay. *Pasta is tricky*, Ben thought. *No more pasta with bread.* He felt Jerry snuggle close to him, and the approach of sleep. He belched softly.

"Your stomach's rumbling," Jerry said.

"Yours," Ben said.

"It's hard to tell." Jerry felt Ben twitch, then relax. "What?"

"I should've asked Dad for some money up front. I was so surprised to see him paying the bill that I forgot."

Montague Cromwell lay in bed. Despite the wine and brandy he'd drunk, he was sleepless. He had the house to himself, something he hadn't been able to rely on for some time since Ben had become an erratic semi-boarder. Ordinarily he'd have been holding a series of small dinner parties for this agent, that collector, this American buyer, that Arab investor. But with Ben likely to stumble in and insult the prospects, his style had been cramped.

He couldn't understand why Ben didn't spend every night with Jerry. *Lucky young devil*, he thought and quickly cancelled the assessment. There was no such thing as luck, and corruption was relative. Brains and guts were what counted. In his fifty-plus years Montague had seen plenty of people who'd missed the bus—some did it at seventeen, some at ten-year intervals all the way to their dotage. Montague knew the signs. To his mind it was mainly a matter of trying the wrong things and then giving up. Giving up inside. He hoped Ben wouldn't join the ranks of the givers-up.

He rolled over in bed, trying to find comfort. It was

hot even under one sheet. Montague liked to sleep next to warm, breathing flesh at least a couple of times a month. It was expensive, but nowhere near as expensive as a divorce. He shuddered to think what a divorce could cost him now. He had this house on a very small mortgage, a good lease on the gallery in Old Brompton Road, fees, clients, consultancies, the cottage in Dorset, the Jaguar. The settlement with Monique had been bad enough. Now it would be unthinkable.

Montague thought about the commission he could get on the sale of the Turner. *The provenance is good, unimpeachable.* It depended on whether it went to an American or an Arab. Prestige was another matter. If he could contrive for the painting to stay in Britain . . . Unlikely. And what if he couldn't find an heir? Well, there were other ways to swing a deal. He'd have to talk to Ben about that, make sure he understood. Almost asleep, Montague thought: *Legitimately is always the best way, and the lawyers are discreet, uninterested in publicity, co-operative. But they're also impatient—people don't understand that these things take time.*

Two days after the dinner in Soho, Ben Cromwell met Jamie Martin in a Charing Cross Road pub. Through contacts at London University, Ben had been put in touch with Jamie, who had handed in his PhD dissertation on time, to the right length and with all other conditions satisfied. There was no doubt, Ben had been told, that Jamie's thesis on the Game Laws—the ancient statutes that preserved millions of pheasants for the guns of the aristocracy and sent hundreds of poachers to gaol and the convict transports—would be accepted. Whether Martin would land an academic job on the strength of it was more problematical. He was applying frantically, and he was desperately short of money.

Ben bought the drinks, flush from cashing his father's cheque for seven hundred pounds, and outlined the project to Jamie. He passed across several documents—photocopies of the *DNB* entry on John Gulliver, a disparaging mention of 'fighting John's painter brother Tom the Gypsy' in *Bell's Sporting Life*, and a parish registry entry of the birth of John Patrick to Thomas Gulliver and Mary *née* Donovan, 10 October 1863.

Jamie sucked on his half pint, the first he'd had since celebrating his thesis submission some weeks before. "Doesn't sound too hard—unusual name, second half of the century when the records are pretty good, south of England. I'll be surprised if I can't turn something up, Mr Cromwell."

"Ben." Ben Cromwell felt vaguely ill at ease employing someone of his own age who had succeeded at something he had failed at. "Right you are. The sticky thing could be distinguishing descendants of John Gulliver I from John Gulliver II, the nephew. Follow me?"

"Yes." Jamie Martin was a compact man, muscular under his shabby clothes. If he'd had money to spend on his hair and teeth he could have looked like one of the pushy, well-groomed professors one saw being expert on television. He knew he could think clearly and talk well. Now he was sitting opposite a lean, dark idler who drank whisky and let the change from twenty quid sit in the slops on the table. Mr Cromwell looked to him like a mercenary without a war to go to. Well, he was at war every day himself, trying to get an interview, an article accepted, a reference. "It could be tricky, though."

"It's a piece of piss," Ben said, "if you're as good as they say you are. Want the other half?"

Over the second drink they came to terms. Ben agreed to twenty-five pounds a day and travelling and copying expenses. He gave Jamie the telephone number at Jerry's flat, where he was more or less living now that he had money to pay his way. When he was broke he tried to stay in Chelsea as much as possible where there was always the possibility of putting the bite on Montague or one of his friends. If the deal his father had outlined to him came off, all that penny-pinching would be over.

Ben paid Jamie for a day's work in advance. "When will you have something?"

"Two days," Jamie said. "No, make it three."

Ben nodded and handed over another twenty-five

pounds. Jamie Martin couldn't remember the last time he'd had fifty pounds in his pocket.

Three days later Jamie rang Ben at Jerry's to request a three-day extension. When they met, Ben hardly recognised Jamie. He'd had his hair cut and it was thick and glossy, freshly shampooed. He wore clean, freshly pressed slacks and a new shirt. He was sitting at the same table looking through the contents of a manila folder; he was smoking a Gaulois and had a glass of red wine in front of him.

Ben got a whisky from the bar and sat down at the table. "Hullo. How'd you get on?"

Jamie took a drag on his cigarette and squashed it out. "Pretty good, I think." He passed several sheets of paper across the table. "Marriage, birth of children, police report..."

Ben nodded. "This is John Gulliver II?"

"Yep. Bit of a lad it seems. He took after his uncle in some ways. Big chap. He did some boxing and was all right at it apparently, but he'd lie down if the money was right. That sort of thing got him into trouble." He handed across a photocopy of a page of newsprint. "Bit of a drinker, kept bad company, as the paper says. He stole a boat for some reason and did a couple of years in Norwich prison for it."

Ben finished his whisky and gestured to Jamie to drink up. He went to the bar for refills. "Thanks," Jamie said. "He got married in 1895 to one Catherine Riebe, German girl. She was a good deal younger than he. I . . . haven't got much about her."

"Doesn't matter," Ben said, "Go on."

"Gulliver seems to have settled down after his marriage. Four children—John born 1895, Carl born the next year, Susannah in 1898 and Edward in 1900."

Ben saw in his mind's eye a spreading family tree with numerous collateral branches. He wasn't sure how many descendants would be best for his father's purposes. Not too many, he fancied. Still, there was always the Great War to carry off a few.

Jamie sipped his wine. Around them men and women

were perched on stools or leaning forward across tables. Newspapers were rustled and folded and the volume of noise went up as the drink flowed. Jamie hadn't been in such a convivial atmosphere since his undergraduate days. He was nervous about some of the news he had to deliver, but he was enjoying himself. "Your John Gulliver eventually got a stall at Leadenhall market. Did quite well."

Ben's mind was running on the influenza epidemic of . . . when was it? 1918? That might have helped clear the decks. The whisky and the good time he'd been having with Jerry made him feel benign. He was impatient for Jamie to get on, but the man was obviously enjoying the telling so much that Ben hadn't the heart to push him. "What'd he sell at the market?" he said idly.

"Everything from books to buttons. Regular jumble sale, but it looks as if the stall was a sort of front."

"For what?"

Jamie smiled. He'd been to the dentist and had his teeth cleaned so he smiled now as often as he could. "He was a pornographer. He and a bloke named Christopher Smale had a stable of hacks churning the stuff out and a printing shop where they ran off the books. They sold some at the stall, under the counter as it were, and had a whole chain of other outlets. Big operation."

Ben was impressed. "Where did you get all this?"

"It made a stink at the time, around 1908 it was. The papers lapped it up."

"I bet. Nothing's changed." *No wonder the other Gullivers weren't too keen to connect themselves with Tom the Gypsy's offspring*, Ben thought. "So he got collared?"

"Not exactly. An outraged wife of one of the well-connected customers found the stuff under the marital bed. She informed and the police closed the whole show down. Gulliver and Smale must've greased a hell of a lot of palms to get the charges against them dropped."

"I see. Well, that's all bloody interesting."

"I've enjoyed it."

"Right. Let's press on, Jamie. They weren't wrong

when they said you were good. I want to track down these kids and their descendants. Can you do it?"

"I suppose." Jamie drank some wine and lit another cigarette. Ben refused the offered packet impatiently.

"What's wrong?"

"Gulliver dropped out of sight after 1908. I had a hell of a job finding anything else. That's why I needed the extra time. It just came to me all of a sudden. Sometimes I *love* research."

Ben understood what Jamie was saying. He knew that the best historical researchers had flair and luck—they made imaginative leaps at the right time and in the right direction. He tapped the papers he'd been given into a neat stack and reached forward for Jamie's manila folder. Jamie hung onto it; he suddenly realised that he wanted to go on with this job, and not just for the money.

"Jamie," said Ben, "what's the problem?"

"I don't want you to think I'm stringing the job out."

"I won't. Hang on, I'll get us another drink."

Jamie sighed as he expelled smoke. He recalled his trip out to the Public Records Office in Kew—the train ride at vast expense to the antiseptic document repository that had replaced the old PRO in Chancery Lane. Older academics had told Jamie about Chancery Lane with its oak panelling, musty carpets and arcane procedures. None of that at Kew. It was more like Murdoch's fortress at Wapping, all departure lounge decor, metal detectors and security checks. Still, it was efficient enough.

"Cheers." Ben had returned with the drinks.

Jamie sipped automatically. "I had to go to the PRO," he said, continuing his train of thought.

"Oh, yeah? Still making everyone use pencils, are they?"

Jamie smiled. "Right. But there's a place for people using laptop word processors and dictaphones. How do you know about the pencils?"

Ben shrugged. "Heard about it. Well?"

"It's slow going. The annual influx of Yanks is starting. You wouldn't believe the amount of stuff they order up. It can take two hours before your documents come."

Ben was getting impatient. "Come on, Jamie. Cut to the chase. What's the problem?"

"How long have we got?"

"A few months."

"I hope it's a *good* few. I'm looking at a lot of work here, and we're going to need some luck. Gulliver must have done a deal with the authorities. It happened in those days. The Board of Trade took over from the Emigration Commissioners in 1872. I suppose Board of Trade blokes could talk to Home Office people. That is, there was a connection to the police."

Ben swallowed whisky. "What the hell are you talking about?"

Jamie ran his tongue over his cleaned teeth. *If this is it*, he thought, *I'm still better off than I was*. He cleared his throat. "John Gulliver and his family emigrated to Australia in 1910," he said.

Jack, Stephen, Georgia

1

Southampton, January 1910

The rain beat down hard and cold as John Gulliver waited with his family for the call to board the Pacific Steamship Line's 16,000-tonner *Southern Maid*, bound for Suez, Colombo and Australia. The Gullivers, as steerage passengers, were the last to be called. The iron roof above their heads leaked and Edward, the youngest at ten years of age, squealed when a cold drop fell on his neck.

"It's terrible cold, Ma," Susannah said. "Will we get hot supper on the ship?"

"Your mother doesn't know, girl," said John Gulliver, "and no more do I." He looked fondly at his daughter, whose dark eyes and tangle of almost black hair reminded him that his own father had been called 'Tom the Gypsy'. He raised his voice as his son Jack darted out into the rain. "Be a pity to break your neck on those cobbles right here, young Jack, and never see the land o' sunshine."

Fifteen-year-old Jack had left shelter to get a closer look at a woman. She was strolling along holding a large umbrella in such a way as to protect her from the wind-driven rain but not to conceal her from Jack. She was tall and wore a long dark coat trimmed with fur. Her hat was fur-trimmed also and her boots had high heels that caused her to walk with a swaying gait on the greasy cobbles. Jack could see her bold, bright eyes and painted face. His excited breath steamed in the cold evening air.

"Jack!" John Gulliver called. *A whore down to see her sailor off, or one of 'em,* Gulliver thought. He looked at Jack as the boy ran back. *I was the same at his age and for a good few years after. And it was whores that brought me down in the end.*

Gulliver looked up at the grey, leaking sky and let his gaze wander across the masts of the few sailing ships drawn up at the docks. The stately clippers were far outnumbered by steamships with their funnels, cargo winches and bulky outlines. The roofs of the warehouses and sheds that fringed the wharves were salt-stained and slick with rain. Smoke rose from braziers used by the chestnut roasters and from a pie and peas stall at the end of the long, open shed in which the steerage passengers waited. The greasy, soapy smell of the sea water hit his nose and he seemed to hear the whole city roaring around him. *I'll not see it again,* Gulliver thought. *I know I won't, nor any of us, most likely.*

"We're near dead with the cold, John," Catherine Gulliver said. "Could you not find out what's happening?"

Glad of the action, Gulliver pushed through the squatting, grumbling people towards the end of the shed. He had to step out into the rain at times to keep moving forward and he pulled his cloth cap down and turned up the collar of his coat. He was a big man, over six feet tall and built wide. His full beard, reddish brown with a good deal of grey in it, gave him something approaching distinction, and his clothes, heavy coat, over a serge suit, woollen scarf and strong boots, were in better condition than those most of the passengers wore. He was used to authority and he asserted it. He pushed through to where he could see the ship through the mist and rain.

The pie and peas man raised his ladle. "Bit for you, mate?"

"No," Gulliver said. "No thanks. How long can they keep us waiting?"

"As long's they please. They've got the quality to board first."

"The quality!" Gulliver's derisive snort brought a plume of steam from his nose. He knew about the quality, knew what excited the gentlemen and some of the ladies. What pictures, what words.

"Say it quiet-like, mate," the pie seller said. "I've heard they drops Marxians overboard at night."

"Rubbish. Anyway, I'm not a Marxian, I'm . . ." He stopped. *What am I?* he thought. *Not a voluntary emigrant, that's for certain.* The smell of the hot peas was delicious, London was delicious but the police and magistrate had made the terms clear—he left England or he went to gaol. They'd stripped him of nearly every penny into the bargain, leaving him just enough for his family's passages. And he couldn't have paid that much, he was ashamed to acknowledge, without the assistance offered to immigrants by the government of the state of New South Wales.

"Give me a scoop," he said.

The pieman had a stack of tin cans beside the stall; they were dented, much used and badly washed. He wrapped one in a square of newspaper, filled it with hot peas and handed it to Gulliver. "Thrippence to you, guv'nor, and good luck to you in Orstralia. There's a farthing back on the tin."

Gulliver paid, took another look at the ship and saw two men advancing towards the shed. Brass buttons gleamed through the mist. He hurried back to his family. "Here's peas for you, my darlings, and I'm happy to say something's happening. I saw the Admiral of the Fleet himself coming towards us."

"John." Catherine Gulliver smiled. Her husband always provided and he had good news more often than bad, until recently when he'd had the worst news of all. He'd been uncharacteristically gloomy for a time and she was glad now to see him back at his joking. She held the can of peas carefully to the mouths of each of the children and tipped it slowly so that they got their share and no more. Jack moved her hand and sucked hard and the tin was suddenly empty.

"You're a greedy one, Jack," his mother said. Jack shrugged. His keen eyes had spotted a pocket knife hanging on a leather thong from a man's belt. The leather was old and frayed. Jack thought that a sudden jerk, perhaps when everyone started to move towards the ship, might not be noticed.

Carl Gulliver, small, fair and quiet, sat on the bag he had packed himself. He was prepared to carry it as far as he had to although it was heavy. Probably, if Jack suddenly vanished as he usually did, he'd end up carrying Jack's bag too. John Gulliver observed his small, serious second son. Every day was an adventure to Jack; Susannah was still caught in the dreams of childhood and Edward seemed younger than his ten years. But Carl worried him. He reached out, took the empty tin from his wife and gave it to the boy. "Here, Carl. Take this to the pieman and you'll get a farthing. You can buy a farm with it in Australia."

"Thank you, Pa," Carl said. "We're moving now. I'll get it as we go past the pie stand. Mother, we're off!"

The crowd was heaving up and moving slowly forward. The rain fell harder and the people in the lead hurried, heavily burdened, towards the *Southern Maid*. John Gulliver held Edward's hand in his left and a heavy suitcase in his right; Susannah twined her fingers in the fringe of her mother's shawl; Carl shouldered his bag and shuffled forward, looking for the pieman. Jack opened the flap on his canvas bag, judged the distance, waited for the jolting that came when someone ahead stopped suddenly, and tugged. The pocket knife disappeared into his bag; he closed the flap and moved out of sight behind his father.

As Catherine Gulliver left the shelter of the roof and felt the rain fall on her bonnet, the baby inside her moved. She almost stopped but forced herself to blunder on through the rain. She hadn't told her husband she was pregnant; she'd confirmed it with a doctor in Camden Town, paid him his fee and ignored the veiled suggestion that he might be able to help her out of her trouble. It *was* trouble, one she couldn't visit on her husband in the midst of his business difficulties. He was fifty-seven and such a vigorous man that it was not surprising, but she was near forty and past the age, she'd thought.

She looked up at the towering mass of the ship. It was painted a dark colour, red perhaps, but she could see things—rails, lifeboats, doors—picked out in cream. She closed her eyes and prepared herself for the slow shuffle up the steep ramp to the steerage deck. The bundle she was carrying cut into her narrow shoulder. She was a small woman, not physically strong, but Catherine Riebe Gulliver had never let any adversity beat her yet and adversity was something she'd seen plenty of. Living more comfortably in recent years, she had grown a little stout. This had distressed her at first but now she was grateful for it. Her condition would not be as noticeable as in the days when she was slimmer. She was, she calculated, not much more than four months gone; the voyage would take two months. She would bear her child in the new country, in the sunshine. She hurried forward and rejoiced when she felt her feet on the boards. England was behind her.

The *Southern Maid* was forty years old. A coal-burning vessel with steam turbine engines, she was, in the language of sailors, 'a fair bitch.' She rolled in heavy weather, was slow to respond to her controls and the hammering of her screw was accompanied by a clanking and grinding metal that tore at the nerves. Many searches and inspections had failed to reveal the source of this sound.

None of this yet concerned the Gullivers as they settled into the quarters they would occupy for the next eight weeks. The hundred and ninety-three steerage passengers had been allotted space which was half that given over to the seventy-five second-class travellers, who had less room overall than the thirty people in first class. John Gulliver and family were packed tightly into a cabin that had four bunks and scarcely enough floor and locker space to hold their baggage. Jack threw himself on a lower bunk, rolled against the wall and feigned sleep. Like his mother, Jack exulted at being aboard ship. He'd worked for six months at the printing trade and hated it. He hoped for better in Australia, but it was not Jack's way to display exultation or hope.

John playfully pushed Edward onto the lower bunk opposite. "You and the young'un down here, Kitty. I'll go aloft and Susannah and Carl'll have to top 'n' tail above you. If Jack snores everyone's allowed to throw a boot at him."

The children laughed as they settled in, falling over their feet and banging their heads when the ship gave unexpected slow lurches. Carl tugged at the bolts that held the porthole closed.

"It smells, Pa," Susannah said.

"Pretty soon it'll smell of coconuts and ivory and you'll see great white whales the size of St Paul's." John Gulliver looked down at his wife's pale, narrow face. She had long features, blue eyes and light hair, and he admired every inch of her. For the first time he realised that intimacy would be impossible between them for the whole of the voyage. At home, in the large comfortable house in Golders Green, they'd made love more nights than not and sometimes in the day when the opportunity presented. "Are you all right, Kitty? You look . . ."

"I'm tired, John. Why don't you take Carl and Susy and find out about the meals? I'll take a rest here with Edward."

"I'm not a baby," Edward said, but he curled himself up on the bunk. Jack turned over, swung his feet free, narrowly missing Carl, and went out of the cabin. John Gulliver spoke to his back. "Jack, it's cabin ten, mind."

"I learned to count at school," Jack shouted.

Gulliver shrugged and made pushing gestures to Carl and Susannah.

Catherine took off her boots and stretched out on the bunk. The cabin was gloomy and she felt rather than saw a pile of thin, rough blankets near her head. She pulled one over herself and the boy and cradled her head on her arm. She felt the baby kick again, harder. She heard a commotion in the corridor and from time to time the clatter of boots on the iron staircase outside the cabin. But she dozed. Close to real sleep, she opened her mind to thoughts of her own parents, Johann and Ilsa Riebe, who had left Germany to come to England for reasons they had never told her. Her father had worked for a succession of pottery manufacturers in the Midlands. The Riebes had moved frequently and Catherine's schooling had been much interrupted. She recalled mean houses and poor food and being taunted at school for her poor English and thick German accent. But eventually Johann Riebe had prospered. She remembered the fields around the town and the flowers in their last and largest garden.

She had first seen John Gulliver as he worked on a barge moored in the canal near her father's house. Stripped to the waist, brown in the summer sun, he had entranced her. He unloaded cargo, the muscles in his body flexing. He whistled as he swung the heavy boxes down. He saw her watching him and she was drawn to him by a force that she still felt every day. When the barge moved north on the canal three days later, she was aboard.

She wrote to Johann and Ilsa from the first town, but she knew that their concern would not amount to tearing grief. Catherine was eighteen years of age and had three brothers and two sisters: Riebes enough.

It was strange to think that she had started life with John on a boat of sorts. And here she was again on the water with him, except that they had the children. Hers had not been an easy life. John Gulliver had worked hard at a variety of trades, always permitting them to live decently by not making a surplus until he had established the mysterious business that had brought them such prosperity.

Catherine Riebe spoke unaccented English now, but she had never learned to read or write the language well. They had moved house abruptly after John had given out the bad news that he was ruined. She had never read the newspaper reports. Her husband's rise and fall remained mysterious to her.

Jack worried and frightened her sometimes; Carl made her feel safe, Susy reminded her of John himself when young and the boy asleep beside her was strong and healthy, which was all you could ask for at ten years of age. And the next one? Who could say?

She was asleep when the lines were cast off and the *Southern Maid* eased away from the dock. Even the throbbing of the engine and the thrashing of the screw did not wake her.

2

Jack Gulliver discovered sex two weeks after the *Southern Maid* left Tilbury; he also confirmed his own opinion that he could whip anyone his own age and size, in a fair or dirty fight. There was virtually no contact between the passengers in the different classes on the ship, but these barriers were much less observed by the children. True, the young second-class and steerage travellers saw virtually nothing of the children in first class on the upper decks, but they mixed freely among themselves.

Trudie Peel was sixteen with green eyes and red hair. She was a Londoner who had lost her virginity three years before, to one of the many 'uncles' who had moved in briefly with her mother. To Trudie the word 'father' was an abstraction, but 'uncle' was all too real. From the second uncle she had extracted a sovereign as the price of her silence and over the three years she she had accumulated a fair number of sovereigns which she had spent mostly on clothes. If Hester Peel, barmaid and *chanteuse*, had noticed that her daughter was often better dressed than herself, she made no comment. She made a point, instead, of leaving her douche bags where Trudie could not fail to see them. Trudie's latest 'uncle' was taking them to a new life in Australia.

Trudie first noticed Jack when she saw him stealing extra food in the dining hall. Jack had no right to be in the second-class dining room, but there he was, big for his age at five feet eight inches tall, strongly built with thick dark hair falling into his eyes. He calmly loaded a plate with bread and meat, sat down, ate a little and transferred the rest to his pockets. When a steward asked for his ticket, by which he meant a wooden token the passengers were supposed to carry at all times, Jack crossed his eyes, allowed saliva to dribble from his mouth and played the idiot.

"Seen that," Trudie said. She joined Jack by the rail where the boy was seated, wrapping the food in newspaper.

Alarmed, Jack looked around to see a handsome girl with a big, exciting soft mouth. "Going to tell?" he said.

"No. What's it for?"

"To sell to the pigs in steerage. Bloody little bread back there an' the soup's thinner an' all."

That was the start. A few days later Trudie lowered her drawers for Jack behind a pile of dirty clothes in the ship's laundry. There was a salty, sweaty smell from seamen's jerseys and socks in his nostrils as he crouched down, unbuttoned his flies and let her guide him. He would remember that smell and the hot, sweet rush through his body for the rest of his life. It was over too soon and the girl held him and put his hand to her small hard breasts and he was soon ready again and it went slower. Trudie moaned with him this time and hooked her legs around him, drawing him further and harder into her.

Jack and Trudie spent every possible minute together. It irked them that they could not eat or sleep together. Jack continued to steal and sell food, with Trudie's help. He was busy with a variety of schemes—selling diluted ship's rum which he got from the few teetotal crew members to the thirsty passengers, assisting the hard-pressed second-class stewards in return for a share of their tips, manufacturing cigarettes from the long butts to be had from a first-class steward for a fee. When a challenge to Jack's possession of Trudie came from a lanky, rawboned Scot, Jack thrashed him with his fists and boots late one night in the crew's quarters. Trudie collected at the door and Jack won six pounds in bets. He also shared a bunk that night with Trudie. Jack was having a good voyage.

John Gulliver observed something of his son's activities but he kept his counsel. He'd been a violent, headstrong youth himself and he expected Jack was running true to form. In many ways it was better to have selfish, moody Jack out from underfoot so that he was able to tend to the rest of his family. The younger children settled well into the ship's routine. Carl had won entry to the library—not available to steerage passengers according to the rules, but the boy's persistence had previled. He pored over books, fact and fiction.

"Did you know the Suez Canal was opened in 1869, Pa?" Carl said as the male Gullivers were taking the sun on a cramped platform above the lower deck.

"I did not, son. Is that a fact? And how deep is it?"

Carl studied his book and looked up, disconcerted. "It doesn't say."

"Well, there's something for you to find out. Ask one of the sailors, maybe. We'll be there in a week or so, I expect."

They were nearing the Straits of Gibraltar. The weather was still cold but the rough seas had abated, and when the sky was blue there was a depth and strength to the colour that was new to him. He lit his pipe and puffed carefully; like money, tobacco was in short supply and had to be carefully rationed. Edward was sitting between his legs playing with a set of farm animals John had carved for him back in England. Gulliver directed his puffs away from the boy.

"I don't think the streets will be paved with gold the way it says in the song, d'you, Pa?"

Gulliver rubbed Carl's fair head. "No, son. I expect there'll be a lot of hard work and a good deal of luck needed, like anywhere else."

"Jack's lucky," Edward said. "He's got a pocket knife with a long blade, and it's so sharp."

"Jack's strong," Carl said. "I've seen the muscles in his arms—they're like rocks."

The Gulliver Fortune

Gulliver grunted and stared at the boiling wake. He remembered the boats he'd stolen. The first when he was just a lad. Where had he meant to sail her to? Ireland, was it? He couldn't remember. And later the one he'd taken to use in smuggling. And the barge he'd worked on for a pittance after he'd got out of gaol. Hard work, but it had led him to Catherine and that was his life's lucky stroke. Thinking of her made him want to see her.

"C'mon, boys. Let's find your mother and Susy."

"Look, there's Jack!" Carl pointed below to the aft deck when Jack walked with Trudie. They were deep in conversation, the dark and red heads close together.

"She's a pretty girl," Carl said.

Edward waved and called out. Jack looked up and scowled but he lifted his hand in a quick gesture of recognition. Trudie waved. "I want to be like Jack," Edward said.

John Gulliver pulled him to his feet, lifted him off the ground a few inches and set him down. "What about me? Don't you want to be like your Pa?"

Edward looked at the giant doubtfully. *That big, that much hair?* he thought. It didn't seem possible. John Gulliver saw the doubt and felt his confidence drop. He was going to need all the confidence he could muster for this new place, and all his seemed to be draining away in the direction of his eldest son. "Let's find the women," he said gruffly.

Catherine and Susannah worked at the laundry trough deep inside the ship. The passengers' use of the troughs and the coal-heated coppers was strictly rostered, and space at the washing lines that crisscrossed a section of lower deck was keenly contested. Susannah rubbed at a shirt collar that hadn't come clean in the wash. Jack's shirt. She glanced at her mother, who struggled to lift a sodden mass of clothes up from the water for rinsing. Susannah leaned across to help.

"What's the matter, Ma? What's wrong?"

"Wrong? What should be wrong, girl?"

"You look so pale and you get tired easily. Pa said something about it the other day."

Catherine wrung a shirt vigorously; her sleeves were rolled up and her forearms were muscular from years of work. She was alarmed. "What did he say?"

"I didn't cotton to it. It was in German, I think."

Catherine smiled. She had taught her husband pet words and phrases in German in the early days of their lovemaking and John would bring them out from time to time. This was probably something about a little flower, *meine kleine Blume*. "I'm all right," she said. "This soap is rubbish!" She scratched at the bar of coarse yellow soap, trying to roughen its surface and raise a lather with it.

"I had a dream that I was in Australia. I met a blackfellow. I was frightened."

"There's blackfellows everywhere," Catherine said. "They do no harm. Remember Willy." Willy was a tall gentle African who had delivered coal to the Gulliver house in Golders Green. The family were good customers, taking many sacks, and Willy welcomed the cup of tea that was always waiting for him when he emerged from the coal cellar for the last time. Susannah remembered that the coal dust had been blacker than Willy's face, but not by much.

"Will we have money again in Australia, Ma?"

"I don't know. I hope so. Your father always finds a way to make money."

"Like Jack."

Catherine Gulliver wrung out a heavy long underwear suit. "No, not like Jack. Your father is a worker, Jack is not. Well, there may be a place for both kinds in this country Australia." She felt weak suddenly and could not get much moisture out of the heavy fabric.

"That won't dry, Ma. Not like that."

Catherine gritted her teeth and wrung it again. "It will be warmer soon. Things will dry more quickly." *And the sun will shine and we will get colour in our faces*, she thought. *So I will not look pale*. She did not like her husband to be worried. He had teased her the other night about getting fat. "Must be the wonderful grub," he said.

Her gorge rose at the thought of food. She was tired of eating and living with so many people—tired of the noisy children and the surly men and the women who talked incessantly, sometimes so fast that her brain seemed to seize up and she could remember only German words. She was tired. She'd have to tell him soon.

The *Southern Maid* passed peacefully through the Mediterranean; the sea was calm and the air grew milder. The passengers spent more and more time above decks, competing for the space, especially for seats in the form of upturned buckets and barrels, and the six precious folding canvas chairs that Jack had stolen from second class and rented for a few pence per day. Where he stowed them at night no one knew, but his manner and the sight of the heavy pocket knife swinging from his belt was enough to deter most from attempting to cheat him. And Jack had let it be known whose son he was—the name of Gulliver still meant something to those who followed boxing and even in his late fifties John had the stamp of a fighting man.

In the Sicilian channel Carl tried to interest his older brother, whose attention he had caught for a few fleeting minutes. He stared at a misty shape visible miles away to starboard. "It's Italy to one side and Africa to t'other, Jack."

"Which be which?" Jack said.

Carl pointed in turn. "Africa. Italy. That's Sicily. It's as big as Ireland, almost."

Jack's interest in both places was nil. "Which way to Australia then, Carl? D'you know that?"

Carl considered the question carefully, as he considered all questions. He scanned the horizon. He knew something of latitude and longitude but not enough. He was an honest boy. "No," he said. "But I can find out."

"That's what matters to me."

"I know the first port of call."

Jack had had his sea legs within minutes of being aboard and he despised the poor sailors, but the thought of land interested him. There was a possibility of trade, or perhaps a present for Trudie. Not that she'd ever asked for one. It was something he wanted to do and he was surprised at himself for having such a feeling. But then, all his feelings for Trudie surprised him. "Where's that?" he grunted.

"Port Said, Egypt."

Jack's policy was never to thank anyone for anything lest it cost the initiative. Even asking questions was dangerous. "And after that?"

"Colombo," Carl said proudly. "That's in Ceylon. Where the tea comes from."

Jack turned away. He had things to do but he couldn't resist. "What's next, Carl, after Columbus?"

"Colombo. Then Australia, I think."

"Good," Jack said.

3

London, July 1986

Ben and Jerry lunched at Garfunkels in Piccadilly because it was close to the bookshop where Jerry worked and because she liked the salads. Jerry was figure-conscious, aware that her present agreeable shape left little margin for error. Ben would eat anywhere he could get wine, as well as salads suited to his diabetic diet. It was also a good place to meet Jamie Martin, something Jerry had been pressing for since she'd heard the news of his successful tracking of the Gullivers. They sat near the window and looked over at the Americans and Australians pouring in and out of the Regent Palace Hotel. The newsstand was doing brisk business with papers carrying the headline: BECKER BLITZ!

"I've tried to read up on it a bit," Jerry said.

Ben sipped his wine. "One what?"

"Emigration to Australia before World War I."

"I thought it was called immigration."

"It's immigration to Australia but emigration to us."

"What about the West Indians and Pakistanis?"

"That's the reverse."

"I see. And what did you find out?"

"Almost nothing. Hang on." Jerry took her plate across to the buffet and heaped it, avoiding the potato salad and starchy beans. When she returned she said, "There's almost nothing written about it from the personal angle. No diaries or letters. Just general works, really. A lot of facts and figures. What're you going to eat? You have to have something to soak up the wine, Ben."

"Mmm. Omelette, I suppose."

"You had eggs for breakfast."

"I don't care. I didn't have wine for breakfast."

"Almost, I bet."

Ben grinned. "Where's Jamie? He's late. You were saying?"

Jerry swallowed tomato and lettuce. She added a few drops of wine to her glass of mineral water. "There doesn't seem to be anything much written on people going to the colonies at that time. And there were *thousands* of them! It sounds like a possible thesis topic." A secret wish of Jerry's had been that Ben would go back to historical research and become an academic. She had almost abandoned the idea in recent weeks, along with the wish that they would get married. Her public ambition, still firmly held, was to get a short story in the *New Yorker*.

Ben's omelette arrived and he poked at it without interest. "With any luck the Gullivers' ship will have sunk and only one of the family will have survived." Ben was three glasses into the bottle. He waved his fork. "The survivor will have returned to Britain, been married and widowed, and his one son is a bachelor living quietly in West Ham."

"Eat something, Ben," Jerry said. "You're getting pissed. Oh, look, this must be him."

Jamie Martin entered the restaurant and peered around. The day was bright outside and his eyes were slow to adapt to the fashionable gloom. When he spotted Ben and Jerry he waved a manila folder in the air and approached quickly. Ben made the introductions and Jerry poured Jamie a full glass of wine to cut down on Ben's reserves.

"Jerry's bookish," Ben said. "She says there's nothing much written on departing Britons pre-World War I."

Jerry looked anything but bookish to Jamie Martin. She was wearing a sleeveless white dress; her dark red hair fell to her shoulders which were, like her arms, lightly tanned. The combination of hair and skin colour was unusual. Jamie gulped some wine, said he would have a rare steak and was suddenly acutely conscious of a wish to impress Jerry. "If you mean personal, primary material, you're right," he said. "There's a hell of a lot of statistical stuff, though. Britain lost more people to overseas countries around the time the Gullivers went than to any other except during the Irish potato famine."

Jerry cherished her remote Irish ancestry. "Is that right? That's interesting, Jamie. How many?"

"It hit a quarter of a million, that is, emigrants, around 1909, 1910."

Jerry leaned forward. "And how many during the famine?"

"Could we skip the history lesson?" Ben said. "What've you turned up that's useful?"

Jerry frowned and worked at her salad. Jamie was saved from having to make a quick answer by the arrival of the steak he had ordered. He cut through the pink meat, forked a piece into his mouth and chewed thoughtfully. "Great," he said, "just the way I like it. I got the passenger list for the ship they went on. Oh, and I found out a bit more about John Gulliver's wife, by the way."

Ben waved his glass, indicating a half-hearted willingness to listen.

"Don't be such a shit, Ben," Jerry said. "This is terrific. Go ahead, Jamie. It's so long ago, how did you find out about her?"

"She's listed as an alien on the passenger roll. The Home Office kept tabs on aliens and the files're open."

"If you know where to look," Jerry said. "Come on, then. What about her?"

"Jewish," Jamie said. "Or her mother was, which amounts to the same thing. Seems there was some sort of pogrom in their part of Germany in the 1860s and her father and mother got out."

"That's fascinating," said Jerry, who had once calculated that more than half the people she admired in history were Jews. "So they all fetched up in Australia, did they? I hope you can track them from there."

Jamie concentrated on his steak for a few minutes while Jerry picked at her salad and Ben considered the pros and cons of another bottle of wine. He decided against. The funds his father was providing were adequate but not princely and he'd have to fork out again to Jamie after lunch, which he'd have to pay for. Save now, spend later, Ben decided. He'd get a bottle of Scotch to take home. Jerry poured the last of the wine into Jamie's glass.

"Thanks," Jamie said. "It could be a bit tricky. I've confirmed that the ship didn't sink." He grinned at Jerry, showing the newly cleaned teeth. "I know a bloke who tried to do research on a ship that traded around China. Went nuts trying to track this particular voyage, only to find that she sank off Lands End."

Ben was swaying in his seat. Jerry smiled. "Let's get some coffee," she said. "Tell us more, Jamie."

Jamie finished his food quickly, leaving only a few scraps of fat and a few bloody streaks on the plate. He hoped Jerry would be able to steady Ben's hand enough for him to write a cheque, or perhaps she controlled the cash . . . He consulted notes in his folder. "Port Said, Colombo, Fremantle was the route. I've sent some telexes off to Canberra and Sydney. Expensive, I'm afraid."

"No object," Ben said. "Nothing spared."

Jamie cleared his throat. "Good. I should have something back pretty quickly."

"What's tricky, then?" Jerry said. "You said it could be tricky."

"Yes. There's a newspaper report. Pretty vague. It seems to come from a Morse code message picked up at sea so there is room for error."

The coffee arrived in a pot. Jerry poured a cup for Ben and virtually forced him to drink it. Jamie took his with milk and sugar. "The *Southern Maid*," he said. "She's described in this newspaper as a fever ship."

4

'Southern Maid', February 1910

Clive Rooney was an Australian who had taken a trip to Britain as a single man and was returning with a 'wife and daughter', to wit, Hester Peel and Trudie. Not that Clive and Hester saw much of Trudie, who spent all her time with Jack Gulliver. Neither minded this much; they were full of plans for their future in Western Australia. Those plans included marriage. According to Hester, a distance of 12,000 miles between her and her husband, whom she had not seen for ten years, constituted a divorce.

"We could have a double wedding from the look of those two," Hester said as she and Clive joined the crowd at the rail straining for a sight of Port Said.

"Steady on, Hes, the lass's only sixteen."

"That's what I was when I got hitched."

"The boy's not even that."

"He looks older."

"Be useful in the pub," Clive mused. "Think his people'd let him get off with us? I wouldn't want to argufy with that John Gulliver." Clive Rooney was a smallish man, stockily built and redheaded but without the temper and cockiness that often go with that build and colouring. He liked to get along easily with people.

"We'll see." Hester Peel was used to her gentlemen paying attention to her daughter. Clive Rooney had never done so and it added inches to his stature and expanded his character in her eyes. The idea of taking Jack Gulliver in charge was another example of his loyalty and seriousness. She squeezed his arm and pointed across the flat, grey sea. "Look, Clive. I can see the land."

Rooney nodded. "Port Said. Saw it on the way over. It's a hellhole and a half. Don't let young Trudie go ashore."

"As if I could stop her," Hester said. "I want to go m'self. You can show me the spicy bits. Do they really sell postcards with . . . you know?"

"To knock your eyes out," Rooney said.

The passengers were told that the ship would be in port for only one hour, to take on more travellers, coal, food and water. This was a lie; the stopover would be for four hours, possibly longer, but bitter experience had taught the Pacific Steamship Company to keep its passengers on a short leash in Port Said.

Catherine Gulliver refused to go ashore. "A rest on the ship when it's quiet would be a tonic to me, John," she said. "The noise seems to go right through me. Listen now, that awful clanking has stopped. What a relief!"

John Gulliver looked at his wife doubtfully. She was puffy and pale, her eyes watered and her hair was lifeless. He'd suggested that she should wear some lighter clothes in the heat but Catherine had persisted with her heavy skirts and shawls. He also thought fresh air would do her good, but from the quick sniff he'd had of it the air of Port Said was none too fresh.

"Well, the children are keen, Kitty, but . . ."

"Go on with you. Children, just mind to stay close to your father. Carl and Susy, you watch Edward now."

"Yes, Ma," chorused the children, including Edward himself.

Husband and wife exchanged smiles. Jack Gulliver appeared in the cabin doorway as his mother was arranging herself, luxuriously alone, on the bunk. "Are you poorly, Ma?"

"No, Jack. Just tired. You can help your father keep an eye on the little ones."

"No," Jack said. "I'm going with Trudie." He put his

hand into his pocket and took out three half crowns. "I'll buy you something nice, Ma, and here's a little for the kids."

Carl nodded gravely and took the coins. "Thank you, Jack."

John Gulliver had noted that his eldest son apparently considered himself no longer a kid. He'd seen enough of Jack and Trudie together to tell that Jack was a man, in the physical sense at least. His pride revolted at the thought of his son providing pocket money where he could not, but he fought the feeling down. "That's handsome of you, Jack. Perhaps we'll see you and Trudie in the bazaar."

"Perhaps, Pa," Jack said gruffly. After a look at his mother, who lay with her eyes closed, he turned and strode away towards the stairs.

Market stalls, crammed with jewellery, leather goods and ornaments, and carpets spread on the ground and covered with trinkets, seemed to flow right down to the dockside. The artificial harbour at Port Said sheltered behind a huge breakwater, built of stone transported across the desert. This 'gateway to the Suez Canal' was connected to Egypt only by a causeway and a spit of sand, but for most sea travellers it was all of Egypt they ever saw. Jack and Trudie walked along the narrow aisles between the stalls and dodged the beggars and hucksters who leapt out at them, pawing and gibbering.

"Ver' cheap, effendi, ver' cheap, young sir!"

"I want something that *isn't* cheap," Jack said.

Trudie held his arm and stayed closed. With her free hand she raised the skirts of her long dress a little. The strange smells, a mixture of dust and palm oil and body sweat, excited and alarmed her. "Everything's cheap here," she said. "I heard a man in the saloon say you can get a woman for . . . a shilling, I think. Look there, Jacky."

Jack stopped and looked at the first building in a narrow street which ran at right angles to the rows of festooned stalls and heaped carts and mats with teetering piles of goods. A woman stood in the doorway; her huge dark eyes were rimmed around with still darker paint and a jewel was set on a band that ran across her forehead.

Her body was covered, but with thin clothes that seemed to emphasize its curves and hollows. Jack felt his mouth go dry, but he was also aware of the warmth of Trudie pressing against him. They moved on. "What were you doing in the saloon?" he said.

Trudie laughed, pleased by his jealous concern. "I was trying to talk that salesman into playing cards with you."

"Will he?"

"I think so. What are you going to buy me, Jacky?"

"Anything you want." Jack had turned sixteen and he had measured himself against his father in the gangway outside the cabin. He thought the difference in their height was small. He sweated inside his heavy shirt and jacket. He pulled Trudie out of the path of a beggar who swayed and muttered. "What about some clothes? I could do with something lighter." They moved in the direction of the clothes stalls.

John Gulliver lifted his eyes to the red-tiled rooftops of the town that had grown up around the port. Palm trees sprouted in pots on the flat roofs, and their leaves brushed against shutters closed against the heat. Ordinarily busy commerce excited and interested him, and the variety of humanity here was a challenge to the merchant—Arabs in long robes, black Africans in loose cotton shirts that reached to their bare feet, heavy-nosed Armenians buttoned into tight suits. The variety was duplicated in the headgear—sun helmets on the Europeans, Arab headcloths, tarbushes and turbans. But the feverish buying and selling in Port Said left him unmoved. He thought of London and felt like an outcast.

The children clung to him, their hands sticky from the sweets they had bought with Jack's money. Suddenly, Susannah tugged at his sleeve. "Pa, we've lost Carl!"

Gulliver jerked from his daydream of London. He looked frantically around the bustling, noisy market for the boy. He saw only dark faces and gesticulating hands, metal and jewels flashing in the sun.

"There, Pa," Susannah said, "by the books."

Carl had wandered to a stall run by an Oriental.

The Gulliver Fortune

Among the bamboo fans and jade ornaments were several palmleaf baskets filled with books. Carl was squatting, half-concealed, reverentially taking the books from the baskets to examine them. He gazed up at his father with an expression of wonder. "Look, Pa, Byron and Shelley, wonderful editions. How much do you think they might cost?"

An experienced market hand, Gulliver took his cue from the stall holder who was ignoring Carl and concentrating on a woman displaying mild interest in a jade brooch. "I think you might have to take them by the basketful."

Carl was shocked. "You can't buy books like that."

"Why not?" Gulliver teased.

"It isn't done."

Gulliver's roar of laughter turned heads. He grinned while the boy haggled for an edition of Shelley and agreed with him that he'd got a bargain. The incident restored his spirits. "Come along, children, I'll buy yez all a lemonade."

On the way to the lemonade seller they passed the street of *houris* where Jack and Trudie had paused. The dark eyes and the full languorous bodies touched off fuses of lust and guilt in John Gulliver. He sweated and stood rooted to the spot while his children called to him to hurry. He stumbled after them thinking of his sick wife on board and regretting for the thousandth time the meeting with Christopher Smale in the Sportsman's Guinea that had made him first almost rich and then an exile.

By the time the *Southern Maid* was approaching Colombo, the living conditions in steerage were giving the ship's doctor concern. Dr Anderson explained to the purser that the rough, wet weather on the Arabian sea passage had contributed. "They couldn't get out on deck and they huddled in together. Coughs and colds, that sort of thing."

"I must say some of them smell pretty bad," the purser said with distaste.

"Well, they couldn't get their clothes dried. The bed linen's in bad order and the rats are increasing."

The purser sighed. "What are you suggesting?"

"Fumigate at Colombo."

"Means putting them all ashore for a couple of days."

"If we arrive in Fremantle like this we could get a rap over the knuckles. I don't think anyone would be too pleased about that. Anyway," the doctor snapped shut the notebook he'd been writing in, "that's my advice and I've entered it in my log."

The steerage passengers, accommodated in four seedy harbourside hotels, sweated, itched and quarrelled. Few had light clothes and fewer still adapted well to the spicy food served in the hotels. On the morning of the second day John Gulliver discovered a chair in a shady spot on the verandah where there was also the suspicion of a breeze. The harbour lay in a heat haze and the sprawling, dusty town seemed to be slowly baking like a huge loaf. The temperature had not dropped below ninety degrees and rose to a hundred and ten in the middle of the day. Gulliver draped his jacket over the chair.

"Ye can't do that!" A big Irishman named Doyle had come onto the verandah. He had climbed three flights of stairs and the sweat was saturating his shirt and waistcoat.

"It's for my wife," Gulliver explained. "Not for me. I'm just going to get her. She's sick."

"We're all sick, sick o' this bloody heat." Doyle twitched the jacket from the chair. John Gulliver's control snapped; he moved forward and his short left hook knocked Doyle down. A Tamil servant heard the crash of the Irishman's fall and ran out to the verandah.

"Bad, sir," he said. "Get police."

"No," Gulliver said. "Don't get the police. I'm sorry, friend. You're right about the heat. Let me help you up."

Doyle struggled to his feet unaided. "Damn your help and damn you." He shoved the servant aside and stumped off. Gulliver shrugged, put his jacket back on the chair and went to fetch his wife.

The children suffered less in the heat. Carl slept and found shady places to read in. Susannah had formed a friendship with a girl of her own age, Mary Welcome, the only child of Digby and Laura Welcome, late of the English stage. "You should see Mama's gowns and Papa's dress suits," Mary said. "They're ever so lovely. Much better than in the pictures." The girls were in the Welcomes' room examining a book of newspaper cuttings. The Whirling Welcomes was a song and dance act that had toured the provinces, with an occasional London booking, for twenty years. Now, with few seasons on the boards ahead of them, the Welcomes had determined to try the colonies.

Susannah was doubtful. She had seen Mary's parents and thought her father as badly dressed, hot and tired-looking as everyone else. Laura Welcome possessed a kind of sheen that lent some support to Mary's claims. "Where're the gowns now?"

"In trunks on the ship. Ever such big trunks. Papa says we can live in the trunks if there aren't any houses in Australia. D'you think there will be houses, Susy?"

"I expect so." Susy was in a dream of chiffon and polished dancing pumps. She turned the pages and marvelled at the fairyland costumes, worn not only by the people on the stage but by those in the audience. The heat in the little room was stifling; she gazed out of the window. The jungle and hills high up above the building line looked even hotter than the town. She swayed as she sat on the bed. Her head felt hot and her mind was wandering. "Where's our Edward, Mary?"

"Don't you remember? He went for a rickshaw ride with Mama and that nice Mr La Vita."

"Is Mr La Vita nice?" Susannah remembered only dark eyes and flashing white teeth.

"Oh, yes. It's terribly hot, but Mama doesn't seem to mind." Mary was fair like her father and her skin blistered if exposed to the sun for more than a few minutes. Laura Welcome was dark, like Mr La Vita. "They'll have such fun. Can't you just see little Edward when he comes back? He'll say, 'Susy, we saw an elephant, and a crocodile, and a python and . . .' "

Mary giggled. "And Carl will say, 'The elephant is found in Africa and is the biggest something or other.' " The girls collapsed into laughter.

Digby Welcome had made his way to the bar of the Oriental Hotel, keeping under shade as much as possible.

He had a weakness not for drink but for well-dressed company. He was the son of a clergyman whose education and prospects had been good until he threw both away for Laura and the stage. It mortified him to travel steerage. Digby was of medium height and trimly built. In the right clothes he could look dapper. Now, in celluloid collar and tie, freshly pressed jacket and with his sunhat on his knee, he sat with a gin and tonic in the relative cool of the bar. A fan stirred the air. Digby lay in wait for a familiar face from the ship.

Dennis 'Rusty' Clarke was about to make his fortune, or so he thought. When he heard he'd been left a plantation by an uncle and that the location of the estate was New Guinea, he thought at first of Africa. Kenya perhaps. Coffee. Occasional trips out there to see how things were going, otherwise a high old life in London on the profits. He'd come down to earth with a bump when he learned that New Guinea was 12,000 miles away on the other side of the world. And no one in the London lawyer's office could tell what crop the plantation produced. It was the London lawyer's first dealing with Sydney, Australia, and Rusty had the feeling that he found the whole thing bad form.

Rusty's prospects in England had not been good. A clerk in the office of a firm that manufactured shoes, he found the work boring and, as the office was well stocked with relations by blood and marriage of the proprietor, advancement was unlikely. Indeed, the job itself was insecure. Rusty's wife Violet had recently lost their first child. The baby, a boy, hadn't lived an hour. The letter from the lawyer announcing the legacy, unsatisfactory as the details proved, offered a chance, and Rusty and Violet grabbed it.

Rusty wandered into the bar of the Oriental after a walk which he called privately 'acclimatisation'. New Guinea, he had learned, was very hot. He was travelling second class on money he'd borrowed and scrounged against the day when he would return as a substantial landowner and producer-investor in . . . Rusty had still not decided. He rather fancied rubber. He was a big man and heavily built with a red face, not at all clerk-like. He got a gin sling and looked around for a seat near the fan.

Digby Welcome pushed a chair away from his table with a highly polished shoe. He raised his glass and caught Rusty's eye. "Have a seat, old man. Scorcher, what?"

Rusty was a sociable soul. He sat and fanned himself with his hat. "More like a hot bath than anything else."

Digby smiled. He'd performed strenuously for years in hot, smoky places, often under lights. Perspiration wasn't much of a problem. He looked cool enough as he refused one of Rusty's cigarettes. Digby was concerned about his wind; Laura was several years younger than he. "Yes," Digby said, "Melbourne might be the place for us. I hear it's quite temperate there. Where're you bound? Oh, I beg your pardon—Digby Welcome. I take it you're on the *Southern Maid*."

The two men shook hands. "Dennis Clarke. Yes, I'm for New Guinea myself, by way of Sydney."

Digby relaxed. This was just his sort of thing. Men exchanging views on matters of importance. "New Guinea, eh? How interesting. What line are you in?"

Rusty puffed on his cigarette. "Rubber, actually," he said.

5

'Southern Maid', March 1910

Dr Anderson diagnosed the first case of typhus when the *Southern Maid* was three days out from Colombo. The sufferer was an eight-year-old boy travelling steerage who had stayed in the same hotel as the Gullivers. Other cases developed quickly, all among residents of the same hotel. Within a week there were twenty-seven cases that were mild and eight that were serious. On the ship, fear and anxiety ran high. The steerage passengers swept and cleaned their quarters obsessively. Patients were quarantined in the ship's sick bay, where the child whose illness had signalled the epidemic died. Two days later the child's mother, an apparently healthy woman, developed the symptoms—fever, chills, pain and a rash in the armpits—in the most violent form. Within a week of her child's death she too was dead.

"I can't understand it," the exhausted doctor told the captain, "the child was weak to start with. His death was no surprise. But the mother . . ." He shook his head.

Roger Duff had been master of vessels like the *Southern Maid* for thirty years. A Scot without vices, one of the most practical breeds in existence, he had seen everything from epidemics to mutiny and his response to the typhus outbreak had been a calm despatch of Morse code messages and the cautious adoption of a policy that would satisfy all parties. He was proceeding to Fremantle at reduced speed, hoping that the scourge would run its course and that quarantine provisions would be met with relative ease.

"Carry on, doctor," Duff said. "I'm sure ye're doing all ye can. It's a bad business but people canna expect t'cross the world without risk."

"Surely they can expect to cross it without dying?" Anderson said bitterly.

Duff raised his eyebrows. "I'll enter y'r opinion in m' log, but I believe it's a novel notion—not more than fifty years old at the most."

Three other children and two adults died. Again, the children were sickly to begin with. The doctor questioned the widow and the widower of the dead adults and learned that both of the deceased had had disabilities

'Dormant tuberculosis and syphilis,' the doctor entered in his journal. 'The typhus appears to be of a not particularly virulent kind but is dangerous to the point of fatality to those who are in any way previously weakened.'

The Gulliver family spent as much time as possible on deck. The doctor examined Susannah closely after her mother reported that the girl had felt feverish in Colombo. He found no signs of the pestilence. The next day Catherine Gulliver fell in a dead faint at the ship's rail where she had been leaning. John Gulliver put the children in the care of whoever would have them and attempted to nurse his wife, but she weakened by the hour. In the sick bay she confided to the doctor that she was pregnant.

Anderson examined her. "Seven months at least."

"Oh, God," Catherine said. "Longer than I thought. My poor children. Doctor," she gripped Anderson's arm with a strength that surprised him, "my husband does not know. I didn't want to worry him while we made this change and we haven't . . ."

"I see. This is very serious, Mrs Gulliver. You must rest."

Catherine convulsed and screamed. The next few hours were a nightmare for the doctor and his assistants and living hell for John Gulliver. The bacteria infecting Catherine's body triggered what the doctor expected to be a painful and bloody miscarriage. He assisted the delivery, paying almost no attention to the foetus and concentrating his efforts on relieving the suffering of the mother. The baby was male and large.

"It's alive, doctor," the nurse said.

"Not for long, I'll be bound. She's haemorrhaging! Don't worry about it, woman. Help here!"

The child, grey-green like a skinned rabbit, dribbled mucus from its pipes and whimpered. The nurse, working frantically in the narrow space partitioned off within the sick bay, attended to it virtually with one hand while she applied towels and cold cloths. The nurse was a Roman Catholic, doctrinally strict. She struggled to save both souls, but the mother bled to death, despite her efforts. The child lived but was given no chance of long-term survival by Anderson, the sceptic, who had had almost no sleep for seventy-two hours.

"This place is a mortuary and a hospital combined," he said. "It can't be a nursery as well."

The nurse nodded. She had washed the infant and swaddled it. She held it in her arms while the doctor drew a sheet over the body of its mother. "I'll have the purser tell Mr Gulliver," she said. "The poor man."

"Hurry, please," Anderson said, "We've others to attend to."

The nurse left the sick bay. If she'd been at home in Dublin she'd have gone straight to the priest; here and now she needed a different kind of help. She crossed herself, said a prayer and hurried.

John Gulliver felt a terrible pain deep inside his body as the purser framed the words. He thought his heart had stopped or that the breath in his lungs would be his last. *Kitty can't be dead*, he thought. *It's not possible*. He shook his head.

"I'm sorry, Mr Gulliver. The doctor did all he could. I'm terribly sorry to have to tell you this, but your wife will have to be buried at sea, and quickly. Do you understand, sir?" It was not the purser's habit to so address steerage passengers but something about Gulliver impelled him to use the word.

"Yes. I understand."

"I'll make the arrangements and inform you." The purser said nothing about the child, of whom he knew nothing.

"Thank you," Gulliver said. "I want to see her."

"I don't advise it, sir. The infection . . ."

"I saw her every day for sixteen years and I will see her today."

The purser nodded. He felt as if he should salute Gulliver or shake his hand, but it would be ridiculous to do so. He went to the sick bay to tell the doctor of Gulliver's wish but Anderson was snatching an hour's sleep in his cabin. He stood, undecided, outside the partitioned corner where Catherine Gulliver had died. Her husband approached and he stood aside.

John Gulliver wandered about the ship. He stood at the stern rail and stared out at the churning water. Scenes from his life with Catherine glowed in his mind. He remembered their first lovemaking on the barge, Jack's birth, the cooking smells in the succession of single rooms where they had lived, slept and eaten, and made love and had more children. His mind flicked to his erstwhile partner and nemesis, Christopher Smale—his easy manners, ready money and way of treating everything as a joke.

Something about Smale reminded John Gulliver of his father, 'Tom the Gypsy', who'd faked a few paintings in his time, forged a signature or two and minted some gold using, for the greater part, lead. Gulliver knew and feared his own larcenous streak and knew that it was only Kitty who had kept him out of gaol. The business with Smale had seemed harmless enough. How could reading or looking at pictures hurt anybody? Smale had told him that the ancient Romans had produced such works and the Chinese and Indians and every race of men under the sun.

Well, perhaps Romans, Chinese and Indians had paid penalties, as he had. The loss of his worldly goods and even the hard fact of exile he'd been willing to endure, but not this. His heart was broken. He could still feel the chill on Catherine's lips as he bent over to kiss her. Sobs shook his body and his strength seemed to diminish with every fresh gust of weeping.

'John Gulliver, aged 57, husband of the late Catherine Gulliver, died this day of typhus,' Dr Anderson wrote in his journal. 'He appears to have become infected from close contact with the corpse of his wife and to have offered no resistance to the disease.' After this entry the doctor wrote up the daily statistics on the course of the epidemic: fatal cases, 9; serious, 5; recovering, 12. He turned the page and a thought struck him. What had become of the infant Catherine Gulliver had given birth to? Was it still alive? He doubted it. He was exhausted and lay down to sleep, pledging to enquire of the nurse the next day. His last waking thought was: What in hell will become of all those orphans?

6

London, August 1986

Jerry Gallagher sat in the sunlight falling on the steps of the British Museum. She had agreed when Ben suggested that she might like to fill in for him and receive Jamie Martin's latest report, and Jamie had suggested the BM as a meeting place. Jerry had become fascinated with the Gullivers and was eager to share the feeling with Jamie; Ben seemed increasingly distracted from the search. He conferred frequently with Monty and once she had caught him abruptly changing the subject and his tone of voice when she came in unexpectedly as he spoke to his father on the telephone. Ben had said that the lawyers were pressing Monty for results, but Jerry doubted the truth of this. If it were true, surely Ben would be pressing Jamie. And he wasn't; he wasn't even very interested in meeting him.

Jerry stood as Jamie approached through the gates. He was almost running and the pigeons scattered in front of him. Jerry noticed how well he moved as he dodged old people and strolling couples.

"Hello," Jamie gasped. "I'm so glad to see you."

Jerry smiled and touched his arm. "Me too. You look as if you've got news."

"Yes, I have. Where shall we go? Inside?"

Jerry shook her head. "Too nice a day. Let's find some grass and sit." Jerry was wearing loose beige trousers, medium heels and a long white cotton shirt belted at the waist. Jamie drew himself up to his full five feet nine and was glad he had worn his clean jeans. He found it hard to take his eyes off her. Twice she had to stop him from stepping heedlessly out into traffic. They walked into the Bloomsbury and found the grass in the precincts of London University.

"How's Ben?"

Jerry shrugged. "Secretive and morose. What's your news? Do I have to take notes?"

Jamie pulled a sheet of paper from his hip pocket. "No. I can give you the gist of it. I'll type something more formal up later. I just got this stuff today. This morning."

Jerry smiled. The mention of Ben had dropped her spirits momentarily, but Jamie's enthusiasm was infectious. "What stuff?"

"The passenger list from the Australian end. A friend faxed it from Canberra."

"You haven't got a fax machine, have you?"

"No, but I know someone who has."

"Well, come on, come on. Did the Gullivers survive the voyage? They must have, or you wouldn't be looking so full of yourself."

Jamie wanted to tell her that just seeing her made him feel good and that he'd feel the same if the ship had burned to the waterline off South Africa. Instead, he assumed a serious expression. "John and Catherine Gulliver died of the fever within a few days of each other. They were buried at sea."

"Oh, God," Jerry gasped. "How awful. Poor things." She knew what Ben would be hoping—that the fever had reduced the Gulliver brood to a more manageable size. *Damn Ben!* she thought. "What about the kids, Jamie? What about them?"

Jamie saw that her distress was genuine. He had felt something the same when he'd seen the black marks on the photocopied sheets, and the words "buried at sea" had an ominous ring of eternity about them. "The children whose names we know all survived, but there's a remarkable thing here—Catherine Gulliver had another child, born just before she died."

"That's sad," Jerry said. "I suppose it died pretty soon after."

Jamie shook his head. "No, it didn't die. It . . . I don't know what sex it was or what name it was given. The list just calls it an infant. Anyway, it was still alive when the *Southern Maid* reached Australia."

"That's amazing," Jerry said.

"That's not all." Jamie stretched and moved a little closer to Jerry. They were sitting on a patch of yellowed grass across which a spindly tree was just beginning to cast some shadow. The sunlight in Jerry's hair created an aura around her head. Jamie wanted desperately to touch her. Jerry didn't move away. She plucked at some leaves on the grass.

"Ben won't be pleased about an extra body," Jamie said.

"Bugger Ben. I don't know what would please him lately."

"He did some historical research himself, didn't he?"

Jerry nodded. "A bit. He gave it up. How did you know?"

"Oh, I heard. It's a small community in a way." He didn't add that he'd heard the suspicion voiced that Ben Cromwell's idea of 'original' research wasn't orthodox. "Have you ever seen the Turner?"

"No," Jerry said. "Why?"

"Are you sure it exists?"

Jerry's mind was jerked to the mysterious phone call. "I'm *not* sure." She didn't want to think these thoughts. She looked at Jamie as he pushed back his thick, fair hair that was starting to curl on his collar. She was suddenly aware that she was smelling him and not getting the stale alcohol smells she got from Ben or the reck of tobacco emitted by Montague.

"Ben told me you smoked Gauloises," she said.

Jamie brushed his hand across the dry grass. "That was an affectation born of having a few quid in my pocket. I stopped it."

Jerry smiled. "Good. You said that the passenger list wasn't all you had."

"Right. Right." Jamie was glad to get off the dangerous ground of the Cromwells' intentions. "I'm going back out to the PRO in Kew tomorrow. I hope they can turn up the medical officer's journal." Jamie glanced at the sheet of paper in his hand for the first time. "Ah, Dr Percival Anderson. I've never seen one of these things, but I expect it could give us a lead. The MO's the most likely person to have made arrangements for the children."

"What about the chaplain?"

"Good point." Jamie pulled a ballpoint from his shirt pocket and scribbled a note. "I didn't think of that. You're not religious, are you, Jerry?"

Jerry laughed. "Me? Come on. No way. Look, I could do with a coffee."

Jamie jumped up and extended his hand to her. Jerry took it and he pulled her up slowly. Her hand was firm and strong; she steadied herself with a hand on his shoulder while she adjusted a shoe strap. They didn't speak until they were back in Great Russell Street. "So the next move is to track the Gulliver kids in Australia?" Jerry said.

"Yep." Jamie took her arm as they crossed at the lights. "All five of them."

7

Fremantle Harbour, June 1910

"I can offer the lad a job and a home," Clive Rooney said.

Jack stood beside Rooney uncomfortably. He was as tall as and more muscular than this man who was volunteering to sponsor him, and during the ill-fated voyage of the *Southern Maid* he'd become used to being his own master. This situation, where men disposed of him simply because they were older, irked him. But he stood and endured it—because of the pain he felt at his parents' death, because of his burning need to get off the ship that had lain quarantined for weeks in Fremantle harbour, and because of Trudie.

"Is this what you want, Gulliver?" Roger Duff said. The captain and the doctor had constituted themselves a tribunal on the disposal of the Gulliver children. The interview took place in the doctor's cabin on the day that the West Australian authorities had agreed that passengers from the vessel could land.

Dr Anderson, who felt a vague sense of responsibility for the whole Gulliver plight, looked at the strong, dark youth whose hard, lean face was set in a way that suggested stubbornness combined with intelligent self-interest. "Jack?" Anderson said. "You can have your say."

"I'd like to work for Mr Rooney," Jack said.

64   *Peter Corris*

The answer did not satisfy Anderson. "What about your sister and brothers?"

Jack shrugged. "They'll have to look after themselves."

The captain made a quick note on a sheet of paper. "Right," he said. "Best of luck to both of you. You can go ashore in an hour."

Rooney and Jack nodded and left the cabin. Roger Duff sighed and turned to the doctor. "Not the most engaging youth I've ever met, but I suppose he's been through a lot of life in a rush. What d'ye think, doctor?"

Anderson drew his journal towards him and flipped it open. "I think he's going to need a deal of luck not to become gaol bait or worse."

"Yes," the captain said. "Well, I wished him luck, didn't I?"

Clive Rooney, Hester and Trudie Peel and Jack Gulliver stood in the hot, dusty street outside their hotel in Fremantle, where the cab had deposited them. Jack was subdued; he had made brief farewells to Carl, Susannah and Edward. For the baby he felt only hostility. He shook his head as if attempting to expel the associations of sixteen years, feelings and memories. He knew he would never forget the sight of his parents' bodies, wrapped in canvas, one so much bigger than the other, sliding into the sea.

Clive Rooney cleared his throat. "Let's get settled. And then we all need a drink."

"Yes," said Jack who had acquired something of a taste for rum aboard ship. "That's what we need all right."

Rooney booked a room for himself and Jack and one for Trudie and her mother, but the four did not even go through the motions of observing these arrangements. Jack and Trudie slept together in a proper bed for the first time that night and, also for the first time, Jack failed at sex.

"What's the matter?" Trudie sat up in the bed, surprised and distressed, while Jack huddled under the sheet.

"Dunno," Jack said. "Too much beer, I suppose. I've gotta sleep, Trude."

He was snoring within minutes, leaving Trudie staring at the wall. *True, he has drunk a lot,* she thought, *but it was a celebration, wasn't it?* They were off the damn ship, in the new country at last, and Clive Rooney had money in his pockets. But Clive Rooney hadn't got drunk as he'd outlined his plans.

"I've got enough to buy a little pub in a nice town," he'd said. "Not too far from here and Perth. We build it up, do everything nice. I never heard of a publican in Australia who didn't make money. Then we expand, see? Get a farm for Jack and Trudie. Me 'n' your mother might give you a couple of brothers and sisters, Trudie."

Trudie and her mother looked doubtful but Clive was full of visions for his future as a man of importance in some provincial locality. Jack had said nothing and drunk glass after glass of the cold, strong beer. Clive Rooney hadn't got drunk. Trudie imagined that she could hear the bedsprings squeaking in the room next door. She sighed and snuggled down next to Jack.

At three a.m. Trudie felt Jack's sour breath on her face. She woke with a start as he kissed her savagely. She felt him press urgently against her. His hands found her breasts, forced her legs apart. She moaned and clawed at him, pulling him close and stroking him with her hands. "Ooh, ooh, Jacky. Yes. Ooh, that's better. Ooh, yes, put it in, lovey. Put it in!"

They made love energetically and inventively, rolling over in the bed and struggling to get closer and to have more freedom for the delicious movements. When Trudie climaxed Jack clamped his hand over her mouth and stifled the sound. He thrust hard into her and bucked and thudded into his own orgasm. He grunted, but made no more noise than a restless sleeper.

"Why did you do that?" Trudie said after they'd finished and lay in a tangle of legs and bedsheets. "Who cares if they hear?"

Jack stroked her hair. "I don't want to live on some bloody farm buried in the bloody country. Do you?"

They packed and left the hotel. Jack had saved money from his enterprises on board ship and by the time Clive

Rooney and Hester Peel woke up, Jack and Trudie were on a train to Adelaide. They looked older then their years and neither was shy. Jack bought newspapers as they travelled, read them from end to end, and rapidly acquired a working knowledge of their new country's manners. Trudie talked to everyone she met and picked up her own brand of knowledge.

"Sydney's the place for us, Jacky," she said as they contemplated their finances in a Melbourne hotel one week after their flight.

"What's there?" Jack said. All he knew about the city was that it was big and busy and on a harbour.

"Shops and factories to work in. Places to have fun."

"I don't want to work in a shop or a factory."

"What *do* you want, Jacky?"

Jacky didn't know. He suspected that he didn't want to work at all. They travelled to Sydney and rented a room in Surry Hills. Trudie found work in a city shop that made and sold gowns to ladies of quality. Trudie's London accent was found 'charming' by the ladies who still thought of England as home—and better, as a country where people who spoke like Trudie knew their place.

Over the next two years Jack found life tougher. He lost jobs through being lazy and quarrelsome. He got into fights; it was after laying out a big foreman on a building site who had criticised his labouring skills that Jack found something he could bear to do.

He was five feet nine and a half inches tall and eleven and a half stone by this time. Mick Riley might have spent most of his time as a bricklayer but he knew a fighter when he saw one. Mick had the contacts and within two weeks Jack had sworn off beer, done some training at Stone's gymnasium and was booked to fight a preliminary six-rounder at Rushcutter's Bay stadium.

"C'n I come, Jacky?" Trudie asked.

Only four years earlier Mrs Jack London had defied tradition by being present at the Burns–Johnson world title fight in Sydney. Since then women had attended fights regularly and in increasing numbers.

"All right, love," Jack said. "But keep quiet and don't wear anything flashy."

"I never wear flashy clothes." It was true; under tutelage from the women with whom she worked, Trudie had become a fashion plate. At the stadium she sat close to ringside with Mick Riley and was perturbed at not seeing Jack's name on the handbill. "I don't want to see any of these others," she complained, "I want to see my Jack."

Riley's broad, broken-nailed finger rested on the paper. "That's him, Jacky Gee."

"Why doesn't he use his own name?"

Riley shrugged. "I don't think he likes it, Mrs Gulliver." Trudie nodded and looked at the brightly lit ring. There had always been things about Jack she didn't understand. She was eighteen, Jack was one year younger. She wasn't Mrs Gulliver yet and she wondered if she ever would be.

Jacky Gee won his fight in the second round with a right that put his opponent down for a full minute. He won his next eight fights and only once had to go the distance for a points decision. A preliminary fighter's purses were small, but Jack was a crowd pleaser and he always got a 'shower' after a fight. The patrons threw coins into the ring and the money was split between the fighters.

After one fight, which he won by a devastating knockout in the second round, Jack asked his opponent why he'd taken the fight.

"You can't punch, mate. You must've known I'd kill you."

The other boxer shrugged. "Yeah, I knew. But youse is alwus good for a shower. Do better from losin' to you than winnin' against some other blokes."

Jack told Trudie about this as she bathed his cuts and massaged his aching shoulders. They were still in Surry Hills, which Trudie liked because it reminded her of life in London, but now they had a small flat and decent furniture. "Can you imagine that? Fighting for the money they throw into the ring?"

"Is it so different from fighting for the purse, or for bets?"

"Yeah, it is, somehow. When I think about it, I'd rather be the one throwing the money."

Jack fought a main event, a twenty-rounder against an up-and-coming country pug named Les Dixon. Neither had much skill, both had strength and courage. Jack's strength lasted longer and he knocked Dixon out in the eighteenth round. After the fight, Mick Riley was surprised when Jack invited him to share a couple of bottles of beer with him. They sat in the old Ford Jack had bought with his winnings.

"Give me that," Jack said. He prised the top off the bottle with his thumb and let half the contents run down his throat. "Christ, that's good."

Riley was alarmed. "Y'never drink, Jacky. You know what the stuff does to a fighter. What's got into you?"

Jack drained the bottle. "I've finished with fighting."

"Finished, is it? Y've only just started, boy."

"Open another couple, Mick. I'm finished."

"Why, for God's sake? It was hard tonight, but y' won."

"Three reasons. One, it's a mug's game getting your brains beaten out; two, they'd match me with this Maitland bloke, Les Darcy, sooner or later and he'd kill me; and three, I've got other plans."

John Gulliver, bachelor, and Gertrude Peel, spinster, were married on 1 August 1914, three days before Australia declared war on Germany and six months before the birth of their son Stephen. Jack had wanted to use his ring name on the marriage documents but Trudie had refused to agree. "I'm not marrying anyone named Gee," she said. "It sounds like an Indian or a Chink or something."

"You've been living with someone named Gee for the last two years."

"Getting married's different. I don't care what they call us afterwards."

Jack gave in, as he always did when Trudie's mind was firmly set. Luckily, it wasn't like that often. After the wedding at a registry office, and the reception in the back room of the Surry Hills Arms, Jack and Trudie went to Manly for a week. They had a spell of Sydney's best winter weather—clear, bright days and cold nights. Jack bought ten hot water bottles and heated the whole of the bed. They made love the way they had four years before, on the ship, when they had no thought for anything but themselves and before Jack had begun to drink regularly. In recent times Jack had been more interested in sleep than love, first because he was exhausted from training and fighting and then because of the beer. But not at Manly.

"Ever think about your mum, love, or Clive?" Jack said as they stood on the pier, well wrapped against the cold wind and looking across the clear green-blue water towards the Sydney Harbour heads.

"Sometimes." Trudie clutched his arm. "Not that often. I think of London a bit but I really love it here. It's good, isn't it, Sydney?"

"If you've got enough money," Jack said.

"What about you, Jacky? Do you think about your sister and brothers? I mean, I suppose Mum and Clive have got their pub and there they are, somewhere. But the kids . . ."

Jack turned away from the water and the wind and lit a cigarette, another habit he'd adopted since finishing with boxing. "When my pa packed us all up and we left bloody England was the day my life started." He blew smoke which was plucked away by the wind. "No, it started when we snuck off from that hotel in Fremantle. I dunno. There was a fresh start somewhere. No, I don't think about 'em."

That night, Trudie lay awake beside the gently snoring Jack until the early hours. She'd seen big houses fringing the harbour, really big, and she wanted one for herself. In the city she saw the women who lived in the houses, heard how they spoke, saw how they dressed and ate. She knew from what they said that some of them had roughneck husbands, but they were worthy of the houses they lived in, and she would be worthy too.

8

Only gradually did the war make any difference to Jack. At first he ignored it, saying it was no business of his. In private, with Trudie, he joked that he was half-German himself so he wouldn't know which side to fight on.

"Don't say that, Jacky. Don't *ever* say that." Trudie's look was fierce. "If they hear you saying things like that they'll lock you up, and then where will we be?"

When talk of conscription began, Jack's other joke, especially when he was drunk, was that he was too young to be conscripted. "Can be called up till nineteen bloody sixteen," he said. "Too young to die."

This angered rather than frightened Trudie; she didn't like attention being drawn to her being slightly older. Jack continued to treat the matter of war service lightly. After Stephen's birth, a long and painful affair for Trudie, whose narrow, boyish lines were bad for childbearing, Jack excused himself on the grounds of his family responsibilities, as the highest people in the land were doing. "My fight is here," Jack said, "against the landlord and the butcher and my bloody wife's shoemaker." At times he mentioned other responsibilities—for a sister and three brothers. "Not a one of them," Jack would say, glass in hand, "yet ten years of age."

Jack's 'plans' involved, initially, the use of his fists and boots. The conqueror of Les Dixon readily secured contracts to protect card games, to persuade defaulting gamblers to pay up and to supervise proceedings when the owners of brothels and illegal gambling establishments made payments to the police. After 1916, when a referendum was passed which closed Sydney hotels at six p.m., Jack moved into sly grog. He supplied the places he formerly guarded, and now guarded the places he supplied.

The soldiers were thirsty. Some were awaiting trans-shipment, some enjoying leave on account of wounds or meritorious service, and some were permanently based in Australia. They needed sex and diversion. They had some money and Jack helped them spend it. By the end of 1916, with the referendum on conscription decisively lost and six p.m. closing firmly in place in the southern states, Jack Gulliver employed eight men and had interests in profitable enterprises around Sydney, which did all of their business at night. He was twenty-one years of age, but boxing scars and the strains of living by his wits and intimidation made him look older. He weighed fourteen stone (beer and easy living having filled him out) and he was having a good war.

The white feathers worried Trudie. They arrived in the mail at the three-storeyed house in Bellevue Hill and were sometimes to be found on the front seat of Jack's touring Buick.

"Forget it," Jack said. "I'm collecting 'em. Soon I'll have enough to stuff a mattress for Stephen."

"Don't talk like that, Jacky," Trudie said. "No one in this street'll have a cup of tea with me."

"Bugger them and their tea. Come out with me tonight. You can drink wine and whisky and eat caviar and they know what they can do with their tea."

"I can't go out. I have to look after Stephen."

"We can get someone in to look after him."

Trudie's face closed. She remembered being looked after—long, lonely nights with drunken women who, like as not, had some man around to look after them. "No," she said.

"Suit yourself."

Jack spent more time in the rough and tumble of Kings Cross than in well-mannered Bellevue Hill. But he paid for everything his son needed. He opened a cheque account for Trudie and left money lying around in the house. He shouted at his wife often, when she refused to 'come on the razz' with him and when she was cold to the people he brought back to the house for chicken suppers with champagne. She objected to the noise that might wake Stephen, although he was two floors above in a room she called the nursery.

One day Trudie found a note which had been folded small and tucked into one of Jack's waistcoat pockets. She picked it up from the bottom of a wardrobe where it had fallen into a shoe. The hastily written pencilled scrawl read: 'Darling Jack—don't worry about it. it happens to a lot of men sometimes. i still love you and we can tri again. Barbara.'

Trudie remembered Barbara, a plump baby-blue-eyed blonde Jack had brought back to the house late one night alone with several men, all of whom were considerably older than the women they escorted. Jack had paid particular attention to Barbara, refilling her glass almost as frequently as his own and ending up very drunk. He had not attempted sex after the guests had left but Trudie was sure what the outcome would have been. *If he prepares himself for Barbara that way,* Trudie thought, *it's no wonder she has to write notes afterwards.*

Trudie made a copy of the note and placed it on Jack's pillow in the bed they shared when he was at home. He saw it two nights later and his high colour faded. He almost fell onto the bed.

"Jesus," he said.

"It's just a copy. I've got the one she wrote put away."

"Why?"

"So I can divorce you."

"Jesus, Trudie, no!"

"Why not?"

Jack rolled on the bed; his collar stud popped and his collar and tie hung loosely around his neck. "You can't."

The Gulliver Fortune

Trudie stood at the end of the bed and looked at him. She was wearing a silk nightdress and there was lace around the edges of the light silk dressing gown she wore over it. "No, Jacky," she said. "You're the one who can't. You can't do it with anyone else, can you?"

Jack wept, burying his head in the bedclothes. "No. No. No, I can't. I can't."

Trudie sat on the bed and drew his head towards her. She leaned down and let her big, ripe breasts fall from her nightdress. She put her nipples to his lips. "Suck it," she said. "I want another baby. I went with twenty men before you, but you're the only one who gave me a baby. Suck it!"

Trudie used her weapon against Jack ruthlessly. She secured the enrolment of Stephen at a private school against Jack's wishes, by sleeping apart from him for a month. She brought an end to the late night carousing visits and forced her husband to take her to the theatre. Jack wrote cheques for paintings and a piano. He permitted a dog, a snarling German Shepherd, fanatically loyal to Trudie and Stephen, to share his home. At Trudie's insistence, as soon as he entered the house, he placed the .45 automatic he always wore in the box attached to the hallstand.

"It's no use to me there," Jack had protested. "Take me half an hour to get to it."

"Jacky Gulliver," Trudie had said coldly, "the day a shot is fired within a hundred yards of this house is the day you leave. And you know what that means."

Trudie lived in fear that Jack would overcome his disability, but he did not. She frequently seduced him because she desperately wanted another child, but this did not happen either. Trudie mothered Stephen, who was a sturdy, cheerful child, closely. Jack appeared to be fond of the boy in an offhand way. In fact his one child reminded him of the fact that he was apparently incapable of fathering more. Jack attended the business. The Gee family rubbed along, to all outward appearances no unhappier than most.

* * *

One of Jack's favourite sayings was that as a businessman he preferred liquids to solids. After the war he continued in the sly grog selling that had served him so well, and included black market petrol and smuggled perfume among the commodities he dealt in. He now employed ten men and hired others on a casual basis—as drivers, warehouse hands and gun carriers—when he needed them. He acquired an office in a building that also housed a greyhound trainer, a dentist and a doctor. The greyhound trainer was a race fixer and bookie, the dentist dispensed cocaine and the doctor did abortions. All four shared a lawyer named James Wright-Wilson, who was a cousin of the chief commissioner of police.

"I'm known to the police," Jack would say. "I oughter be. I buy the buggers drinks every day an' put the bloody petrol in their tanks."

Trudie devoted herself to a minute study of 'respectability' and to an obsessive concern for Stephen, his health and his happiness. She became the mainstay of Carnley, the small private preparatory school he attended. Trudie's cheques arrived on the principal's desk regularly—for double glazing to insulate the building and make it quieter, for first aid equipment in the infirmary, for sets of encyclopaedias. Trudie served on committees, hired caterers for school functions and personally resolved the dispute over whether the Reverend Angus Cameron, a Presbyterian clergyman, should be permitted to minister to the spiritual needs of the students, as well as one from the Church of England. The Reverend Cameron was an ambitious man.

This debate, which raged within the school and among the parents, provided one of the few opportunities for Trudie to seek Jack's help. They talked about it at home one night, after dinner and after Trudie, against her usual practice, had taken a drink or two.

"I don't want the Prezzos in on it," Trudie said.

"Why not?" Jack was expansive, well-oiled and smoking his fiftieth cigarette for the day. "What the hell difference does it make? It's only make-believe anyway, all that religious sh—rubbish."

"Of course it is Jacky, But it's a question of tone."

"What?" Jack said.

"Tone. The look of the thing. Really good schools don't have Prezzos around. It'll affect Stephen's chances of getting into Shore."

"Christ." Jack's soul revolted at the school's name and everything associated with it. But Trudie, at twenty-eight, with leisure and money to spend on her appearance, was still the most beautiful woman of his acquaintance. And if he played his cards right and didn't get onto the brandy he could have her tonight. "What's this parson's name?"

"Angus Cameron."

"Forget about him," Jack said. "Let's go to bed."

Ten days later the Reverend Cameron was under a cloud, the nature of which he never quite understood. His neighbours in the fashionable suburb of Centennial Park began to avoid him, his housekeeper resigned and his wife took their two children on an extended holiday to Scotland. Angus Cameron began to wear a neglected look and he impressed Carnley's Presbyterian-leaning parents less and less. When he was removed to a posting in the Riverina Trudie took Jack to bed, giving him the lace underwear and all the trimmings.

"How did you do it, Jacky?" she said after he'd collapsed following his second orgasm within an hour.

Jack gulped air and waited for his pulse to slow. "It's who you know in this town," he said when he had the breath. "What've we got here? A couple of hundred thousand people and only a few of 'em matter. You can always find someone to squeeze and he'll squeeze someone for you."

Trudie nodded. She was lying on the bed, brimming with Jack's sperm and trying to calculate how long it had been since she'd enjoyed sex with him. Too long. And she'd had no one else; she wouldn't dare. She looked at Jack as he slid towards sleep. His belly was large and his second chin rested flabbily in folds on his neck. He rolled onto his side and snored. Trudie seldom smoked but she had a craving for a cigarette just then. She eased herself off the bed, straightened the nightdress over which Jack had slobbered and hitched at its torn shoulder. She went quietly to her wardrobe and took out a plain dark dressing gown. Jack's clothes were lying in heaps around the floor. She found his jacket and extracted a packet of cigarettes and a petrol lighter.

The bedroom was big, as wide as the house itself, and deep. It had two large bay windows, one of which was equipped with a small padded settee and a satin footstool. Trudie sat and smoked and looked out at the dark starless night. Jack snored on the bed.

School committee work had taught Trudie the importance of a properly prepared agenda. She understood the necessity for priorities, ambitious claims and positions to retreat to. Over the next eighteen months she worked carefully. First, she ensured that Jack had a substantial life insurance policy and that his will was in order. One of the benefits of her sexual hold on Jack was that there were no mistresses around, no mothers of illegitimate children to be taken care of. Jack's will left his estate in its entirety to Trudie. But there were subsidiary arrangements—an endowment to Shore Grammar to smooth Stephen's path and an educational trust fund for the boy.

Jack's business interests now ranged from racehorses to pie stalls. He was a partner in various enterprises such as a gymnasium and a factory that produced motor car tyres. Trudie found ways to involve herself in many of these businesses. She was aware of the other activities, those that generated helpful cash, but she never acknowledged their existence.

"You could've handled the books in Clive's pub," Jack said one night after Trudie had resolved an accounting problem. "I wonder if they made a quid. D'you think we should try to find 'em, Trude? Might be able to help 'em out a bit if things didn't work out so well."

Trudie looked at him cautiously. It was rare for Jack to extend consideration to anyone. He wasn't drunk. She observed him closely for any changes in his moods and attitudes that might signal a new sexual confidence. She saw no such signs. She poured drinks for them both. *The last thing I need is for Hester and Clive to turn up*, she thought. *She's probably the size of a battleship by now, and God knows what color her hair'd be.*

"They'll have done all right," she said. "Don't go soft, Jacky. You've got too much on your plate. By the way, I think you should discharge the mortgage on the Avalon beach house. You can afford it."

"All right, love." Jack sipped his brandy. "Did I tell you I might be going into politics?"

"What?"

"Yeah. No joke. Couple of men around town think I could be useful."

"Which party?"

Jack was surprised. "Labor, a'course. I'm a Lang man."

Trudie shuddered at the thought of Stephen's father as a wheeling and dealing Labor machine politician. Besides, she didn't want him in the public eye. She pressed on with other aspects of her preparations. These involved hiring two men who had seen service in the war and fallen on hard times: tough, resourceful men who wanted capital to establish themselves as coffee planters in Africa. Hearing of Jack's plantation interests in Fiji, they had applied to him for a loan and been refused.

Jack had laughed about them. "Africa, my arse," he said to Trudie. "Remember passing the bloody place on the way out here? Africa! If we could still buy and sell niggers I might be interested."

Trudie made contact with the aspiring planters. She sold jewellery Jack had given her, skimmed from the household accounts and made apparently foolish mistakes with her cheque book.

"I'm forever forking out for you and the kid," Jack complained.

"He's your future," Trudie said.

Jack poured more brandy and lit another cigarette. "My future's in my own hands. John Gee, MP." He laughed and got very red in the face.

On 12 August 1925, at nine p.m., two hours before the *Wilhelm Weber* sailed for Mombasa, a Buick tourer, travelling at speed, went out of control on a steep, wet road in Dover Heights. The car broke through a barrier and plunged sixty feet onto the surf-lashed rocks. The body of John Gee, aged thirty, was recovered from the water the following morning. It was identified by Gertrude Gee, his widow. John Gee was buried in the Church of England section of the Waverley cemetery.

9

New Guinea, July 1945

First Lieutenant Stephen St John Gee crouched over the Bren gun in the shallow trench, taking care not to touch the breech, which was sizzling hot, steaming in the damp New Guinea air. Spent cases had sprayed from the gun and lay glinting in the thick, mud-matted grass. One live man squatted down beside him, but three other men, clad in the same khaki as Gee and his companion, lay dead in the depression.

"How many d'you think we got?" Private Frank Lewis asked.

Across a clearing which had been sprinkled with saplings and bushes before the murderous fire had cut them down like wheat, was thick jungle. A path appeared as a darker blur in the deep green background. Down this path the Japanese had come, more of them than Gee had expected, almost more than he'd been able to stop, even with the element of surprise on his side.

"I don't know, Lewis. Quite a lot, but there's no point in kidding ourselves. There's more in there and they'll come again."

"Yeah," Lewis wiped sweat and mud from his face and was surprised to see blood on his hand. "I got hit."

Gee turned to look at him and grinned. His teeth were even and showed white against the skin of his face which was yellowed by the constant taking of atabrine.

"You've got a scratch on your cheek. Probably one of your own shell cases. You were really pumping them out."

"Mention me in despatches, will you, sir?"

Both men smiled at the joke. They knew Gee would write no more despatches, no more letters home, and Lewis would win no more darts tournaments, hit no more jam tins with a .303 at four hundred yards.

"They'll come around us if they've got any sense," Gee said. "They can get pretty close, over there and over to the right. I'll take the right with the Bren. See what you can do."

Lewis nodded and wriggled around so that he sat with his back almost touching Gee's. It was early in the afternoon, night was many hours away. *Too many*, Gee thought. The rest of their unit was far down the track now, heading for Lae. Would there be stragglers who might come up behind the Japanese? No, *they* were the stragglers, limping back with two men wounded. Good men. After the battle on the ridge, which A Company had won, Captain Lipmann had given the officers the gist of the latest intelligence report. "Detached groups of Japanese hiding in the hills to the west. None between here and Lae."

Gee was sceptical about intelligence reports; in his four years of war he'd found them wrong as often as not.

"Got a smoke?" Lewis asked.

"Sorry, I don't."

"That's right. You don't. I forgot. Why's that? You don't smoke?"

It was on the tip of Gee's tongue to say, "Because my mother told me not to," but he didn't.

"Do you drink?"

"Not much. But I wouldn't mind one now."

"Bloody right." Lewis had filled the magazine of his rifle and had two more magazines, also full, ready to hand. "How many rounds have you got for the Bren?"

Gee felt that the difference in rank between Lewis and himself had disappeared. He was glad of it. "About a hundred."

"Think we've got any chance of getting them all?"

Gee laughed. "No."

"Didn't think so. Get a few, though."

"Yes." Gee was tired; his shoulders slumped and he leaned back until he and Lewis were spine to spine. "There's one thing, Lewis," Gee said.

"What?"

"Sitting like this we can't possibly shoot each other."

Both men laughed. Gee stared at the jungle growth, imagined he saw a movement, looked again and relaxed. Nothing. There was nothing to see. He could hear birds in the trees behind him and a light wind was moving the leaves. The quiet was welcome after the days of thumping mortars and steady rifle and machine-gun fire. An insect buzzed near his ear and settled somewhere, possibly on his helmet. It was peaceful and Lieutenant Gee, with time to spare and nothing better to do for the first time in years, remembered . . .

It had been wet for weeks, and the rain didn't let up for his father's funeral. The cemetery was all puddles and grey, stony mud. His mother wore black clothes that day and for a time afterwards, he wasn't sure how long. Somehow, everything was different for him from that day. It wasn't that he missed his father; he scarcely knew him. It wasn't the moving house from Bellevue Hill to North Sydney, although that had brought changes. The new house was smaller and his life seemed to shrink too. His father had constantly brought people to the house, usually late at night. He had heard their noise from his bedroom. Now few people visited.

"A gentleman, be a gentleman." It was a refrain he seemed to have heard from his mother for the next fifteen years. So he tried to be a gentleman. He attended gentlemen's schools and played gentlemen's sports. Trudie came to see him perform in the school swimming carnival, where he won three sprint races, and she took an interest in his golf. She bought him expensive woods and irons, and wouldn't hear of him joining any club other than Royal Sydney.

"It's the club for gentlemen." she said. Trudie's cockney had long since been replaced by an accent she had acquired from listening often and carefully to clergymen and certain actresses in British films.

"Yes, mother. But . . ." In fact he found other courses more interesting to play on and he did, while maintaining his membership at the gentlemen's club, where the course was still called a links. In fact, Stephen had already learned to conform to his mother's wishes on the surface, while going his own way. He had played some rugby on the quiet and enjoyed it. He studied classical piano but played jazz whenever he could. He left the house dressed like a gentleman, always, but often in his bag he carried what he called 'smarter togs'.

He had few friends, none close. Trudie discouraged visits by other boys and forbade staying overnight at other houses. This restricted his opportunities for bonding. With no relatives in Australia, there were no country houses or sheep properties for him to visit, such as his schoolmates had and seemed to take for granted. Stephen went to organised camps in the mountains or by a lake where there was proper supervision and not much fun.

It was in the matter of his career that he had his first direct confrontation with Trudie. She had been generous with money and praise all his life, and now she wanted her reward.

"The law," she said. "You must study law. I want you to be a judge. You'd look wonderful in the robes and you have the brain for the job."

It was true that Stephen was over six feet tall, with a long, wise-seeming face, and he had matriculated with honours in a range of subjects. He was a little weak in mathematics but none of the professions appeared closed to him. He had a place at St Pauls, the oldest and most Oxfordian of Sydney University's colleges.

"I don't want to study law, mother. I want to study literature."

"You mean read novels," Trudie snapped "You do too much of that already. It probably cost you a second class in mathematics."

"No. I hate mathematics and I should hate law. I'd probably fail."

The word brought Trudie up short. She couldn't recall hearing Stephen ever use it before. She certainly never used it herself. An instinct told her to go carefully. "You mean do an arts degree?"

"Yes," Stephen said.

"With what end in view?"

"I don't know."

It was 1932. The dole queues stretched along the streets and in some parts of the city more than half the shops and businesses were boarded up. Trudie's investments had been sound but even her returns had shrunk. She could feel the contraction of hopes and dreams around her. She looked at Stephen and saw the stubborn set of his long jaw. Suddenly, and with much alarm, she saw signs of Jack in him. She had a vision of Stephen defying her, refusing to go to university, taking to the track. "A compromise," she said. "Would you consider a compromise?"

It was the first time Stephen could recall his mother backing down over anything. "I might."

"You can study arts and law—do a combined degree. It'd take longer but when you've finished things might be better. There might be better prospects for . . ."

"A lawyer?"

Trudie smiled and reached up to pat his cheek. She was stylishly dressed, not yet forty, and with Stephen about to leave the nest she was contemplating the selection of a husband. It would take time and care and she didn't want the complication of a fractious son. "As a lawyer, or whatever your study of literature might fit you for." She sighed. "Though God alone knows what that might be."

Though overindulged and overprivileged, Stephen was neither stupid nor unreasonable. "Right you are, mother," he said. "There's the small matter of a car to be settled."

"At the end of your first year," Trudie said. "If you do well enough."

Stephen did very well. To his surprise and his mother's gratification he did better in law than arts, and preferred wrestling with casebooks than novels and poems. He dropped arts and charged ahead in his legal studies, picking up a prize or two each year. Trudie bought him a car which he drove carefully and well. He was drunk at the end of his second year and once or twice in the years following but he did not acquire a taste for alcohol. This was something Trudie watched for, knowing the signs so well. She bribed Stephen not to smoke until his twenty-first birthday with the promise of a better car, after she read that this was done in fashionable American circles. As a consequence, Stephen never acquired the tobacco habit.

Usually, it was to America that Trudie looked for example and inspiration. She even considered moving to the States but gave up the idea when Stephen expressed no interest. Like many first-generation Australians, he was a passionate nationalist.

"This is the greatest country in the world," he told his mother over dinner one night when he was taking a rare night off from study in his final year. "I'm so glad you and Dad decided to come here."

"How did that come about, Gertrude?" The speaker was Alexander Courtney, a widower of fifty-five and manager of the bank that handled some, but by no means all, of Trudie's financial affairs.

"My parents came out for the business opportunities," Trudie said. She had given such vague explanations for so long that she half believed them herself. Stephen, who had seen old photographs of young Jack and Trudie, suspected that there was more to the story than this, but he had never asked for details.

"Ah, yes." Courtney folded his hands comfortably across his stomach. "Australia was doing wonderfully well before these socialists put their oar in. Don't you agree, Stephen?"

Stephen smiled and took another spoonful of soup to avoid answering. He was amused by politics, amused by his mother's careful vetting of her suitors, amused by almost everything.

* * *

The Gulliver Fortune

The afternoon rains came. Stephen Gee and Private Lewis sat stolidly through the drenching, knowing that the hot sun would soon dry them and that conditions were the same for the Japanese. They covered the mechanisms of their weapons and waited. Soaking wet, skin itching and muscles cramping, Stephen began to think about the comforts of his prewar life and the discomfort of his 'problem' . . .

After graduating with first-class honours and just missing the university medal, Stephen was articled to a prominent Macquarie Street firm where he performed with distinction. He moved back into his mother's house and continued to live with her for reasons neither of them quite understood. Trudie had not married Alexander Courtney or anyone else. She always found something to dislike about the men she met—their cigar smoking, throat clearing or eagerness to manage her money. She preferred to cook several times a week for Stephen, to attend to his laundry and to go to the theatre with him occasionally. She endured Shakespeare and enjoyed Noel Coward. She described herself as 'living quietly'.

Stephen changed firms, attracted by an offer from a barrister who specialised in criminal cases.

"I'm not sure that's the best move for your career," Trudie said. "Wouldn't something more commerical or even academic be better?"

"Dull," Stephen said. "Working with Mr Easy could be fun."

Geoffrey Easy was a law book and courtroom addict. He lived for his work and did nothing else. "Plenty of work about, young St Gee," he told Stephen. "As long as you're not too fussy."

"It's just Gee, Mr Easy. Not St Gee. I feel I've had a rather fussy life so far and it's time for a change."

"Spotted that in you, St Gee. Sort of thing I'm looking for. To start you off, I've got a brothel keeper here the police want to put in gaol. Most unreasonable. The lady's willing to pay a fine. See what you can do with it."

Over the next few years Stephen defended madams,

SP bookmakers, defaulting solicitors, violators of the liquor licensing laws and wealthy kleptomaniacs. Geoffrey Easy's practice was busy and chaotic, with a high turnover of staff. Easy gave alcoholic lawyers their last chance, often to his cost, and took chances with brilliant eccentrics. Stephen was a steadily good performer. He earned a lot of money and enjoyed the work. After he had successfully defended a newspaper publisher against a libel action, Easy took Stephen to dinner and then to a select brothel in Rose Bay.

"No," Stephen said.

"What d'you mean, no?" Easy pointed with his cigar at the blonde, the redhead and the brunette who stood in the middle of the tasteful room. They were young, elaborately made up and wore expensive clothes that accentuated their good figures. "These are the cleanest girls in Sydney. I've been coming here for years and never caught a thing. Well, small case of the crabs once, but . . ."

"I'd rather not," Stephen said.

Easy eyed him shrewdly. "How old're you, St Gee?"

"Twenty-four."

The redhead giggled.

"Shut up," Easy growled. "It's just a matter of taking the plunge, boy. You couldn't get better swimming teachers than these lasses."

Stephen shook his head miserably. Easy went up the stairs with the brunette. Stephen attempted conversation with the madam but soon ran out of things to say. Easy came down the stairs whistling; he gave a generous tip to the young woman who had taken custody of his and Stephen's hats and left an envelope on the highly French polished table by the door. Later, walking through the streets with Easy, Stephen admitted that he had never spent any time alone with a woman. "Except my mother," he added.

Easy grunted. "And why's that?"

Stephen shrugged. "Shy, I suppose."

"Not a nancy boy, are you?"

Stephen had drunk more and experienced more powerful emotions than he was accustomed to. He faced the question squarely as he walked. He'd played sport with men, seen their bodies in the locker rooms. "No," he said.

Easy walked on. He was a thin, small man, very spry and sure of himself. Stephen had to hurry to keep up. "I'll take your case, St Gee. You can buy women or you can meet 'em. I prefer the former but there's no accounting for taste. Leave it with me."

That was how matters stood on 1 September 1939. Two days later Australia followed Britain in declaring war on Germany. On 10 September, Stephen St John Gee, ignoring protests from his mother and words of caution from his employer, joined the army.

The rain stopped but water still fell heavily from the trees for many minutes. The sky remained overcast so the heating and drying Stephen had anticipated would not occur. It hardly mattered. He eased his back away from Lewis's and felt the soldier stir.

"Nodded off," Lewis said.

"You could've got nipped in the bud."

It was an old joke but they both forced a laugh. Stephen stared at the path, which he knew was a mistake. That was not where they would come from. He almost wished they would hurry . . .

Stephen was trained, commissioned and received his overseas posting all within six months. His mother pleaded with him to take a staff job, but he refused.

"You're my only child," she said. "I don't want to lose you."

He looked at her trim, well-dressed figure. She was forty-six but looked much younger. *You could have had other children,* he thought, *and it's not my fault that you didn't.* He kissed his mother goodbye, promised to write and boarded the ship. Trudie watched him until he disappeared from sight. She thought he looked smart in his uniform and she particularly liked to see him being saluted. She went home. For the first time since the last occasion when she'd dutifully kept Jack company while extracting some agreement from him, she got drunk. She slept and dreamed of her mother and felt sick when she awoke. The years began to show on Trudie's face from that day.

Stephen wrote dutifully from Egypt, Greece and Italy. He wrote from London when he was there on leave. Trudie opened the mail from England nervously, fearful that he might encounter a member of his family from either side. But he never did. Her hopes rose a little when he wrote, in November 1944:

> *Dear Mother,*
>
> *I appear to have survived the European war. I am being sent to New Guinea, which should please you as I will be able to get home on leave. I can't tell you much more on account of the censorship. I think Geoffrey Easy could probably establish that censorship is illegal, but there you are.*
>
> *You ask about promotion. No, I am a lieutenant still. It doesn't seem to come my way. Perhaps I will cover myself with glory in New Guinea and return home a captain.*
>
> *Your loving son,*
> *Stephen*

Trudie had her hair done a different way and bought some new clothes. Stephen took her out several times while he was in Sydney on leave. He had aged, grown thinner and acquired frown lines. Trudie painted artfully and fancied that they could almost be taken for lovers.

"Can't be long, sir, can it?" Private Lewis asked.

"No. Not long."

"Got anything to write on? I'd like to leave a note for my missus and nipper."

Stephen passed him his notebook and pencil. He could feel the movement of Lewis's back as he wrote. After what seemed like only seconds he heard the page being torn from the book.

"Thanks. What about you? You got a wife?"

Stephen smiled. "Yes, I have."

He had met Tess in Wewak or, rather, she had met him. She was a nurse, Brisbane-born and three years older than he. She fixed her eye on the lieutenant on the day of his arrival at the base and her pursuit of him had been relentless. She had herself rostered to the medical inspection of Stephen's platoon and contrived a chance meeting in the canteen. The rest was child's play. Stephen had maintained his innocence of women while killing men in different parts of the world. Tess found this exciting and a boost to the strong attraction she felt for the tall, quiet man who carried books in his battle jacket pocket.

Tess's comparative maturity reassured Stephen and made him less nervous. He talked to her about books and London and showed no great fondness for beer. These things made him unusual among soldiers. He had never been to Brisbane and she told him about the city. She talked well, making it sound like an exotic tropical creation, manmade. They began to spend their off-duty hours together, walking along the jungle tracks around the town and on the dark, mangrove-fringed beach.

"I'd like to see Brisbane when this is all over," Stephen said one night as they sat on rocks by the water.

"If it's ever over."

"Can't be long. We've dislodged the Japs from most places. They've lost their grip on the place and they're losing the people."

Tess looked at him with surprise. "You mean the local people supported them?"

"Some of them, yes. Why not? I can't see that we've ever done them much good."

Tess thought him a most unusual man and never more so than when she finally got him into her tent. It took weeks of her cigarette ration to bribe the other nurses to keep clear for a couple of hours. She made tea while Stephen sat on her camp bed. She brought the mug of tea across and held it to his mouth. He put his hands up to take it but she shook her head. She moved so that his hands touched her breasts.

"Please, Stephen. Touch me. I want you to."

Tess's brassiere was in her locker; there was only the thin material of her nurse's dress between her body and Stephen's gently moving hands.

"God," he said. "That's wonderful."

"Inside."

Clumsily he undid the buttons and opened the dress. Her breasts were high and firm. He put his hands on them and the nipples hardened. Tess put the mug aside and moved his head so that his lips brushed against her breasts. "I want to make love."

"I can't," Stephen whispered. "I mean, I never have."

Tess was delighted. She sat on the bed next to him and opened his shirt. She kissed his chest. "Lie back. Relax."

Tess had had two American lovers in Brisbane, one officer and one enlisted man, one married and one single. She had learned a great deal from them, particularly ways of taking sex slowly and by degrees. Patiently and calmly she showed Stephen how to explore her body. He became erect and she slowed everything down, forcing him to concentrate on her reactions, not his. He was awkward and hurt her with his urgent fingers. She took his hand and guided it. Stephen felt as if he had doubled in strength and wisdom. They kissed and he moved on top of her on the narrow bed. She lifted her knees and spread herself.

"Go deep, darling, and stop when I tell you."

He entered her, plunged and exploded. He collapsed and put his face in her hair. "I'm sorry. I couldn't."

She laughed and kissed him. "I didn't think so. Don't worry. Wait. You're still there. I can feel you."

They made love twice more before her time of bought privacy expired. He held her and kissed her hard. "I love you."

"Do you?" she said. "We'll see."

Stephen St John Gee and Teresa Savage were married in Brisbane on 8 May 1945. They were on short leave and agreed not to complicate their service lives by making the marriage public. Stephen put off telling his mother and Tess had no close family to inform. They spent a week in Brisbane, with Tess showing her husband the sights. They stayed in a city hotel and made love every night and at least once during the day.

"I've got a lot of time to catch up on," Stephen said.

"I started well before you. That's not hard to tell, is it?" Tess lit a cigarette and waited for his reply.

They were both naked on the bed. Their faces and arms were brown and there was a vee of tanned skin below their necks. Stephen kissed her on the point of the vee and went lower. Tess squashed out her cigarette. When they'd finished Stephen got a towel and wiped the sweat from their bodies. "I don't care how many men you've had," he said. "You brought me to life and I'll love you forever."

She put her finger on his lips. "Don't say forever. It's bad luck."

"There's no such thing."

They walked around the city streets debating where Stephen would have his office and took taxis to the suburbs to plan where they would live. They drank beer and ate Chinese food and went dancing.

"How is it you can dance and never got to know any girls?" Tess asked.

"Lessons. I've had lessons in everything." Stephen turned her expertly to avoid a half-drunk American who was trying to put some vigour into his steps.

"You're a good learner."

Tess was dark with a round face, big eyes and a full mouth. Everything about her was generous and easy. She smoked a lot and drank much more than Stephen but he didn't care. They were happy. At the end of the week they returned to New Guinea and soon after Stephen's company was despatched south to participate in the mopping up of the Japanese units still active between Lae and Buna.

The jungle seemed suddenly to have become quieter. The interval between the bird calls seemed unnaturally long. Stephen uncovered the Bren and checked the action. He adjusted the angle of the belt feeding into the breech and made sure that nothing would obstruct it.

Lewis's voice was high and shaky. "See anything, sir?"

"No." Stephen opened the notebook and began to write.

"See anything?"

"No." He wrote: 'Darling Tess'.

"That's the bloody trouble, isn't it?"

Stephen didn't reply. The pencil touched the paper again and the bullets hissed and thudded around him. The range was shockingly close; dirt and shredded leaves stung his face. He swivelled the gun in the direction of the fire and squeezed the trigger. A dozen bullets hit him like hammer blows. His finger locked the trigger onto automatic fire and the gun rattled on for seconds after he was dead.

10

Many times Georgia Gee had heard the story of her mother's arrival in North Sydney to introduce her to her grandmother. As Tess told the tale, it was a bright, sunny day and she had Georgia dressed in a yellow smock and a white sunhat. The child was not quite one year old.

"You were gorgeous," Tess had said. "With your black curls down to here and those eyes. I didn't see how anyone could resist you."

Tess had been two months pregnant when Stephen was killed. She went into a kind of trance when she got the news. The bloodstained notebook with 'Darling Tess' written in it was given to her and she wept over it for hours. She was discharged from the nursing corps, given her severance pay and found herself alone and pregnant in Brisbane. The shock took a long time to wear off; she knew nothing about Stephen's will and very little about his circumstances. She knew he had a mother alive but she did not know her address or even whether she lived in Australia. Stephen had been vague about such things.

The war ended a few weeks after her discharge and the celebrations left her unmoved. She rented a room in the Fortitude Valley area of Brisbane and prepared for the birth of her child, doing all the things she'd learned about in her training, automatically, almost without thought. The doctor she consulted was helpful; he questioned her gently and learned that she had her marriage certificate and the official record of Stephen's death in action.

"You'd be entitled to a pension," he said. "And other health benefits and such."

A small flame of independence flared in Tess's mind. "I'm an ex-servicewoman. I can claim those things on my own account."

"Only for yourself," the doctor said. "Not for your child. The child's father died for his country, and the country is grateful."

"You could've fooled me," Tess said. She observed a very quick return to all the old ways—the end of a kind of civility that had operated in wartime. Louts made comments on her condition in the streets, women who had held jobs and achieved some pride were turning back into household drudges. The Americans with their free-spending easy ways left. It was all going to be the same again.

But the doctor was persistent. He booked Tess into a hospital for her confinement and, among other arrangements, he saw to it that application papers for a service widow's pension were forwarded to her.

"What the hell," Tess said, pouring herself a glass of stout. She had lost weight through the pregnancy and the doctor had recommended stout in moderation; Tess tended to double up on the doses. She filled in the forms and after she had written her name—'Teresa Gee'—on the back of the envelope, she took out a photograph of herself and Stephen standing by the Brisbane River and pointing to a spot in the trees high above the water. It was where they said they would build a house. A stranger had taken the picture of them and wished them luck. Tess wept as she looked at the picture; tears fell on the sealed envelope. She finished the bottle of stout.

Army and Repatriation Department wheels turned slowly. Not until after the birth of her child—a healthy, dark-haired girl weighing eight pounds whom she named Georgia—did she receive a response to her pension application. She was back in her room with the baby quiet in its bassinet when she read the letter.

* * *

Dear Madam

With respect to your application for a service widow's pension I regret to inform you that some complications have arisen. Although your marriage to Lt Stephen St John Gee is authenticated, the army received no notification of the marriage and you and Lt Gee were, technically, in breach of certain provisions of the Service regulations in not seeking official approval for your marriage.

I have further to inform you that Mrs Gertrude Gulliver, of 4 Claremont Street, North Sydney, New South Wales, the mother of Lt Gee and sole beneficiary under the terms of his will, denies all knowledge of her son's marriage. She has announced her intention of seeking legal advice and it is the opinion of the Army and this Department that you should do the same.

It is proposed that a hearing be held in Sydney at some time convenient to yourself, Mrs Gee and your legal representatives to resolve this matter.

I await your further communications.

The letter was signed by an official of the Repatriation Department.

"Bastards!" Tess opened a bottle of beer and began to draft an angry letter in reply. She drank some beer and finished the letter. The baby slept on. Tess napped briefly and when she awoke she read through her letter and tore it up. She underlined the address given by the bureaucrat and spoke to Georgia, who woke up when she heard the bottle clink against the rim of the glass.

"Time for you to meet your grandma," Tess said.

But Georgia developed jaundice and associated illnesses and it was almost a year before Tess made the trip south. She bided her time, writing a few letters to the Army and the Department to keep her claim alive, but putting no faith in the results. She took part-time work in a hotel, leaving Georgia with a neighbour. She worked hard, drank a lot and firmly rejected all propositions from the pub's patrons. "I had a real man," she'd say. "A hero. None of you blokes measure up." It was an effective statement.

"What was Grandma wearing when you showed up at her house?" Georgia would ask later, when what women wore was one of the most important things in her young life.

"A silk dress," Tess would say. "A grey silk dress and white shoes."

"Did she look like the Queen?"

"No, she just looked elegant . . . fierce."

Tess was over thirty when she rang the bell in Claremont Street; she'd lived all her life in the tropics and had been smoking and drinking for more than ten years. To Trudie Gee it must have seemed impossible that this woman could have claimed her son, whose smooth, boyish face looked out at the world from a photograph on the top of the highly polished piano he used to play. Stephen was eternally twenty.

"I'm Tess Gee, and this is your granddaughter."

Trudie tensed to slam the door against the creature, standing there in a cheap cotten print frock with a wild head of grey-streaked hair and too much lipstick. She glanced down at the child in the stroller. A pair of dark eyes looked up at her, a babyish smile, slightly sly, spread across the face, and Trudie saw the reincarnation of Jack Gulliver. She felt faint and leaned against the door jamb. Tess's strong arm steadied her.

"You must come in," Trudie had said. "I'm sorry. This is a terrible shock."

"We got along like a house on fire," Tess told Georgia. "She dropped all the nonsense about me not getting the pension. In we moved. We were on clover."

"Why did she change her mind?" Georgia asked, although she'd heard the answer many times.

The level in Tess's bottle would be well down by this time. She'd take another cigarette, light up, blow smoke and answer in her cracked, hoarse voice. "She reckoned you looked like your father's dad. I've seen the photos of him but I'm damned if I could see any resemblance. Still, it did the trick."

The Gulliver Fortune

Life was comfortable for Georgia in North Sydney. Her grandmother doted on her, bought her clothes and paid for her curricular and extra-curricular education. Sydney changed rapidly in the postwar years, especially for the affluent. They built tennis courts, installed swimming pools and hired talented European migrants as tutors for their children. By the time she was twelve Georgia could swim, dance, ride and play the piano. She was quick to grasp things and eager to learn more. Up to a point: her instructors agreed that she was adept but none thought that she would ever put in the work required to lift her performance to excellence. Trudie had no objections; she wanted accomplishment in her granddaughter, not brilliance. The brilliance, she determined, would be acquired through marriage.

Tess found life less pleasing. "I hate this place," she complained to her cronies in the ladies' bar of the North Sydney Returned Soldiers' League Club. "I miss Brisbane."

For an answer a finger would point out the window. "Sydney's got the best harbour in the world."

"What good is it to me? I don't sail on it, and you can't bloody drink it." Liquids to drink had become the main focus of Tess's existence.

"I could give you an allowance, Teresa," Trudie said. "You could buy a house in Brisbane if you're so fond of the place."

Tess squinted through her cigarette smoke. "And leave Georgia with you, I suppose?"

"Yes."

"No chance."

"Why? What's wrong with me?" The thought of having Georgia to herself excited Trudie so much that she temporarily forgot the modulation of her vowels and other careful speech habits she'd acquired over the years. The words came out roughly, but Tess didn't notice.

"You're too lah-de-dah. No offence. But I want Georgia to know what life's really like."

Trudie was amused by that, but didn't show it. *If she only knew where I came from and the things I've done*, she thought. "And what is life really like, Teresa?"

"Up and down. Tell you what, though. If you could help me out a bit I could get a flat of my own in Sydney. Georgia could stay with you in the holidays and at weekends."

Trudie's vowels were back under control. "That sounds like a nice arrangement."

So Georgia became, and remained, a bargaining chip between her mother and grandmother. She went on to school at Abbotsleigh and lived her weeks with Tess in the flat in Milson's Point and spent holidays and most weekends with Trudie. It was a divided existence: North Sydney housed many people like Trudie who gave the appearance of having deliberately moved across the harbour to greater respectability. There, life was all table manners, clean clothes and polite outings. Like a lot of Milson's Point residents, Tess seemed to have just got off the ferry there on a whim and settled. She worked occasionally at a variety of jobs but her pension and the allowance from Trudie took away the necessity so that she stopped work when she pleased. She drank heavily and smoked every waking moment. Occasionally, prompted by something she overheard or by watching *Ben Casey* on television, she thought of going back to nursing, but she knew that she couldn't take the hours and the responsibility. A few drinks would remove the idea effectively.

Georgia loved both women for different reasons. She admired her grandmother's calm and control and she liked her mother's affection and easy-goingness. In North Sydney she could be assured of money, plentiful food and taxi rides to her activities; in Milson's Point she had loud music from records and the radio, hasty snacks and ferry rides. Georgia saw the signs of the men who were around when she was not—socks, shaving soap, hand-rolled cigarette ends—and she knew her mother couldn't have consumed all the bottles on her own. She didn't mind. She seldom saw Tess under the influence and was never personally inconvenienced by any arrangements Tess might make with her friends. Besides, there was the hunger in her for knowledge of her father and her past, and Tess could almost always be persuaded to come up with the stories. Especially if she was well-oiled.

"Was my father good-looking?"

"You've seen the photos. He was very good-looking."

"Could he dance?"

"He was a wonderful dancer and a terrible singer."

"He looks too young to be a father."

Trudie had no photographs of Stephen in uniform; all images of him dated from his days as a young lawyer about town. He looked impossibly young, even standing proprietorially beside his Austin Seven.

"He was old enough to be a father and old enough to die for this country." Tess would start to cry at that point and Georgia would comfort her. It was a ritual. By the time she was sixteen, Georgia was sharing the beer and sherry with her mother. This interfered only slightly with her success at school: she was a prefect but did not display quite the steadiness required for the school captaincy. She did well at sports and, despite occasional sloppy essays and moments of inattention in class, matriculated with honours in English and history. Her grandmother had hopes of her following her father's profession but Georgia had an announcement to make at the small celebration Trudie organised when the examination results were announced.

Only the three Gee women were present. It was December 1962 and hot. They sat under shade in the leafy yard of the Claremont Street house. Trudie had a gardener who tended the flower beds and trained the vines over the pergolas. They had coffee and cakes. Trudie ate nothing and took her coffee black. She was sixty-eight years old and still trim in a pink frock. She had protected her complexion from the Australian sun and it had stayed fresh, although somewhat doll-like. Tess, at fifty, had spread. She ate several cakes quickly.

"I want to be a journalist," Georgia said.

"A what?" Trudie gasped.

"I want to travel all over the world and meet lots of famous people and write about them for the newspapers."

"Terrific." Tess was wondering if she might take her

coffee inside and pop something in it from her handbag to get it on its feet. "Great idea, kid. You do it. 'Scuse me, nature calls." She heaved herself up and walked into the house, balancing her cup and saucer.

"Wherever did you get such an idea, Georgia?" Trudie felt she was replaying the scene with Stephen and she knew she had to go carefully.

"From reading papers and magazines." Georgia smiled and ran her fingers through her thick dark hair. She had grown into a tall, strongly built young woman with an arresting face. She was not beautiful but nothing in her features was unsatisfactory. Her smile, which seemed to have thought behind it as much as amusement, enlivened her face. "To tell you the truth, Grandma, I like them more than books."

Trudie sipped her coffee and thought about it for a few minutes. Jack had known a few journalists—seedy, down-at-heel men who smelled of beer and cigarettes and dropped the names of important people. "It's such a shabby life," she said.

"Ain't it the truth." Tess had fortified herself perhaps more generously than she intended and she felt reckless. She dropped back into her chair and lit a cigarette. "As you know, I'm an orphan. I could be the illegitimate daughter of . . . somebody important. But most likely not. But don't you think it's time Georgy found out something about your side of the family, Gertrude? Now that she's embarking on a career?"

"I want to go to uni first," Georgia said. "Then take up journalism. C'n I have a cigarette, Mum?"

"Georgia!"

Tess smiled lopsidedly and lit her daughter's cigarette. "Bad blood will out, Gertrude. I don't think Stephen ever smoked a cigarette in his life."

"Your father was a gentleman, Georgia," Trudie said.

Georgia waved her cigarette. "What about *his* father?"

"He was a businessman."

"What about my great-grandfather? You must've known him, Grandma."

Trudie recalled the burly commanding figure of John

Gulliver striding around the deck of the *Southern Maid*. She remembered his beard and the force of his manner which softened when he was dealing with his wife and children. What had Jack told her about him? Precious little. Had Jack been afraid of him? No, Jack had never been afraid of anyone. He had not been afraid of her and that was a mistake. She raked back through her memories, searching for a phrase, a word.

"He was a . . . publisher," she said.

"There you are, kid," Tess said. "You're going into just the right game. Maybe you'll end up a publisher, like your great-grandpa."

11

Georgia entered the University of Sydney in 1963. She lived in the women's college in her first year and shared a house with other students in Paddington after that. She had a Commonwealth Scholarship and Trudie gave her a generous allowance. She worked sufficiently to earn good honours marks but her real passion was the university newspaper. She wrote on all subjects from sport to theatre, edited the letters page, attended university meetings that concerned the paper and became a well-known name and face on campus.

Three successive editors of the paper—one of them a woman—attempted to seduce her and failed. Georgia drank with her mother on her increasingly rare visits but not otherwise, especially not at parties. She was too busy for sex, and too careful.

She went into her final year at twenty, still a virgin and with a fair prospect of getting a First. In April a batch of national servicemen left Australia for Vietnam. By May more than five thousand Australians were fighting in Vietnam, one-quarter of them conscripts. By August Georgia had lost her virginity to Paul Lucas, a radical lecturer in politics, who helped her to organise anti-Vietnam activities. She was deputy editor of the paper; she smoked forty cigarettes a day and drank flagon wine from noon to the early hours on most days. She ate nothing.

"Georgia, you're ruining your health," her grandmother told her when Georgia squeezed out some time to pay a visit and to extract some money. Trudie was resolutely anti-war although her sympathies for all things American caused her some pangs over this one.

"I'm strong, Grandma," Georgia said. "I'll be all right. The men are getting killed, the women can take some chances with their health at least."

Trudie remembered Jack and the white feathers. "Your grandfather was a pacifist," she said.

"Was he? Good for him. I suppose it was different for my father. A different sort of war."

"Yes. Why do you wear those dreadful clothes? What's wrong with a nice frock?"

Georgia was wearing black trousers and boots, a long black sweater and dark glasses. Her hair was twisted into a greasy knot. "I have to go, Grandma. Thanks for the tea and the money and everything."

"What would you like for a graduation present?"

Jesus, graduation, Georgia thought as she hurried for the train. *I haven't been to a lecture or opened a book for weeks.* Paul Lucas came to the rescue; he helped her organise the random notes she'd made for her thesis on Australian women and the Spanish Civil War and he fended off interruptions while she dashed off a draft. This he took away, polished and had typed. As the exams drew closer he took her through an intensive course in her subjects, reading aloud to her, forcing her to study the introductions to the texts and throwing questions at her while she got on with her newspaper and Vietnam work. Georgia fortified herself with wine and cigarettes.

Underslept, overstimulated by wine, coffee, tobacco and sex, Georgia stumbled through the examination fortnight. She presented for each paper, although she failed to complete several of them. Twice she fell asleep. Her thesis, somewhat fraudulently attested by Georgia to be 'my own independent work', was submitted on time.

"A Third at best," she said to Paul in the pub after the last exam.

"A First for sure," Lucas said. He was worried about

Georgia's appearance—she was pale and thin with hollow eyes—especially as he was considering leaving his second wife for her. But he had to spend Christmas with his family, and Georgia lived on her nerves waiting for the exam results. She visited Trudie and Tess but was driven away by their exclamations of horror at her thinness, the nicotine on her fingers and her nervous twitches. She suffered through the early months of a very hot summer, became ill, took massive doses of aspirin and tried to wean herself off wine with marijuana.

This brought Georgia into her first contact with the law as an individual. She'd been arrested after demonstrations but there was solidarity in the paddy wagons and holding cells. She and the others sang songs and shouted slogans at the uniformed police. When the drug squad detectives knocked at her door in Paddington she was alone in the house. One of the cops waved a folded paper.

"Warrant, miss. We have reason to believe there are illegal drugs in this house."

Georgia was stoned and giggled. The cops exchanged looks and tried to push her aside. Georgia stood her ground. "Let me see the warrant."

She examined it but could not focus on the print. The police moved quickly through the house. They found the grass Georgia kept in a Chinese jar in her room, the plants growing in the backyard and those curing in the bathroom.

"Big bust," Georgia said. "You'll be hero pigs."

Georgia was arrested, charged with the cultivation, possession and use of Indian hemp and released on bail put up by Trudie. At the end of January the examination results came out. Georgia had been awarded Second Class Honours, division one. She spent a weekend with Lucas in a Kings Cross motel drinking and smoking dope. On the Monday morning she collapsed and was taken to the hospital. She was diagnosed as suffering from malnutrition. She was also pregnant.

The climb back was long and hard for Georgia Gee. She miscarried and had to be drip fed. She was totally dependent on Trudie financially and this added guilt to her despair. She refused the offer to become Mrs Paul Lucas

III, a decision she later regarded as the first smart thing she did in the sixties. The court proceedings dragged on, much adjourned on account of Georgia's ill health. Eventually her solicitor received word that the police might have trouble producing the evidence. He made application to see the confiscated Indian hemp and when the police could not comply, the charges were dropped. Tess brought her the news in hospital.

"Can't see anything in that stuff myself," she said. "Never did anything for me."

"You're too pickled."

"Probably. How're you feeling?"

Georgia considered. "Better," she said. "How're you and Grandma?"

"She'll outlive me," Tess said.

This was prophetic. Tess's lung and liver cancer was discovered a few days later and she was dead within two months. Georgia left hospital and moved in with Trudie. Here, at first, she did nothing but read novels, lie in the sun and try to eat. She gained weight slowly and her looks improved. The gloss returned to her dark hair; her teeth, which had been smoke-stained and had turned a greenish grey during her illness, whitened. She enjoyed her grandmother's company and spent hours talking to the alert old lady about the Sydney of fifty years before.

"The air smelled different," Trudie said. "The water tasted different and the harbour was wonderful. There were places you could go in a boat and look over the side and see the bottom."

On impulse, Georgia wrote an article she called 'A Day in Sydney, 1917' which was based on Trudie's incredibly precise memories of transport, shopping, prices and the details of domestic life. Georgia sent the article to the *Sydney Morning Herald*, where it was accepted. Seeing her name in print in the most authoritative newspaper in Australia thrilled her and revived her old ambition. By June she was working for the paper as a graduate cadet; she weighed nine stone, drank Scotch and water and smoked ten thin black cigarillos per day.

12

London, September 1986

Ben Cromwell looked glumly at the telex Jamie Martin had received from Perth, Western Australia. "The upshot is," Jamie said, "that while Peel and Rooney are on record, there's no sign of a Gulliver. We know from the medical officer's journal that John Gulliver junior got off the boat in Fremantle with Hester Peel and Clive Rooney. Peel and Rooney later married in Perth and had a few children, but that's no help."

"Bugger all," said Ben. "What d'we do now?"

"If we had unlimited time and money we could go out there and do the research. Australian records are pretty good, they tell me."

"I need a drink," Ben said. They were in the sitting room of Jerry's flat. He got up and went into the kitchen. Jamie could hear him pushing things around, opening the refrigerator. After a few minutes Ben was back, dark-faced and swearing. "Bloody woman's run out of drink, or poured it down the sink. We'll have to go out for a drink."

Jamie struggled against a wish to tell Cromwell that he loved Jerry Gallagher and didn't want to hear a word said against her. But he'd made no approach to Jerry. His situation, he felt, was absurd. "Coffee'll do me," he said.

Ben reached for a coat hanging on the back of the door. "Well, it *won't* do me. This is a real bastard. Monty's not going to be pleased."

Jamie nodded, but his training had accustomed him to disappointment and patience. "I'd really like to get a look at the picture, Ben."

"Why?"

"I'm interested, and we're going to a lot of trouble to locate these people so the painting can be handled properly. Isn't that what this is all about?"

"Fuck the picture."

"Steady on, Ben."

"That's all I ever hear, 'Steady on, Ben'." Ben took the coat and threw it on the chair. "Look, this is a farce. Old Gulliver cashed in a hundred-and-twenty-odd years ago. We don't need to track down every Tom, Dick and Harry descended from his nephew. We need to find one fucking colonial who fills the bill. That's all. Wake up!"

Jamie Martin turned slowly away from his contemplation of one of Jerry's bookcases. He'd never seen so many short story collections on one shelf before. "What d'you mean?" he said.

But Ben was rummaging in a cardboard box. He lifted out a bottle and crowed, "Hiding it, the bitch! I knew there was some Irish around. Make some coffee, Jamie old boy, and we'll toast Collins an' O'Casey an' all those other idiots!"

Jamie went to the kitchen and made the coffee. Alarm bells were ringing loudly in his head. He wished that Jerry was there to add balance to the situation. It looked as if the Cromwells were bent on short-circuiting the inheritance process. The historian in Jamie rebelled. He took the coffee into the living room and watched Ben pour Irish whisky into the cups.

"Cheers," Ben said. "You'll catch up with someone."

"Someone?" Jamie said.

Ben drank his coffee in a gulp. He poured the whisky into his cup and drained it. "Bound to be a crook, isn't he? Tainted genes."

Jamie said nothing.

"Anyway," Ben said, "I've accelerated the process. We'll soon get some results." He punched the air like a boxer and poured more whisky.

Jamie wanted to punch back. He wanted Jerry to understand the dark places that were forming around the piece of research they were both following so closely. *Not yet*, he thought. He poured more coffee for himself and added a few drops of the whisky. "What're you up to, Ben?"

"We c'd keep sending messages off to Australia—Victoria an' Queensland—all the other godforsaken places—'n' get the same results, right?"

"Yes."

"We need the media," Ben picked a newspaper up from a chair and displayed the headline. "Look, everyone in the world knows that Reagan and Gorbachev are going to have a chat in Iceland."

"Yes," Jamie said. "Whether they care's another thing."

"Doesn't matter. We've been too low-key." Ben drank more whisky and picked up the paper. He folded it back clumsily, fumbling with the sheets. "Look at this. I gave the interviews the other day. Now we'll get some action."

13

Sydney, September 1986

Georgia Gee was forty years of age when her grandmother died. She had been a newspaper reporter for twenty years. She had been engaged twice but never married. She had had two abortions and no children. She had worked in Britain, China, Argentina and the United States. Her book, *Experiencing Argentina,* in which she told the story of her two years in the country passing as an Argentine by virtue of her dark appearance and near-perfect Spanish, had been a minor bestseller. Her reports on life in the country during and after the Falklands crisis had won her a coveted Walkley Award, the highest prize for excellence in journalism.

After a stint as foreign correspondent in Beijing she was back at the *Herald* as a leader writer and editor of foreign news. Her contract with the paper allowed her to freelance in certain areas. She was in demand on radio for commentaries on South American politics and literature. Her reviews of the fashionable writers—Borges, Marquez, Puig—regularly appeared in newspapers and magazines.

Through it all, through the heady days of following Whitlam on the campaign trail in 1972, through the letdown of 1975, through the overseas postings and the lovers, foreign and domestic, her grandmother had remained Georgia's truest friend. Trudie was critical only of superficial things; Georgia could sense that she held the old lady's unstinting approval deep down, and she responded with loyalty and affection. She suspected Trudie of an instinctive feminism and once accused her of it.

"I think you must have known Emily Pankhurst back in England. Go on, admit it. You went to suffragette meetings."

"Never," Trudie said. "I was too young."

Georgia laughed; she was not quite sure how old her grandmother was and she was too polite to ask. Trudie stood straight and walked easily, if slowly. Her face was crisscrossed with tiny lines which she concealed with makeup. Her eyes had faded to a very pale blue but they remained bright and alert. Her white hair was thick and expensively cared for.

"I don't really trust women," Trudie said once. "We're too emotional. We let ourselves and each other down."

"What about men?" Georgia asked.

"They let everybody down."

This conversation took place at a time when Georgia was able to repay Trudie for some of her support. Trudie's investments had dwindled and the North Sydney house required expensive repairs. Trudie sold the house when Georgia was in China and, through bad financial advice, lost a good deal of the proceeds. When Georgia next saw her, she was appalled to find the normally calm and composed old woman in a state of high anxiety. She overcame Trudie's pride, teased out the story of mismanagement and put her affairs in the hands of a trustworthy accountant. In the end, Trudie's capital had dwindled but she was comfortable, and grateful.

"I never gave you that graduation present."

Georgia laughed. "I never graduated, not really."

"That's right, you didn't. You were working, you said. You were always a rebel."

"I wasn't, Grandma. Not really. Look at me now. How respectable can you be?" Georgia wore tailored jackets and trousers, silk blouses and smart shoes to work. She relaxed in sweaters and jeans. Her wardrobe contained two formal outfits for rare ceremonial occasions. Her current, undemanding lover was a safely married TV newsreader.

"You've done well. I always thought you would. You're your father's daughter, although you look like *his* father."

"Mum said you thought that. She couldn't see it."

"She never met Jack."

"Jack. Was that his name? You never talk about him, Grandma."

Trudie sighed and Georgia afterwards wondered how her ears could have played such a trick on her. She could have sworn she heard her grandmother say, in the sighing expulsion of breath, "I murdered him."

This conversation was on Georgia's mind the next time she drove her Honda Civic from her Mosman flat to the unit in Kirribilli where Trudie lived, still independent and caring for herself. She did not expect to hear anything so dramatic over the tea and cakes this time, but lately Trudie had been more than usually inclined to ramble about the past. The television set was on when Georgia arrived, showing pictures of the yachts off Fremantle preparing for the America's Cup defence. Usually Trudie switched the set off immediately she had a visitor but this time she gazed at the blue and white images, bathed in fierce sunlight.

"Jack and I got off the boat at Fremantle," she said.

"Did you?" Georgia paused in her tea making. "Were you married in England? For some reason I thought that wedding picture looked like Australia."

Trudie looked at her and a smile came slowly to her pale, carefully preserved face. "We weren't married on the boat. But we should have been."

Georgia laughed. "I see. Pretty daring for those days. When was this?"

"Nineteen ten. You don't know the half of it."

Georgia made the tea and brought the cups and plates across to the armchair where Trudie sat. "Did you read my book on Argentina, Grandma?" she said.

"Some of it."

"Do you think I'm a good writer?"

"Yes, like your father. He wrote wonderful letters."

"Why don't I write your story and my grandfather's, Jack's? It sounds . . ."

"No!" Trudie sat straight suddenly and tea slopped into her saucer and over her dress. She put the cup on the table with shaking hands. She dabbed at her dress with her handkerchief, agitated.

14

After solemnly promising not to think of researching her family history, Georgia took some time to calm Trudie down. She did not feel bound by the promise and the idea interested her but she did nothing about it. She saw her lover and wrote her articles, struggled to remain the non-smoker she had become ten years before and to keep to her limit of three drinks per day. She was at her desk when Trudie's doctor telephoned to tell her of her grandmother's death.

"I saw her yesterday," the doctor said. "She seemed to be fine. She was ninety-two years old, you know."

"I didn't know," Georgia said calmly. She had seen death in Argentina and other places, deaths of the young and the old, and she was not shocked by it. "What happened, doctor?"

"She was sitting at her escritoire and she had a cerebral haemorrhage. She just fell forward across the desk. It must have been very quick."

"Thank you." Georgia put down the phone, and the tears came. She cried for her grandmother, whose life had been so busy and full at first and then so empty and strange, and for her mother who had thrown hers away, and for herself. When she realised that she was crying for herself she stopped. Known in the office for her good humour and unflappability, Georgia, weeping and snuffling into a tissue, was unsettling for her fellow-workers. She left the office and held a private wake for Trudie, going considerably beyond her self-imposed limit of three drinks.

Trudie's funeral showed Georgia how alone she was in the world. She was the only family member present at the rather florid Anglican service held in the church at Mosman. Trudie had left instructions for this to be done and had, over the years, been a benefactor to the church. The doctor attended, and two neighbours, and Georgia was accompanied by a female friend from the office. It was a small, sad procession to Waverley cemetery where Trudie was buried alongside her late husband in a plot that had long been booked and paid for.

Georgia had to bend down and peer closely to read the old, weathered headstone: JOHN GULLIVER 1895-1925. AT REST. Georgia puzzled over the name, but this was definitely the right plot.

Her friend was standing back. "What're the dates?" she asked.

Georgia read them out aloud.

"That's young."

Georgia looked at the headstone and the fresh earth beside it. "The men in my family die young and the women die old, very old."

She was, as she had expected, the sole beneficiary of Trudie's will. The estate amounted to the Kirribilli flat and an investment portfolio worth sixty thousand dollars, returning an annual income not big enough to live on. Georgia was grateful for this—she could live here or sell the flat and buy another. To be free of the burden of rent or a mortgage would be a relief. She could have used more, though. With other journalists who were concerned at the change in ownership of Australia's media and a growing conservatism that resulted, she'd considered the idea of starting an independent magazine. Georgia was no blinkered radical, but she knew that the corporations and governments colluded and collided in ways that the public, directly affected and needing to be informed, knew nothing about. The magazine would require more money than any of them had. Georgia had entertained the idea that Trudie's legacy might be sufficient.

Well, the old girl would have hated the idea anyway, Georgia thought. So she'd have to keep on working within the system. Perhaps it was best; she didn't know how well she'd handle total independence. At least the extra money would allow her to travel at will. Thanks to Trudie. Everything was thanks to Trudie.

Two weeks after the funeral, on a bright, warm Saturday, Georgia drove to Kirribilli to inspect the flat. She had happy memories of its light and views and she entertained thoughts of living there herself. Trudie's ghost, if such there were, would not upset her. She got the keys from the neighbour who had found her grandmother, endured the condolences and let herself into the flat. The blinds were drawn but the rooms were still full of a muted light. Georgia felt herself drawn towards the writing desk, which had not been disturbed since Trudie had slumped across it. A copy of the *Sydney Morning Herald,* covered by a thin film of dust, lay on the polished rosewood surface of the desk. It was dated the day of Trudie's death and folded so that a small item on an inside page caught Georgia's attention:

LONDONER SEEKS GULLIVER IN AUSTRALIA
Mr Benjamin Cromwell of Chelsea, London, has announced that he has very good news for descendants of John Gulliver who migrated to Australia with his family in 1910. Mr Cromwell said he was not at liberty to reveal details but that 'a very exciting legacy is in prospect'. Mr Cromwell, an historian and ex-army officer, also said that media interest in the legacy and the story that went with it would be considerable. 'There's a film in it, for sure.'

Specifically, Mr Cromwell is seeking the direct descendants of John Gulliver's five children but he stressed that information would be welcome from any parties. Although only the de-

> *scendants could benefit directly from the legacy, he was prepared to offer rewards for useful information. Mr Cromwell said, 'The beneficiaries may choose to share their good fortune with anyone who has been of service.'*

"Gulliver," Georgia said. "Nineteen ten." She began to open drawers in the old writing desk.

Carl, Mikhail

15

'Southern Maid', Sydney, June 1901

"How old are you, Carl?" Dr Anderson asked. "It appears from these papers that you're fourteen, but you don't look it."

Neither Carl Gulliver nor Dr Anderson was a fool. Both knew that a fourteen-year-old new arrival in Australia would be treated as a near-adult by the authorities. He might possibly be provided with some temporary accommodation, but he would be expected to find work quickly and support himself. Carl was undersized and pale. Anderson had observed that his favourite occupation was reading, of which he had done more and more since the deaths of his parents.

"I'm twelve years of age, sir," Carl said, "and I want to go to school."

"I thought you might. Leave it to me."

Anderson arranged for Carl to be admitted to the orphanage at Petersham, a residential suburb close to the city of Sydney. It had been his melancholy duty to inspect the belongings of John and Catherine Gulliver after their deaths. He had found no will and very little of value. As Carl was the oldest son on hand, Jack having left the ship in Fremantle, Anderson felt free to sell John Gulliver's watch and a few of his wife's trinkets. The small sum raised he deposited with the orphanage authorities; it was his experience that this ensured better treatment than was meted out to the destitute.

Carl packed his few possessions in a small suitcase and carefully tied his personal library of nine books with a leather strap. He bade Susannah and Edward a solemn goodbye and left the ship with the doctor. Since the deaths of their parents and the departure of their older brother, the Gulliver children had spent little time together, as if the demolition of the foundations of their family had brought down the whole structure.

"I'll give you my address in London, and you can write to me," Anderson said as they travelled by horse cab along Parramatta Road. "And I'll come and see you when I'm next in port."

"Thank you, sir." The cab drew up outside a forbidding red brick building surrounded by a high iron railing fence. THE PETERSHAM ORPHANAGE FOR BOYS was printed in severe letters on a faded board above the gate. "I'm an orphan," Carl said. "I really am."

Anderson glanced at the boy to see whether there was any crack in the shell of his reserve, but he could see none. "It's a hard start for you, Carl, I won't deny that. But you've got the greatest advantage nature can bestow."

"Sir?"

"Brains, lad. Brains."

Carl settled quickly into the routine of the orphanage, which was administered by Mr Joseph Stubbs in an authoritarian manner. Corporal punishment for infringement of regulations was a feature of the institution's emphasis on discipline. Carl shared a dormitory with six other boys, all younger than himself although similar in size, and he attended Petersham junior school. It soon became apparent to Stubbs and the teachers at the school that he was a gifted pupil. He grasped all subjects quickly and worked willingly and effectively.

"This is the best school report one of our boys has ever had," Stubbs informed Carl at the end of the second term.

"Thank you, sir."

"What . . . ah, what do you wish to do when you leave school, Gulliver?"

"I don't want to leave, sir," Carl said. "I want to be a teacher."

Stubbs nodded, dismissed the boy and entered the general comment from the report on the record sheets he kept for each of his charges. 'Intellectually outstanding—performing well above junior school standards.' No inmate from the orphanage had ever attended high school and Stubbs had never before had to consider such a possibility. Clearly, he now did.

Carl was not popular with the other orphans or the children at school, who mocked his London accent. They sensed a difference in him, a deep seriousness, and resented his easy annexation of top place in all subjects. He tried to be friendly but his efforts failed. He was not arrogant because he knew that he was two years older than those he was competing with, and he wondered whether he would be so successful if placed on equal terms with his peers. The doubt made him work harder and perform better.

The orphans were rostered to a range of jobs—sweeping and scrubbing, laundry and kitchen work, gardening, filling the coal buckets. Carl did his share of these tasks but was annoyed by the inefficiency of the system. The boys swapped jobs between themselves, filled in for each other for various reasons and attempted to monopolise the more favoured jobs. Slowly, by a process no one could quite explain, Carl came to organize this side of orphanage life.

"Gulliver," a boy would say, "Williams won't swap coaling for potato peeling with me. I'm sick of coaling; I've done it four times in a row."

"It's a harder job," Carl would declare. "And dirty. It's worth two potato peeling duties. Offer him two for one. That'll give him some time to skive off."

Carl came to know who was lazy and who energetic, who stubborn and who reasonable. He kept lists and rosters of his own, supplementary to the official ones, and helped to make things run smoothly. This activity was noted by the custodians, who were at first amused and then appreciative. More approving comments were entered on Carl's sheets.

Towards the end of his second year Carl was summoned to Stubbs's office, made to wait outside for half an hour and entered a room made chilly by disapproval. Carl had grown to five foot seven inches and filled out a little, but he was still pale and his features were immature.

"You've gone too far, Gulliver," Stubbs said. "What's the meaning of this?" He stabbed his finger at two foolscap sheets on his desk. The sheets were covered with writing and pinned together at one corner.

"It's a petition, sir."

"I know it's a petition. I can read. 'We, the undersigned inmates of the Petersham Orphanage for Boys, respectfully request that corporal punishment be no longer administered without the written consent, in each case, of a clergyman or other responsible person from without.' You've become a troublemaker, Gulliver."

"No, sir."

"Yes. You may be sure I will inform Dr Anderson of your appalling behaviour."

"I have already written to Dr Anderson, sir."

"Gulliver, you are fourteen years of age. I have here a list of employers. I will make application to them on your behalf. You will accept the first one to accept you and you will leave this establishment. I am disappointed in you."

"I'm sorry, Mr Stubbs," Carl said quietly. "I've made other arrangements."

"Arrangements?" Stubbs was a fat man whose collar cut into the folds of flesh around his neck. These folds now swelled and reddened.

"Mr Thodey from the junior school has agreed to take me into his house. I have a place at the high school and I intend to become a teacher."

"We'll be well rid of you."

"If you look at the bottom of the petition, sir, you will see that a number of copies have been made, and that it is the petitioners' intention to send these to interested parties."

Stubbs flipped the paper over and saw listed the

names of office holders in education, religion and politics. "H-have these been sent?"

"No, sir, and they won't be if you agree to the petition."

Stubbs agreed. Carl left the orphanage and his name was carved deeply and appreciatively into the tops of many desks.

Hector Thodey and his wife Diane were childless, which was a sadness to them. Carl was the third child they had fostered: they kept photographs of Roger and Patricia, now grown and independent, in their parlour like any proud parents. Hector Thodey was the English master at the junior school; his wife taught piano at home to the sons and daughters of the middle class. Although he was not aware of it, Carl had modelled himself on Thodey from the first. He admired the teacher's good humour and firmness. Thodey controlled his classes with a sarcastic wit and the occasional violent verbal outburst. He never used the strap.

Thodey had seen the scholarly potential in Carl from the first time the boy had read aloud in his class. Like the best readers, Carl's eye and mind leapt ahead of the print, allowing him to read with full comprehension and expression.

"Very good, Gulliver," Thodey had said. "Have you read this before?" The book was Scott's *The Heart of Midlothian*.

"No, sir. But I've read *Rob Roy*."

There were sniggers in the class but Carl and Thodey ignored them.

Books and music so dominated the Thodeys' large untidy terrace house in Petersham that there was little conversation. Diane Thodey had a moderate private income and the couple lived well. Hector Thodey's mild socialism kept him in the public school system although he could have had a more agreeable and better paid career at the sort of school he had himself attended.

When he arrived at the Thodey house, but not before, Carl confessed that he was two years older than he had represented himself. "I may not be as clever as I look, sir," he said.

An inveterate reader of novels, Thodey loved an intrigue and a deception. He was a stocky man with a plain, good-natured face and keen, intelligent eyes. He smiled at the nervous-looking boy who was all bones and awkward angles. "I'll just have to give you a test then. You're sixteen, you say?"

"Almost, sir."

"You should be sitting for the fourth year exams straight off. Tell you what, I'll give you a few of the papers from last year. That'll tell us what's what."

Carl struggled with the mathematics and science papers but passed the English, history, and geography tests easily.

"Fourth form," Thodey said. "With some coaching in mathematics and science. What d'you say to that?"

It was rare for Carl to show emotion and demonstrations of physical affection were unknown to him. His eyes grew moist and Thodey put a hand on his shoulder. "You're too thin," he said. "We'll have to fatten you up."

"How can I thank you, sir?"

"Be happy," Thodey said. "And do well."

16

Carl attended Fort Street high school and passed the fourth year examinations without difficulty. At first he had been dismayed to find that he had to study a language, but some instinct told him to choose German and he discovered that he had some grasp of the language from exposure to it as a child. More than he had realized, his mother had used German in her dealings with the household and the children. Mathematics continued to be difficult for him but his marks in the other subjects were outstanding. He entered his final year still resolved to become a teacher, which was gratifying for the Thodeys.

At seventeen Carl was five feet eight inches tall and weighed nine and half stone. His hair had darkened a little and his features, dominated by a large nose and a wide mouth, had set into a serious cast. He travelled from Petersham four miles to the school, which was near the harbour at the north end of the city, on foot and by tram. This was all the exercise he got; otherwise he read and studied. On two evenings through the week and on Saturdays he worked in a lending library, stamping the books, collecting the halfpenny and penny borrowing fees and returning the books to their precise places on the shelves. He was paid two shillings when the library closed at five p.m. on Saturday and he often spent half of it in borrowing books himself.

The Thodeys fed and housed him; they took him to the doctor when he became ill, which was not often, and they encouraged him to study. They did no entertaining and seldom went out. Carl withdrew into himself and the world of books. He had imaginary conversations with the characters in the books and plays he read—with Hamlet and Lear, David Copperfield and Sam Weller, Sherlock Holmes and Raffles. He had no awareness of living in Australia. Apart from occasional visits to Centennial Park and the zoo, he saw no native flora and fauna. The yew trees of English country churchyards and the wolves of the northern European wastes were more real to him than eucalypts and kangaroos. He disliked the climate—the long, hot summers oppressed him and he found the snowless, clear-skied winters undramatic. He was nostalgic for London's fogs and chill winds.

At school, he endured cricket and football stoically. He thought of them as English games, which helped to make them acceptable. His hand-eye co-ordination was only fair but he was a fast runner and could keep up with a pack, and field on the boundary effectively enough to avoid making a fool of himself. At the high school there was no scope for the organisational talents he had employed in the orphanage, and his passion for lists and schedules found expression only in his re-ordering of the library's borrowing cards and in his study plans.

One night as Carl was carrying a book and a cup of tea upstairs, Diane Thodey stopped him. "Are you sure you're not overdoing it Carl? Do you have to study quite so much?"

Carl fidgeted on the stairs. He was nervous with women, having had very limited contact with them since his mother died. He knew no girls of his own age and treated the women in the library simply as cardholders. "I want a scholarship to the teachers' college," he muttered.

"I know, dear. But Hector says you are assured of one. It will be of no use to you if you impair your health."

Carl smiled at her and went up to his room. In fact his long incarcerations with his books were not all for study. He had discovered the Russian novelists and was reading them voraciously. In a secondhand bookshop he found an edition of Dostoyevsky's *The Gambler*, in which the text on the right-hand page was in English and the left in Russian. He bought a Russian primer and was attempting to pick his way into the language, deciphering its strange, and to him fascinating, script. He could spend hours on a single page, totally absorbed.

Carl earned honours in all subjects for the Leaving Certificate with the single exception of mathematics. He won a full bursary to the teachers' college and began his two years of training in February 1914. He was watchful and diligent. The lecturers marked him down as promising. Several female students tried to befriend him but Carl kept them at a distance. His images of women came principally from literature—they were alluring, dangerous, frivolous. The earnest young women at the teachers' college seemed to be none of these things, which threw Carl into confusion. The men he treated as he had his fellow students at Fort Street—as rivals. The competitive instinct, combined with ambition, conspired to make him aloof and unpopular.

None of this mattered to Carl, who had discovered Vladimir Pavel one day when he was out taking a walk, as advised by Diane Thodey who worried about his pallor. Carl had heard muttering coming from behind a hedge that grew luxuriantly in front of one of the substantial houses of Stanmore, a suburb adjacent to Petersham. By now, Carl's grasp of the printed language was good. He had never heard it spoken but the mumbled words seemed like music to him.

He stopped. "Russian," he said.

A big, bearded face appeared through the untidy top of the hedge. "I am. This is a crime now?"

"No, no, of course not. It's just that I've studied Russian for a few years but I've never heard it spoken. Say something else, please."

In Russian Pavel said, "I am not a parrot."

"You are not a peacock?"

"Parrot!"

"Parrot. Parrot? Oh, I see. I'm sorry. Yes, parrot."

Carl searched his memory and attempted a stumbling phrase. "You have a fine garden."

Pavel laughed. "Dr Archibald has a fine garden, also a fine fat wife and a cellar full of fine wine. I have none of these things."

"You're speaking too fast for me. I understood wife and wine, that's all."

Pavel snipped some straggling shoots. He repeated the sentence slowly and then said the same thing in English. He watched the pale young man absorb the lesson. *An interesting fellow*, he thought. In his experience most Australians were reluctant to learn anything, especially from a foreigner. "Do you have any other languages, young sir, as well as your terrible Russian?"

"German," Carl said. "And you?"

"German, French, Hungarian, some English—not much."

Carl gaped at him. Grey, grizzled hair appeared to grow all over Pavel's face, leaving only space for his eyes, nose and mouth to function. Carl found it impossible to guess his age. Then Pavel smiled; his teeth were tobacco-stained but strong, his eyes were clear and keen. "I'd like to learn those languages," Carl said.

It was the beginning of an association that had elements of a teacher-student relationship, strong bonds of comradeship and was almost a love affair. Pavel and Carl met often, in the evening and at weekends. They went for walks and talked endlessly, switching languages and framing ideas. The Russian made no secret of his radicalism and hatred for the old regime in Russia. This at first alarmed Carl, whose notions of Russia, as of everything else, were romantic.

"Culture will be stronger after the revolution," Pavel insisted. "Books will be better and music will be sweeter, because they will be written by free men and read and heard by free people."

Carl could find no counter-arguments.

Pavel lived in two rooms in a boarding house in Glebe. He cooked on a gas ring, ate, smoked endless hand-rolled cigarettes and slept in one room, keeping his books in the other. The book room was a mecca for Carl who spent hours there browsing, reading and helping Pavel protect the books against the rising damp. There were only chairs in the room, no tables, and no writing materials. One day Carl asked Pavel whether he planned to write about his political and philosophical notions.

"No," Pavel said.

"Why not?"

The Russian shook his head. "Because I found out some years ago something that more people should find out. Would stop so many bad books from wasting time."

"What did you find out?"

Pavel laughed and poured himself another glass of wine. "That I would rather read than write."

Carl would not join Pavel in his wine drinking, nor would he go with him to the Darlinghurst brothels Pavel used frequently.

"Only a man who gets drunk and has women knows his true vocation," Pavel said.

Carl believed he knew his vocation. He smiled and asked Pavel to explain further.

"Why do you think the Catholic Church insists on celibacy for its clergy?"

"To save them from the distractions of a home and family."

Pavel smiled. "Not really. The church fears that if its priests went with women their faith would falter. To hold a woman's breasts in your hands is a pure thing, perhaps the purest."

"You talk a lot of nonsense, Vladimir. The church allows its priests to drink, anyway."

Pavel grunted. "To forbid both would be impossible. They allow one as a consolation for denying the other. You should come with me. There is no experience like it. I have sometimes read five hundred pages at a sitting after making love."

Carl had heard Pavel claim that he had done the same after drinking three bottles of wine but in his observation the claim was a fantasy. "I know my vocation. I want to be a teacher. That's one reason why I *don't* go with you."

"Explain, please."

"I have to pass a medical examination when I finish my training. If I have a disease I will not be allowed to teach."

Pavel nodded; he recalled his own itches, sores and cures. "That is one reason."

"One's enough," Carl said.

Pavel denounced the European war as an imperialist conflict, interesting only if it brought down some of the repressive monarchies. He thought it might speed revolution in Russia but feared that it might come too soon for the backward peasantry. "Revolution must stem from the bourgeoisie, as you know," Pavel said.

"As Marx says, you mean," Carl corrected him. Carl was interested in events in Europe and, aware of his German heritage, he was somewhat uncertain about his allegiance. He felt like a European and was distressed that 'his country' was tearing itself apart, but he was more concerned with the examinations and period of classroom training that were approaching. Hector Thodey was obsessed by the war; he picked over the news daily and frequently regretted that he was too old to enlist. Diane Thodey, deeply relieved that this was so, expressed sympathy. Carl's frequent absences from home she attributed to his having met a young woman. She was tolerant of Carl's quiet and secretive ways and assumed she would meet his choice when the time was right. The Thodey household continued to be comfortable.

Carl sat his exams well prepared and confident. None of the papers presented him with any problems and he expected a good result. On Monday, 10 November 1915, aged nineteen, with his wiry hair plastered down, his boots polished and wearing a new suit, he presented himself at the Lewisham public school for a three-week period as a trainee teacher. Carl watched the assembly, stood to attention as the anthem was played and heard the headmaster address the school on the subjects of inkwells, nits in the hair and the conflict in Europe. An hour later he was standing in front of thirty-eight fourth grade students.

The subject was history, the exploration of the Australian continent. Carl could draw freehand an accurate map of Australia; he could position the major rivers and other features, give the dates of their discovery, and name and describe the journeys the explorers had undertaken.

He drew the map and turned to face the class. That moment he would remember for the rest of his life. He felt his throat dry and his body began to shake. He clasped his hands to stop them flying wildly about; sweat broke out on his forehead; there was a roaring in his ears, and the classroom seemed to narrow in front of him and stretch away into the far distance. The closest desk, not fifteen feet from him, seemed fifty yards away. He shut his eyes and made harsh, croaking sounds. Some of the pupils laughed—the sound pierced him like a needle through the eardrum.

"Mr Gulliver," the class teacher said. "Mr Gulliver, are you all right?"

Carl dropped the chalk. His shirt, freshly pressed by Diane Thodey that morning, was a limp rag. Most terrifying of all, he felt his bowels loosen. He stumbled forward and would have fallen had not the teacher caught him. The teacher glared at the gigglers and led Carl from the room.

After recovering in the infirmary, Carl was excused from the school for the day. There had been a lot of talk around him which he only half heard through mists of shame and misery, but he had caught a few words. "The worst case I've ever seen," the class teacher had said.

He wandered the streets for hours, looking in the gardens where Pavel worked and not finding him. It was a hot day and he was exhausted, parched, sunburnt and light-headed when he arrived at the Glebe boarding house. He stood below Pavel's window and spoke the first words he had uttered since he had turned from the blackboard in the classroom. "Pavel," he croaked, "let me in, for God's sake. I want a drink."

17

Carl went on a bender that lasted three weeks. He drank in every dive Pavel knew in Sydney and accompanied the Russian into the brothels. He was drunk when he did so and the results were less than spectacular, nor did they ease the anguish that consumed him. It was as if his character was dissolving, as if he was dissolving it himself with each drink and cigarette and entry into a dimly lit, smelly room with a girl or woman he had laid eyes on only minutes before.

One of the whores allowed him to gather her flaccid breasts in his hands and kiss them; he licked her nipples and she moaned professionally. When he bit them, she jerked away.

"What the hell d'you think you're bloody doin'?"

"Pure," Carl muttered. "It's supposed to be pure."

"Pure my arse. What are you talking about?"

Carl stared at her. The heavy makeup concealed a coarse, pitted skin that was heavily lined. "Pavel said it was pure."

"Pavel," the whore snorted. "He's an animal. He does it up the bum. He likes it that way. You should know."

"What do you mean?" Carl said.

"Hasn't he done it to you? Up the rear end?"

"No, he hasn't."

"He will. Give it here, lovey, I'll give you your money's worth this way. Pure? That's a laugh!"

Carl watched miserably as she attempted without success to stimulate him. He paid her and left while Pavel was occupied in another room. It was very late at night when he entered the Thodeys' house in Petersham. He packed some clothes and documents, and agonised over the selection of books. Eventually he decided in favour of the most portable—some paperbound editions of Russian and French novels and essays. He spent some time composing a letter to Hector and Diane Thodey and was reduced to tears by the inadequacy of the result. He tore up several drafts and left only a few lines:

> *Dear Mr and Mrs Thodey*
>
> *I will never be able to thank you for your kindness to me but one day I will try. I have suffered a great disappointment as you will have heard from the Education Department, and something like a nervous breakdown following that. I feel well in my mind now and am planning to travel for some time. Please do not worry about me.*
>
> *Despite my recent lack of consideration for your feelings, I hope you will think well of me as I shall of you—always.*
>
> *Affectionately*
> *Carl Gulliver*

At ten a.m. Carl presented himself at the recruitment office in Pitt Street. After a wait of nearly three hours in the company of scores of men whose ages ranged from sixteen to sixty, he shuffled forward to the recruiting officer's desk.

"Name?"

"Charles Gulliver."

"Age?"

"Nineteen."

"Parents' consent?"

"I'm an orphan." Carl put the paper he had received

on being discharged from the orphanage on the desk. The officer glanced at it and then at Carl. He saw a stocky young man, pale but with several days' reddish stubble on his face. Carl's recent dissipations had aged him and given him a tough, shabby look. He wore a collarless shirt and his jacket had acquired some food stains and lost a button.

The officer banged a stamp down on a form and handed it to Carl. "Medical. Through there."

The doctor found Carl to be sound of wind and limb and to have perfect eyesight. He was free of venereal disease and his teeth were good. He was ordered to take off his boots, put his feet in a bucket and step on a tiled floor. The footprints showed well formed arches.

"Accepted." Another stamp hit the form and Carl was invited to sign his enlistment paper. He bent forward to read it and the officer jabbed him with his stick.

"What do you think you're doing?"

"I'm reading the paper."

"Say 'Sir', you're in the army."

"I'm reading the paper, sir."

"Are you a troublemaker? I can tear this bit 'a paper up, you know."

"I'm not a troublemaker. I just . . ."

The officer pointed to the stack of forms on the desk. "Sign it. If it's good enough for them, it's good enough for you."

Carl signed.

After eight weeks in a training camp at Bathurst in western New South Wales Carl, as a private in the Second Brigade, First Division, AIF, embarked for Egypt. From the minute of his enlistment he had been paid five shillings a day with one shilling deferred until the end of his service. The pay rose to six shillings after embarkation. Like the other soldiers, he spent most of the money on beer, tobacco and food to relieve the monotonous army diet. Unlike the rest, he spent some of the money on books.

The training period had been hard and dull. Carl's wiry physique had enabled him to keep pace with the other men at all exercises and his strength had increased. He was a first-class rifle shot almost by instinct and he found ways to occupy his mind through the endless drilling: he recited to himself verses he had memorised and composed vocabulary lists in English, French, German and Russian. He was not popular with the other men, who regarded his reading and manner of speech with suspicion, but he was respected for his shooting and increasing ability to hold his beer. They called him Charlie.

"See this, Charlie?" Col Andrews, newly promoted to lance-corporal, flopped down on the next bunk and produced a bayonet that had been honed to a razor sharpness. "I'm gonna stick a Hun with it and then skin 'im."

Carl nodded. He thought of his mother with her soft voice and mild manner. *She was a Hun, and I am half a Hun*. He had done a good deal of work with the bayonet on wheat bags stuffed with straw, but he doubted he would be able to use one on his fellow man. "Don't cut yourself," he said.

The lance-corporal rolled a cigarette. "I'm goin' on deck to wave goodbye to me mum. Comin' up?"

"Later," Carl said. He did not go on deck; there was no one to wave to. He had not communicated further with the Thodeys or with Pavel at all. The shame of his failure in front of the class still tortured him. He knew it was absurd but he punished himself by cutting off all his existing human contacts. If he could not be a teacher, he did not know what he could do. For now, he would be a soldier; it suited him because, one way or another, there was no future in it. He lay on his bunk and did not hear the clatter around him as men stowed their gear, dropped rifles, played cards, shouted and swore. He felt the lurch and tug beneath him as the ship pulled away from the dock. He smiled as several of the young soldiers paused in what they were doing, lost colour and rushed away to be sick.

"What're you grinnin' at, Charlie?" Andrews was rolling a cigarette but he was unsure of his ability to smoke it. His stomach felt loose under his belt, heaving as if he'd had twenty beers.

"I was thinking that I came out here on a boat something like this. Only five years ago. Now here I am going back."

Andrews lit the cigarette. "We're goin' to Egypt."

Carl shrugged. "That's closer."

"Mad bastard." Andrews jumped from the bunk and rushed towards the door.

Carl watched him go and examined his own feelings; he had not been seasick on the voyage out and he felt no uneasiness now. He was not frightened of the fighting because he did not fully believe it would ever happen. This was the twentieth century; civilized nations would not throw themselves madly against each other. There were no Napoleons now, no Wellingtons. The whole thing, he concluded, was like a giant play: the armies would posture and wheel about to avoid each other; the monarchs would confer with their ministers; the diplomats would talk and the correspondents would scribble. He was an actor with a tiny part in a vast panoramic spectacle in which men would be transported, trained, fed and shouted at. No shots would be fired although rifles would be cleaned and polished. He was going to Egypt, the land of the Pharoahs, where Caesar's legions had marched. And Europe was just across the Mediterranean. He felt better. He was going to enjoy himself.

"Where's the bloddy kip?"

"Polish 'em up, mate. Let's go."

"Come in, spinner."

Men gathered in a circle and the two-up game started. They yelled as the pennies rose and fell, letting off steam, comrades in a great adventure. Carl felt at one with them. He scrambled off his bunk, feeling for the banknotes in his pocket.

Three years later Carl Gulliver was, physically and mentally, a different man. He had seen more fear and suffering and blood and death than a normal human being could comprehend. Gallipoli, he had thought, was as bad a place as men could make, but the Somme and Flanders were worse. He had been wounded in the jaw, in the right leg and arm. He had lost two toes from his left foot to frostbite and an exploding mortar at Passchendaele had permanently impaired the hearing in his right ear. He had lain semi-conscious in the freezing mud of a shellhole at Ypres and a rat had gnawed away the little finger on his left hand.

He counted himself lucky. He had seen unprotected men claw their eyes from their sockets and others vomit blood and pale, shredded lung tissue, but his gas mask had been effective. He breathed normally and he was alive, but he could not sleep for more than two hours at a time and he ducked instinctively at any noise louder than a handclap. The years in the trenches had bent him a little and he smoked so much he could scarcely taste food. He ate almost nothing and was, consequently, wasted and thin. His pale skin had a greyish tinge and his once fair hair had turned a sickly brown, the colour of the Flanders mud. He wore a reddish beard to cover the white scar on his jaw. He had a slight limp.

He was convinced that his books had saved him. He saw men throw their lives away in despair at the torments they were enduring. Instead he snatched minutes, seconds even, to read. He retained his excellent eyesight through all his tribulations and could read in the dimmest of lights. On his infrequent leaves and several hospitalizations he bought books, the more densely packed with words the better. He read Milton and Shakespeare, Hugo and Proudhon, Goethe and Marx, Tolstoy and Gogol. When he could not read he repeated memorised passages to himself, translated them backwards and forwards between four languages. Often he was unaware of his surroundings; he might have been crouched in a trench with the water seeping into his boots and the lice colonising his body hair, but his mind was free of it all, locked in theological debate with Newman, probing for weaknesses in Kant's metaphysics.

Carl no longer read for pleasure. He read in a desperate, anxious way, rapidly and impatiently, searching for meanings and explanations. He pursued the ambiguities of words through his several languages, trying to track down kernels of truth. He read for information and argument, passion and political purpose. He trusted nothing. He had been baptised in a Methodist chapel in Spitalfields, but the Gullivers in London scarcely attended church. The mild agnosticism he had acquired in the Thodey household had hardened into a resolute atheism. He read sceptically, trying to throw light on certain questions that changed, almost daily, in his mind. What are the proportions of good and evil in the world? Does luck exist? Is pain physical or mental? News of the success of the Bolshevik revolution had filled him with a kind of joy. Could freedom supplant tyranny?

On a practical level, Carl's abilities as a sharpshooter and message runner had contributed to his protection. Snipers were afforded cover and a kind of camaraderie developed between them. Carl had often fired dutifully at intervals, aiming at sandbags and wooden supports, and he knew that his German counterparts had done the same. As a runner, relaying messages between the trenches, he had been spared more than a few advances across territory jungled by barbed wire and made deadly by bombardment and machine gun fire. He had obeyed orders, volunteered for nothing, avoided promotion . . . and survived.

After the breach of the Hindenburg line and subsequent Allied successes, colonial troops were pulled out of the fighting as if the imperial power wanted to reserve the final triumph for itself. Carl did not care. He awaited the resumption of the slaughter and was shocked at the news of the armistice. He saw men around him weeping, getting drunk and scribbling frantic letters. He began letters to Dr Anderson, the Thodeys and Pavel and failed to complete them. But the attempt at writing helped him to order his thoughts. Four miles from Amiens, huddled over a fire with two tots of rum warming his blood against the winter cold, he made decisions. He would not go back to Australia; he would apply to be demobilised in Britain; he would go to Russia.

18

Carl travelled in the summer of his twenty-third year. It was 1919. The Allies harboured fear and hatred for the Soviet state, which had deserted them in their struggle against the might of Germany and had repelled their own invasions at Murmansk and Archangel. No facilities were provided for travel there. No boats left Britain for Russian ports, and Carl was obliged to travel overland. Europe was like a gaping wound with maggots crawling in the flesh. Towns and cities were devastated, roads and railways were cut, and everywhere people were on the move. It was as if half the population had been turned into gypsies. In fact Carl met gypsies for the first time in his life, travelled with them for a time and learned something of their strange language. Travel under adverse conditions was nothing new for the Romany people and many of the things they taught him—how to live off the country, board moving vehicles, cannibalise stolen bicycles, purify stagnant water—helped him to make his way north and east.

Years of soldiering had toughened him and he could walk all day without difficulty despite his limp. He slept outdoors most of the time because he was apt to wake yelling and trembling, to the great alarm of anyone who might be within earshot. Influenced by the gypsies, he abandoned cigarettes for a pipe. He regained some appetite and put on weight, although there was little to eat inside Russia except bread and soup. Still, when he stepped from the train which had taken him from Riga to Moscow, he was a desiccated figure, with a pale skin stretched tight over sharp bones. In the pocket of his jacket was a paper that had been hidden in the lining until he produced it at the Soviet border. The paper was signed by Maxim Maximovich Litvinov, Soviet diplomatic agent in Britain, and it introduced Carl Gulliver, 'a friend of the revolution'.

Letters had passed from London to Moscow. Carl was met by Ian Armstrong, a Scot who had deserted the Allied force that had invaded north Russia to oppose the Bolsheviks. Armstrong noted Carl's single canvas bag. with approval.

"You travelled light, comrade."

Carl stared at the massive dome of the terminus and the rushing crowds, a motley mixture of soldiers and civilians, swarming over the platforms and down onto the railway tracks. He had expected order and discipline and saw instead the same sort of chaos he had witnessed elsewhere. But he heard shouts and questions and answers in Russian—it was the first time he had heard the language spoken by more than a couple of people at once. He shook Armstrong's hand warmly.

Carl spoke in Russian. "I've dreamed of this moment."

Armstrong shook his head. "You'll have tae speak slower with me, lad. M' Russian's nae a patch on yours."

"I'm sorry."

"Aye, maybe you will be. They'll distrust you for it."

Carl shouldered his bag and the two men moved slowly along the crowded platform. Armstrong was a tall, rawboned man who did not hesitate to shove when he saw a gap. "Not the leaders, not Lenin or Trotsky, they speak English themselves. The others—they'll no' be able to talk freely in front of you an' whisper behind your back."

"Why should they whisper?"

"Have you not heard? There's enemies everywhere. The war here's no' yet won."

"I've been travelling. Out of touch."

They passed out of the Vindau station onto a busy street. The air reeked of factory smoke and petrol fumes, although there were more horse-drawn vehicles than motorized ones. Carl was surprised to see men and women pushing heavily loaded handcarts. Armstrong hailed a *droshky* and when they were settled, he waved his hand at the buildings. "Well, you're here now, comrade, and right in touch. What do you think of it?"

Carl loosened his collar. "It's hotter than I thought it'd be."

Armstrong laughed. "Aye, everyone thinks of ice and snow in Moscow. Me, I've been more sunburned in Russia than . . . in other places."

Carl nodded. He was used to men who didn't want to be specific about places they'd been. He noted that many of the buildings had not a single pane of glass intact and he remarked on it.

"That's the work of looters, mostly," the Scot said. "The distilleries were smashed by order. The reactionaries were getting the workers drunk and turning them against the police and the Red Guards. It was bad there for a while."

"What's the state of the city now?"

"There was more fighting here than people realize. It wasna all in Petrograd. Whole streets were flattened by our artillery. The most bourgeois streets, I'm happy to say. Och, it's all right. There's kids on the streets will cut your throat for a kopek but we had that in Glasgow."

Carl gaped at a Rolls-Royce cruising effortlessly past them. The big car's suspension smoothed out the rough ride the cobblestones were causing the *droshky*.

Armstrong grunted. "Cheka, most likely. Bloodsucking secret police. I hope your papers are in apple-pie order, comrade."

Carl fingered the paper signed by Litvinov. It had been like a magic wand at the border, but would it have the same effect here? He shrugged. Life was uncertain. Who knew that better than he? He grinned at Armstrong. "The secret police? They're everywhere. Probably had them in Glasgow too, Jock."

"Aye," Armstrong said. "I suppose they're nae worse here than anywhere else."

Armstrong relaxed as Carl sat calmly beside him, asking an occasional quiet question. The Scot, starved for congenial company, became almost chatty, and Carl learned that the country was still almost on a war footing. Food shortages were grave; power was rationed; looters and black marketeers were summarily shot.

"But ye'd be surprised," Armstrong said. "They tell me the Bolshoi ballet school at Theatre Square's still open and the horses're running."

"Horses?"

"Aye. The Skatchki racetrack's operating and I hear the betting concession is privately owned."

"I don't recall much in Marx about gambling," Carl said.

Armstrong signalled the driver to stop. "The Whites were mad for it. I'm against it myself."

Bitterness had crept into Armstrong's voice when he spoke of the Whites. Not until January of the following year would the White admiral Kolchak be captured and executed, and the conflict with Poland would continue for another two years. Armstrong's talk of the White armies and the border wars worried Carl because his only practical experience was in soldiering. He feared that he could be useful only as a soldier to the new socialist country he admired and wished ardently to serve, but a soldier was the very last thing he wanted to be. He voiced the fear to Armstrong as the Scot was settling him into his room. Carl's first home in Russia was on the fourth floor of a barrack-like building on Sukharov Square in the shadow of Moscow's giant twin water towers.

"Dinna worry," Armstrong said. "They'll have other uses for you than at the thick end of a rifle."

"What do *you* do?"

Armstrong ran the tap over the cracked, stained basin in the draughty room. He nodded, satisfied with the thin, brown flow. "I do this. I help men like yourself find roofs and keep them supplied with bread an' cabbage."

"What about tobacco?"

Armstrong grinned. "Aye, we're all o' one mind on that. Lenin an' Trotsky an' all."

The Gulliver Fortune

* * *

Carl need not have worried that he would become, once again, a piece of solid flesh to be thrown against meatmincing machine guns. The day after his arrival in the capital he went before a committee that subjected him to a rigorous ideological and linguistic examination.

"You speak Tsarist Russian, not Marxist Russian," the chairman told him.

"I'm sorry," Carl said. "I learned from old books and from a man who left Russia many years ago."

"His name?"

Carl was alarmed. "Vladimir Pavel," he blurted.

The chairman's pen scratched. "What do you want to do, Comrade Gulliv . . . Gulliver?"

Carl would later think back on this interview as a miniature of his life in the Soviet Union. A barked command followed by an invitation to speak like a free man. There was a balance in it that suited his nature and tapped deep levels of energy and ability in him.

At first, his linguistic abilities were of most use to the state. He translated political messages received from and despatched to foreign countries. He acted as an interpreter for the steady stream of foreigners who were making representations to the Bolsheviks—French and English trade unionists, German industrialists, American journalists and film makers, even the occasional eccentric philanthropist. Early in this phase of his career occurred a brief but important meeting. An official beckoned Carl across from his desk and he was awestruck to find himself in the presence of the stocky, bald, sharp-eyed President of the Council of People's Commissars. Lenin leaned heavily on a cane and held his head oddly, a legacy of the assassin's bullets that had severely wounded him the year before. He said nothing, but inclined his head stiffly towards the man with whom he had been speaking.

"Hugh Williams." The accent was Welsh. Carl shook Williams's hand. "Does Mr. Lenin speak English or what?"

"He does," Carl said, smiling at the singsong lilt in the voice. "I think it's your accent giving him trouble."

"And who might you be, then?"

"I work here, comrade." Carl had been instructed not to give his name to foreigners, and his natural diffidence made this easy for him. "Tell me what you have to say and I'll try to help."

"It's to do with modernising the coal mines here." Williams spoke at length on methods of draining mines and improving the operations of extraction. Lenin listened carefully and quickly mastered the accent, appealing to Carl only for enlightenment on a few words and phrases. He asked questions in his guttural but accurate English. His voice, also affected by his recent wounds, was breathy and harsh.

"Thank you, Comrade Williams. Very helpful to us."

Lenin shook hands with Williams and nodded his thanks to Carl before moving away. He glanced back as Carl and Williams shook hands.

"I did not catch your name, comrade," Williams said.

Carl smiled and went back to his desk. He was surprised to find Lenin standing beside him a few minutes later.

"You need a name, comrade. People do not like to deal with nameless men."

"My name is Carl Gulliver, Comrade President."

"Mine is Vladimir Ilyich Ulyanov. I mean a revolutionary name. *Gulliver's Travels,* a book by the English writer, Swift."

"He was Irish, Comrade President."

Lenin's eyes flashed angrily behind his spectacles. "So Swift is *bystryi* in Russian. You are very swift with your information. A good name for you, Comrade Bystryi."

"Yes, Comrade President. Thank you."

Lenin used the name when mentioning Carl to another bureaucrat, and it stuck. Dealing with experts in all branches of industry, agriculture and economic management gave Carl Bystryi a breadth of knowledge and expertise that was quickly recognised by the members of the committees overseeing the reconstruction of the Russian economy. He was co-opted to serve as secretary to bodies as various as the Committee on Motor Traffic Planning and the Committee for the Rehabilitation of War Veterans. He quickly absorbed the Russian practice of treating every post as a personal as well as public benefit. He learned to drive a motor car and he received first-class treatment for his own disabilities.

Armstrong's prediction that he would be worked hard and mistrusted was borne out. As a foreigner, Carl was kept clear of all matters with a direct political import. He was instructed to report any approaches to him that smacked of intelligence gathering or giving, and he obeyed the order to the letter. No sensitive political material crossed his desk and he was ordered from the room when discussions turned from practicalities to policy. This irked him and he complained to Armstrong, who had become his friend and to whom he gave Russian lessons.

The two men sat hunched over the coal fire in Carl's two-room flat on Entuziastov Road. As a secretary to busy committees, he rated two rooms. It was a practical matter. He needed space for books and writing materials, light to write by in the daytime, a fire to permit him to work at night so he would be prepared for his morning meetings. His flat had to be on an accessible road, not too far from the administrative offices in the centre of the city. Not too many floors above street level, because the messengers who delivered papers and sealed envelopes to him had only so much strength. On the other hand, as a single man, he needed only a narrow bed, and a twentieth share in a toilet and bathroom was generous. All this had been explained to him when he was given the key. The explanation was unnecessary because the allocation of resources, the planning of budgets, the fitting of things and people into spaces, had become his work and his obsession.

"They don't trust me," Carl said. He poured the last of the tea into the glasses. If he broke a glass it would be months before he could get another.

Armstrong carefully shredded hard-packed tobacco on an enamel plate with his pocket knife. "What can you expect, laddie? The country's surrounded by wolves looking to tear its throat out."

"*Volki*," Carl said. "We're talking Russian here."

"Bugger Russian," Armstrong said. He packed his

pipe and pushed the plate towards Carl. "We're men talking here. Christ, it's cold!"

"Losing heart, Jock?" Carl carefully mixed his dottles with the fresh tobacco, leaving some for Armstrong.

"I'm not. We're living in the future right here. I'm sure of it, an' the centuries o' misery an' want'll seem like they happened on another planet."

"Aye."

"Dinna mock me, lad."

"No, Ian, I know you're right. I just . . ."

"You want to be loved, son?"

Carl laughed. "I want to be trusted."

"They'll come to it, and you'll know when."

"How?"

"You'll see. Meanwhile, what you need is a woman. Now, that's where I can help you. How long since you had a woman?"

Carl had not repeated his experience with the Sydney whores in any of the cities he had been in since. "Five years," he said.

"Christ, man, that's damned unhealthy. I can find . . ."

"No," Carl said.

"And why not?"

Carl found it hard to explain; he spoke of the bloodshed and the cruelty he'd seen—the dead children and raped, bleeding women begging to be shot. Armstrong listened stoically. "We've all been through that. You can't let it twist you. Life goes on."

"I agree, my life goes on. I want to do something useful with it. I don't want to be burdened with a wife and children."

"Who's talking about a wife an' bairns? In the long run of course, but I'm on about the question of a man's needs now."

"I tried that. I didn't much like it."

Armstrong stirred the few dying coals back into life. He used drink and women to blot out the horrors of his own war, but he had the imagination to see that other men might use other ways and was curious about what they might be. "You've never spoken of your mother and father," he said quietly.

"They died within days of each other."

"Were they happy together?"

"Yes."

"Don't you want that for yourself?"

The room was lit by an oil lamp set on a table in the far corner; Armstrong couldn't see Carl's features clearly by its dim glow. He saw a well-shaped head set on a strong neck, a red beard growing thickly, pale skin. Slowly, the face hardened and turned as if made resolute by the force of the realisation that had come to Carl at that moment. "He destroyed her," he said.

Carl continued to work as a translator and interpreter for another two years. Nothing changed in his life. He worked long hours and was preoccupied by the work. For relaxation he read, almost exclusively in Russian, books on economics and political philosophy. From time to time the imaginative, sensitive side of his nature rebelled and he went on binges of novel reading—Dickens and Zola, highly approved of by the Soviet authorities, and more erratic choices such as Thomas Hardy and George Sand. By chance he acquired a battered copy of Scott's *Redgauntlet*, the romantic story of the last flickering of the Jacobite cause, in English. He read it and wept and did not know why.

In the summer of 1925 Carl was summoned into the presence of Pasha Chuchin, whom he knew to be a senior official of the security service. Chuchin was a fat man, tightly buttoned into his grey uniform with its red collar tabs. He was clean-shaven as was the recent fashion in the higher ranks of the bureaucracy. Chuchin eyed red-bearded, drably dressed Carl Bystryi with distaste.

"An investigation has been carried out, Comrade Bystryi," Chuchin said softly. "A thorough investigation."

Carl stood nervously in front of the big polished desk. He made the decision to test the water. "May I sit down, comrade?"

Chuchin inspected the notes in front of him, decided,

and nodded. He made no protest when Carl packed his pipe and lit it. "Did you know, comrade, that your mother's mother was a Jewess?"

"No. That's interesting."

"If you think so. It is of interest to Comrade Trotsky apparently."

Carl smoked and said nothing. The room was a vast Tsarist chamber in the administrative block on Kaunin Prospekt. It had been stripped of its trappings, was too big for its current use and was, consequently, cold and impersonal.

"It has been decided, comrade, to offer you Soviet citizenship."

Carl felt his breathing constrict and he fought to puff casually on his pipe. "That is a great honour, comrade," he said.

"It is." Chuchin prodded his notes with a sharpened pencil as if he wished to push them off the desk into the wastepaper basket. "Further, if you accept that honour, an important service for the state awaits you."

19

The job for which the newly accredited citizen, Comrade Bystryi, had been selected was nothing less than the secretaryship of one of the major committees whose operations would spearhead the first of the Soviet Union's Five Year Plans. Carl's apprehension that he was an unwitting part of a Trotskyite clique, in which Jewishness was a factor, was quickly dispelled. He followed the events that succeeded Lenin's death in 1924 in *Pravda*, but not otherwise. Trotsky left the country in 1927 and Stalin assumed control. Carl took no interest in politics, avoided discussions that could lead to complicity in any political manoeuvring. Comrade Bystryi studied and worked.

The work became his passion. The task of transforming a mediaeval economy into a modern one was monumental, requiring thousands of decisions, thousands of meetings, thousands of tons of paper and, as it eventuated, millions of lives. Carl's single-minded capacity for work, his ability to read and absorb lengthy and complex reports quickly and advise on appropriate strategies, made him a key figure in the devising and execution of the Five Year Plan. Trotsky's vision of a rapidly transformed agricultural sector feeding a modernized, urban-based economy had a natural appeal to Carl. As a child in England and an adolescent in Australia, Carl had had very little exposure to the joys of the countryside. As a soldier he had seen deserts, hillsides and forests enough and had found them all dangerous. Rivers had to be crossed under fire, valleys were possible traps, grassy plains concealed landmines. Carl worshipped cities.

"Think of it, Jock," he said to Armstrong one night as they ate dinner in a Moscow cafe. "We make an industrial revolution, as complete as the political one, and without the horrors that happened in Europe."

"Aye," Armstrong said. He had recently married and was feeling secure and comfortable. He had put on weight and had come to value his friendship with Carl all the more because his status as a senior bureaucrat admitted him to cafes like this. "If it can be done."

"You're sceptical?" Carl pushed away his plate and took a sip of wine. He had never become very interested in food or alcohol; the long rationing of both in Russia had never bothered him; tobacco was his vice but he resisted lighting his pipe until Armstrong had finished eating.

"I am." Armstrong was a minor functionary now, a railways administrator. He found the work dull but enjoyed the opportunities to deal in black market goods— furs, jewellery, brandy, cigarettes and medicines— that were transported around the country by train.

Carl packed his pipe. He kept his voice low by habit. "You've lost faith in socialism?"

Armstrong laughed, he chewed vigorously and swallowed. He wiped his face before emptying the last of the wine into his glass. Carl had put his hand over his own half-full glass. "Not a bit of it. Look at us, eating caviar in style. Clean tablecloth and we have this to drink." He tapped the bottle. "Rumanian. It's horse's piss, but that's better than cow's piss."

Carl sighed and lit his pipe. "I'm talking about a new world and you're talking about wine." He felt in his pocket for matches. He never had any; most of the members of the various committees on which he sat were smokers, and matches were quickly expended. Armstrong passed him a petrol lighter.

"How old are you, Carl?" Armstrong accepted the return of the lighter and lit his own pipe.

"Thirty-one."

"You look forty. Natasha has a sister, twenty-five. Tits out to here."

"No."

"Why not?"

"Sometimes I work at home until three a.m. I have four hours' sleep with two nightmares, get up and go to work in an office. I come home at eight, eat some bread and cheese and start work. What would Natasha's sister think of that?"

"You wouldn't do it if you had her."

"Exactly. And if I were you, comrade, I wouldn't produce my French cigarette lighter with such a flourish. You didn't buy that in GUM."

In the summer of 1936, on 26 August shortly before his fortieth birthday, Carl Bystryi awoke in his apartment near Moscow University. The move to this district, not premature or the result of any string-pulling or queue-jumping, had pleased him. The apartment was old but well built, with high ceilings and a skylight in the small room that served as a laundry and kitchen. Carl had a refrigerator, a gramophone and radio, modern furniture and a view of an ancient seat of learning. He cherished an ambition to teach in the university one day, and to that end he had taken up two new projects in addition to his heavy administrative workload—he met regularly with a group of students from the university to discuss foreign literature, and he was translating Child's *English and Scottish Popular Ballads* into Russian. The university authorities had approved his informal classes and the State Publishing House was supporting his translation.

Carl looked out cheerfully at a clear blue sky, unusual for Moscow, but which could herald a spell of bright weather. He left his bed, put on a dressing gown and prepared coffee—another privilege attaching to his status. *Life is good,* he thought as he sipped the coffee. With the Second Five Year Plan well under way, the modernization of Russia was being accomplished according to schedule. The peasants had resisted the collectivization and many had been dispossessed. This Carl knew, but he regarded it as a regrettable necessity. If pressed he would have declared that many had died, but that most had been relocated or re-educated, and were now productive members of the Soviet state. Moscow-based, he had seen nothing of the butchery in the Ukraine; he was totally ignorant of the mass graves of Georgia. He knew that the cities were being fed and that more than eighty per cent of Russian industry was operated with plants less than ten years old. He believed that Russia was on a course to outstrip the rest of the world economically, as it had politically, and he was proud to have played his part. And there was much still to be done.

On a personal level, he felt his life to be expanding dramatically after years of stasis. Work on the massive Child collection had revealed to him his ignorance of Russian dialects, of Ukrainian and the Turkic tongues spoken in the south. He felt that he had to capture at least the flavour of these to do justice to the ballads, and he had resolved to travel when he could be spared from his endless committees and reports.

And there was Vitalia.

Vitalia was the illegitimate daughter of Rachel Kylenko, a dancer and musician. She had been born in Odessa in the Ukraine and had been protected, with her mother, by Colonel Udanov when the city was taken by the Red Army in 1920. Later, Rachel joked that Udanov, the only man who had ever treated her well, was her only lover at the time who could not possibly have been the father of her child. She claimed to have slept with twenty men in the month in which Vitalia was conceived. In that month Udanov, who had operated as an undercover agent in the city for almost a year, was not in Odessa.

It made no difference to Udanov, who distinguished himself in the fighting around Odessa, was rapidly promoted to general, and from 1925 kept Rachel and her daughter in comfort in a small flat in Minsk. Here Rachel, starved for attention and artistic outlet, drank herself to death in seven years after the move from Odessa. Udanov, a solid family man whose one passion and aberration Rachel had been, arranged for Vitalia to be fostered by a discreet family of displaced Ukrainians in Moscow. Her outstanding scholastic record earned her a place at Moscow University without Udanov's intervention, although he had been instrumental in arranging a scholarship for her.

Vitalia was a member of the second instruction group in foreign literature Carl took at the university. He would never forget the first words he heard from her: "How can you tell a Scotsman and an Englishman apart, professor?"

He looked at the strongly built, dark-haired young woman who sat with the others in the university courtyard. Carl had been promised a tutorial room 'when available'. For now, the weather encouraged learning *al fresco*. "By their accents primarily," Carl said. "You," he looked down at his typed class list, "Vitalia Kylenka, are from Minsk."

The girl's smile lit up her dark, sombre features and made her beautiful. She shook her head. "From Odessa."

"Originally perhaps, but lately from Minsk."

The other students watched the exchange doubtfully; they were accustomed to vast distances being daily maintained between their teachers and themselves. "And you, comrade professor, are you an American?"

"No," Carl said. "And I am not a professor either."

They had gone on from there, with bantering and teasing that they had learned to repress in class because it embarrassed the other students and interfered with instruction. They had met for coffee and cake outside the university. For the first meeting, hesitantly arranged after a class, Carl trimmed his beard and moustache, had his hair cut and wore a new shirt. Vitalia brushed her hair until it shone dark red in the sun. She chose her prettiest blouse and wore a light patterned jacket over it that matched her full skirt. She wore a pair of ankle-strap shoes that hurt her feet.

They met at an outdoor cafe on a street that bordered Gorky Park. They talked for four hours and drank six cups of coffee each. Carl smoked one pipe and made himself late for an important committee meeting. As he talked and listened, new unfamiliar feelings warred inside him. He noticed the swell of her breasts under her blouse and the smooth brown skin of her throat. At another time, in another country, Carl might have been embarrassed by the mutilation of his left hand, but not in Russia in 1936. Men with missing eyes and limbs, with terrible scars and prosthetic devices substituting for shattered bones and flesh were a common sight. Carl's disfigurements were minor. He was glad that he had a full head of thick hair, although he regretted that it was streaked with grey. His stomach was flat, that was good; his eyes were surrounded with lines and wrinkles—bad.

"You have seen the world outside?" Vitalia had said.

"Yes." Carl forced himself not to stare at her full red lips, the dark wisps that grew on the nape of her neck below the point where her hair had been gathered and swept up.

"Tell me about it." Vitalia's lips were parted and her eyes shone with something like the fanatical light Carl had seen in some of the planners and executors he had dealt with for the past decade. He knew he should be cautious—these were the signs of unrest and dissent—but he could not help plunging forward to tell her what she wanted to hear. He wanted to say what he had felt to be the truth until then, that there were good people in the world but that the world itself was rotten. He could not say it; old images swam up before his eyes and the words formed without his bidding.

"I rode on an elephant in Ceylon," he said. "I was frightened. It was so high and it swayed, but the view was wonderful. We bought bananas and threw them into the elephant's mouth."

"How wonderful," Vitalia said. "Who is 'we'?"

"My brother and I." Carl felt his eyes growing moist at the memory of Edward. He had not thought of him for more than fifteen years, almost the lifetime of the girl sitting across from him. He shook his head, trying to clear away the thoughts and emotions, but they would not go. "I haven't talked of these things, ever."

"I understand." Vitalia had her own memories—of the photographs of the White Russian officers her mother kept hidden in the Minsk apartment, of the men who arrived late after General Udanov had left and whom Rachel turned away scornfully because she would rather drink than take risks for love.

"Do you?" Carl felt an overwhelming need to talk. He spoke mainly of the sea—of the passage through Suez, of the blue waters of Sydney Harbour and the Dardanelles, the grey blustery English Channel. Vitalia knew only Odessa, Minsk, Leningrad and Moscow, but Carl hung on her words. They did not touch at the first meeting or the second. The third time they walked beside the river and crossed bridges they had crossed often before, but never feeling like this. They found the city beautiful. On the fourth meeting Carl kissed her. He had not touched a woman since he had fumbled and failed with his last whore more than twenty years before. He felt his body tingle with a new life, and years and months and weeks and days fell from him like grains of sand spilling in an hourglass.

"I love you," Carl said.

Vitalia kissed him hard. "I am eighteen in two weeks," she said. "We can be married."

Carl finished his coffee. He was too happy to eat and he wanted to remain slim. He looked around the sitting room carefully to make sure no papers were in evidence. He took a towel and went out of the flat to the bathroom he shared with two others. This was a great luxury; three single men could roster for a bathroom so that no one ever had to wait, which was what Carl and his fellow residents had done. He bathed and shaved. Back in his flat he packed his briefcase and selected some of the Child material he would work on in the library that night.

A firm knock on the door startled him. Sometimes a car was sent for him when he had to conduct a meeting in a remote part of the city. Sometimes there were packages and messages. But he was expecting nothing like that today.

"Who?" Carl said.

"Security, Comrade Bystryi. Open please."

Carl felt a shiver run through him and his hands shook as he unbolted the door. Three men stood on the landing; they wore the grey and red uniforms of the security police. Pistols in hard leather holsters sat high on their hips. The senior officer, with gold badges on the lapels of his coat, stepped forward, forcing Carl to retreat into the room.

"What?" he said.

"You are under arrest," the officer said.

"A mistake," Carl stammered, "I am . . ."

"I know who you are." The officer omitted the word 'comrade' and Carl felt the omission like ice water being dashed into his face. "You are Carl Bystryi, and you are being placed under arrest for anti-revolutionary activities and subversion."

20

The man who limped through the gates of Kazan station into Komsomol Square on 1 August 1955 would have been unrecognizable to anyone who had known him twenty years before. He had shrunk in size, barely five feet six inches now, and was painfully thin. His hair was still thick, but it was white, and his features were pinched and sunken. His skin was grey and he coughed harshly with every few steps. The coughing brought some colour to his cheeks but racked his body and made his limp seem more pronounced. He carried a cardboard suitcase in one gloved hand and the other hand was clenched tight around a piece of paper.

Carl Bystryi wore an overcoat, gloves, a scarf and a hat, although it was a mild day in the Russian capital. He had been cold so long that he felt it would be impossible ever again to be too warm. He looked at the hurrying, normally busy people in the square without interest. At the sight of an MVD militiaman, striding along in his smart uniform, he shrank back against the wall. People stared at him curiously, noting the bloodless lips and the awkward, shuffling gait. They knew him for what he was—a person who had been brought to justice in the People's State, punished and set free. No one wanted to speak to him, but Carl stopped the first man walking slowly enough for him to clutch his sleeve. He showed him the paper.

"This address, comrade, can you direct me?"

The man recoiled from the discordant foreign accent wrapped around the quick, colloquial Russian sentence. He glanced at the speaker, then at the paper, and pointed. "It's three blocks that way. Go right before the bridge, and it's two, no, three streets down on your left."

"Thank you, comrade."

The man nodded and walked on more quickly. He had registered almost nothing apart from an uneasy oddness about the old man in the greasy overcoat, but Carl had taken in every detail about him—the shoes made of thin, flexible leather, the soft-collared shirt and the large, loose tie knot, the generous sweep of the lapels of his suit jacket—much had changed in twenty years. People smelled different, as if they used different soap and ate different food.

Carl, the ex-bureaucrat, pondered these questions as he plodded through the streets absorbing the sights and sounds—noisily contending traffic, the rounded shapes of the motor cars, the light clothes worn by the younger women, many hatless, tieless young men, cigarette butts littering the pavement and dry gutters. He fancied the children were taller.

His eyes were still keen; he did not need glasses to read the street signs, and although he was thin and small he was strong: he carried the bulging suitcase in his right hand the whole way without apparent effort. When he was satisfied that he was in the right street, he put the suitcase down and sat on it. He wiped his face with a handkerchief and smoothed his hair. He took off his gloves and checked that his fingernails were clean. His boots were cracked and one sole flapped; he could do nothing about that. He unbuttoned his overcoat.

"You smell like a horse," he said. He spoke in English, a habit that had gained a hold on him lately. Three children playing with a ball against a tin fence giggled at the old man making such odd sounds. He picked up his suitcase and entered the lobby of a grey concrete block of flats. Work on the building had been interrupted and the seventh storey was just a frame of steel and concrete.

There were thirty-six mailboxes but most of the slots had two or three names written beside them, indicating that the flats were shared. An elevator stood open, its doors held apart by a chair. Carl looked at his piece of paper, sighed and began to climb the stairs. At the third level he stopped outside a door, put down his case and went through the ritual of smoothing his hair and straightening his clothes again. His heart was racing, but not from the effort of climbing the stairs. He was accustomed to exerting himself much harder than that, and for hours on end.

Carl almost left at that point. He realised that he was more afraid than ever before in his life—more than at the Somme when the sky above was full of death and the ground was shaking from the bombardment; more than when he'd faced the cold-eyed men of the tribunals; more than when he'd first seen the icy wastes stretching off into the far distance. Close to twenty years of suffering and hope were concentrated in this single moment. If he'd been able to pray, this would have been the consummation of tens of thousands of prayers. He knocked at the door and was angered at how puny the sound was. He turned his bunched fist and hammered with his calloused knuckles. He heard noises behind the door, footsteps.

The woman who opened the door was almost middle-aged and almost stout. Her hair was tied back and covered with a bright red headcloth. Her olive skin was smooth, but faint white lines sprang into life around her shocked eyes and mouth as she looked at the man in the doorway.

"Vitalia!" Carl's lips trembled. His mind was flooded with English and French and German. He struggled to find words in Russian.

The woman stood as if she was frozen to the spot. Her dress was blue with small yellow flowers on it. He felt like a child; his tongue was slow and awkward in his dry mouth.

"Vitalia. What a beautiful dress."

She did not answer and for one ghastly second he thought he had made a mistake—that his deepest dread, the darkest nightmare he had been able to conjure, had come true. Then he felt rather than saw her move towards him. His heart pounded in his chest and his vision clouded. Years of pain and anguish seemed to be erased as he felt her fingers on his face.

"Carl," she said. "Oh, darling. Oh, my love. Oh, Carl."

21

Carl and Vitalia did not leave her room for three days. They scarcely slept. When Carl removed his coat, Vitalia held her nose. She put him in a bath and washed him thoroughly. She touched every inch of his skin and his body seemed to come to life under her touch. They talked and she led him to her bed where they made love for the first time. The final spasm shook him and produced a deep, searing cough. Vitalia held him in her strong arms like a child.

"Oh, God," she said. "What is that?"

"My lungs. I think they are damaged."

"You must see a doctor."

"Yes." He smiled in the semi-darkness, and she felt the movement of his face.

"What?"

"It was wonderful. I dreamed it ten thousand times, but it was better. I'm sorry if I was clumsy."

She clutched him. "You weren't clumsy. You are so thin, it's exciting. Rudi . . ."

Carl freed himself from her arms and pulled her close so that her head was on his shoulder. He stroked her thick brown hair. "You have had other lovers, I know that. I even know the names of two of them. It doesn't matter as long as you are mine again now."

"I am. But how could you possibly know?"

"The gypsies told me. The gypsies who travel to . . . that place. I can speak their language a little. I talked to them. I helped them with some of their problems and they helped me. They found you for me, they told me what you were doing. Not everything, just some things. I always knew you were alive, that was the main thing. Sometimes I would hear nothing for two years."

She had stiffened. "You could have got a message to me. I thought you were dead."

"I *was* dead. I didn't want you to wait for me. I wanted you to be happy. I was jealous when I heard of your lovers, but I was happy for you."

"Carl, darling . . ."

"I'm not a saint, Vitalia. I thought of it often, but it would have been madness to send you a message. If it had been intercepted you would have been in trouble. You could have been sent to the same sort of . . . place."

They were silent under the blankets for a while. She kissed him gently and stroked him. He responded, and they made love again, and Carl did not cough. Vitalia brought tea back to the bed; Carl rested and watched her plait her hair. She wound the thick braids around her head.

"They cut it off," she said.

Carl kissed her large soft breasts. She dabbled her finger in the sugary dregs of her tea and wet her nipples. He sucked them and they kissed and cried a little.

"It was four years before the gypsies found you," Carl said.

"Tell me what happened."

The anti-Jewish, anti-Trotskyite purge that had swept Carl up had also touched Vitalia. As the illegitimate daughter of a displaced Jewess of doubtful political background, Vitalia was vulnerable to the paranoic wave that swept through the Soviet bureaucracies in the 1930s. Administrators vied with each other in hunting out individuals whose backgrounds seemed not to fit the Stalin-approved model of the loyal, suffering Russian. Vitalia's interest in 'foreign literature' was suspect; her university career appeared to be frivolous; she was not a diligent student; she was not deserving of a scholarship.

Her double misfortune was the association with General Udanov. The hero of Odessa had fornicated in the same bed as White Russian officers; he had protected a Jewish whore and constantly failed to suppress black marketeering and smuggling in the districts he had controlled. He had pardoned young deserters, approved pensions to malingerers and arranged uncomfortable postings for officers whose zeal in the pursuit of the goals of General Secretary of the Communist Party Joseph Stalin exceeded his own. Fat, contented, easygoing General Udanov fell rapidly when the time was right for his enemies to denounce him, and in falling he took Vitalia with him.

"It was nothing to do with you, darling," Vitalia said. "Nothing to do with your teaching."

"I had scarcely started," Carl said. "How many classes had we? Three, four?"

Vitalia smiled. "I don't remember a thing about them. Only that we were in love."

Carl massaged the place at the side of his hand where the finger was missing. It hurt him sometimes. "I've done some teaching since. I'm not a bad teacher. But what did you do after you left the university? You said they cut your hair. Were you in prison?"

She nodded. "Just for a few months. That was when I lost my hair. I think they feared to keep us in gaol. There were so many, as if half the university population was imprisoned. We had some wonderful talks."

Carl nodded. "Yes, I know. We . . . yes, something like that."

"General Udanov was shot. His wife too, I think. But they let me go. I was not allowed to go on with my studies. I was sick for some time. I could not find out anything about you. They wiped the slate."

Carl nodded. "They would. A foreigner, a Jew . . ."

Vitalia's eyes opened. Carl nodded. "My mother. I knew nothing about it until I was an adult. My mother died when I was young. She was small and fair." He looked at the dark-eyed, dark-haired woman beside him in the bed. He smiled. "Jews are as different as horses, apparently. Go on, my love."

"When I got better, everything had changed. I had nowhere to live, no work, no money. I had some bits and pieces of my mother's jewellery and I sold them. That kept me alive for a while. Then I got a job at the university library."

Carl looked surprised.

"Cleaning," Vitalia said. "Just cleaning. I was useful because I knew how a library worked. I could tell the difference between the books the students brought in to the library and forgot and the ones that belonged there. I knew what was scrap paper and what was important. I could put books back where they belonged, and after a while I stopped cleaning and did other jobs, like repairing and rearranging shelves and sections."

Carl nestled against her as she spoke. He realised that he was warm, truly warm in body and mind for the first time in many years.

Vitalia's usefulness had acted as a counter to the disfavour that attended her. She graduated to classifying books and eventually to accessioning them, and then into other branches of library work. She was paid the minimum possible, which meant that she was often hungry.

"During the war was the worst. The university closed several times and there was no work."

"What did you do?"

She shrugged. "Starved, sometimes. People were kind. We shared, we stole. We went with the soldiers in return for food. We didn't care. We thought the Germans would come and kill us all. What did it matter?"

After the war, Vitalia returned to the library and the same work. She had no qualifications, and all avenues to get them were closed to her. She had her wages and no security.

"But I was able to read, Carl. Anything I wanted. I read all the authors you had mentioned in our classes— Dickens, Balzac, Scott, Conrad, all of them."

Carl smiled. "I know. The gypsies called you 'the lady with the books'. They told me that you were never without a book. I was glad of that."

Vitalia eased herself down in the bed and pressed against him. "You looked so frightened when I opened the door."

"The last report I had was ten months ago. I didn't know that you would still be here."

"What else did the gypsies tell you about me?"

About the men—I mentioned that. Do you remember an old woman coming to see you when you were ill one winter? I think it was 1951."

"Yes. She cured me."

"A gypsy woman. It was arranged."

Vitalia kissed him. "So you were watching over me. I knew you were a wonderful man the first time I saw you. Do you remember, darling? In the courtyard?"

"Yes."

"That is enough about me," Vitalia whispered. "You must tell me about yourself, my poor wonderful man."

But Carl was asleep.

Four months later Carl received an official letter noting his request to be repatriated to Great Britain along with his wife, Vitalia Kylenka. The letter said that the matter was under consideration and would receive attention in due course.

"It could take years," Vitalia said.

Carl shrugged. "A few more. After so many, what difference does it make?"

They were living in Vitalia's room, which had given her slightly less than the official housing space allowance of nine square metres per person, and they were happy. For Carl the physical freedom was a luxury. Money was short, since Vitalia's wages had to feed both of them. She ate less but more healthily as she tried to build up her husband's strength. They went for long walks through the city, often for pleasure, sometimes in search of shorter queues for better food. Vitalia lost weight and looked more beautiful.

They both read, sometimes went to the cinema and continued to make love every night. Carl was disturbed at his dependence on Vitalia, but his political record would have made it difficult for him to work, even if suitable work had been available. His health was uncertain. He applied to the State Publishing House for a position as translator and received no reply. He considered writing to England or Australia for assistance.

"To whom?" Vitalia asked.

"I had a rich uncle in England, I think. I had a sister and two, no, three brothers."

Vitalia was knitting. Her hands stopped as she looked at him. "You are not sure how many brothers you had?"

He told her the story of the voyage on the *Southern Maid*. His memory was excellent. He could recall the face and kindness of Dr Anderson. "He would be dead by now. They might all be dead."

"Idiot! The baby brother would be only a few years older than me."

"I don't even know his name," Carl said.

Vitalia resumed her knitting. "It would be no good anyway. Your letters would never leave Russia."

Carl smiled. "Oh, I could get letters out."

"How?"

"The gypsies. They can do marvellous things. And they'll be here soon. You can meet them. There'll certainly be a party."

The gypsies came at Christmas. It was the safest and best time for them in the city. Food was in better supply and people were willing to buy the trinkets and craft goods the gypsies had to sell. Around Christmas the militia and other authorities were most lenient and people generally were more tolerant than usual. A note was handed to Carl one day when he was buying bread. A note and a few quick, whispered Romany words, that was all.

That night Carl showed Vitalia the note.

"It means nothing to me," she said. "What language is that?" She pointed to a collection of pencilled marks on the paper.

"It's not a language at all. This is a map. Look, this means bridge, these marks indicate distances and turnings to left and right. Only a gypsy or someone who has been taught by them can understand it. It would mean nothing to the police or the KGB."

"Don't be too sure," Vitalia said. "The KGB have people everywhere. I am sure they are in the library."

In a few short years the *Komitet Gosudarestennoi Bezopasnosti* had become a known and feared element in Russian life. Carl shook his head. "Not the gypsies," he said.

Mere mention of the secret police sobered them for the rest of the evening, but the next day Carl was making plans. "We'll have to dress warmly and take blankets."

"How long will the party last?"

Carl inspected the note. "Two nights."

"I can get money for that," Vitalia said. She knew of at least three sets of young lovers who would pay for the use of her room.

"I know," Carl said. "And with the money we can get the only thing we'll need to take to the party."

Vitalia raised her eyebrows.

"Brandy," Carl said. "Two bottles."

The party was held in an abandoned warehouse on the western edge of the city. The area was marked for redevelopment and the authorities tolerated the temporary presence of the gypsies, who would burn a lot of crumbling, splintered wood, clear away and stack rubbish and leave the area cleaner than they found it. On Christmas Eve Carl and Vitalia travelled by train and then walked for nearly a mile, burdened by the blankets, some food and the bottles that had been carefully wrapped to prevent clinking. A couple walking at night through this part of the city with clinking bottles would not be safe.

The warehouse was a huge burned-out shell. They skirted around it and saw more than fifty wagons arranged in a wide semicircle around several large fires. The wagons were hung with lanterns. They could hear music—strange warbling notes from a fiddle and quick, surging phrases from a button accordion. The night was still and cold with a promise of snow.

"Smell the food," Vitalia said. "They're roasting meat. How do they get it?"

Carl smiled. "They steal it. It's the perfect crime. You steal and then you eat the evidence. The dogs eat the bones."

As he spoke a pack of thin dogs came yapping towards them. Carl uttered a couple of quick sibilant words and the dogs were silent. A tall man loomed up out of the shadows.

"Hello, brother," the man said. "I've been watching for you."

Vitalia watched in surprise as Carl, who rarely showed emotion except at intimate moments with her, reached out both arms towards the man. The two embraced; Carl's head fitted under the man's chin.

"Isadore," Carl said. "It's good to see you." He hugged the man hard and then stepped back. "Isadore, this is my wife. I think you know her."

Vitalia looked at the huge man; his beard grew almost to his eyes and bristled out above his scarf and coat collar. She shook her head. "I'm sorry, I . . ."

"Isadore Laza, Madame Bystryi." The giant extended his hand. "I am happy to have been of service." He gripped Vitalia's hand with his right and lifted the bag free of her shoulder with his left. He shook the bag. "As I thought, brother, as I told you—books."

"Isadore kept watch over you, darling," Carl said, "for many years."

"Now is not the time to think of that, brother. Now is the time to sing and dance and drink and sing again."

The party lasted for two nights and a day as promised. At the end of the time Carl had been drunk twice but had sobered up quickly from the cold and the food and the strong, sweet gypsy coffee. Vitalia had joined in the singing but had drunk almost nothing and danced little, which surprised Carl who knew she was good at it. But he had never seen her looking more beautiful and happy. Most of the talk Vitalia had not understood but some she had—scraps of information about men still imprisoned, about the hardships they endured, the anguish of the separations from friends and family that stretched on, seemingly forever. Carl had told her almost nothing about his exile, saying he could not bear to think of it. From the talk Vitalia gained some understanding of what he had suffered. The bond between Carl and Isadore Laza was like that between father and son, but it was hard to tell which man filled which role.

After the final farewells a gypsy drove Carl and Vitalia to the station in one of the horse-drawn wagons. It was snowing and they huddled close together under the canopy.

"What wonderful people," Vitalia said.

"Yes. They've suffered for centuries, like the Jews, but they survive."

"Will they take the letters?" Vitalia whispered.

"Yes."

There was hesitation in his voice. Vitalia gripped his arm. "What is it? What's wrong?"

"Isadore wanted us to stay with them. They are going south. He said he could get us out of Russia."

"Could he?"

"Possibly, but I don't have the courage. If we were caught, we would be punished. They would separate us, and I couldn't bear it."

The horses' hooves thudded in the snow while Vitalia considered what was in her mind. She decided. "I'm glad you said no."

"Why? I feel like a coward. The letters will be slow. We may not hear anything for years. This way could have been quick."

"I don't want to travel south with the gypsies. Not now. I'm pregnant. You are sixty, darling, and I'm nearly forty, but we're going to have a child."

22

When Mikhail Bystryi was eleven years of age his father asked him to make some tea and bring it to him in the bedroom. Carl was ill and almost bedridden. The Bystryi family had moved to Leningrad after the birth of Mikhail. Vitalia had got a job in a scientific library and Carl did piecework translations for academics. They had a flat with three rooms—Mikhail slept on a divan in the living room. They pulled a bamboo screen around it at night and called it 'the Chinese room'. They had a small kitchen where they lived and worked in the cold months.

Mikhail read a book as he brewed the tea. He was a dark, serious boy, tall for his age and graceful. Everybody said he was old for his years. In looks he reminded Carl of his older brother Jack. Carl found himself thinking of his brothers and sisters more often lately. He wondered what had become of them. He hoped that Mikhail would not resemble Jack in character—sixty years had not removed Carl's memory of his brother's ruthlessness.

The boy put lemon in his father's glass and sugar in his own. He took the tea into the bedroom and sat on the bed.

"Thank you, Mickey," Carl said. "How's school? How's everything?"

"Fine," Mikhail said. "How are you, Papa?"

Carl sipped his tea. "As you see me—old. It has been

hard on you having an old father, hasn't it? Not to play football together and so on?"

"Sometimes, but there are other things. The kids at school tell me their fathers hit them and fight with their mothers. You don't do that."

Carl smiled. "No. My father didn't do those things either."

Mikhail looked at the old man with interest. "Your father? You've never spoken of him."

"I'm going to speak of him now, and of a lot of other things. How's your memory?"

Mikhail made a circle of his thumb and forefinger and jabbed the air affirmatively. He had seen the gesture in foreign films.

Carl laughed. *Jack again,* he thought. He coughed violently. When he had recovered he drained his tea glass and began to speak. He told his son about the Gulliver family's departure from England and the ship voyage. He told him about the death of his grandparents and described them in detail when Mikhail put questions. He spoke of Sydney, Australia, the orphanage and the Thodeys. He omitted Pavel from his narrative and did not explain why he had gone to war. The boy's eyes widened at Carl's account of Gallipoli.

"I didn't know you had fought in the war. Many of the boys boast of their fathers' bravery."

"I wasn't brave," Carl said. "I was lucky and I survived it." He touched the grey mottled flesh on the side of his hand and told Mikhail about the rat. The boy's tea grew cold in the glass as he listened. Carl told him how he had come to Russia after the revolution and of the work he had done.

"You met him? You really met him, Papa?"

"I did. We spoke. He gave me this name—Bystryi."

Carl answered a volume of questions about Lenin's manner and appearance as best he could, and then he went on to his arrest in 1936. Mikhail's face grew still and his hands moved nervously as his father spoke.

"I have never told anyone of these things, Mickey. Not even your mother. But I want you to know."

The labour camp was on the upper reaches of the Lena River in southern Siberia. The land was frozen for much of the year and sometimes even missed out on the short, warm Siberian summer because of winds from the high plateau to the north. The prisoners mined salt and limestone which was transported by rail and barge. They repaired railway tracks and locks. Sometimes, when the locomotives broke down, they pulled the carriages along the lines. They hauled the barges over sandbars and through log jams. They cleared snow and broke ice.

"It was very bad," Carl said, "and I was there for nearly twenty years. Almost twice as long as I have had with you and your mother."

Mikhail said nothing. He was not sure whether to believe or not—he could not imagine his old, frail father having the strength to haul a barge. But he had never known him to lie.

"Well, it ended," Carl said. "And with the help of the gypsies I found your mother in Moscow, and here we are today. But I want you to know about the Gullivers, in England and Australia. They are your people and one day, if things keep changing in the Soviet Union, you may be able to visit them."

"Did you not want to see them, Papa? Your sister and brothers?"

Carl told him about the letters he sent with the gypsies in 1958. Letters to the orphanage, to Fort Street high school, to the *Sydney Morning Herald*, to the immigration authorities and to the Australian Army, in which he told his story, requested help in locating his relatives, and asked for advice about repatriation to Australia. "The letters were posted in Turkey," Carl said. "Isadore posted them himself, but there was no reply. And my requests to our government were ignored."

Mikhail felt the tears coming and he sniffed loudly. Carl did not seem to hear. "So you are still a prisoner, Papa?"

"What?" Carl jerked out of his mist of memory to see his son's distress. He reached for him and hugged him. "No, my boy, no. I've been happy from the instant I saw your mother again. It didn't matter where we were, and to have a son like you is a great gift."

"You have had a hard life, Papa."

Carl nodded. "At times. But what joy I've had. I would like to know what happened to Jack and Susy and Edward and the baby. But I never will."

"Because it was so long ago and so far away?"

Carl nodded, but that was not what he meant.

Carl Gulliver Bystryi died six weeks after he had told his son his history. This helped to stamp the account in all its detail in the boy's mind. He questioned his mother but could learn very little more. Yes, she had met Isadore Laza. Once only. Yes, he and Carl had stayed in touch through the next ten years, but she did not know where he was now. No, she did not know the name of Carl's youngest brother, nor where any of the Gullivers were to be found.

"Probably in Australia," she said. "But the girl would have changed her name if she married. The brothers close to your father's age are probably dead, and they may not have had children. There may be no one."

Australia seemed to Mikhail like another world. He read the standard accounts of it in encyclopaedias but learned little. It sounded like a backward place. His mother recovered from her grief and continued her work. Books and her son were her consolations.

"On your father's side there is no one and on my side the same," she told Mikhail. "You will have to make your own way in the world, my son. What do you want to be?"

She dreaded his answer; if he said 'diplomat' or 'teacher', she knew he would be doomed to disappointment. The child of non-Party members, the son of a father who had been punished for political reasons, could never hope to fill such positions of prestige and influence.

"I want to be a doctor," Mikhail said.

Vitalia was relieved. *Not a highly ranked occupation*, she thought. *They are training more women in medicine than men these days. And no political overtones.* "Study hard, Mickey," she said. "I'm sure you can do it."

Mikhail Bystryi did study hard, and qualified for entry to the Leningrad Medical Institute. After three years of intensive training, he was posted to a series of hospitals around the Soviet Union. He performed creditably, showing a flair for diagnosis. A quiet, undemonstrative man, with inherited linguistic abilities, he told no one that he read widely in foreign medical literature. This reading assisted him with diagnosis; his modest publications in Soviet medical journals helped him to obtain a post, as Provisional Assistant Medical Superintendent, at the tropical diseases clinic in Tashkent, capital of the Soviet socialist Republic of Uzbeck.

"You have done well, Mickey," his mother said when they met in a Moscow cafe for her sixty-seventh birthday. Vitalia had been retired for seven years and now lived back in the same district as she had thirty years before. She had a small pension and a room and a half in a large block mostly occupied by pensioners. She liked the markets; she liked to look at the trains at Kazan station. Mostly she read. She and Mikhail corresponded regularly, and she worried that he was not married.

"It's as well as I'll ever do, mother," Mikhail said. He poured coffee and pushed the plate of cakes towards Vitalia. She was watching her weight and refused.

"Times are changing," she said. "The old days when things your parents did were held against you forever are going."

"It's not what they did, it's what they are." Mikhail told her of the prejudice against Jews that was rife in the medical profession where so many Jews were to be found. "None at the top," he said.

Vitalia studied the lean, intense young man. He wore a dark moustache which made him look older than twenty-eight, but his hair was thick and his body was firm. He earned three hundred roubles a month; he did not smoke and rarely drank. "Why have you not married, Mickey? You are a catch."

Mikhail crumbled a cake on his plate. "Something always held me back. Recently I found out what it was. I want to marry another Jew. I'm learning Hebrew, also Arabic."

"Be careful," Vitalia said.

A year later Mikhail had been confirmed in his job; he had advanced in his Semitic studies. He met Sofya Vertova, a nurse in Tashkent's largest hospital. Sofya was Jewish. They planned to marry. In October 1986 he received a letter from his mother; enclosed was another communication, which had been posted in London. The sender was Benjamin Cromwell.

23

London, October 1986

The arrival of Georgia Gee's telegram had sparked a row between Ben Cromwell and Jerry Gallagher that threatened to end their relationship. They were spending the afternoon in Montague's Chelsea house. Ben had read the cable, said, "Shit!" and passed it across to Jerry. As she read it she heard the unscrewing of a bottle cap that was the inevitable accompaniment lately to Ben's moods, high or low.

Jerry read the brief message which informed Mr Cromwell that the sender was female, an Australian citizen and a journalist with ironclad proof of her descent from the exiled John Gulliver.

"That's great," Jerry said. "What's wrong with you?"

Ben tossed off a stiff whisky. "A journalist! Terrific!"

Jerry was tiring of Ben's cynicism and self-absorption. He seemed to be more like his father every day—affable when not under pressure, self-indulgent and exuding a whiff of self-satisfied conspiracy. "I suppose you'd have preferred a little old lady in some nursing home or an illiterate dingo hunter?"

"Yeah," Ben said. "Female journalists are all bitches, and most of them are dykes."

Jerry crumpled the telegram and threw it at him. She left the room and the house and it had taken several humble and contrite phone calls from Ben to get them back together again. He promised to cut down on his drinking. Jerry didn't believe him. She began work on a short story about an alcoholic and she had coffee several times with Jamie Martin.

Ten days after the contact with Georgia Gee had been made, Jamie and Jerry met under a striped umbrella in a patch of sunshine outside a coffee bar off Carnaby Street. Jamie showed her a postcard of the Turner painting "Approach to Venice".

"It's beautiful," Jerry said. "I haven't seen the Gulliver painting, have you?"

Jamie shook his head.

"I wonder if it exists. I'm worried. They'll defraud that woman if they can."

Jamie waited while the iced coffees were set down on the red and white checked tablecloth. "I wouldn't worry too much about that. I looked her book up in the library. She's a pretty highpowered lady—over the Alps in Argentina, all that sort of thing."

"Andes," Jerry said.

Jamie smiled. "How's your story coming?"

Jerry wanted to touch him. She felt gratitude and something else. Ben never asked about her writing. "It's coming."

"That's good." Jamie sucked up some froth. "Is Montague running short of money?"

"I don't know, Jamie. Why d'you ask?"

"Ben cut my rate. He said Monty had cut his."

"He never said anything about it to me. God, they're so *devious*."

"I feel as if I'm getting out of my depth," Jamie said. "I really don't know what to do."

"About what?"

"About you, for one thing." Jamie pushed the near full glass aside. He had lost weight and the skin along his jawbone was stretched. Although his clothes and hair were clean, something of the careless, unkempt look had come back over him.

Jerry reached across the table and laid her hand on Jamie's forearm. "Well, we can talk about that."

"I want you to leave Ben," Jamie blurted.

"I have, more or less. What else are you out of your depth in?" She laughed. "Over? Under? Whatever."

"I've found another one. Another Gulliver."

"Jamie! Tell me."

Jamie grinned. "Okay. It's a strange one. I wrote to a few people I know in Australia, historians and researchers and such, and I got this reply out of the blue from a bloke who's been working on the Cold War."

"Yes, yes," Jerry said.

"Seems he got hold of some army files, correspondence no one thought was worth classifying or something, and lo and behold there's a letter from one Carl Gulliver. It's dated 1956 and you'll never guess where it came from."

Jerry attempted an Australian accent. "Ayers Rock."

Jamie stirred his iced coffee with a straw. "Russia," he said triumphantly.

"Russia!" Jerry's voice went up and the people at the next table stopped talking.

Jamie moved his arm back and took hold of Jerry's hand. "Carl Gulliver got off the boat in Sydney. He was in an orphanage there for a while and then he got adopted. He went off to World War I in the Aussie army and he finished up in Russia just after the revolution. He wrote a letter in 1956 to the Army, enquiring about a pension and repatriation to Australia."

Jerry groaned. After what Ben had told her about military procedures, she wouldn't have liked to rely on an army for anything. "What did the Army do?"

"Nothing. Filed it. It was the Cold War, remember? The Aussies wouldn't want to have anything to do with some renegade who'd decamped to the Soviet Union. The letter got passed around a bit, but there was no action."

"Typical," Jerry said. "So, where are we?"

"I've got a photostat of the letter. Seems Carl's wife was pregnant in 1956. We've got an address in Moscow."

"Thirty years old," Jerry said, "address and child, if there was a child."

Jamie nodded. "But it's something. Carl doesn't give

any details about his brothers and sister, but he seems to think they'd be in Australia. He also wrote to a Sydney newspaper. Doesn't say what about, but my contact might be able to get onto that."

"Looks like we've got to write to Moscow," Jerry said.

"Yep." Jamie released Jerry's hand, took some folded photostat sheets from his pocket and passed them to her. "Sounds like an interesting chap, this Carl. D'you realise what you just said?"

"What's that?"

"You said *we* have to write to Moscow. Do you mean us, or Ben?"

"God," Jerry said. "I was forgetting about him." She read the sheets and handed them back. "Monty paid for all this."

"Yes, but how's he going to use it? How will this news affect Ben?"

"He'll hate it. A Russian? It means complications and delays. They're the last things he wants."

Jamie reached for her hand again. "That's great. Let's tell him right now."

Susannah, Margot

24

'Southern Maid', Sydney, June 1910

Susannah had spent all her time since her parents' death with the Welcomes and their *de facto* adoption of her went unquestioned. Dr Anderson, a man not accustomed to attaching much importance to females, contented himself by simply entering 'S. Gulliver' alongside the Welcome name in his list of passengers cleared by the health authorities.

Susannah waited patiently through all the arrangements that preceded their leaving the ship. It was late in the afternoon before they stepped ashore at Woolloomooloo. Susannah still had in her possession a shilling of the half crown Jack had given her at Colombo. When the family were settled in a cab, with the large trunks, which were as imposing as Mary had said, piled up behind them, Susannah handed the coin gravely to Digby Welcome.

"Well, well," Laura said. "Now, there's a wonderful thing. We'll have to tell the cabbie to take us to a better hotel."

"Don't tease the girl, Laura," Digby Welcome said. "You keep the shilling for a treat, Susy. We're all old troupers here. We'll make do, won't we, darling?"

"Less of the 'old'," Laura said. The driver whipped up the horse and the cab jolted over the rough paving outside the dockyard. Digby stretched his legs, wondering how much strength and agility he'd lost during the voyage. "I can't wait to get into a bed after that bloody bunk. Excuse the French, ladies."

Mary giggled and Susannah smiled carefully. For some years she would watch other people before smiling or laughing herself. She didn't want to do the wrong thing, particularly in the eyes of Laura. She guessed rightly that it was Digby who had been most responsive to Mary's plea that they take Susannah with them. Mary gripped her hand and whispered, "We're like sisters." The day was warm and Mary's fingers were sweaty but Susannah returned the pressure. She alone among the Gulliver children had seen her baby brother, a tiny red-faced thing sleeping quietly under the protective eye of the nurse. She wondered briefly at the time whether the Welcomes would take the baby too but she sensed that they would not. And she knew that she had to look out for herself, as Jack had done.

The Welcomes and Susannah spent the night at the Metropole Hotel opposite the Botanic Gardens. In the morning Digby telephoned for an appointment with Harry Rickards, manager of the Tivoli Theatre. Laura and the girls spent the next few hours in the hot, dusty city trying to see the sights, frequently having to retire under shade to recover from the heat. Mary Welcome suffered greatly and spent much of the afternoon lying on her bed, but Laura and Susannah adapted quickly. By evening, when a cooler breeze got up, they had persuaded Mary to join them for dinner at a fish restaurant salubriously situated in Elizabeth Bay. Laura left the name of the place at the hotel for her husband, who had not returned by six o'clock, although his appointment had been for ten in the morning.

"It's very bad of Digby," Laura said. She sipped iced water and looked out across the harbour to the few lights showing dimly on the opposite side. She was in the habit of talking to children as if they were adults. Children in the theatre were precocious. "He should have returned by now."

"It's not a very big city," Susannah said, "nothing like London. I don't suppose he'll get lost."

"Where was he supposed to see Mr Richards?" Mary

asked. She felt better and was beginning to think about food.

"Rickards," Laura corrected. "At the Tivoli, I imagine."

"It sounds grand," Susannah said. "Oh, look, here he comes."

Digby Welcome was stalking towards their table; he moved rapidly but unsteadily and bumped into a waiter. He did not apologise. A wide smile was set on his face.

"Oh dear," Laura said. "Digby's been drinking."

Digby planted a kiss on his wife's cheek and smiled at the girls as he sat down. He waved to a waiter and ordered champagne.

"Can I have some, Papa?" Mary asked.

"Yes."

"Digby! She's far too young. Now, what's this all about? Did you get some kind of splendid contract out of Mr Rickards? Been celebrating, have you, dear?"

The questions seemed to deflate Digby a little. He waited until he had champagne in his glass before he answered. "Not exactly, my sweet. D'you know what that wretch Rickards had the nerve to offer us?"

Laura sipped some champagne and shook her head. The girls listened closely.

Digby hiccupped. "Bottom of the bill in a country town tour. A pound a week."

"You told him we were the Whirling Welcomes? You showed him the notices?"

"Scarcely looked at 'em. Fellow's not a gentleman." He rubbed his hands briskly. "Devilish hot day, wasn't it? I nearly roasted in the shipping office."

"You seemed to have cooled off in the bar," Laura said evenly. "What shipping office? Digby, we have to work. A country tour's better than starving, just."

Digby smiled and said nothing. A waiter took their orders for fish, the names of which none of them had ever heard before. Digby worked on his second glass of champagne. He poured an inch for Mary and Susannah, who sipped carefully. Mary giggled at the taste. "Ooh, it's sour."

"Dry, dear," Laura said. "Digby!"

Digby's smile had faded, but he was determined not to let his spirits slump. He reached into his pocket and pulled out an envelope. "We're going to America. We sail the day after tomorrow!"

Susannah's eyes widened at the news. Life among the Welcomes was certainly exciting. She was a little troubled; she'd had vague thoughts of seeing Carl and the others at some time in the future, imagining that they would all be in Sydney. Mary Welcome's geography was poor; her schooling had been much interrupted by her parents' touring and she was by no means sure where America was in relation to Australia. She judged it better to remain silent. Her mother did the same.

The food arrived and Digby and the girls ate heartily. Digby finished his second glass of champagne and defiantly poured a third. Laura ate and drank little. When the meal was finished she ordered coffee and told the girls to go across to the piers and look at the boats. She spoke sharply, as Susannah noted she almost always did, and added a sting. "And don't fall in, because you can't swim."

"Don't look at me like that, Laura," Digby said after the girls had strolled away. "We didn't come here to starve in the outback." He wiped his mouth and tried for an air of dignity. He was still a little dusty and his hair was unruly. The sun had put some colour in his face and Laura could see something of the old, optimistic Digby in him. She remembered the hangdog air he'd adopted in London. This was better. He was a brave man after all, but her faith in him had been badly dented and the close acquaintance she had with several other men during their stage career had left her wondering why she had married him. "I have two questions, Digby. If you can answer them satisfactorily I won't offer any objection to your plans, although God knows I don't want to get back onto a bloody ship."

Digby sipped his coffee. "Shoot, old girl."

"What are we going to do in America?"

"We're going to act in the films. They've got a place called Hollywood in California where they're going to turn out films by the hundreds. They're desperate for English men and women with stage experience."

Laura drank some coffee as she absorbed this news. She'd never heard of Hollywood and had seen very few films. She had a vague idea that American films were made in New York; still, it was possible that Digby's information was correct. The fact that Digby had no use for films, saying that they were a fad and that the vaudeville stage would still be alive when films were forgotten, was now, it seemed, conveniently forgotten.

"Where did you get this idea?"

"From this chap Williamson. He runs the other big theatrical show here, competitor to Rickards. He's an American—James Cassius Williamson. Would you believe it? Said we were perfect for films."

Laura looked at her husband. Despite her disaffection, she had to admire him; he'd dashed about this strange city with the temperature in the nineties, trying his best. She loved him and regretted her dalliance with Mr La Vita aboard the *Southern Maid*. She reached for his hand. "And where did you get the money for the tickets, Digby?"

"Ah hah, that's not fair. That's three questions. You said only two."

"Digby?"

"I borrowed some from Williamson. Very decent chap, for an American. He gave me some names to look up, too, he . . ."

"And the rest?"

"I sold the costumes, and the sashes and prizes and the trunks and my father's watch and your jewellery. I sold everything we had."

25

The Welcomes arrived in San Francisco aboard the *Pacific Pearl* in April. It had been a rough passage in a vessel better constructed for cargo than people. Digby and Mary had been seasick continually, but Laura and Susannah were unaffected. With her husband still pale and weak, Laura had to take charge. She bought tickets on the Southern Pacific line for Los Angeles and food to eat on the journey. Susannah sat with the others at the busy rail terminus, waiting impatiently for the train. She was tired of travelling and wanted to stop somewhere, anywhere.

"At least we're travelling light," Digby said, "don't need one of those niggers."

Susannah looked at the black men handling the passengers' bags. They wore blue jackets and red caps and had very white teeth. People rushed around the station checking notice boards and shouting for porters. A big man with a white, wide-brimmed hat strode past her. His long-tailed coat blew open and she saw the pistol thrust into his broad belt. Susannah had seen only two films, both Westerns, in London. "It's like a film already," she said.

The Welcomes arrived in Hollywood, a dusty little town separated from Los Angeles by eight miles of rough road, after a day and a night on the train. J.C. Williamson, in fact, had given Digby Welcome only one contact—that of William N. Selig, who had moved his film studio from Chicago to Hollywood the year before. As soon as they got down from the branch line train Digby wanted to contact Selig, but Laura was firm.

"We're hot and dusty. You need a shave and a change of clothes. We have to find a hotel and then you can telephone this Selig. I have to tell you, Digby, he sounds like a Jew and you know what they're like. Also, this Hollywood doesn't make a very favourable impression on me."

Susannah looked around at the unpaved streets with their one- and two-storeyed wooden houses; the hills seemed very close and the air smelled of grass and trees. The sky was an intense blue and the people moving leisurely about on the streets cast dark, clear shadows. "It's a lovely day," she said.

Digby enquired at the station. He was told the name of a hotel that would take 'movies' and was two blocks east. They walked, glad of the exercise after the hot, cramped train.

"I'm sick of summer," Mary said. "We've had summer for months and months, ever since Colombo." She glanced at Susannah to see whether mention of the place upset her, but Susannah was staring off into the distance.

"I want it to be cold," Mary whined. "I want to see some rain."

"It doesn't look as if it ever rains," Susannah said. "Everything's so dry."

Digby pondered on what a 'movie' might be but he had reached no decision when they found the hotel, a wooden-framed clapboard structure that looked as if it had been built yesterday. The weekly tariff for two rooms almost exhausted the Welcomes' funds. They were on the second floor with a view to the east across houses and stores, clustered where streets crossed, and vacant lots and dusty roads. Susannah looked out of her window at the long range of blue hills; big, dark birds swirled up above them, hovered in the sky and swooped. "I like it here," she said.

Mary sneezed. "I don't. This dust is going to make me sneeze. I just know it."

Susannah continued to enjoy things. She liked the hot, spicy food, cooked by a fat Mexican woman and served in the hotel's long, cool dining room. The food made Mary ill. After dinner Digby went off to the bar to drink beer and 'sniff out the lie of the land' as he put it to Laura. When he came to bed late he smelled of beer and was cheerful.

"We're in on the ground floor, girl," he said. "The thing's just getting going, and this Selig is the top man."

"Are there others?" Laura was cautious about top men.

"From what I can gather there's a few about to start and plenty more interested. Making Westerns mainly, but before long they'll be making all sorts of movies."

"Movies? Isn't that what the man at the station called us?"

"That's right. It seems that people in town who don't like the films call the people who work in them 'movies'."

"Why don't they like them?"

Digby rolled into a comfortable position. "Haven't an earthly. I met a few tonight. Seemed like splendid chaps to me."

Laura remained restless while Digby slept. *He's always meeting splendid chaps and making a splendid chap of himself*, she thought. *But perhaps this time he's right.* She had seen a few tall, dark men on the streets who'd be worth a second look if she got the chance. Prices in the town seemed high, and she'd seen a few big cars roaring through the Hollywood streets which indicated that there must be money about. In her heart Laura knew she was tired of 'whirling', and she suspected that Digby's wind and legs wouldn't be up to it much longer. She slid down in the bed and turned away from her husband. Her mind strayed to thoughts of the soft, dark moustache of Mr La Vita. A fine gentleman who had taken a great shine to Susannah's brother; what was his name? Edward. And Susannah was a charming child, and good company for

Mary. As Laura was drifting optimistically off to sleep Mary sneezed loudly in the next room.

Digby Welcome, spruced up and exuding confidence, made a good impression on William N. Selig. The producer was a little vague about who J.C. Williamson might be but he let it pass. As it happened, he was casting for his production of *Daniel Boone* and he had a perfect part for Digby.

"What is it?" Laura asked when Digby showed her the card indicating that he was an employee of the Selig Polyscope Company.

"Dancing," Digby said. "An Indian war dance around a campfire."

Laura laughed. "Oh, Digby, can you do it?"

Digby took out one of the cigars Selig had given him and lit it. "There never was a dance Digby Welcome couldn't do. I'll give them the best bloody Indian war dance they've ever seen."

Digby's performance in *Daniel Boone* was a success and he was in constant demand thereafter. He learned to ride a horse and, more importantly, to fall off one. His sense of timing and the conformation of his body made him a natural stuntman. Selig worked his crew hard: a stuntman, limping after a fall, was pressed into service as a crippled waiter; a twisted ankle did not prevent a jump from a building into a net; a man with an arm in a sling was a point of interest in a crowd scene. Digby acquired a Model T Ford and sometimes drove it using walking sticks to manipulate the controls because of his injuries.

The Welcomes installed themselves in a frame house in one of the cheaper of the new residential sections springing up around Hollywood. 'Movies' were still unpopular in the older more sedate neighbourhoods, which was a matter of regret to Laura. She had a few small roles in films such as *The Merry Wives of Windsor* and she was considered for a part in *Kathryn,* Selig's long-running serial, but she disliked filming. The constant noise, the waiting around and the short, jerky bursts of work did not suit her temperament.

Laura devoted herself to maintaining a home for Digby

to recuperate in, and to Mary and Susannah. Her sole recreation was a series of highly discreet affairs with actors, producers and directors who were interested in squiring an English lady who did not want them to divorce their wives, could dance like a dream and did not get crying drunk in public.

Until 1913 Westerns were still being shot in New Jersey, but when Cecil B. de Mille chose Hollywood rather than Arizona to film *The Squaw Man*, the steady movement west became a rush. Hollywood grew fast as the New York-based industry shifted its operations west to benefit from the cheap land and the sunshine.

After a seriously mistimed fall from a buckboard, which put him in hospital for several weeks, Digby Welcome abandoned stunting for production. He worked for Selig on the *Kathryn* serial and for Cecil B. de Mille on *The Virginian*.

"The pay ain't much but no bones get broken," Digby told Laura and the girls. He had become very Americanised and Laura found him increasingly tiresome. Mary and Susannah attended school in Hollywood and developed into beauties of a contrasting kind. Mary shielded her skin from the Californian sun, brushed her fair silky hair a hundred times a night and cultivated an imperious, unapproachable manner. Susannah's dark hair tumbled around her face; she seldom wore a hat and her skin was tanned to a golden brown the year round.

"Your face'll be like an alligator bag when you're forty," Mary told her.

"Then I'll move to Florida and live in a swamp," Susannah said. She'd acquired a knack of deflecting Mary's more hurtful remarks.

Mary wielded her hairbrush. "I'm going to live in London." London was a topic of conversation in the Welcome household at that time.

Early in 1917 the United States entered the European war and Digby Welcome volunteered. He had wanted to fight since 1914 but his new devotion to all things American had made him uneasy about fighting for England in a 'foreign' war. Isolationism was a strong sentiment in Hollywood, where it was felt that wars were bad for business. The entry of the United States resolved his dilemma. Although almost forty, he was accepted and was among the first contingent to leave from the film capital. Laura and the girls farewelled him at the station. It suited each of them to be there.

Mary had taken time off from her job at a fashion jewellery store on Sunset Boulevard. Her 'real' life, however, revolved around the lessons she was taking at Professor Louis's acting academy in Hollywood. The Professor had told her to involve herself in 'real-life' situations and play the part. Today she would play the tearful daughter waving her gallant father goodbye.

Susannah was a cadet reporter on the *Hollywood Evening Star*. She had taken the job while waiting to hear from the several state colleges to which she had applied for scholarships. She had been accepted by Washington State, two universities in Chicago and two in the east, but in the meantime she had come to like journalism and was undecided about her future. She had formed in recent weeks a strong wish, unrevealed to anyone, to go to Paris. She went to the station along with one of the *Star*'s senior reporters to cover the heroes' departure. Digby Welcome had been away in training camp for several weeks; she wanted urgently to tell him to send her a postcard from Paris.

Laura travelled to the station in a Pierce Arrow driven by Samson Harkness, a New York stage director who had recently arrived in Hollywood to work for the Famous Players—Lasky Corporation. Harkness was a sleek, confident man pleased to have acquired a handsome mistress so quickly. Laura stepped down from the big, shiny car and placed her gloved hand against Harkness's smooth-shaven cheek.

"Just you wait here and have a cigarette, Samson," she said. "This won't take long."

The mayor of Los Angeles made a speech, the band played and the soldiers were hugged and kissed. Digby, still chagrined that he had not been offered an immediate commission and putting it down to a prejudice against limeys, perched on a hard seat in a narrow space. He was hot in the thick uniform and his bladder, always a problem since a heavy fall from a burning wagon, was giving him trouble. Also he was puzzled. *Why is Mary screwing up her face like that?* he thought. *And why does Susy want a postcard from Paris particularly, rather than London?* Most of all he wondered why Laura's embrace had been so passionate. Moments of passion between them had been few of late, and he was struggling to recognize the smell that hung around her well-groomed head. The train was halfway to San Francisco before he identified the aroma as bay rum.

Things at the Welcome house ran on looser lines after Digby's departure. Laura's association with Harkness became an open affair; she spent as much time at his house in Beverly Hills as in Hollywood, and she began to take an interest in real estate. Contrary to what had been thought, the war proved to be a bonanza for Hollywood. There was a demand for patriotic war pictures which was readily met. With Douglas Fairbanks and Mary Pickford leading the war bonds drives, Hollywood and love of country became synonymous and the town boomed. Laura had an offer for her house, the size of which surprised her; she immediately took out a mortgage and bought another house in the street. She persuaded Harkness to lend her money and bought more property. Finding the juggling of rents and bank loans profitable and engrossing, she fell into the habit of leaving sums of money and hastily written notes in the house in lieu of her presence and authority.

Mary, caught up in dreams of a life on the stage, scarcely noted the absence of either parent except when she had to cook or when a tap leaked. Susannah covered weddings and dog shows for the *Star* and dreamed of Paris. Her first news of Digby was not a postcard but a telegram from the Secretary of the US War Department. She opened it carelessly, expecting it to be an announcement of Digby's commission which, he had told them, was a certainty. She read, "It is with deep regret that I must inform you that Pvt Digby Welcome of the Second Division died of wounds sustained in an action against the enemy. Pvt Welcome was buried with full military ceremony at Argonne, France. On behalf of the American people I extend my sympathy to you and your family. Pvt Welcome's sacrifice will not be in vain and will never be forgotten by this nation. Further communications from this office will follow." Susannah wept for the kindly man who had sheltered and provided for her for almost half her life.

Laura wore black, which became her. She did not let widowhood interfere with her plans to open a realty office on Vine Street. "I have to provide for my girls and get on with a useful life," she told anyone who would listen. "It's what Digby would have wanted." The office was an immediate success. Laura discovered that black was bad for business, and she was out of her widow's weeds within a month.

A week after the armistice was signed Mary went to Triangle Film Corporation for a screen test. Susannah accompanied her, partly because she could drive the Ford and Mary could not and partly because she thought there might be a story in it for the paper. Professor Louis had coached Mary carefully. "Project," he had said, jutting his jaw and blinking fiercely. "Project!"

After the test Susannah drove Mary to Harkness's house. She stood under a vine-covered pergola while Mary sobbed in Laura's arms. Laura had been examining contracts while taking the sun beside Harkness's pool. She endured Mary's weeping as long as she could and then pushed her away. "Whatever's the matter, Mary? One screen test isn't the end of everything. I thought you wanted to be a stage actress, anyway."

Harkness was bringing drinks from the house. He stopped in his tracks when he saw the scene by the pool, and Susannah standing straight and poised in the shadows.

"It isn't that, Mama," Mary sobbed. "That horrible man frightened me and made me forget everything."

"Happens, kid," Harkness said. "It's . . ."

Mary wailed, "Then he grabbed Susy and made her act for the camera and he said she was wonderful. Susy's got a contract, and I want to *die!*"

26

Susy Welcome's life history was written for her by the publicity office at Triangle Pictures. She became Suzie Welcome, the daughter of the late 'respected producer and war hero', Digby Welcome, and the 'former dancer turned successful realtor, Laura Harkness, whose marriage to the Broadway, and now Hollywood, director had been one of the social events of the year.' The Welcomes, the publicists claimed, had originally signed contracts with William N. Selig in London and had come to Hollywood to 'breathe the air of freedom and success'.

The biography handed out to the newspapers, radio stations and magazines trimmed a year off Suzie's age, added an inch to her height and endowed her with a beloved sister named Mary, 'a blonde beauty who will sell you a thousand-dollar bracelet, with a million-dollar smile thrown in for free'. Susannah was amused by the fiction and did nothing to contradict it. Her happy memories of life as Susannah Gulliver had faded and only the pain of loss and separation remained. She was happy to have the shelter of what was virtually a new identity and she was surprised to find a new confidence in herself, as if she had become a person in her own right.

"Of course *I* can manage you, darling," Laura said over lunch at Harkness's house. "It's just business, after all, and business is my cup of tea."

"You couldn't do better," Harkness said.

Susannah thought she could. She spoke to several journalists who worked the movie industry beat. She hired Dan O'Connor as her agent and David Jacobsen as her business manager.

"A mick and a kike," Harkness said.

"Dan's honest and has charm," Susannah said. "David is fairly honest and has brains. That's what I need. You don't think I imagine all this nonsense will go on forever, do you?"

Harkness was troubled by any suggestion of impermanence. He turned to Laura. "What does she mean?"

Laura shrugged. "I'm so shocked by your ingratitude, Susannah, that I can hardly think. After all I've . . ."

Susannah had finished her lunch. She put on her dark glasses and stood. "This won't last. It's too silly. I'm going to make the three pictures I've contracted to make and get as much money as quickly as I can. Then I'm going to college, or I might go to Paris."

Laura sneered. "Which?"

"Both. Thank you for lunch, Samson." She giggled. "It's such a funny name. This is a town full of funny names. Suzie Welcome!" She burst into laughter, waved and left.

Suzie Welcome's madcap comedies for Triangle Pictures were hugely successful. She specialized in roles that permitted her to laugh at everyone else in the picture and finally at herself. *Flying Feathers* was one of the biggest-grossing movies of 1922, putting Dan O'Connor in a strong position for the renegotiation of Susannah's contract.

"Do the best you can, Dan," Susannah said, "but remember three pictures or three years, that's the limit."

"Five or five'd be better," O'Connor said. He was a small man, a pale-faced Celt with blue black hair. His weakness was drink, and the Volstead Act that made alcohol consumption a crime was an affront to him. He prided himself that he could persuade almost anybody to do almost anything, but he found Susannah Welcome an exception. It was as if his charm went into reverse and he outdid himself in trying to achieve what *she* wanted.

Susannah stood by the window of O'Connor's office on Hollywood Boulevard. "Not for me. Three's my lucky number."

"How's that, then?"

"There's the three of us in this silly circus, you, David and me. D'you know how many times three divides into the letters that make up my name?"

"No."

"Exactly four. That's significant."

O'Connor laughed, and Susannah laughed with him. "You're crazy," he said.

"That's what they pay for."

In her films she wore outlandish costumes, makeup and wigs; in the street, wearing dark glasses and a white linen suit, with her hair coiled in a dark bun, she was unrecognizable even to the most ardent fan. She was careful with money and drove a Ford.

No one paid any attention as she drove from her bungalow on Alessandro Street through the town to pick up the desert road. As she drove she thought about two people in her life who were giving her very different kinds of trouble—one wanted to marry her, the other wanted to see her dead.

Lou Faraday was a scenario writer for Triangle. After watching Susannah do some scenes for *Flying Feathers,* he caught up with her outside her dressing room.

"I'm onto your act," he said.

Susannah looked with interest at Faraday, whom she'd noticed around the studio. He was a short, stocky man with a craggy face. Unlike most of the young men in Hollywood, he did not put brilliantine on his hair. Faraday's thick, dark blond hair curled around his ears and fell into his eyes. The eyes were blue and knowing.

"What act?" Susannah said.

"You think all this is a joke. Underneath, you're a serious person." Faraday grinned at her. "Look me up if you ever want to use words with three syllables, but don't worry—I won't tell anyone you've got a brain."

Susannah had looked Faraday up. On their first date they talked until five a.m., mostly about books but also about the world at large. Faraday had served in the army for a few months at the end of the war. He'd been to Paris.

"What's it like?" Susannah asked.

"Lousy. Spoils every other place in the world for you."

"So when are you going back?"

"When I can earn enough money in this dump to finance it."

"Me too."

Faraday nodded. "I thought you had more on your mind than movies."

"Movies are okay, they're fun and people like them."

"Right," Faraday said, "but I think they'll make better ones in Paris than here."

On the second date Faraday brought along a banned book of French poems, a bottle of illegal wine and a packet of condoms, and they went to bed. Susannah was a virgin and Faraday was inexperienced so the event was not an initial success. "It's harder than it looks," Susannah said after their first attempt.

Faraday laughed nervously. "That's part of the problem. It's not as hard as it should be."

They both laughed, tried again and were much more successful. Later, as they lay naked under a sheet in Susannah's bed, Faraday caressed Susannah's face and kissed her. "Well, I believe it can get better than that for you. We'll have to work on it."

"How was it for you?"

"Wonderful."

"When can we start working on it?"

"Pretty soon. I . . . what's that?" A door slammed inside the house.

"Oh, God," Susannah said. "It's Mary, my sister. She comes over here when something else has gone wrong for her."

"What goes wrong?"

"Everything."

"What could go wrong at three a.m.?"

"I hate to think."

The door was flung open and Mary stood in the doorway; her hair was dishevelled and her face was a pale, twitching mask. "Oh, Suzie," she wailed, "He said I was a . . ." She saw Faraday in the bed and stopped. Her slightly protuberant eyes bulged and her jaw dropped. She moaned, turned and ran from the house.

"Christ, she looks dangerous," Faraday said.

"She isn't, she's just disappointed."

"She looks crazy to me." Faraday reached over for a blanket, drew it up and put his arms around Susannah. She curled herself into him and they slept for three hours. When they woke they made love again and Susannah had her first orgasm.

She was still feeling good about it at nine o'clock, after Faraday had left and she was preparing for her day. She intended to go to the library, take her car to the garage for a service, have a quick meeting with O'Connor, and play tennis. As she was leaving the house she noticed an envelope pushed under the door. It was addressed to S. Gulliver; inside was a note: 'I hate you. You have everything I want and I have nothing. You took it all from me. I hate you. I wish you were dead.' The note was signed 'Mary Welcome'.

She went back in the house and sat down. The use of her name, which she had not heard or seen written for so many years, disturbed her. She remembered various vicious acts of Mary's, physical and mental cruelties practised on younger children, and her ruthless manipulations of Digby when there was something in particular she wanted. *Perhaps Lou was right*, Susannah thought. *Perhaps there had been something dangerous in those bulging eyes.* She shivered and telephoned Faraday at the studio.

"There's only one solution," Faraday said.

"What's that?"

"You've got to marry me. Then I'll be around night and day to protect you."

"D'you really think I need protection?"

"Look at it this way—if you marry a sawed-off, poor-as-dirt writer, she'll take pity on you. She won't hate you any more."

"Be serious, Lou."

"I am serious. I'm asking you to marry me. On the telephone. This may be a first."

Susannah laughed and felt better. "Well, that helped."

"I mean it, Suze. Think it over till lunchtime."

Susannah thought it over and rang Dan O'Connor to tell him about the proposal.

"Nix, kid," O'Connor said. "It'd queer everything for you just now. In a few years, maybe. As it is, the studio put a no-marriage clause in the contract."

"How binding is it?"

"Fairly tight. That's the way they feel about it."

"Who?"

"The public. The great unwashed. They don't want to think of you with diaper pins in your mouth. Not unless you're going to swallow 'em. Don't do it."

"Listen, Dan, I'm going to Palm Springs for a week or so. Don't tell anyone where I am. I need time to think things over."

"When're you going?"

"Today. Now."

"Artistic," O'Connor said.

Susannah left the houses and streets and trolley tracks behind, and the desert opened up around her. After a few miles she found the light and the clean air relaxing. The sagebrush looked blue in the distance and the sandy soil sprouted bright flowers in sudden, unexpected clumps where a few drops of water collected. She thought about Laura, who had grown thinner and more intense as ambition and money making had gripped her, and Mary, almost breaking down under the weight of her disappointment. She wasn't sure she could spend much more time in Hollywood.

The San Bernardino Mountains were looming larger ahead when Susannah noticed the dust in her rear vision mirror. A car was travelling fast behind her, so fast it was careening off the narrow road and throwing up dirt. She slowed and saw a yellow Packard emerge from the dust cloud. Lou Faraday was at the wheel. Susanna didn't know whether to be pleased or annoyed. She kept moving and the Packard was forced onto the dirt to travel beside her.

"Be careful," Susannah shouted, "you'll break your ankles."

"That's axles," Faraday yelled.

"I'm the comedian. Where are you going?"

"Palm Springs."

"How did you know where I was going?"

"I threatened Dan O'Connor with a glass of water."

Susannah laughed. "Where'd you get the car?"

"I stole it from one of Doug Fairbanks' dentists."

Susannah laughed again, swerved and threw dust up in front of the Packard.

"Christ!" Faraday wrenched the wheel to avoid a rock.

Susannah screamed, "Be careful!" She suddenly realised that she wanted Lou Faraday to stay safe and sound. She glanced at him as he brought the car back into line. His large head looked ever bigger because he was wearing driving goggles and a peaked cap. He looked indestructible. She felt a sexual tremor run through her. She eased off the accelerator and the two cars moved together slowly.

"We'll never get there at this rate," Faraday said. "Wanna race?"

"No. You follow me."

Faraday grinned. "Let's make it fair. We'll swap the lead every five miles."

Susannah cheated at the second exchange and took six miles; at the third, Faraday took seven. The Ford and the Packard drove into the main street of Palm Springs side by side.

27

Lou booked them into the Crystal Hotel as Mr and Mrs Faraday. "That's the advantage of being a nobody," he said. "Nobody cares what you do."

Susannah kissed him and drew the drapes together to shut out the last of the desert sunlight. "You're not a nobody, you're a somebody-to-be. When you write your novel everyone who can read will have heard of you."

"Dat ain't many in Hollywood," Lou said.

After a highly charged lovemaking session, they went down to sit under lights around the pool. Susannah showed Lou Mary's note.

"What's this Gulliver business?"

Susannah jumped into the pool and swam lazily around while Faraday smoked a cigarette. She was wondering whether to tell Lou her story. It might help her come to terms with it and with the uncertainties it had left in her. Or it might fix it as part of their relationship, something she could never get away from. She was still uncertain when Faraday wrapped a towel around her and handed her a cup of coffee.

"It's got a shot in it," he whispered, "to keep out the cold." Susannah sipped the coffee and brandy gratefully. The odds were, she decided, that Lou would have some good jokes about being an orphan. She leaned forward and took his hand. "My real name's Gulliver, and Mary's not my sister. Let me tell you about it."

Susannah talked through dinner and afterwards. Faraday asked an occasional question but he mostly listened. "That's a great story, Suze," he said when she finished. "I'll write it someday."

Susannah nodded. "Give it a happy ending."

They stayed in Palm Springs long enough to improve their technique in bed and to be married. She wrote to O'Connor who wrote back addressing his letter to S. Faraday: 'Good luck. We'll need it. There's a half-million-dollar contract for a spinster at stake, I hope you've got an understanding husband.'

"That's a lotta loot," Faraday said.

"It's just for a couple of pictures. I hope they make them fast."

"They will. Then we'll go to Paris on your money and get married again."

"And you'll write?" Susannah said.

"Yeah. What will you do? Remember that you can get a three-course dinner in Paris for about twenty cents. That half million's going to last a long time."

"First, I'll learn French. Then I'll learn German."

"Why?"

"My mother's family was German. I want to go there and find them. Then I'll go to England and look up my father's people. Then I'll try to find my brothers."

"You mean go to Australia? What language do they speak down there?"

"English, stupid. Sort of slowly though and through their noses. You can hear it around towns. There's a couple of Australians in the movies. I can't imagine Carl talking like that but I suppose he does by now."

"You realize your brothers might've been in the war, Suze? And . . ."

"I know. Jack and Carl might have been, but not Edward or the baby. They'd have been too young."

Faraday didn't tell her that he'd encountered sixteen-year-olds in the army and had heard of soldiers even younger. He watched his wife carefully as she spoke, but he saw no signs of obsession in her. If she wanted to trace her family that was fine by him, but he had another idea to plant. "There's something else we'll have to think about," he said.

Susannah was stuffing clothes into a bag. "What?"

"Having a family of our own."

She dropped her bag and hugged Faraday. In her three-inch heels she was taller than he. "Of course we will. And grandchildren and everything. We'll live to be a hundred and there won't be any orphans. I told you I wanted a happy ending."

"Yeah. A hundred years old sounds about right. They'll probably have sound to go with pictures by then."

"D'you think so?"

"Why not? I hear they're working on it."

Susannah shrugged. "Well, it won't worry me. I'll be finished with pictures in a few years. If they get sound it'll be all singing and dancing, won't it? I can dance but I can't sing. Can you sing, Lou?"

Faraday burst into a few bars of 'Camptown Races'.

"No," Susannah said. "Poor kids. Tone deaf on both sides."

They drove back to Hollywood in the Ford and Packard. Faraday did not tell Susannah the news he'd heard of Mary from a friend he'd run into at the Crystal Hotel. The day after she burst in on Susannah and later left the note, Mary had gone to work at the jewellery store. She had become hysterical when dealing with her first customer, attacking the woman, smashing a glass display case and damaging some of the expensive items. She had cut herself on the glass and daubed blood over the customer, herself and those who attemped to restrain her. Laura had arranged for her to receive treatment in a private hospital.

The Hollywood to which Susannah and Lou returned was humming with activity and optimism. Mary Pickford was making the second version of *Tess of the Storm Country*; de Mille was warming up for *The Ten Commandments* with *Manslaughter*; Griffith was shooting *Orphans of the*

Storm on closed sets so he could extract the maximum emotion from his players. *Photoplay* was the most popular magazine in town and the days when 'movies' were excluded from hotels and clubs was a memory.

"She's out of harm's way," Laura told Susannah coldly when she enquired about Mary. "Somewhere she won't have to look at your good luck every day."

"What about your good luck?"

Laura sniffed. "I work for every dollar."

"You never said a truer word." Susannah left the mansion Laura had recently acquired in Beverly Hills. It was larger than Harkness's house, as Laura's income was now larger than his. Susannah had the feeling that Harkness might not hold his place much longer. She intended to stay on Alessandro Street, and Lou would continue sharing with three other scenarists in Venice. They were together, publicly by day and privately by night, as much as they could be. Welcome and Faraday were an 'item' for the gossipers, which did Lou's career no harm and some good for Susannah's.

"At least they can't say you're a dyke," O'Connor said. "I give it that. And he's not a lush. I give him that."

"Gee, thanks, Dan," Susannah said. "You can come to the wedding."

O'Connor shuddered. "Don't even talk about it. How's the picture going?" Suzie Welcome was working on the next of the films O'Connor had contracted for her. It was a comedy called *Short Skirts*. "It's stupid," Susannah said. "The camera never goes above my waist."

"You got nothing to worry about," O'Connor said, but *he* looked worried.

"What's the matter, Dan?"

"There's this guy Hays, ever heard of him?"

Susannah shook her head.

"He's the three Ps in my book—a prick, a puritan and a Protestant. He's going to clean up the screen, he says."

"What does that mean?"

"Six inches less leg. Don't worry, kid. It probably won't amount to anything."

Susannah and Lou got together late that night in her

bungalow. She'd got into the habit of wearing her black silk stockings home from the set, to Lou's great appreciation. After they'd made love she peeled off the stockings and told him about what O'Connor had said about Hays.

Lou nodded. "He's going to take the sex out of it. Could be okay if the movies go serious for a while."

"What if they just stay silly without the sex?"

"Or if they start making more dog pictures. God! The westerns are bad enough." Faraday was writing a Tom Mix western for Fox Film Corporation and finding the work tedious.

"I wish we could go to Paris tomorrow," Susannah said. "That's what you need."

"Yeah." Lou ran one of the silk stockings through his fingers. He'd been working on his novel between times but found inspiration elusive. The book dealt with the lives of some Americans left behind in Europe after the war. Faraday himself had caught a boat home soon after being demobbed. He felt he needed to get back to the scenes he was writing about.

"Maybe they'll cancel the other two pictures if Hays causes too much trouble. We've got enough money now. We could go."

"Nah," Faraday said. "They'll put you in something with a dog. I saw them training some out on the lot the other day. They'll use the good ones and the others'll get shot."

Susannah was disturbed by the bitterness of his tone. He wasn't quite the good ol' fun-loving Lou any more. He'd stopped throwing his fedora at doorknobs and hatstands. She wondered why.

28

"It seems just like the last picture I made, except that it's not funny," Susannah said to Jacobsen on one of their regular meetings. "How're we doing for money?"

"Fine," Jacobsen said. "Your net worth's getting close to a million. 'Course it's mostly tied up in stocks and bonds, but you could lay your hands on it if you wanted to."

"Enough to buy the studio off for the next picture?"

Jacobsen looked horrified. He shook his head. "No. And they'd keep you in court for the rest of your life. If *Short Skirts* lays an egg they might talk about it. But . . . what's on your mind?"

"I want to get away. Lou's not happy and . . ." Susannah broke off to light a cigarette. She put the match in the ashtray on Jacobsen's scarred desk and blew smoke at his slightly soiled walls. Jacobsen liked to give off an air of economy.

"Since when did you smoke?"

"Lately. I'm on edge. I'm thinking of going onto heroin like Barbara la Marr."

"Work out the contract and take a break. It makes good sense all round. What's that mick O'Connor say?"

"He says ask the kike his opinion."

Jacobsen spread his hands in an exaggerated Semitic gesture. "What more can we say?"

The Gulliver Fortune

"It's all right for you. You don't have to do all those dumb things in front of the cameras. They've cut out the sex and the movies can't show people under sixty drinking any more. It's going to die, the whole thing."

"Sound'll save it," Jacobsen said.

"That's all I hear. What good's that to me? I can't sing."

"Plus you gotta funny voice. Not really American. If sound comes in you'll have to be a serious actress."

"Jesus," Susannah said, "I'd rather sell cars."

"You want one? I gotta Dodge . . ."

Susannah laughed. "Go on with your adding up. I want to retire rich."

"Will do. Wanna hear something interesting? Your mother's made an offer for your house. Seems that area's going up. You did the right thing buying there."

"She can't have it," Susannah said. "She's got enough houses."

"She'll never have enough. Word is she's gotta few houses of the other kind. Know what I mean?"

"I wouldn't be surprised. She probably does a shift herself."

"Why're you so down on her?"

Susannah stubbed out her cigarette and lit another. "I don't know. Where's she living now?"

"Still at Beverly. I hear she's got a tennis court and two pools. Who needs two pools?"

"Is Mary, my . . . sister there?"

"I don't think so. Just tennis players and truck drivers and tango dancers."

Despite Susannah's misgivings, *Short Skirts* displayed enough of Suzie Welcome's figure and zany sense of fun to be a success. She went into rehearsals for *Let's Get Married* almost straight away. She hated the script for its sentimentality and the message it preached—marriage equals happiness. Susannah had seen enough of the world in her twenty-five years to know it wasn't true. Mary was much on her mind as she went through the boring costume fittings and rehearsals. She wondered whether Mary would have enjoyed acting as much as she had expected to. She doubted it.

"Where d'you think Mary is?" she asked Lou one morning when they were breakfasting together behind drawn blinds.

"Don't know. I'll try to find out if you like, sweetheart."

The cheerful note in his voice was a pleasant change for Susannah. She looked at him and saw that he was grinning with something of the old Faraday charm. "That would be good," she said. "I suspect Laura did dreadful things to her at various times. Ah, Lou, you seem . . ."

"Happier? I am. I've quit on the novel."

"Lou!"

"But I've started another one. It's *your* story, baby. The Gulliver story. 'Course I'm going to have to make up a lot. Make you good-looking and so on, if I want sales."

Susannah hugged him. "You make up whatever you like. Just be sure to give it a happy ending."

"Sure."

"Oh, what about Paris?"

"We'll still go. It's a cheap place to live and a good place to write. And I'll be taking my inspiration along with me. Doesn't really matter where I am."

After breakfast they went back to bed.

Susannah went to work on *Let's Get Married*, which changed its title to *Let's Get Rich* as the scenarist and director wrestled with some of the instructions coming from the Hays office. Hays had announced his intentions to the cigar-chewing picture moguls thus: "Above all is our duty to youth. We must have towards that sacred thing, the mind of a child, towards that clean and virgin thing—that unmarked slate—the same care about the impression made upon it, that the best teacher or the best clergyman, the most inspired teacher of youth, would have." If the moguls sniggered about virgins and about what they used to write on their own school slates, they didn't let Hays hear them. They jumped to do his bidding.

Lou and Susannah sneaked away to a friend's beach house in Santa Barbara for a weekend in November towards the end of the shooting of the film, now entitled *Many*

Happy Returns. They walked on the beach and made love in front of the open fire in the cabin. They wrapped the blankets around their shoulders and smoked and drank bootleg red wine.

"They changed the guy in the picture to a widower yesterday," Susannah said.

Lou stirred the fire with a stick. "Christ, why? I thought he was supposed to be a life-of-the-party type."

"He was, but there's a double bed in his apartment. They can't reshoot the apartment scenes so he has to have been married. Single guys don't have double beds."

"Some married guys don't have 'em," Lou said.

Susannah leaned over and kissed him. "Not for much longer."

"Yeah. Well the picture's just about finished and you'll be off the hook."

"Not a moment too soon. How's the book going?"

"Fine. Hey, what d'you mean, not a moment too soon?"

"We got careless, baby. That night at your place, remember? When Bud and Charlie were out?"

"What're you saying?"

"I'm pregnant, Lou. Fairly well along. That bastard of an assistant director, West, made some comment about it the other day, 'Lay off the sweet rolls, honey' or something such. To hell with him. How d'you feel about it, Mr Faraday?"

Lou reached over and took Susannah's glass and cigarette. He drank the wine and threw the cigarette on the fire. "It's terrific." He pulled her towards him and kissed her throat; his hands went down her breasts and she let the blanket fall away. She reached for him and stroked him while his hands moved over her body. She opened her legs and he entered her.

"Hey," he whispered. "We don't have to . . ."

"That's right. Come on, darling. Come on!"

Afterwards, Lou poured her a small glass of wine and allowed her one drag on his cigarette. "You're going to have to be careful. No boozing, give up cigars, no bareback riding. Any more stunts in that piece of junk you're working on?"

Susannah snuggled closer to him under the blankets. "No. I've just got to get married and throw a cake at the widower."

"Jesus."

"It'll be a turkey, Lou. Then we can forget all this and get on with our lives. Tell me about the novel."

Faraday talked until Susannah fell asleep. He arranged some cushions, put more wood on the fire and left her wrapped in blankets. In the fireglow her skin looked smooth and soft; like a true Californian she never lost her tan. She had never looked more beautiful to Faraday, and he went off to his typewriter feeling himself to be the luckiest man in the world.

Over coffee the next morning Lou winked at her. "Any cravings yet?"

"Just for more of what we had last night."

"Don't let Will Hays hear you say that. Hey, I forgot. I found out where Mary is. She's here in Santa Barbara, in some kind of clinic. D'you want to go see her?"

Mary crouched in the small room as if she was trying to hide. The room was almost a cell. The wide blue Pacific was outside, and a clear Californian sky, but the small window was set too high for Mary to see the view. The glass was thick, reinforced with wire, almost opaque. Only a thin, pale light penetrated.

"Mary, it's Suzie."

Mary turned dull eyes on her. She pushed back some dirty, dry blonde hair and licked her lips. "What?"

"It's me, Suzie. Mary, what are they doing to you here?"

"Careful, Miss Welcome, you don't want to excite her." The supervisor of the clinic in Santa Barbara was a heavily built man with a dark moustache. Like the clinic itself, at a distance he looked solid and reliable. Up close both man and institution were seedy and rundown. Susannah had been appalled at the grime and smell. Only her well known name got her past the door.

"Excite her?" Susannah said. "She looks as if she gets beaten every day."

Mary cowered back at Susannah's raised voice.

"Nothing like that, miss, they all get the best treatment here."

"She's drugged," Lou said quietly. "Up to the eyes."

"She's violent." The supervisor tidied some clothes that hung limply over a chair. Mary retreated from him to the back wall.

"She's terrified." Susannah pointed at two heavy leather straps that dangled from the sides of the bed. "What're they, for God's sake?"

The supervisor coughed. "She has to be restrained sometimes."

"Christ," Lou said.

"Don't swear, sir, please. It upsets them."

Susannah shook her fist at him. "You bloody bastard. You should be in gaol. You bastard."

Mary stopped scratching at her hair. "Fuck," she said. "Bastard, fuck, fuck, fuck." Her voice was a harsh crackle.

"You see? Quietly now, Mary." The supervisor took a step towards the woman, who was drooling slightly and rolling her eyes.

"Don't touch her!" Susannah yelled.

Mary rushed forward with her hands raised, the fingers clawlike. She raked at Susannah's face but Lou's upthrust arm blocked her. The supervisor grabbed Mary in a bear hug, forced her to the bed, held her and tied her down. "Watch her, watch she doesn't swallow her tongue." The fat man gasped for breath as he levered himself off the bed. "I'll get the doc to give her a shot. You shouldn't have come here, Miss Welcome. You upset her." He left the room, still panting.

Mary writhed on the bed; her eyes were wide and staring and spittle foamed in the corners of her mouth. Susannah watched her although she wanted to run from the room. Suddenly Mary fell quiet; she stopped struggling and her features, still pretty but altered by pain and distress, became composed.

"Mary," Susannah said. "Oh, Mary."

"Suzie?" Mary whispered. "Is that you?"

"Yes, it's me. Mary, what's happened to you?"

"I must look awful."

"What?"

"My hair's a mess and I'm all dirty. I need a bath, Suzie. I'll have a bath and put a nice dress on, and we can have tea. Who's the gentleman?"

"This is Lou, my husband." It was the first time Susannah had introduced Lou in this way, but the words came naturally to her. Mary tried to smile, but her face muscles seemed to have lost the ability. A grimace was all she managed.

"Pleased to meet you." The words came out coquettishly. Lou made a half bow and tried not to stare at the evidence of a young life ruined. "You look different, Suze. What have you been doing?"

"Oh, this and that. We'll take you out of here, Mary, to somewhere you can get better."

Terror showed in Mary's eyes. "No, no. I like it here. I love it here!"

"You can't."

"I do! I do! Go away!"

"I must ask you not to disturb my patient." A white-coated man entered the room. He shouldered Lou aside and went to the bed. Mary's arms strained against the straps as if she wanted to embrace him. Susannah moved forward, but Lou pulled at her arm.

"Come on, Suze, we can't do any good here. Not now."

The supervisor stepped aside to allow Lou and Susannah to leave the room. Susannah could smell the whisky on his breath as she passed him. "You'll be hearing from me," she said.

"She's doped up," Lou said as they drove away from the clinic. "Probably addicted. There's not much chance for her, Suze."

"She's got no chance there. I'm going to see Laura, then a lawyer, then the police if I have to."

When she got back to Hollywood, Susannah found

that Laura had gone on vacation to the east coast. The lawyer she approached through David Jacobsen was unhelpful. The private investigator she hired learned that Mary had been moved from the Santa Barbara clinic but he wasn't able to find her whereabouts. Susannah raged and two days' shooting on the film was lost. O'Connor told her she was in danger of being sued unless she calmed down. Lou told her she had to think of the baby. Susannah cursed them both but she finished the film and got on with being pregnant.

Lou probed for more details of Susannah's life—London, the boat, life with the Welcomes. He asked about her relationship with Mary but Susannah found the subject confusing and painful. Otherwise, she contributed happily.

"I feel I'm having twins," she said one night when Lou had finished a chapter.

"What!"

"I mean the baby and your novel."

Lou picked up the pencil and made a note. "Hey, that's not bad. Maybe I can use that."

29

Many Happy Returns was a flop. Even the sensational announcement that Suzie Welcome had been married to Lou Faraday for a year and was now expecting their child failed to stimulate interest in the picture.

"I'm sorry, Dan," Susannah told O'Connor when he gave her the news that the major studios in Hollywood were no longer interested in her. "For you, not for me."

"It's okay, kid. We had a nice ride. It's sort of good to be associated with someone normal after all the freaks you meet in this business. So you 'n' Lou're settling down, eh? Where you going to live?" They say Malibu's the place now."

Susannah looked around the living room of the Alessandro Street bungalow where she'd invited O'Connor to lunch. It was plainly furnished; she'd never acquired the taste for high living. "After the baby's born we're going to Paris. We'll stay there for a while. Lou'll write his book, and I'll look after the baby and do . . . other things."

"Wish I could go to Paris myself. A man can get a drink legit there."

"You get enough as it is. If it was legal you'd kill yourself."

"Uh huh. Well, you'll know where to find me if you want to get back in the business."

"Don't hold your breath."

"Where's Lou?"

Susannah cocked her head. "Hear that typing? He'd rather write than eat."

Jacobsen told her about her investment portfolio, which had made her a wealthy woman. "Triangle could sue you for breach of contract, marrying on the quiet like that. But they ain't. I talked them outa it."

"Thanks, David," Susannah said. "Are there papers for me to sign or anything?"

"Not much. You should make a new will. I suppose you want to leave everything to Lou and the kid?"

Susannah nodded. "Maybe something for Mary."

"I'll work on it. You know where she is?"

"No. I haven't seen Laura for weeks. I suppose she knows but I doubt she'd tell anyone. I'm worried about Mary, David."

"I'll keep on it. When's the baby due?"

"A month. Look." Susannah proudly showed her stomach. Jacobsen, the father of six, patted it absently, thinking of stock options.

Margot Catherine Faraday was born at Los Angeles General Hospital on 4 April 1924. She weighed eight pounds and, apart from a slight case of jaundice that gave her skin a golden sheen, she was strong and healthy. Susannah had had a trouble-free pregnancy and there were no complications to the birth. The Faradays had rented a house in Culver City on a short lease. Their plans to travel to Europe when the baby was old enough were well advanced. Lou completed the tenth chapter of his novel before going to the hospital to fetch his wife and daughter home.

"Today's the day Mr Welcome," the ward sister said.

"That's Faraday, sister," Lou said. "The name is Faraday."

"I never saw a more beautiful mother and baby. You take good care of them both."

"I plan to."

Lou had brought a baby carriage with him but Susannah wanted to carry the child in her arms. Lou loaded the carriage into the new Buick station wagon and opened the door for his wife.

"We're sort of on our way to Paris right now, aren't we, Lou?" Susannah said.

"That's right, honey. You 'n' me 'n' Margot."

"I hope the grammar's better in your book. When can I read it?"

"When it's finished."

Margot was christened at home by a Congregationalist minister. Lou was an atheist but he said he didn't mind playing it safe. David Jacobsen and Dan O'Connor were godfathers.

"That's really playing it safe," Susannah said. "A Catholic, a Jew, a Congregationalist, an atheist and an I-don't-know."

"Kid's got bets all covered," Dan O'Connor said. "I'd like to drink her health."

"Sssh," Susannah cautioned him. She thanked the minister, to whom Lou had already given a generous cheque, and went into conversation with Leo, Lou's brother and only relative. At twenty-four, Leo was five years Lou's junior. He lived in San Francisco and admired his older brother. He was a policeman and Susannah thought it only fair to sound out his views on prohibition. Leo Faraday said he thought the Volstead Act was "the dumbest thing this country's ever done". The party following Margot's christening lasted eight hours. Clara Bow dropped in, along with William Fox, Lillian Gish, Tom Mix and others.

The baby thrived. Lou and Susannah were happy. Families were 'in' and the Faradays received a lot of publicity from the Hollywood newshounds. In June Dan O'Connor paid a visit to the house and found Susannah taking in the winter sunshine in the courtyard. Margot gurgled in a bassinet in the shade.

"Kid," O'Connor said, "you're hot again. We've got a hell of an offer from Paramount."

"I'm not interested, Dan. We're going to Paris in August."

"Very hot there in August, so they tell me."

Susannah laughed. "We're leaving here next month,

getting the train to Chicago and the 20th Century Limited to New York. Then the boat to London and Paris after that. It won't be hot in London. It never is. I *know!*"

"Yeah? How d'you know?"

Susannah had never told O'Connor her life story. "Never mind. I'll tell you one day. Anyway, that's what's happening. I hope you haven't made . . ."

O'Connor held up his hand. "Would I? I mean, would I do the wrong thing by you? I'm hurt."

Susannah kissed him. "Let me give you a drink for the pain."

"That'd help."

She brought out a tall Scotch and water and O'Connor took off his hat and sat in the shade near the bassinet. "Bottoms up, kid. Cute little thing you got here. I could get her some baby spots if you wanted."

"I don't want. Can't you get it through your head, Dan? I've quit."

O'Connor shrugged. "I guess I have to. Thing is, all this baby business and going to Europe is great publicity. They're licking their lips."

"Sorry."

O'Connor drank. "I never had this problem before. A client with things happening in her life that're real interesting and she won't let me do anything with them. I'm usually making crap up, excuse me, Margot, about noble blood and titles and stuff. Here you are, with a husband writing a novel . . . say, could I do Lou some good by giving the press a bit about the book?"

"No. He'd kill you. It's all a secret. Even I haven't read it."

"Can I say you are catching the Century? I give that to a guy at the *Star* and I can lean on him for something else. You were in the business, you know how it works."

Susannah looked at her daughter, checking that the sun wasn't in the child's eyes and that she was properly covered. "Sure, Dan," she said. "I know. You can tell them we're leaving on July the tenth at eight p.m. I can hardly wait. You can tell them that too."

30

Susannah placed the baby in a carry basket on the seat in the Pullman car, checked that it couldn't easily be dislodged, and collapsed onto the plush leather. She lit a cigarette. "God, I thought we were going to travel light?"

"We are," Lou said. "By the standards of this town we're gypsies."

They had loaded four suitcases and two crates, mostly containing baby equipment—crib, bassinet, toys, foldaway play pen—onto the Chicago train. The black porter showed them to their compartment, jotted down their requirements for food and drinks, accepted Lou's generous tip and left.

"This is really it," Susanah said. "I wonder if we'll ever come back here."

"Who knows?" Lou said. "Via Europe and Australia? It seems unlikely."

"My whole life seems unlikely to me sometimes."

Lou laughed. "Don't say that, honey. You're talking about my novel."

"Where is it?"

Lou patted the briefcase beside him on the seat. "Right here. All two hundred and eighty pages. First draft, of course."

"You're not telling me I have to wait for a fourth draft before I can see it?"

220

"No. You'll see it when I finish the first draft. I want you to tell me how to make it better."

Susannah blew smoke carefully away from the sleeping Margot, butted the cigarette and stretched. "Nice compartments, these. You should have seen the train we travelled to Tilbury Docks on."

Lou got out a notebook. "Yes I should have. What was it like?"

"Not now sweetheart. Sometimes I think you're writing as we talk."

"Bad habit. Tired?"

"Mmm. We're moving! No, false alarm. What time is it?"

"Eight. Fifteen minutes to go."

"I thought those reporters'd never go away. I thought they were going to make us miss the train. Was I too rude to them?"

Lou grinned. "No, you weren't rude. Think what they put up with from de Mille and Zukor."

"I think that's one of the things I don't like about Hollywood—being compared with people like that."

"Who *would* you like to be compared with?"

Susannah thought about it. She had very few female friends; Mary had provided her with most of her adolescent companionship. And Laura had been there. "My mother," she said.

The woman who showed the platform ticket at the barrier was wearing a fur coat, although the night was mild. She wore high-heeled shoes that made her totter a little and her blonde hair was disarrayed. But she was carefully made up and the guard couldn't smell any liquor on her breath.

"Is that the Chicago train?"

"Yes, miss. Leaving in ten minutes."

"I want to say goodbye to someone."

"You can do it if you hurry. There'll be two calls for people not travelling to leave." As he spoke a voice could be heard shouting something above the hubbub on the platform. "There's the first call. Do you know what carriage your friends are in?"

"Yes, yes." The woman hurried past the guard and began to move quickly along, peering at the carriage numbers. She almost lost balance and a man had to steady her as she rushed past. She flashed him a glowing smile. Her eyes glittered in the bright platform light and the man stepped back in surprise. "Are you all right, miss?"

"Oh, yes, thank you. I'm fine." Her voice suddenly swung off key into a high-pitched screech. "Now let go of me, you bastard!"

"Take it easy."

"Eat shit!" The woman pulled her too-long, too-big, too-warm coat around her and hurried on.

"Nuts," the man said. He turned to his companion, a fat woman who was fanning herself with her newspaper. "Did you see that?"

"Yes, Clarence," the woman said. "I saw your gallant act. You got what you deserved. I'll be glad to get back to Chicago. This town is full of loose women."

"Crazy women, you mean."

"I mean loose and worse," the fat woman said. "She had nothing on under that coat. Not a stitch."

Clarence peered along the platform. He saw the skirt of the fur coat flap as the wearer boarded the train two carriages further on.

"Five minutes," Lou said. "How's Margot?"

Susannah looked. "Perfect."

Lou surveyed the brass fittings, the mirrors and the silk window curtains. As he reached to draw the curtain he caught a flash of a face outside—a woman's face, upturned and searching. He thought he recognized it but it was gone too quickly for him to be sure. He smiled at his dark, handsome wife. "Pretty fancy." He looked at the diagram that indicated how the seats were rearranged to form bunks. "You reckon we could do it here?"

Susannah kissed him. "I plan to try, and on every other train and boat we catch. How about we agree on it? We make love at least once on every kind of transportation."

"Won't there be bark canoes in Australia? And what d'they call them—bullock drays?"

"You're crazy. They have Buicks and Fords. I can see some of that book's going to need rewriting. Oh, why can't we *go!*"

Mary Welcome pulled the fur coat tightly around her and fumbled to fasten it up at the neck. She was confused about almost everything—about how she'd escaped from the house in Santa Monica while the party was going on; about how much money had been in the pocket of the coat; about where she'd spent the previous day and night. How long ago had she read the newspaper report about Suzie Welcome, twelve hours or twenty-four? Only two things were clear in her mind—that Susannah was on this train with her husband and child and that there were six bullets in the .38 pistol she'd found in the coat along with the money.

She'd stood outside the room in which Susannah and Lou Faraday had met the press. She'd seen Suzie hold up the baby and the look on her face. The photographers, crowding forward for their shots—they should have been taking pictures of *her!* The baby should be hers and the compact, amused-looking man standing by Suzie's side should have been hers too. And now she'd seen his face again in the train window.

She moved along the corridor, pushed past the stragglers heading back to the platform. Her hand clutched the gun. She'd examined it carefully in the taxi and worked out where the safety catch was. She slipped the catch to the off position and took the gun from the coat pocket. When she calculated she was at the right place she slid open the compartment door. An old man and woman looked at her with tired, myopic eyes. She rammed the door shut and pulled at the next.

The compartment was brightly lit and everything in it seemed twice normal size to Mary. She raised the pistol and fired twice at Susannah, and twice more at the wrapped bundle on the seat beside her. The shots were huge, crashing booms, like a cannon going off inches from her ear. Lou Faraday rose from his seat and moved towards her, but time had slowed for Mary; she seemed to have aeons to level the pistol and shoot him between the eyes. Faraday fell away from her, still slowly, still huge. Mary put the pistol in her mouth and fired the last bullet up through her brain.

31

Palo Alto, California, September 1986

Lou Faraday had been named for his uncle who had been shot to death, along with his wife and baby daughter, in a compartment of the Chicago train at Los Angeles railroad station in 1924. Leo Faraday, the brother of the murdered man, had a long and distinguished career in the San Francisco police force. He rose to the rank of assistant commissioner. He married happily and late; the son he named after his brother was born in 1955.

When his father died in 1975, Lou Faraday was an English major at San Francisco State. The police fund saw him through college and supported his mother until she married again a few years later. Lou graduated in 1977, missed Vietnam the way he'd missed Flower Power, and drifted into journalism. He wrote on sports for magazines around the country, although he'd never had any sporting ability himself.

"Jocks're easy to interview," he told one of his numerous girlfriends. "They've got nothing to say so you can make it all up. They can't read so they never find out what you've done."

Among his father's effects, handed over to him by his mother when she went off to Florida to live with her new husband, were several boxes of books and papers and a briefcase that had belonged to Lou Faraday I. Lou Faraday II stored these things in the basement of his apartment in Berkeley unopened. He wrote his articles and began to dabble in short stories—mostly ironical pieces about sports and journalism and girls who preferred their men taller than five foot seven.

"You're not five foot seven, are you?" one of the girls asked after reading a story in the *Atlantic Monthly*.

"Just," Lou said. "On a good day."

The stories received critical acclaim in the right quarters. In 1985 Lou won a place in the Stanford Creative Writing Program.

"Two years," he told another girl, "and enough money to starve on."

Lou took various things with him to Stanford, including his uncle's books and briefcase, for no better reason than the university was paying for their packing and removal. He settled into the routine of writing stories, reading other people's stories, criticising them and defending his own. After six months and eight stories he got a panicky feeling that he might run dry. He was living in East Palo Alto on the edge of the black ghetto, but the neighbourhood did not inspire him. One night, on a whim, he pulled out the briefcase and set it on the rug in the middle of his tiny living room, which was also his sleeping quarters and study.

The briefcase was made of soft cowhide and the first thing Lou noticed was the dark brown stain that ran from the handle down one side. He remembered reading the account of the shooting in the *Hollywood Star* and realized with a shock that the stain was his uncle's blood.

"Son of a bitch," Lou said. He took a swig from his can of Coors.

Inside the case was an old-fashioned binder, the kind that held the leaves by snap rings. The rings were tarnished and dull and the paper had yellowed. The covers of the binder were brittle and the edges of some of the pages that were slightly out of alignment were dry and crumbly. When Lou opened the binder these unprotected edges flaked off, but the manuscript was intact. The type was big, rounded and antique-looking, but every page looked readable, maybe.

The Gulliver Fortune

"Light," Lou said to himself. "Strong light."

Under the light the type was faded but clear enough.

"New ribbon," Lou said. "Thanks, Uncle Lou." His hands were shaking; he drained his can and went out to the kitchenette to get another. He found himself walking backwards, reluctant to take his eyes off the binder. When he got back to the typescript he took it off the floor and dumped it on the table that served him as a desk and eatery. A cloud of fine dust arose from the pages and made him sneeze.

"Okay," he said, "you're an antique. Don't worry, I'll treat you right."

He stayed up all night reading his uncle's embryonic novel. Trained now in the ways of professional writing, Lou could see a hundred flaws—point of view wavered; the author was unsure of whether to go with first or second person and did some experimenting along the way; the pages recounting the heroine's brief stay in Australia were unconvincing. But the book had life.

Lou closed the binder shortly before dawn. "Christ, Uncle Lou," he said. "You were a hell of a writer. Hollywood was fucking you over, but you had *it!*"

Over the next few weeks of the semester Lou wrote almost nothing. The manuscript obsessed him. In the briefcase he discovered sets of notes his uncle had used to build up the story. Mostly, they were in the form of recorded conversations with his wife Susannah. The name 'Gulliver' appeared in these notes although the name of the fictionalised heroine was Susan Gully. Her brothers' names were John, Carl and Edward. The baby, born at sea and orphaned within hours of his launching into the world, had no name.

Before the semester ended, Lou had won the affections of a woman, as he always did. She was a fellow student, Rachel Hattie Brown. Rachel was black, hailed from Queens, and her one aim in life was to get back to New York with some kind of ticket that would win her a job. She called Californians 'airheads' but made a partial exception for people who were from San Francisco. Lou showed her the typescript and told her the story.

"Simon and Schuster," Rachel said.

Lou sipped some generic white wine which was all he could afford. It gave him a headache but he was prepared to put up with that for Rachel's sake. She was a big, coffee-coloured girl with impressive breasts and she seemed willing and able to drink copious quantities of anything. "Huh?" Lou said. He felt his head throb.

"It's their kinda material. *Sell* it to them, man. I know a coupla agents'd jump at it."

"It's not mine. I didn't write it."

"Got the same name, haven't you? Inherited it and the material, didn't you? What the hell, baby? It's dog eat dog."

"I might try to get a couple of stories out of it."

"That's minor league ball, man," Rachel said. "Go for the big one."

"It's only fifty thousand words."

"Ever read *Gatsby*? That's forty thousand, tops. Any more wine?"

It was Rachel who showed Lou the item in the *San Francisco Courier* that had run in papers around the world. They were resting after a bicycle ride in the hills around the Stanford campus. Lou had sold his Volkswagen after he'd learned what a Palo Alto garage charged for repairs. As a New Yorker, Rachel was contemptuous of automobiles. "I slept in a car once," she told Lou. "I wouldn't want to have anything to do with something smells that bad."

Now they were out among the pine needles and eucalypts and sassafras. Rachel pulled the cutting from the pocket of her jeans and handed it to Lou. "Read yourself rich, man."

Lou read, "Mr Benjamin Cromwell of Chelsea, London, has announced that he has very good news for descendants of John Gulliver who migrated with his family to Australia in 1910." He looked enquiringly at Rachel.

"Forget about the novel, honey," Rachel said. "And read on. You gotta get in touch. We talking movies here."

32

London, October 1986

Montague Cromwell rubbed his hands together as he looked around his drawing room. *Scruffy character*, he thought, averting his gaze from Jamie Martin. He favoured Jerry with one of his most Monty-like smiles. "You're looking marvellous, Jerry. Marvellous. What about you help with the drinks while . . ."

"The men do the talking? No, thank you, Montague. I'll just get myself a drink." She poured a small gin and topped the glass up with tonic. She refused lemon. "And I'll put my oar in as required. You've done us proud here, I must say."

"Yes, Dad. Great spread." Ben poured a whisky and took a smoked salmon sandwich. Montague had laid on the drinks and eats to fuel what he called 'a review of events'. Ben had introduced Jamie Martin as his 'research associate', a title which Montague, who liked titles, found mystifying. Also, he was made uncomfortable by the obvious distance between Ben and Jerry. Sensitive to the ebb and flow of human feelings, Montague could feel a strong ebb on Jerry's part away from Ben. *In whose direction, though?* he wondered. *Surely not to this nuggety blond fellow who is drinking beer from a can? Chap looks like a Welsh bricklayer.* Montague took a stack of colour transparencies from his pocket and handed them around.

Jerry held hers up to the light and squinted. "Is this the Turner? It's not very clear."

"It's not meant to be clear," Ben said. "It's meant to be intriguing." Ben would have preferred Jerry not to be at the meeting but Jamie had insisted. Ben didn't push it; he wasn't going to cause dissention over a woman. He suspected that Jamie and Jerry were lovers and was surprised to find how little he cared.

Montague was urbane. "When the time comes we'll be preparing a kind of press kit. I thought you'd all like to see the transparencies. Of course they don't do the painting justice. To business—first, I'd like to congratulate Jamie on his work. We've made remarkable progress."

"Too bloody much progress," Ben said. "I'm in favour of calling it a day with the Australian and the Russian. Two's company."

Jamie shot a glance at Jerry. This was what they'd feared. Jerry's mind raced, searching for an objection. She clutched the transparency and the idea came to her. "That would be stupid," she said. "Can't you see the possibilities in this for film or television?"

Ben downed his drink and poured another. "What are you talking about?"

"Look, we've got a lost masterpiece and international ramifications—Britain, Australia, Russia, America. It's an epic."

Half drunk, Ben smelled money. Montague stroked his nose and thought of the publicity and prestige involved. "Who would own those rights?" he said.

Jamie Martin sipped beer. "Good point."

"Legal point," Montague said. "Does any of you have legal training?" Three heads were shaken and Montague felt he'd gained the high ground. He took another sip of sherry and fiddled with a cigar. "I know several lawyers."

Jamie pushed aside a plate of vol-au-vents and spread some papers on the table. "The American's going to want to be in on anything like that. This Faraday chap."

"Yeah," Ben grunted, "that's what I mean. He's in, but let's make that the cutoff."

Jerry drew a breath. "I think we're going to have disagreements. Would you mind clarifying that?"

"Right." Ben reached across the table and scooped up Jamie's papers. "We've got the Australian woman, Georgia Gee. Great-granddaughter. All looks above board. Documentation's okay."

Jamie nodded. "Bright woman, to judge from her letter. Very keen and willing to come to London. Wants to be in up to her neck."

"What about the Russian?" Montague said. He was of an age to fear Russians, whoru he still thought of, somewhat confusedly, as cossacks and revolutionaries. *Glasnost*, he suspected, was an invention of the Sunday papers.

"That's tricky," Ben said. "We've only got the one letter. There isn't any hard evidence . . "

"Come on," Jerry said. "Carl's wife is still alive."

"Only just, from what he says." Ben located his drink and took a heavy pull on it. "There's a lot of snags. He can't get out of the country, for one thing."

Montague's nod signified agreement. "And the American's bound to hate him, for another."

"That's a stereotype," Jerry said. "Not all Americans are unenlightened. God, it's a great story."

Talk of stories worried Montague, who wanted to keep everything on a factual level. "You're investigating the Russian's claim, are you, Jamie? Going to the Australian Army and so on?"

"Yes," Jerry said. "He is. Try calling him Mikhail, Montague. He sounds like a decent man."

After the initial letters had been sent, Ben had delegated to Jamie the job of writing to the discovered Gullivers, and he was now unfamiliar with the correspondence. Jamie repossessed his papers. "Mikhail works very hard. He doesn't get much time to write or to investigate his family background. They work doctors hard in the Soviet Union, it seems. The Jewish angle's interesting."

Montague grunted. He approved of making doctors work hard and there was a Greenberg in his own family tree. He poured more sherry and turned slightly to get a better look at Jerry. She wore a white silk blouse with several buttons undone. Her dark red hair was loose. Her eyes were on Jamie as he riffled through the file. Montague sensed that the meeting was going badly and he coughed to get attention. "I've talked the lawyers around somewhat. Two heirs is enough. We can negotiate a sale now. I'm not at all sure about this film business."

"No!" Jamie said.

"Let's cut the crap," Ben said. "Forget the bloody films. Monty's got a buyer. We can fake an auction, flog the picture and walk away with a whacking commission."

"Fake an auction?" Jerry looked away from Ben's glowering face. Jamie had turned pale and had bunched a thick sheaf of paper in his hand.

"For the Yank," Ben said. "To kick the story along. One heir from the east, one from the west. A buyer from . . . wherever. English knowhow delivers the goods. Monty and I have agreed to divide the commission up four ways—lion's share for him, of course, but healthy whacks for the rest of us."

"Crudely put, Ben," Montague Cromwell purred. "I have expenses to recoup. This research has cost me a fortune."

"I don't *believe* this," Jerry said.

Jamie moved from his chair to stand beside Jerry. "Speaking of research," he said. "Aren't you forgetting that the MO's log gives us a good lead on the third son? The way it looks, Ferdinand La Vita took an interest in Edward."

"La Vita," Montague Cromwell said. "What sort of name's that?"

Jamie pulled a chair up and sat beside Jerry. Ben was staring into his glass, apparently uninterested in the discussion.

"Bolivian," Jerry said, "according to the passenger list. That's colourful." She shot a glance at the silent, detached Ben. "I don't think the story can do without the Bolivian."

Montague rolled his eyes. "South America. God help me. Ben, what've you got to say?"

Ben could feel the approach of hypoglycaemia. When

his blood sugar level dropped suddenly, he was subject to fluctuations in moods and distortions of perception. Now he felt the obvious harmony between Jamie and Jerry as a bitter personal attack, a reproach against his entire life. *They'll get fuck all out of this*, he thought wildly. *I'll take the lot, the bloody lot.* He reached into his pocket and took out a glucose tablet, which he held up for Jerry, in particular, to see. "I've had my say," he mumbled. "Got enough bloody Gullivers."

Montague watched his son crunch the tablet and slump back into his chair. "Ben's not well," he said. "This has been a big strain on him."

"He shouldn't drink," Jerry said.

Montague put his sherry glass on the nearest surface. "I agree. But he's right on this point. It's time to bring things to a head, and . . ."

Jamie's voice was hard and without the polish that years of university had put on it. He sounded like the east Londoner he was. "If you try to cut things off now I'll go to the newspapers, and you won't like the story they print one bit."

Ben wiped sweat from his forehead and blinked as he waited for the glucose to work. Montague bit his bottom lip. Jerry looked at them as if they had confessed to torturing animals and burning books. "I can't believe you could be so, so . . . immoral and, and . . . unimaginative. Don't you want to know what happened to the *baby?*"

"I don't give a shit," Ben said.

"Well, I do!" Jerry got to her feet and took a step towards Ben.

"What're you going to do about it?" Ben said.

Jamie moved smoothly between them. "We can write to Australia, Russia and California and tell them how you and Montague are trying to fix things."

This was enough for Montague. He got up and put one hand on Jerry's shoulder and one on Jamie's. "Now, now. Let's not be hasty. I withdraw the proposal. Jamie, you say you think we can find the Argentinian?"

"Bolivian," Jerry said.

Edward, Juan

33

'Southern Maid', *Sydney, June 1910*

Ferdinand La Vita sat under a canvas canopy on the deck of the *Southern Maid*. His face was in shadow under a wide-brimmed hat; he wore a crumpled white suit and fanned himself occasionally with a folded newspaper. The heat and glare were intense. The ship's rail was too hot to touch and paint bubbled on the deck. La Vita puffed on his cigar and watched with some regret as the Welcome family left the *Southern Maid*. He felt sure that if the voyage had lasted a little longer he would have succeeded in getting on even more intimate terms with Laura Welcome. She had interested him. She seemed to possess a sensuality that simmered under the reserve and formality all the English seemed to wear like a cloak. He flicked his cigar butt into Woolloomooloo Bay, crossed his legs and instantly forgot Laura. That was another of his characteristics—quick recovery from wounds to the heart.

"Well, Eduardo," he said in his heavily accented English to the boy sitting beside him, "time we looked at this funny country, don't you think?"

"Yes," Edward Gulliver said. He had been puzzled by almost everything that had happened since the ship left Colombo. His mother and father dead, his two brothers and sister whisked away by unseen hands. Only Ferdinand La Vita was left in his life. He did not understand why the tall, dark man had stayed close to him and made sure that he was fed.

"But first we have to see the doctor again."

"I don't want to see him. He took Carl away."

"The doctor is *simpatico*," La Vita said. "All will be well."

La Vita stood by as the doctor and quarantine officers prodded and examined Edward. They went into a huddle after the examination; the doctor accepted several printed forms from the government men and nodded his agreement to their proposal.

"The boy will have to spend some time at the quarantine station," Dr Anderson said.

La Vita protested. "Why? He is perfectly healthy."

"It's for his own good. The authorities need time to decide what's to be done with him."

"His father entrusted him to me."

Anderson looked sceptically at La Vita. His linen suit, although threadbare and soiled, had been cut with too much care for the doctor's taste, and his waistcoat had a suspicious sheen to it. "Do you have anything in writing to that effect, Mr La Vita?"

La Vita turned haughtily away, cursing at the arrogance of the Anglo-Celts. Although born in Bolivia, he had been partly educated among such clods in London and he knew that their prejudices were immovable. "I will try to explain your attitude to him," he said over his shoulder. "Perhaps we could have a few minutes in private."

Anderson was touched. The plight of the Gullivers tempered his deepest prejudices. "I'm grateful for your concern, Mr La Vita. These children have suffered a terrible loss. I'll leave Edward in your care for a day or so if you're willing to remain aboard."

La Vita nodded and beckoned to Edward. "Twice around the deck, Eduardo, for your health."

The man and the boy left the doctor's quarters; they enjoyed the privilege of passing along the second class corridors, now almost empty of passengers, and climbed the iron steps to the deck. When they were out in the afternoon sunlight La Vita lit one of his few remaining cigars. "We are going to have an *avventura*," La Vita said. "You'd like that, wouldn't you?"

Edward had grown used to La Vita's accent, his strange words and odd pronunciations. "An adventure? Yes, sir."

"Call me Tio. It means uncle. That's easy to say. Tio. You remember the word for yes?"

"*Sí*, Tio," Edward said. "I'd like an *avventura*. What is it?"

La Vita laughed and clapped the boy on the shoulder. "We're going to jump ship. Get your things together."

La Vita had anticipated the official line and bribed one of the *Southern Maid*'s crew to make a dinghy available to him at sundown when the watches were slack. It meant landing illegally in the country with almost no money, but that was no novelty to Ferdinand La Vita. He packed his own bags—a valise and an old but good leather suitcase with solid straps. Among other things, the valise contained a Webley .45 revolver.

Under the cover of near darkness La Vita and Edward descended an iron ladder near the stern of the *Southern Maid* and dropped down into the waiting dinghy. The seaman had been untroubled by providing the boat. "It's the swimming off to get it that worries me," he told La Vita.

"Why?" the Bolivian had asked.

"Sharks."

Although he thought of himself as a man from the mountains, the Altiplato of Bolivia, La Vita could handle a boat. He had rowed on the Thames and the Cam and, as a natural athlete, all specialised physical co-ordinations came readily to him. He stroked easily towards the finger wharf a hundred yards from the ship. The seaman had told him about the loose security arrangements at the wharf gate, especially at eight p.m. on a Friday night when honest Australian workers were expected to be drunk, or nearly so. Alcohol was not one of La Vita's vices, a fact for which he had often had cause to be grateful. He had never yet been in a situation where it was a disadvantage to be sober, and Ferdinand La Vita had been in a large number of tight corners.

The dinghy bumped against the piles; there was just enough light left in the sky for La Vita to sight the ladder that led up to the wharf. "So, Eduardo, we are about to step ashore in Australia."

Edward hunted among his recollections of the many books Carl had read him for a parallel to this experience. "It's like *Treasure Island*," he said.

"*Si*," said La Vita, also a reader. He stood, and his head was not far below the level of the planking. "But we are not pirates. I'm tying the boat to the *embarcadero*. Climb up and I'll pass the bags to you."

Edward went up the ladder and hauled the bags after him. He was a sturdy boy, already strong like most Gulliver males and none of the bags—his own cheap suitcase, La Vita's valise and leather bag—gave him any trouble. He had expected La Vita's bags to weigh more and was troubled. "Mr La Vita, I . . ."

La Vita hauled himself onto the rough wharf, "Tio," he said.

"Tio. I'm afraid."

La Vita opened his valise and took out the Webley. "Don't be afraid, Eduardo. This place is nothing to us. We are looking for something *muy grande*, much bigger."

"What?" Edward whispered.

"You will see. Remember, this place was settled by *los presidarios*, the prisoners, and we are free men."

"Men?" Edward said.

"*Si*." La Vita took his bags; he made a loop with a piece of rope and slung the valise over his shoulder. This left him a free hand for the revolver. He jabbed it in the direction of the lights and the noise washing down to the wharf from the streets above. "*Avanzar!*" he said.

Ferdinand La Vita's mother had been a member of the Fochsted family. This meant that she was born into immense wealth, for the Fochsteds were one of the three families who controlled the Bolivian tin mining industry. Like the Patinos and Arameyos, the other tin plutocrats, the Fochsteds never lived in Bolivia and few members of the family ever visited the country. Isabella was an exception. After a French education she had gone on a tour of what her governess and chaperone, Mme Duroc, called 'le monde nouveau'. Her travels had taken her to Bolivia, where she met Jose La Vita, a teacher at the San Andres School in La Paz.

"*Il est un socialiste,* Isabella," Mme Duroc said.

"*Il est beau,*" said Mlle Isabella, whose school reports had all noted that she was 'strong-willed'.

She was married to Jose in La Paz on 8 May 1879. Mme Duroc was dismissed from her post by Isabella's father when news of the wedding reached Madrid in November. She was unconcerned, having found a husband herself, a wine merchant who attended the wedding. In February 1880, Isabella La Vita was delivered of a nine-pound male child who was christened Ferdinand Luis after his maternal and paternal grandfathers. The former was not placated; Jose La Vita was stabbed to death in a tavern fight within weeks of his son's birth. No culprit was apprehended and low-life characters in La Paz remained drunk for weeks after the affray.

The widowed Isabella La Vita returned to Spain with her infant son. Life continued normally among the expatriate land and mine owners. At little more than twenty years of age, Isabella's emotional, social and intellectual development had been frozen by the power her family exerted. She went into a mental and religious retreat, leaving her son to be raised by his grandfather. When Ferdinand La Vita was fourteen years of age the money spent on his upkeep and schooling amounted to twenty-five per cent of Bolivia's annual national spending on education.

Looking back, La Vita could discern no sign that he had ever spared a thought for anyone but himself before he turned twenty-four. He excluded family, to whom duty and loyalty were ingrained from birth. He loved his quiet, withdrawn mother and his stern, commanding grandfather but, he later realized, this was an unthinking love. There was no room in it for criticism. Similarly, the love he received was automatic and unearned, and the only obligation it carried was that he should not bring disgrace on the family.

In 1904, after spending several years at various universities, including the Sorbonne and Cambridge, without taking a degree, La Vita followed in his mother's footsteps to Bolivia. He would later claim that it was his name that drew him there, as someone named Washington might be drawn towards the District of Columbia. Certainly there was no more sinister motive; he had been told that his father was a scholar who had died of consumption when Ferdinand was an infant. This romantic image had satisfied La Vita. He had no thoughts of revenge. He arrived unannounced in La Paz by way of Lima with money in his pocket, a normal level of curiosity, and with his libido high after a month of arduous travel that had afforded him no amorous opportunities.

He put up in a tavern that had been recommended to him by a Peruvian who dealt in coffee. "An interesting place," the Peruvian had said. "Good wine, good beds and women to go in them, at a good price."

"From what I have been told," La Vita said, "that is not unusual. What makes this place interesting?"

"Colourful characters," the Peruvian said. "Gamblers, *banditos*, or men pretending to be such. Do you carry a *pistola*?"

"Of course."

"Put it in your baggage. In this place you may be challenged to use it."

La Vita stayed several days in the tavern. When he emerged he was a changed man. He had learned nothing new from the whores he had slept with but a great deal from an old, alcoholic *rufian* who had told him a long and involved twenty-four-year-old story about a schoolmaster who had enjoyed visiting the tavern to spend time with the mine foremen and other workers. "His name was the same as yours," the drunk said.

"A common name here, surely?" La Vita said.

"Not so common. And this was an uncommon man and an unfortunate one."

La Vita was eyeing a dark woman pouring wine for

one of the pseudo-*banditos* and only half listening. "How so?"

"An assassination was arranged. Very sad. He was newly married with an infant son. Poor *hombre*, he had married above him—this is as great a misfortune as marrying below."

"An assassination?"

The old ruin tilted his glass. "You are interested in my story, *señor*?"

La Vita signalled to the dark woman to bring the wine jug. When his glass had been filled the man resumed, glancing around him to make sure he was not overheard. "You have the look of an educated man, *señor*. Perhaps you are a priest?"

La Vita smiled and shook his head.

"Still," the man said, "the learning is the thing. You understand that I am making a confession." He was very drunk and mumbled the last few words.

"A confession?"

"I shared in the money. I helped. Blood money from the Fochsteds."

La Vita had prepared himself for a fanciful story and the request for a certain number of pesos, but the name shocked him. "When did this happen?"

"It was when the pig Daza was replaced by the pig Campera."

La Vita had read up on Bolivian history. He identified the year as 1880. Thoughts of women and wine were swept from his mind. He questioned the old drunk closely but he would respond only when his glass was filled, and he was very soon incapable. Ferdinand La Vita slept not at all that night. The next day he made enquiries around the town, very discreetly, not identifying himself, backing off at the least sign of inquisitiveness. He learned nothing to confirm the drunk's story of an assassination but he positively identified Jose La Vita, the murdered schoolteacher, as his father. A photograph taken of the staff members of the San Andres school in 1878 left no room for doubt.

"I don't like this place, Tio," Edward said.

They were tramping up a steep street away from the docks. There seemed to be a public house on every corner and from most of them came a stream of abuse directed at the foreigner and the child.

"Neither do I," La Vita said. He sniffed. "It stinks. I like the mountains. The air is clean there."

Edward was tired and close to tears. "Carl would know."

"Know what, Eduardo?"

"If there are mountains in Australia."

La Vita patted the boy's shoulder. They reached a broad street where the gas lights dispelled the dark. La Vita saw lighted shop windows along the street, some imposing buildings to the left and more light beyond them. "There's the city," he said. "Don't worry, Eduardo. We're not staying here. We're going to Bolivia. That's where the real mountains are."

A tram rattled down the hill. Edward watched it, fell into step with La Vita and felt better on the downward grade. They walked by a park, gaslit and ghostly. He drew closer to the man.

"How long will we stay here?"

"Not long. I am expecting to get some good news."

Edward yawned and shifted his bag from one hand to the other. "What news?"

La Vita glanced at him. Edward favoured his father, his oldest brother and his sister; he was dark and strongly built, with a thick lock of hair falling in his face. He looked older than his ten years.

"I am waiting for the news that someone has died," La Vita said. "Can you understand?"

Edward considered the question. He was not quick and intuitive like Jack and Susannah, or gifted with a swift, analytical brain like Carl; he thought slowly and usually found more questions.

"My mother and father died. How can dying be good news, Tio?"

"Evil people also die," La Vita said. "Fortunately."

34

Eduardo La Vita, as he became known, soon knew the story by heart. He knew that after Ferdinand La Vita had discovered the secret of his birth and the treachery of the Fochsteds he had been drawn into radical politics in Bolivia. Supporting the tin miners and the landless Indian peasants, he had become a thorn in the side of the government—a petitioner for the release of prisoners, a character witness, a raiser of funds from sympathizers in other parts of the world. He turned his expensive education against those who had provided it, becoming a writer of newspaper articles and pamphlets that criticised a system in which only literate males, amounting to less than ten per cent of the population, had a voice in the formation of the national government.

"Finally, I had to go into hiding," La Vita told Edward.

"Why, Tio?"

"My grandfather put a price on my head. He did not want to, but I left him no choice. I was trying to destroy him."

Eduardo nodded and watched the horizon. The conversation was one of a great many that took place on the tramp steamer carrying La Vita and Eduardo across the Pacific to Chile. La Vita told the ships' officers, and the other passengers that he had been investigating the possi-

245

bilities of coffee planting in Australia and was returning to make his report.

"What's your opinion on that, sir?" the more commercially minded would ask. La Vita would smile without replying.

As the voyage progressed, La Vita told Eduardo how it was in Bolivia where the few had everything and the poor had nothing. The boy had seen poverty in Whitechapel and things he could scarcely understand—men pulling carriages—in Colombo. He asked if conditions were worse in Bolivia than in Colombo.

"Worse," La Vita said, "the people in Ceylon have land, they can work their gardens and live in the open air. The tin miners live and die in hell, and the Indians have no land."

Eduardo came to understand that La Vita was returning to fight for the rights of the poor of Bolivia. "I have inherited money," he said. "My grandfather tried to have me killed and forced me to wander the world penniless. But in the end he would not leave me a pauper. This is the stupid pride of the *hidalgo*."

Fighting for the rights of the poor had little appeal for the ten-year-old, but La Vita's description of the beauties of Bolivia and his stories of the excitement to be found there were thrilling. As any boy would, Eduardo had been impressed by the pistol, especially when La Vita had said that he would have to use it to rob a bank if there was no telegram for him in Sydney. But there *had* been a telegram, with the news of the death in Madrid of La Vita's grandfather. Money, good beds, food and boat tickets had followed.

"Would you really have robbed a bank, Tio?" Edward asked.

La Vita shrugged. "It would have been nothing new for the pistol. Have you heard of Butch Cassidy, Eduardo?"

"No, Tio."

"He gave me this pistol in the Grand Hotel in La Paz, to keep safe for him. I never saw him again, or the other one."

"Who?"

"Harry, the Sundance Kid."

"Who are they?"

"Americans. Outlaws. I met them several times in Bolivia. They robbed banks and mines, which was good, but they spent all the money on themselves, which was bad. I tried to interest them in politics, but it was no use. Ignorant men."

"Will I meet them?"

La Vita laughed. "Not if things go well. I am not an outlaw and I don't intend to be one, but the government may force it on me."

"And me. Being a *bandito* would be fun."

"You will be at school. Being a *bandito* is only a slow way of dying."

The boy sighted the Chilean coast within a few minutes of this exchange, which helped him to remember it, to recall the exact words. They stayed with him, to be laughed about or cried over, for many years.

From Valparaiso they travelled north to the railhead at Antofagasta. Here they boarded a train which climbed east, away from the coast, traversing Chilean territory, up through the mountains to the Bolivian border and on to the Antiplato. For Eduardo the time passed quickly, in a haze of heat followed by biting cold. He remembered it later as a time of cigar smoke irritating his nose, and hot, peppery food burning his mouth. The broad-faced, flat-nosed Indians spoke languages he could not comprehend and this accelerated his grasp of the Spanish La Vita spoker.

La Vita watched the boy closely as the train skirted the large Uyuni salt marsh.

"What's the matter, Tio?"

"How do you feel, Eduardo?"

"Hungry."

La Vita laughed and hugged him. "You will be a good Bolivian. You don't suffer from the *soroche*, the height sickness. Some of the people who come up here . . ." La Vita grinned and drew on his cigar. "Let us say they are happy to go back down again."

Nothing gratified Eduardo more than winning La Vita's approval and, as this happened easily, he was mostly happy. He grieved for his mother and father and sometimes missed his brothers and sister. For Jack he had no fears and his respect for Carl's brain closed off the thought that any harm might have come to him. Susannah had been like a sister to Mary Welcome. Interested in his surroundings and well cared for himself, he naturally imagined similar circumstances for the others.

He gave a lot of thought to La Vita. His mentor smiled and laughed a great deal, which was good. Eduardo was puzzled that the smiles came even when serious matters were being discussed. Even when he was playing cards, a matter apparently of the greatest seriousness, to judge from the faces of most of the players, La Vita was good-humoured. Eduardo noted that La Vita did most things—ate, drank, played cards—in moderation. The exception was his behaviour towards women. To Eduardo, brought up in the inhibited ways of the English, La Vita's courtesies towards women old and young seemed excessive. Only when the company of a woman was involved did La Vita indicate to him that Eduardo might take himself off somewhere for a time.

"Tio," Edward said after La Vita had reluctantly parted company with a young widow who left the train at Oruro, "are you married?"

"No."

"Why?"

"Haven't you noticed? I like women too much to be content with one."

"What about children?"

"Do you mean have I got any? None to my knowledge." Eduardo was confused. "No, I mean, I . . ."

"I understand you. Excuse me, Eduardo, I was making a silly joke. You mean do I *want* my own children?"

"*Sí.*"

"No, I do not. One half of my blood is Fochsted, and I do not want to bring any more Fochsteds into the world."

35

Ferdinand La Vita bought a house in one of the valleys below the city of La Paz. In this fashionable residential district he surrounded himself with liberal-minded people and plunged into political work. Eduardo attended the San Andres school, along with the sons of the Spanish landowners not wealthy enough to live in Europe, and of the rich *mestizos* who were happy to be big fish in a small pond. It was a time of massive adjustment for the boy, who heard radical opinions argued out with much table thumping at home and conservative political, social and religious doctrines preached at school.

Two instincts guided him in childhood—to please La Vita and to stay out of trouble. He quickly mastered enough of the Catholic ritual to avoid being conspicuous at school and at obligatory religious ceremonies but, like his mentor, he was a total sceptic.

"It's all make-believe, isn't it, Tio?" Eduardo proposed after he returned from school with an account of a particularly terrifying hellfire sermon from one of the priests.

"Yes," La Vita said. "That's a good way of putting it. Interesting, though, don't you think?"

Eduardo smiled and nodded. He did not find it interesting. All instruction at the school that was not taught by rote—mathematics, chemistry, grammar—was slanted in a religious direction. The only interesting things about religion, to his eyes, were the processions and festivals of Holy Week in which people dressed in their brightest clothes and marched and danced down the Prado, the steep main thoroughfare of La Paz. La Vita informed him that the brightest moments on these occasions had more to do with the old religion of the Indians than Spanish Catholicism.

Indians came to the house sometimes and talked and smoked with La Vita and his friends. Eduardo found it impossible to equate these calm, quiet people with the 'benighted, godless savages' described in the texts that celebrated the Christianization of South America. The depiction of England as a country of lost souls amused him. He kept silent, but he knew better.

La Vita permitted Eduardo's presence at his table when such things were being discussed and kept him at a distance only at certain points during a serious love affair. Eduardo was encouraged to contribute to political discussion and to observe flirtation.

"Why are there no schools for freethinkers?" Eduardo asked during a dinner party in which the main subject up for discussion was Bolivia's neutrality in the Great War.

"There will be," a white-bearded guest replied, "by the time of your children, Eduardo."

"Why will it take so long to happen?"

"It's the Bolivian way. When you are minister for education you can change things."

In fact, Eduardo would have had more interest in being minister for the army. Military matters became his obsession—history, personalities, equipment, insignia. He was nine months younger than the century and when he turned eighteen he made preparations to go to the United States to enlist. In 1917 Bolivia had abandoned its neutrality in favour of a guarded support for the Allies. Eduardo's intentions were applauded. The armistice was a grave disappointment to him.

"Never mind," said La Vita, who was tolerant of Eduardo's militarism as of everything else he did. "We will have wars of our own before long."

But the martial phase passed. La Paz was an exciting

city for a young man with money. Eduardo spent his share of time in the taverns and brothels, often waking in a strange bed with a hangover and feelings of guilt he did not understand. His cures for the fits of depression that followed carousing were to walk in the Indian market in San Sebastian, savouring the smells of food and freshly tanned leather and the deafening noise of hucksters' shouts, chanting street singers and the banging of metal on metal to attract buyers. Then he would pack a haversack and walk in the Cordillera Real, hiking along the pre-Colombian highways and then leaving them for tracks in the cold, clear air high above the treeline.

In villages such as Choquekota and Takesi, Eduardo spent time with the stoical Indians who herded llamas, made rope and cultivated crops as they had for thousands of years. Wrapped in his poncho, he slept on the dirt floors of adobe huts. He smoked the local tobacco and learned a halting, pidgin Quechua. From these retreats he would emerge thoughtful and serious, devoting himself to his books until the next binge.

This phase lasted for almost two years, during which time Eduardo struggled with medical studies. Late in 1920 he returned from a tramp that took him through the mountain pass above La Cumbre, down a broad trail with snow-covered peaks on either side into the subtropical Yungas area. He stayed in the village of Chairo where the people grew coffee and citrus fruits and spent any surplus centavos they might gather on *festas*. He talked for most of the time with an old man who had returned to the village after twenty years of working in the mines at Potosi. He was forty years of age and looked sixty. He chewed coca leaves and drank *aguardiente,* raw cane alcohol, to ease the aches and pains he suffered from numerous injuries sustained in the mines. His pain was all he had taken away from the mountain, which yielded two billion dollars' worth of silver. Eduardo had seen mine foremen and engineers, inspectors and medical officers. He knew how bad the mines were, but he had never before met an actual victim.

Eduardo abandoned medicine for law at the University of San Andres. He graduated in 1924 and went into practice in La Paz, specializing in the sorts of cases approved by his mentor. He represented miners attempting to form trades unions, Indians petitioning for land grants, evicted tenants. The work intensified his radicalism and drew him into his first real dispute with Ferdinand La Vita.

"How can you continue to use Fochsted money, Tio? You know that it comes from the sweat of the workers."

"I do. From their blood too."

"Then how?"

"You will agree that I use the money well? That I help people?"

"Yes. Many, many people. But . . ."

"If I renounced the money it would go to one of my cousins in Europe. He would use it to buy an automobile that would go five kilometres an hour faster than the last one. Does that make sense?"

Eduardo agreed that it did not, but he moved out of La Vita's house as soon as he could afford to. He rented a small apartment near his office, worked long hours and was careful not to get into debt or to call on La Vita for financial help in any way. He knew that Ferdinand channelled cases to him but he also knew that he performed well for his clients. The Bolivian economy boomed after the war as a rebuilding Europe bought its minerals. None of the prosperity penetrated to the workers and peasants who, more than ever, needed protection from the laws that were designed for the rich and influential.

Occasionally, through the 1920s, Eduardo had thoughts of his siblings, whom he imagined to be in Australia. He felt sure that Carl would be a man of note by now, especially in a backward and small country, and that he could locate him. But he never took the first step. He was busy; he was tired; he was seriously ill with a mysterious blood disorder; he recovered; he argued with Ferdinand; he fell in love and was rejected absolutely. His English had become halting through disuse and his passion to see a just society in Bolivia intensified.

Political and practical matters, quietly conducted, dominated his life until 1932 when the Chaco war erupted. After the discovery of oil in the Chaco region of the southeast, where Bolivia shared a border with Paraguay, skirmishes between the citizens and militias of the two countries were common. In 1932 Bolivia despatched 100,000 troops, largely armed and provisioned by the Patino tin mining interest, to the Chaco to secure control of the area and win a route to the Atlantic for Bolivia.

Eduardo was a violent critic of the war.

"It is unjust," he asserted to Ferdinand.

"Yes."

"It will cripple our economy."

La Vita puffed on a cigar and nodded.

"How can you be so calm? It's a disaster. It will cost thousands of lives."

"Listen, Eduardo, it could be the best thing that has ever happened for the people of this country. Salamanca is weak and unpopular, right?"

Eduardo nodded. The president was a laughing stock and the government was unusually corrupt and inefficient.

"This war will be lost. The Paraguayans are better fighters than the Bolivians and they have more to fight for. The war will be expensive and disruptive. This government will fall and the next will be no better and the one after that will be the same."

"You seem very sure, Tio."

"I've studied history. This is the beginning of a change for Bolivia, a big change."

"*Revolucion?*"

La Vita shrugged. "Who knows? Men will be trained to fight, some of them will have ideas of their own. Trained fighters with ideas are hard to control."

Eduardo looked at the man sitting on the other side of the big polished table. Around them were the trappings of affluence—ancient Peruvian rugs, copper and brass that had taken hundreds of manhours to fashion, European glassware. La Vita smoked Cuban cigars. Eduardo had never known him to perform a mean act, never heard malice from his mouth or seen him act violently. He felt impatient, irritated by the comfort surrounding the man to whom he owed so much. He felt an irresistible urge to hurt him.

"All this will go in a revolution."

"I know that. I do not think Bolivia is a country for violent revolution."

Eduardo lit a cigarette and expelled the smoke derisively. "You should go more to Potosi, Tio. See the people there. See the men of my age who look older than you. You will not see any who have reached your years."

"I have been to Potosi," La Vita said quietly. "Many times. I've walked around this country just as you have done. I have seen it all."

"It is ripe for revolution."

"No. The priests have twisted the people's emotions so that they cannot see the world as it is. You agree?"

"There are some good priests," Eduardo said grudgingly.

"The good ones admit that a bandage or a tooth extraction might be of more use than a prayer. That is as far as they will go. The bad ones still defend the *conquistadores'* dashing out the brains of Indian children to send them to heaven the quicker. They would do it themselves."

"The workers . . ."

"The workers are patriots. We are a landlocked country. There are no revolutions in landlocked countries. Look at Switzerland."

Eduardo felt that this was superficial, but he did not reply. La Vita appeared to be unusually animated, as if he was gathering himself for something. Eduardo felt he should proceed warily. "The Indians cannot endure much more. They must have rights, they must . . ."

"No! They must have land!" La Vita butted his cigar savagely in a beaten copper dish. He leaned across the table and reached for Eduardo's hand. Eduardo extended it and the two men gripped hands across the table.

A question, nothing to do with the discussion, leaped for the thousandth time into Eduardo's mind. "Tio," he said, "why did you take me with you?"

"I'll tell you one day. Not now. Listen, I need your help. The workers must own the mines and the Indians must own the land. You agree?"

"Yes. But..."

"There are many who think the same. We are organising. You must join us, Eduardo."

36

In November 1952 Eduardo La Vita was appointed Minister for Education in the government of Dr Victor Paz Estensorro. His election to the Chamber of Deputies to represent an industrial area in the capital was a formality. Behind Eduardo lay twenty years of political activity, all dedicated to the aims of overthrowing the corrupt oligarchs, nationalizing the tin mines and restoring land to the dispossessed Indians. He had been in gaol twice as a result of these activities. The National Revolutionary Movement, led by Dr Paz, had won government in 1951 but the army junta then in power had attempted to resist the will of the people. Along with many other MNR members, Eduardo had been officially declared a *bandito* with a price on his head.

This was the period of his life which most interested Juan, Eduardo's son.

"Did you have a carbine, Papa?" Juan crossed his thin arms across his chest. "And ammunition belts, so?"

"Yes. And a beard, but no earring."

"He smelt," Yolanda La Vita said, "your father smelt like a *mofeta*. That was what they called him in the gang, *el mofeta*, the skunk."

Eduardo laughed. "Not true, Juan. Don't listen to her. They called me *el canguro*, the kangaroo, because I have been to Australia."

"The Minister is a liar," Yolanda said. "No one has been to Australia. Describe a kangaroo, *el mofeta mio*."

"I've never seen one."

"There. I told you. All lies."

At various times Eduardo told his young son about his voyage to Australia and the death of his parents, and how Tio Ferdinand had taken care of him and brought him to Bolivia. Juan listened dutifully, but was always likely to ask a question about his father's brief period of banditry. Eduardo sensed a recklessness in his son, which alarmed him. He attempted to emphasize the hunger and discomfort that went with living off the land and the danger of being betrayed to the militia. Although he was a Bolivian in speech, dress and manners, Eduardo retained a reserve more appropriate to an Englishman. He would not tell Juan that the worst part of being a bandit was the separation from Yolanda.

He had met her shortly after making his commitment to his uncle and the group of men who were to join other liberals and form the MNR. Yolanda was the daughter of Dr Carlo Borota, who was of Basque extraction, although his family had lived in Bolivia for a hundred years. Borota's views matched those of Ferdinand La Vita closely, which meant that he was frequently in conflict with the more progressive Eduardo. But Eduardo was able to forgive the conservative doctor everything on account of his daughter. Yolanda was eighteen years of age and still at school. Eduardo asked her to marry him on their second meeting and she told him that she had no intention of marrying until she had finished her studies.

"I'm thirty-two," he said.

"In four years I will be twenty-two, only ten years younger than you."

"But I'll be . . ."

"Pooh," Yolanda said. "What does it matter?"

She completed her science degree and married Eduardo in 1937. Their son was born five years later after Yolanda had suffered several miscarriages. The birth was difficult and damaging, and Yolanda did not become pregnant again. This was a sadness to them.

But the 1940s were a time of elation and despair for Bolivian liberals. The first MNR government under Colonel Gualberto Villaroel attempted to make the changes sought by Ferdinand La Vita, Dr Borota and the liberals, but the mining and landed interests proved too strong. The bloody coup that overthrew Villaroel sent many MNR supporters into exile. Yolanda joined her father and Ferdinand La Vita in Paraguay. Eduardo spent a brief period in jail then, and again three years later, when President Urriolagoitia took a hard line with liberals.

Through this time Eduardo visited his wife and infant son in Paraguay, but the brief taste of victory intensified his desire to see a progressive government in his country. The death of Ferdinand La Vita in 1950 inspired him further.

"This is temporary," he told Yolanda, after a brief funeral and burial in a churchyard on the outskirts of Asuncion. "We will bring him home soon and do it properly."

Yolanda nodded. The next time she saw her husband, he was no longer the neatly dressed, well barbered lawyer, but a stinking, hairy rebel worn thin by effort and near-starvation. She expected hourly to hear that he had been shot on a hillside or executed in prison, but the day came, as he had always said it would, when the miners rose in a revolt that sparked the revolution. Dr Paz and the MNR were swept into power.

Eduardo was offered several government posts and chose the education job because he knew it would have pleased Tio. It pleased his father-in-law and wife too. It smacked of offices and desks and quiet meetings, of careful planning and gradually achieved results. As Eduardo fulfilled these tasks he sometimes thought of Ferdinand's insistence that Bolivia was not a revolutionary country. He certainly did not feel like a revolutionary now. *But you were not quite right, Tio*, he thought, *it took a revolution to bring you home so that you could sleep in the mountains*.

Juan Gulliver La Vita had his first serious fight at the age of ten years. A boy at school called Juan's father a *comunista*. Juan left him with a black eye, a broken nose and three cracked ribs. The rib damage was done when Juan kicked his opponent several times as he lay on the ground. For this he was threatened with expulsion from the school and the Minister had to go personally to the reactionary principal and eat humble pie to avert the catastrophe.

"He insulted you," Juan told his father.

"Thank you for defending our honour, but you went too far. The eye or the nose would have been enough. The ribs were a mistake."

"I got excited, Papa. The way you must have done when you shot it out with the militia."

"I did not shoot it out. I mostly ran away."

Juan shrugged his disbelief. "You're being modest, Papa."

"It's not a bad quality. I'm worried about you, Juan. You are doing well at school, better than me, perhaps not as well as your mother . . ."

"School is fine, but I can't stand idiots."

"Get used to them, boy. You're going to meet a few."

Apart from disquiet about Juan's wild behaviour and the health of Yolanda's father, things ran smoothly for the La Vita family. A minister's salary permitted them to live comfortably and Yolanda's earnings as a teacher allowed extras—a cabin in the mountains about Choquekota, a car for Yolanda and a very belated two-month honeymoon trip to the United States. Juan, now fourteen years of age and attending an experimental school for the children of liberal parents, stayed behind with his elderly grandparents. They saw little of him. He spent most of his time on the streets of La Paz and around the market. Severe neglect of his schoolwork dated from this period.

Yolanda endured the unexplained absences from home, the stumbling arrivals in the early hours, the scruffy companions and adverse school reports for as long as she could. Eduardo worked an eighty-hour week and she was protective of him, but eventually she was forced to share her distress.

"He is uncontrollable," she reported to her husband.

Eduardo was working on papers at home. He looked up. "Who?"

"Your son, Mr Minister. If he goes on this way he will become a client of your colleague, the Minister for Justice."

Eduardo sighed. It was 1959 and a difficult time for the government. The bottom had fallen out of the world tin market after the nationalization of the Bolivian mines, almost as if by cause and effect. Land reforms had thrown agricultural production into chaos and Bolivia was importing more of her food with less money to pay for it. In many branches of government the demands of the conservatives were being heard; in his own department the problem was with the radicals. On every side he heard the cries—reduce the influence of the church; increase teachers' salaries; amalgamate the teachers' union with a workers' union; allow student participation in school government. He was finding difficulty in keeping sympathy with progressive thought, and this alarmed him.

"I have a Cabinet meeting tomorrow. I must be prepared for it. After that I can do some delegating and find more time for the boy."

"Good," Yolanda said. "He still respects you."

"When he finds I am not recommending equal representation for students on the school board, he may not."

Yolanda kissed her husband's neck. Eduardo's dark hair was streaked with grey and he looked older than his fifty-nine years. She hoped he would not accept another term in the government but she knew there was pressure on him to do so, even to move up in the ranks and assume more authority. After Dr Paz's first term, Hernan Siles Zuazo had become President. His elevation was seen by many as merely an MNR ploy to allow Dr Paz, constitutionally barred from a second consecutive term, to return to office. Dr Paz, Yolanda felt sure, would have plans for her husband.

"You have always spoken of a trip to Australia, *querido*, to find your family. Is there any chance of it soon? It would be good to take Juan away from the *locos* he hangs around with now."

"I don't know," Eduardo said. "Perhaps. Or maybe to the mountains for fishing?"

"He refuses to go to the mountains. He says it's dull."

Eduardo laughed and reached to embrace Yolanda. She came close to his chair and he put his arms around her. "Dull? He should try my job."

"You should retire next year, Eduardo. Go out with Zuazo. You have earned a rest."

His age was a sore spot with Eduardo. He dreaded being sixty; he did not want to underline the fact with retirement. "Too much to do," he muttered. "The Americans want this, Lechin and the mine workers want that. It's a balancing act and I am an old high-wire artist." He realised that he had said 'old' and he made an impatient gesture. He lit his forty-fifth cigarette for the day and coughed. "I have to work."

Yolanda left him. She was worried about the health of both her husband and her father, and about her son's social and psychological condition. She had understated the case to Eduardo: Juan had become a rebel on all fronts—in manners, morals, politics and hygiene. *Men are fools*, she thought. *If only we could do without them.*

Eduardo worked, reading and making notes, until his eyes ached. His head throbbed and his throat and mouth were dry from smoking. He poured himself a glass of water and sat back in his chair. He tried to keep his mind on matters of policy and administration, but he found it impossible. As often happened, he recalled one of the last conversations he had had with Ferdinand La Vita. It had taken place in Paraguay during Ferdinand's exile. They had drunk a lot of wine and Eduardo asked the question again.

"Why, Tio? Why take a boy you scarcely knew halfway across the world?"

Ferdinand's hair and moustache were white; his skin had turned sallow and was stretched thin across the bones of his face. He was in his sixties but looked older; the hand holding the wineglass trembled a fraction. "*Un experimento*," he said.

"I don't understand."

"I wanted to find out whether it was possible for two strangers to love each other. No ties of blood, no common language, no obligations. If I did the best I could for you, would you do your best for me? Would it work out?"

"It has, Tio."

"Sí. You must remember this lesson—if you treat people well, they will treat you well."

"Not always, Tio."

"No, not always. People are not machines—they do not always do what they are designed for until they break down. But generally. And the reverse is true, generally."

Eduardo nodded and poured more wine. His mother and father had been dead for more than thirty years; they were a memory with no substance. He could not recall a word from their mouths or a movement they had made; they were fixed in his mind like still, faded pictures. And he had suffered no loss, never felt betrayed by life because of this man. *If I have a son,* he thought, *will I do as well?*

Well, you have the son. How is it going? Eduardo reached for a file and pledged himself. *After this meeting, Juan comes first.*

He returned home tired and depressed. More concessions than firmness; more losses than gains. Yolanda stood at the door, her face streaked with tears.

"I have been trying to telephone you for an hour. Where have you been?"

"Drinks," Eduardo said wearily. "After the meeting. Very boring. Yolanda, what . . ."

"Juan has been arrested." Her voice trembled and sobs shook her. "They say he has killed a man with a knife."

37

"Why, Juan? Why?"

Juan shrugged. "It was political."

"Explain that, please," Eduardo said.

"You would not understand."

Eduardo fought down his resentment and anger. To be told after two decades of political life that he would not understand something political was galling. But the boy was seventeen.

"You must try to make me understand. You'll have to make a lawyer understand and he will have to do the same to a court. It's important. Why not start with me?"

"Have you got a cigarette, Papa?"

These were the first non-aggressive words Juan had spoken during the interview. Eduardo passed his son a cigarette and matches through the grille that separated them. It would not have been allowed at the Prison Centrale in La Paz, but Eduardo's influence had secured Juan's removal to a gaol at Sucre. It was a newer institution with a more enlightened management, but still bad enough. Eduardo knew that prisoners had to harden themselves to survive the system, and the hardening was the chief contributing factor to recidivism. He watched Juan light his cigarette with a rock-steady hand and he knew that the hardening had begun.

Juan passed the matches back through the grille. "Thanks." He blew smoke over his father's head.

They sat in a small room divided down the middle by a long bench with chairs on either side. The heavy grille, on a metal frame, extended from the centre of the bench up to the ceiling. Influence again had secured Eduardo a special interview; ordinarily the room would have held ten prisoners and their visitors. Nevertheless, a guard stood only a few feet behind Juan, and his pistol holster was unfastened.

"Tell me, son," Eduardo said.

Juan puffed. "We were drunk and arguing about politics. He spoke well of the Americans."

"For that you stabbed him?"

The shrug again. "It was his knife."

Juan leaned forward. "You weren't armed?"

"No. But if I'd had a gun I would have shot him. He is . . . was an informer for the militia. He hangs around with the miners and the students but he betrays them. Perhaps he is a policeman himself."

"An *agent provocateur?*"

"I don't know."

"I don't understand how you could have . . . stabbed him, knowing these things about him. If he is a paid informer his opinions are of no consequence. He is not even worth arguing with, let alone killing."

"I didn't know it then, Papa. I know it now. I was told in the other place." There was a slight tremble in Juan's voice as he mentioned the Prison Centrale. The memory of it seemed to unnerve him slightly. "They can't hang me."

"No. At least we have done away with that barbarity. But are you saying he attacked you with the knife?"

Juan shook his head. "He pulled it out, but I took it from him. I was drunk and wild."

"It was a workers' bar, wasn't it? The witnesses will support you."

"We were at a table with some men I did not know. They could have been *denunciantes,* like him."

"The knife was his. That helps."

Juan butted his cigarette on the benchtop, as a thousand prisoners appeared to have done before. "It depends where the knife is now. It was an ordinary kind of knife. I . . ."

Eduardo passed him another cigarette. "Go on."

"I've carried one like it at times. Papa, I'm sorry for bringing this on you. How is Mama?"

"Brave and ready to help you in any way she can. But your grandfather Borota has died. She is very upset."

"He didn't know . . . ?"

Eduardo shook his head. "Nothing of this, thank God."

"God!" Juan snorted.

"Well, I'm with you there. Juan, I think we can get the charge reduced to manslaughter, and your youth will help. But you'll have some time in prison. Perhaps here, perhaps worse.

Juan nodded. "There are comrades in prison, it's not so bad. And, forgive me, Papa, but the system you serve cannot last for very much longer."

Eduardo stared at his son. Dark stubble sprouted on his chin and cheeks and his hair was long and lank. He registered that one of Juan's large white teeth was chipped in the front, giving him an older, more experienced look. His son was a man, and he scarcely knew him. The guard moved forward and touched Juan on the shoulder. The boy gave his father a short salute with his arm bent in front of his chest and his fist clenched.

Juan was sentenced to eight years' imprisonment for the crime of manslaughter. As Eduardo had expected, his youth was taken into account but his claim to have been unarmed was viewed sceptically by the court. By the end of the trial, through which Juan had shown increasing contempt and defiance, Eduardo was unsure on the point himself. Yolanda was distraught; she visited Juan in the Sucre penitentiary and was appalled by his attitude.

"He has no remorse," she told Eduardo. "He feels no guilt, no shame. No, that's not true. He regrets having made *us* suffer, but that is all."

Eduardo did not tell her of the psychological changes

which imprisonment brings. He had seen it many times in his legal work—the protective barrier built up of defiance, self-justification and egotism. Remorse and guilt would be seen as weak places in the wall and denied.

The publicity given to Juan's case had had an ambivalent effect on Eduardo's career. Initially he had suffered vilification as the parent of such an animal, but in time the mood had changed. The Minister whose son was paying the price demanded by the law without favouritism or special treatment became a useful symbol for the party.

Dr Paz returned to power in 1960 and Eduardo and Yolanda considered their options while the President was deliberating over the composition of his government.

"You wanted me to resign," Eduardo said. "I could do it now."

Yolanda's face was serious. She had aged markedly since the day of Juan's arrest. Still handsome, she seldom smiled now and appeared to find all questions grave and weighty. "You are in good standing?"

Eduardo nodded. "Better than ever. I worked hard through all our trouble. It was the only way I knew to stay balanced. Some good things happened. My department presents Victor with fewer problems than most of the others."

"What is he likely to offer you?"

Eduardo shrugged. "The toughest, possibly. The economy."

Yolanda shuddered at the thought of the workload such a job would involve—the long hours, the meetings, the telephone calls at all hours of the day and night. Eduardo was sixty and looked that and more: he had lost weight and no longer moved vigorously. His cigarette cough was alarming and he was often short of breath. She tried to remember when they had last made love and could not; it had been before the trouble with Juan. She loved him still, but another instinct was stronger. "Whatever it is, you will have to take it."

Eduardo reached for a cigarette and stopped. His doctor had warned him to cut down, had mentioned emphysema and some signs of heart weakness. "I know," he said. "I know I must."

The notion that Juan had been treated like any other citizen who had broken the law was a fiction. He was lodged in a medium-security institution in Santa Cruz de la Sierra. Six hundred kilometres southeast of the capital, situated in the temperate lowlands, the place held few hardened criminals. To Santa Cruz went the husbands who had killed their adulterous wives, delinquent professionals, dishonest priests and foreign-born offenders awaiting arrangements that would take them out of the country. It was Eduardo's influence which had permitted Juan's placement in Santa Cruz. If that influence was withdrawn, the chances were good that the boy would be transferred to a tougher penitentiary. And there was the question of parole to be worked on by Eduardo, slowly and quietly. He was tired and had had his fill of government, but he knew as well as Yolanda that Juan's sentence was his sentence also.

Juan settled in at Santa Cruz after an initial period of rebellion, which brought him spells in solitary confinement and withdrawal of privileges. Santa Cruz is the richest agricultural district in Bolivia and, with unpaid labour to draw upon, the prison was easily made self-sufficient in fruit, vegetables and dairy produce. The inmates worked the farm, hoeing, weeding, picking, milking, maintaining and repairing fences and equipment. For many, the fat, defaulting lawyers and soft-handed school teachers, this was a torture. They fought for jobs as bookkeepers and cooks; anything that would keep them out of the sun and rain.

Juan gloried in the farm work. He became proficient in all branches of it and his thin frame filled out with the abundant food and constant exercise. He chopped wood for recreation and set himself the seemingly impossible goal of doubling a prisoner's daily fruit and bean picking quota.

"Why do you do this?" Jose Ramirez, Juan's cellmate,

asked him. "They won't make you a trusty, you're just a kid."

"I don't want to be a trusty," Juan said. "I don't want to join the oppressors."

Ramirez chuckled as he rolled a cigarette. He was a railway official who had taken bribes from freight companies. Ramirez had taken small bribes, but his superiors had taken large ones, and he was the scapegoat. "It is political?"

"*Sí*. political. Now be quiet, please. I want to read."

Juan was supplied with books by his father to supplement the small holdings in the prison library. Like educated prisoners everywhere, he read law books, but Juan's literary diet included political works that would normally be disapproved of in prison. He read Proudhon, Machiavelli and Gramsci, and C. Wright Mills in English, a language none of the prison officials knew. He was thus able to get some radical texts past them but his attempts to read Marx, Engels and Mao Tse-tung failed—even a monolinguistic bureaucrat could recognize those names. But his subscriptions, again facilitated by his father, to English and American magazines—the *New Statesman*, the *New Republic* and others—helped to supply the lack.

"We live like peasants here, do we not?" he said to Ramirez after lights out.

Ramirez was still smoking, even in the dark. "Less wine and no fat women to fuck, but yes, if you like, peasants."

"And what is an educated, radicalized peasant?"

"A freak," Ramirez said.

"No. A revolutionary."

"Oh, God."

"Do you know what Castro did?"

"I know, but you are going to tell me again."

"With a handful of men he regained his liberty and the liberty of the Cuban people. With a handful!"

"They must have been an exceptional lot."

"Yes. Do you know about 'Che' Guevara?"

"Refresh my memory."

"He was from the middle class, like me. He was of

mixed parentage, Irish and Spanish. I am English and Spanish. That man is a hero."

Ramirez sighed. "Juan, you are young. You have only eight years to serve—with your father to help, probably four. You are educated, you speak well, you look good. It's no disgrace in this country to have been in gaol. You should be thinking ahead—you could be a union leader, a politician, a big man in La Paz."

"I will burn La Paz to the ground if I have to," Juan said.

38

The prison was a simple structure—a grey concrete block surrounded by an asphalt exercise yard. The yard was fenced with watchtowers at each corner. The administration section, workshops and infirmary were located at the east end of the block. The kitchen and eating hall, guards' quarters, rest rooms and armoury were in the centre and prisoners were housed in three tiers of cells in the western section. The farm covered seventy-five hectares, most of which was cleared, both for cultivation and to remove possible hiding places. When the prisoners worked outside they were supervised by armed guards in teams of two and three.

Juan dreamed of escape.

"You're crazy," Ramirez told him. "You don't even have to shave every day. You've got your whole life ahead of you. If they catch you trying to escape they'll shoot you. And for what?"

"A revolutionary has an obligation to try to escape, like a prisoner of war."

"*Loco*," Ramirez said. He peered at the young man sitting in shadow in the corner of the small cell. It was late afternoon, when the daylight was dying and before the electricity was turned on. "Where are you from? I mean your family. You don't look Spanish or *mestizo*."

"My father is English. I told you that."

"Ah, that accounts for it." Ramirez tapped the side of his head. "English. *Loco*."

Eduardo La Vita continued to serve in the MNR government but he found himself increasingly at odds with its aims. Juan Lechin, Vice-President of Bolivia and leader of the mineworkers' union, was becoming increasingly disaffected. Dr Paz had hinted that he wanted the constitution amended to permit him to serve a second successive term. The lawyer in Eduardo bridled at this and the progressive reformer in him worried at Paz's increasing leniency towards the army.

"It is becoming intolerable," Eduardo told Yolanda. "I don't know how much longer I can continue."

"The parole?"

"Coming, possibly. A slow process."

Yolanda devoted herself to her husband's mental and physical comfort, attempting to help him to remain at his post until Juan was released. Sometimes she felt that she was in a race in which the finishing line receded with every forward movement she made. Eduardo worked hard and slept badly, and continued to smoke too much and eat too little.

When Yolanda returned from a visit to Santa Cruz, she was shocked to find Eduardo at home during office hours. He sat by the living room window in an easy chair. A cigarette burned unnoticed in an ashtray beside him.

"You haven't . . . ?"

"No, no, of course not. Two days' leave. I can hardly breathe sometimes. I got a lungful of petrol fumes in the street and I had a collapse." He paused for breath. "I'm all right now. How is the boy?"

Yolanda could see that he was far from all right. In pyjamas and dressing gown he appeared shrunken; the cords in his neck stood out and his hair had lost colour and texture—it lay white, flat and lank across his skull. She stubbed out the cigarette and rested her hand lightly on Eduardo's shoulder. The bones felt fragile. "He is physically very well," she said. "Taller and stronger. He is a wonderful-looking man. Eduardo, it has been four years. He is a man."

"But what kind of a man?"

Yolanda removed her hat and gloves; she made coffee and brought the cups into the living room. Eduardo had lit another cigarette. He was staring out the window at the tall white house opposite. Its dark shutters banged in a wind that promised a late-afternoon squall. Yolanda handed Eduardo a cup. "He is very well informed," she said. "A student of politics."

Eduardo grimaced and drank some coffee.

"He appears to think that big changes are coming."

"Change is always coming. That is not very profound."

"He expects a coup. He thinks the army will take control."

"He could be right. What does he hope to gain from that?" Eduardo coughed once, lightly, then a gust of coughing overtook him. He struggled against it. "An amnesty?"

Yolanda reached out to touch his face. "You must rest, *querido*."

"No, tell me."

"He is in touch with people who want the coup to happen. Revolutionaries. Cubans. Eduardo, I think he plans to escape."

Eduardo's hand shook and he dropped the cup. Before it hit the floor he was convulsed by a fit of coughing. The coughs racked him, jerked him upright and shook him in long, shuddering spasms. He collapsed into the chair and was still. Yolanda grasped his wrist and probed for the pulse but felt nothing. Her hand closed around the thin wrist, and her head fell forward into her husband's lap.

Juan took the news of his father's death stoically as, he imagined, behoved a true revolutionary. He grieved for his mother, who visited him soon after the funeral, but he was scarcely able to talk to her. He welcomed her news that she was going to Paraguay.

"I have friends there," she said. "From the old days. You must come when you are released, Juan."

At an earlier time Juan would have told her that she

should not leave Bolivia because a new age was about to dawn, a revolutionary time that would bring justice for all. But he could see that his mother was beyond thoughts of justice. And perhaps the wives of former government ministers would not fare so well. It was better that she should leave. He would then be unhampered in the work he had to do. "Yes, Mama," he said.

Yolanda was not deceived; she could see the hard set of his face and the fanatical light in his eyes. She cared, but grief had eroded her will. She put her hand to the grille; Juan did the same and their palms touched through the gaps. "Take care, my boy," she said.

As Juan had expected, Dr Paz overplayed his hand. Late in the year his attempts to continue in office and to court the favour of the army backfired. His deputy, Rene Barrientos, joined other army officers in a coup that sent Paz into exile once more. Political ferment in the country reached a new pitch and touched all institutions, schools, colleges, the army and the trades unions. The penitentiary at Santa Cruz was also affected. Political groups of varying persuasions formed among the inmates, many of whom were highly educated. Others saw personal advantage in political alignment; still others conspired secretly and reported their discoveries to the authorities. Some reported accurately, some did not.

The military regime offered no amnesties to prisoners and the new administrators of justice granted few paroles. Discipline within the prison tightened to the point of harshness. Juan offended often, was beaten and served periods of solitary confinement. He revelled in the atmosphere. He continued to work hard on the farm, proud of the callouses he built on his hands and the muscles in his arms and shoulders. He affected rough speech punctuated with frequent obscenities. Yolanda was correct in her assumption that her son had made contact with Cuban revolutionaries. Certain elements in Castro's new state made no secret of their intention to export revolution throughout Latin America. The prisons were seen as fertile soil and Juan stood out among the inmates of Santa Cruz as a possible recruit. He was approached, and he listened.

"Ramirez," he said one night, "can I trust you?"

"No," Ramirez said. "You cannot. I am utterly untrustworthy. I was a dishonest official. I betrayed my trust. I cannot keep a secret. I cannot withstand torture. Even the threat of it makes me spill my guts."

Juan smiled in the darkness. "I think I could trust you, but I will not."

"Thank you," Ramirez said. "If you must trust someone, you can probably trust your mother."

"She has gone to Paraguay."

"Then you cannot trust anyone. Goodnight, *chico*."

The next night Juan made his first entry in his 'revolutionary diary'. In microscopic letters on a leaf of toilet paper, he wrote:

20 February 1967: *The plan is made. I have the pistol. Tomorrow I perform my first revolutionary act. I call on all the heroes of the socialist cause to help me. I want to set the plan down now as an exercise. I want to see how reality matches theory. If they are too far apart I will die. If they can be made to coincide exactly I will be free and with my brothers fighting for the great cause. He is here! He has been seen! It is like a religious moment! A disturbance in the eating hall; solitary confinement; I subdue the guard with the pistol; take his uniform and walk out. So simple. This paper will be in my hand. Tomorrow it will be in my pocket or in my shit.*

At two minutes past midday on 21 February Juan La Vita stood in his place in the eating hall. He hurled his plate against the wall and shouted: "*Viva la revolucion! Bolivia libre! Vive Che Guevara!*"

39

Extracts from *The Revolutionary Diary of 'El Chico'* (Juan La Vita) translated from the Spanish by Roget Valdez; Free Press, San Francisco, 1981

25 March: We are regrouping after the recent fight with the army. Some of our weapons did not perform properly and we are spending much time on them. To talk while working is wonderful; to talk freely to comrades after the years in prison is like making love, being bathed and having a bad tooth fixed all at the same time.

E. [Ernesto 'Che' Guevara] is much troubled by his asthma but as long as he can get the medicine for it he will be all right. He should not smoke and I told him so. He laughed and said, 'Comrade, we are making a new Vietnam here. Uncle Ho does not expect to survive his war and I do not expect to survive mine.' I must have looked alarmed at these words for he laughed and patted me on the shoulder. 'But if I do survive it,' he said, 'I promise you that I will stop smoking. You can hold me to that when we are in triumph in La Paz.' We then spoke about the victory in Cuba. I never tire of hearing those stories.

> *Morale is good. J. ['Joaquin'—Juan Acuna Nunez] is a fine leader when E. is indisposed. On a patrol today he was able to re-create for us the entire agenda of a meeting of the central committee of the party in Cuba, of which he is a member. Inspirational! I long for the day when such councils will be held in this country.*
>
> *11 April: We have defeated the reactionary forces again. We were on our way to G.[utierrez], proceeding up the N.[ancahuazi River], when the scout saw a party of soldiers coming downriver. E. established a perfect guerrilla ambush. We caught them in a crossfire and killed the lieutenant and two of his men. Six soldiers were wounded and we have taken six prisoners. Our only casualty was the Cuban, El Rubio, who was shot through the head. His rifle had jammed. There will be more weapon maintenance drill.*
>
> *The prisoners tell us that there is a company of soldiers established at our old camp near E. [l Pincal]. E. organized another ambush and this time we repulsed more than fifty soldiers who were at the head of the column. We took twenty-two prisoners, including the commanding officer, a Major R.[uben] S.[anchez] and several junior officers. The rearguard and some newspaper reporters escaped. We suffered no losses. A great victory!*
>
> *We demonstrate the difference between a just and an unjust cause by giving medical care to their wounded. In this way, so the leader tells us, their morale is worn down and doubts arise in the minds of the ordinary soldiers.*
>
> *I.[nti Peredo] interrogated the prisoners and we learned their plans. Then we helped them to construct stretchers for their wounded and set them free. They have ten kilometres to walk on bare feet which will give them time to contemplate their mistakes.*

The Gulliver Fortune

* * *

15 April: *E. has decided to split the band. I had hoped to stay with him but I have been assigned to Joaquin's group. Orders are not to be questioned and the reasons are good. We are fourteen and many of us are too ill to march. M.[oises Guevara] has suffered a severe gall bladder attack & T.[ania] has a high fever. The group needs some able-bodied fighters for its protection and I am one such.*

I have not been afraid in the fighting, even when bullets have hit the trees and rocks quite close to me. I do not feel as if I can be killed fighting in this cause. This is irrational, but if it helps me to remain brave and cool I welcome it.

E. wishes us to remain in this area to harass the soldiers and protect the base camp. He has learned from the prisoners that G. is fortified, so he marches on M.[uyupampa] in the south. We will join forces again after this operation.

30 April: *Two weeks without action. We see no signs of soldiers in this area, so it is difficult to carry out the leader's orders. The sick are recovering and we patrol daily but the routine is dull. This, J. tells us, is an essential part of guerrilla training. There were many dull times in the Sierra Maestra.*

Some of my comrades have criticized me for keeping this journal. They say it could betray us if I am captured. I explained that it is in code but they say I could be tortured and made to reveal the code. I showed them the poison capsule I carry at all times. If I am captured I will betray nothing.

10 May: *Still no activity and no news of the leader. We debate tactics and ideology among ourselves at every opportunity. J. is an orthodox communist. E.'s views would be welcome.*

> *Relations with the peasants are worrying. There appears to be little support for us and we cannot gain access to the towns, where there is much sympathy for us. The militia is strong around the towns, too strong for us to enter.*
>
> *Morale is declining among some of my countrymen, I am ashamed to say. J. and A. [lejandro], the Cubans, provide backbone. I attempt to do the same, but C. [ingolo], in particular, is becoming sceptical about our prospects. 'Without the miners and the peasants we are lost,' he said. 'Is any of you a miner or a peasant?' I have the hands of a peasant now but I remained silent.*

> 30 May: *Life is uncomfortable, as it should be at this stage of a revolution. We have caches of ammunition, medicine and supplies in two places along the N.[ancahuazu] and we move between them, with no fixed base camp. This is a good tactic to avoid betrayal and ambush.*
>
> *Betrayal is much on our minds. We have bought pigs and other food from the peasants (paying them well in American dollars), but they continue to be indifferent or even hostile. Yesterday, near the southern supply base, a group of peasants shared their food and drink with us and appeared friendly. But P.[aco—Jose Carrillo] overheard them talking about informing on us to the soldiers. Naturally, one thinks of punishing such people but one cannot. They are ignorant men and not to blame for their ignorance.*

> 15 June: *Everyone is fit again now and ready for action. Our weapons are in good order and discipline is tight. The men all wear fatigues and boots; we keep the clothes clean to avoid skin irritations and sickness. Tania wears civilian clothes for comfort and to allow her to approach people on the roads and farms.*
>
> *J. has proposed that we establish a camp*

and attempt to make contact with the leader with a view to reuniting with our comrades. We are heavily armed and carry documents and papers with us which are becoming burdensome. A clear majority favours the idea of a camp.

8 July: We had word of a great propaganda victory for E. at Samaipata. A truck was commandeered and two policemen in the town subdued. Then an army post surrendered and the commander and his men were left naked in the countryside.

Many people witnessed this action, which took place so close to the city of Santa Cruz, and we can expect a boost in our stocks as a result of it. Our informant tells us that the leader is suffering badly from his asthma and lacks medicine for it. We have supplies of the medicine and must make contact with our comrades.

11 July: We have been fighting and moving for three days. Our camp was discovered by the troops who seem to have entered the area in force. Possibly we were betrayed. We managed to escape encirclement but we were forced to leave behind many documents and supplies.

A.[?], one of my countrymen, was killed. I have a slight shoulder wound. In the flesh only—it is nothing.

30 July: We have been informed that the army has mounted an operation named 'Cynthia' against us, in reprisal for E.'s victory at Samaipata. They are in great strength, hampering our movements. We travel at night to avoid detection, but the soldiers also despatch night patrols which are aided by the local people. It should be the other way around.

My shoulder is sore but healing.

15 August: *This is the low point of our campaign, J. assures us. From this point we will build strength towards victory The army has been pressing us hard, forcing us to march when tired and anticipating some of our movements. My countryman and close comrade P.[edro] has been killed. We had many long talks about politics and life. He died bravely, covering our escape from a near ambush,*

Two days later a further disaster. E.[usebio] and C.[hingolo] were captured. They led the soldiers to the caves where we had hidden documents, photographs and E.'s medicine.

These reverses have lowered morale, but the Cubans urge us on. My wound opened in one of the fights and is very painful.

28 August: *We must cross the Rio Grande and rejoin the leader. In unity is strength. We must make a serious demonstration if we are to rouse the peasants and we cannot do it with such a small band. We need food and information, and the time has come to act vigorously. We took two peasants captive and compelled them to act as guides, but we are not familiar with techniques of oppression and they escaped. It is worrying that they may have deduced our destination, although they were very stupid and frightened for the time they were with us.*

We have bought a cow from a peasant named Rojas who expresses sympathy with us. He tells us that the best place to cross the river is at a ford called E.[l] V.[ado] d.[el] Y.[eso], where we may wade across the river.

I dreamed of my father last night. I dreamed I was with him in Australia as a small boy. Everything he had told me about Sydney and how Tio and he escaped from the ship happened to me. A strange dream.

* * *

The peasants knelt with their knees in the dust. Each felt a pistol barrel press in behind his right ear.

"Tell me," the captain said.

The older man vomited and fell forward into his own mess. The other squared his soldiers.

"I hope you are not going to be a hero," the captain said.

The man trembled. "No, captain. I was drawing breath to speak."

"Good. You have seen Joaquin?"

"*Sí*, captain."

"And how many others?"

"Difficult to be sure, captain. Seven, perhaps eight."

"In what condition?"

"Armed, captain."

"*Imbecil!* In what physical condition?"

"Very tired, captain. And one of the young men, the one they call El Chico, is wounded here." The peasant touched the shoulder of his faded workshirt.

The captain moved the pistol several inches away. "Good. And now, where are they going?"

The peasant hesitated. He had no respect for the guerrillas who had treated him well but seemed not to understand anything about the country or the life working people led. They had offered to pay him with American dollars. How could he spend American dollars with every soldier in the Nancahuazzu area asking questions about *Yanqui* money? Still, if the guerrillas should win and learn that he had informed on them . . . he felt the pistol bite his neck again. "To cross the river."

"Where?"

"The best place is El Vado del Yeso."

"Congratulations, you have just saved your own life." The captain was content: two sources of information—one, the peasant who had sold a cow to the guerrillas, and now another. Confirmation. He planted his foot in the ribs of the man who still lay snuffling on the ground.

"Get up, *peon*. You will lead us to this place."

* * *

The captain deployed his men in the bushes across from the point where the guerrillas were expected to cross the river. They waited, cursing the insects and the heat until the afternoon began to cool and a slight breeze stirred the leaves and the surface of the water. The captain checked his position again: good cover for his men and a clear view of the rocky edge to the water; the fording place was narrow. *They will move in single file and for a time they will all be in the water and concentrating on the crossing*, he thought. *That will be the time.*

He beckoned for one of his men, a soldier who had once been a prisoner of the guerrillas, to come forward. The soldier had been left on a road without any clothes in broad daylight. He said he hated the guerrillas like a whore hates a virgin, and he had been one of the best prepared and most efficient soldiers in his unit since his humiliation. Now without speaking he crouched beside the captain and peered at the break in the brush where the path led to the edge of the river.

The time passed slowly. They waited through the tepid afternoon rain and in the heat that followed it. Steam rose from the ground like a low, warm mist. The captain's skin, inside the damp, drying-out army clothing, began to itch. He frequently had to gesture angrily to silence his impatient men. He was sweating and impatient himself. He checked his watch—almost six o'clock.

He wiped sweat from his eyes and felt a tug at his sleeve. He looked. A man wearing fatigues and carrying a knapsack on his back had stepped from the brush. He had an automatic rifle with a short barrel in his hands. He swivelled slowly, looking upstream and down. "Braulio," the soldier said. "Cuban bastard."

The captain nodded and signalled for his men to hold their fire. One by one the guerrillas followed Braulio into the water. They stepped carefully on the rocky stream bed, maintaining their balance. All were heavily laden with packs, weapons and ammunition. The soldier's breath stank of garlic close to the captain's ear as he whispered the names: "Gueva . . . Joaquin . . . El Negro . . . Paco . . . El Chico . . . Tania."

When they were all in the water, the captain sighted his carbine on the white blouse of the woman. He held his weapon steady to his shoulder, took his finger from the trigger, held up his fist and suddenly splayed out the fingers.

The crashing volley of shots sent birds screaming into the sky; hot lead hissed into the water and thudded into the bodies of the guerrillas. Tania's arms flew up and she collapsed face down into the river; Joaquin fired once and fell; the others crouched, shed their packs and splashed downstream. The shots became ragged as the excited soldiers ran along the bank firing at the figures wading and flailing through the water. A bullet passed through Paco's shoulder and Juan felt a spume of blood on his face. Paco groaned and threw down his rifle. The water around him was turning red; Juan sprayed bullets at the river bank. He felt a blow to his chest as if he had been hit by a giant floating log, and then the world tilted and he slid off it. The soldier who could identify the guerrillas moved slowly along the line of bodies laid out on the river bank. Paco was sitting under a tree; blood oozed from his shoulder into his sodden shirt. The soldier bent and pushed hair away from one of the faces. He nodded. "Joaquin," he said.

He bent again and wiped mud from another still, upturned face. "El Chico," he said. "Hey, he's still alive!" He unslung his rifle and pointed the muzzle down.

The captain struck him viciously on the ear with the butt of his pistol. The soldier's long, greasy hair cushioned the blow, but he reeled away and stared at the officer with frightened eyes. "Leave him. We'll need one of these bastards for interrogation. We've got two. Let us see which one of them makes it."

40

San Francisco, September 1986

Wade Phillips studied the newspaper article carefully. He read for the third time the outline account of the history of the immigrant Gullivers, and wondered for the third time why the item touched some chord in his memory. He sighed, pushed the paper aside and pulled another file towards him. Phillips was a research officer for Amnesty International, the organization that agitates for the release of prisoners of conscience worldwide. He made notes on the South African case in the file, but found it hard to concentrate. He lit a cigarette and got up from his desk.

His office was in a building on Powell Street close to Union Square. He walked to the window and stood there smoking and looking down on the people hurrying about in the crisp fall air. Phillips was thirty years of age. A slim, small man with a neat head and a quiet, contented and as yet childless marriage, he had become interested in Amnesty while doing his PhD in mathematics at Berkeley. By one of the chances that sometimes happens in his field, the equation he had been set to examine had unravelled itself for him in a matter of weeks. His dissertation virtually wrote itself and he was left with at least two years of scholarship and study time. He wrote several mathematical papers but found the relative inactivity galling after eight years of hard undergraduate and graduate study. A friend mentioned Amnesty International to him. He attended a meeting, became involved in a case and was hooked. He graduated *magna cum laude*, but Dr Phillips did no more mathematics. He was an atheist and no idealist; he explained his dedication to the organization by saying that he'd had more than his share of luck and wanted to spread it around a little.

He watched the people moving freely along the street. *Not one in a thousand of them values the actual freedom,* he thought, *which, if they only knew it, is their sweetest possession.* He moved back to his desk to ash the cigarette and his eye fell on the newspaper. The word 'Gulliver' jumped out at him. It was what had been nagging at him. Like most people he'd heard of Swift's book and never read it. But there was something else. Something to do with his work . . . He butted the cigarette, and the connection leapt into his mind.

"Bolivia," he said. He banged his fist down on the paper. "Bolivia!"

Ten minutes later he had the file of Juan Gulliver La Vita scrolling on the screen of his desktop IBM computer. He moved through it quickly, absorbing the contents with a speed born of having done the same thing hundreds of times before. He noted the birthdate, the parents' names, the date of imprisonment, the reports of various investigative committees, correspondence with authorities, petitions. There were many cross-references to Amnesty's vast computerized data base and library of printed material. Phillips scribbled notes, printed out pages from the files and sent out for books and newspaper cuttings. When a colleague put his head around the door and said, "Lunch?", Phillips did not even hear him. His ashtray filled and overflowed. The colleague put a cup of coffee and a doughnut on his desk and tiptoed away. Wade was notorious for his capacity for concentration and involvement.

By early afternoon Phillips had assembled enough information to convince himself. The standard reference work on Latin American politicians had been vague about the birthplace of Eduardo La Vita but his odd and temporary nickname, *'el canguru,'* had been recorded. Ferdinand

La Vita was known to have travelled to Australia around 1910. He had never married, yet Eduardo had his name and was said to be sixty-four years of age when he died in 1964. Yolanda La Vita had visited her son in prison in Bolivia. Along with other members of her family, she had moved to Paraguay in 1964 and had died there in 1970. Juan La Vita now had no known living relatives in Bolivia.

El Chico, after recovering from his wounds, had attempted suicide by swallowing a cyanide capsule, but the poison had degenerated and the effect had not been lethal. In February 1968, four months after the summary execution of Che Guevara at La Higuera, Juan La Vita was sentenced to twenty-five years' imprisonment for the crimes of escape from legal custody, murder and armed insurrection. Governments had come and gone in Bolivia, but Juan was still in prison. He had spent long periods in solitary confinement, had lost privileges and had had years added to his sentence for infringement of prison regulations. Official records described him as 'rebellious', 'seditious', 'a malign influence', 'unrepentant', 'irredeemable'.

Juan's *Revolutionay Diary* had been smuggled out of prison and published by a radical press in 1981. It had attracted little attention in the year of the return of the US hostages from Iran, assassination attempts on Ronald Reagan and the Pope, the assassination of President Sadat, hunger strikes by IRA men in Ireland and the rise of the Solidarity movement in Poland. But the book was in the library of Amnesty International, along with similar works by scores of incarcerated men and women around the world.

Phillips had several photocopied sheets—pages from Juan's decoded and translated journal—in addition to his notes. The diary mentioned Australia, the name Gulliver and contained other clues which convinced Phillips that El Chico was the grandson of John Gulliver and, therefore, a person of great interest to Mr Benjamin Cromwell of Chelsea, London. Phillips turned back to his IBM computer, lit a cigarette and began to compose a letter.

41

London, November 1986

Jerry hammered on the door to Jamie Martin's room. The house, an ancient terrace in Islington, seemed to shake to its foundations and Jerry heard ill-tempered protests from several of the other residents. Jamie opened the door to see Jerry, gasping for breath and trembling with impatience, standing on the gloomy second-floor landing. Jamie was wearing a threadbare, faded Japanese kimono he'd picked up in a street market. An old Arsenal scarf served as a tie. Jerry gaped at him. Jamie pulled her inside and kissed her.

"Jerry," Jamie said. "Jerry. Oh God, I'm happy!"

Jerry enjoyed the kiss but she broke free and pulled two sheets of photocopy paper from her jacket. "Look at this."

Jamie recovered quickly from his disappointment. He and Jerry had been to bed in her flat several times, with highly satisfactory results for them both. But Jamie understood that Jerry, as well as being wary of a rebound relationship, was obsessed by the search for the Gullivers and very serious about her own writing. Jamie was content to bide his time. He took the sheets of paper and flipped them out of their folds. "What's this?"

"Just read it. It's a photocopy of a letter to Ben."

"From Amnesty International," Jamie said. "I imagine it's a while since Ben spared a thought for Nelson Mandela."

"Or for anyone but himself," Jerry said. "Read it!"

Jamie shuffled across the bedsitter's thin carpet towards the gas ring as he read. He stopped dead by the hand basin. "Christ," he said, "The Bolivian connection."

Jerry elbowed him aside, filled the kettle at the dripping tap, and put it on the gas. "What a family, eh? Che Guevara, my God."

"He's forty-four and he's spent more than half of his life in gaol," Jamie said. "The story just gets better and better."

Jerry glanced at him sharply. "Or worse and worse. Mikhail won't be able to get out of Russia and . . . Juan's in prison. That family was cursed."

The kettle boiled and Jerry fossicked for cups and instant coffee in the chaos of the shelves above the gas ring. "How did you get this?" Jamie said.

Jerry rinsed two cups and spooned in the coffee. "I went to Montague's house to collect a couple of things I left there. I also wanted to leave the key Ben gave me. There was no one home and this letter was lying on a table. I rushed out and made the copy. Then I put the original back. I forgot to collect my stuff."

Jerry poured the water into the cups and added long-life milk to both. Jamie took his cup and they sat on the unmade bed. Books dominated the room; several bookcases were crammed full and books lay in piles on the floor and in cardboard boxes around the room. Jerry's eye was caught by a silver trophy sitting on top of a pile of books. She pointed at it. "What's that?"

"For football," Jamie said. "I'm not just a bookworm."

Simultaneously, they put their cups on the floor. Jerry slipped her hands inside the kimono and felt Jamie's ribs and hard, flat muscles. They kissed. Jerry stood and shrugged out of her jacket. She unzipped her skirt and took off her blouse. Jamie watched her as she shook her hair free. She seemed to float down towards him, but in fact he was rising to meet her, reaching for the top of her pantyhose and searching for her nipples with his mouth. They fell onto the bed and wriggled free of their remaining clothes. They kissed and explored each other and locked together in a hard, pounding rhythm that made the floorboards creak and brought a soft shower of plaster down from the old, cracked ceiling.

Later, they sipped the cold coffee and reread the letter.

"This arrived two days ago and Ben didn't tell us anything about it," Jerry said. "They're so greedy and impatient."

"You gave them something to think about when you brought up the idea of selling the story to the movies."

Jerry shook her head. "Ben wasn't convinced. I wouldn't put it past him to steal the painting somehow and defraud the Gullivers."

"I'll ring Faraday," Jamie said. "I'll tell him everything. It's the story aspect he's most interested in, so he'll want every bit of information that's going. The Bolivian angle's great for him."

Jerry recovered the Arsenal scarf from the foot of the bed and draped it around her neck. "What about Ben?"

"I'll tell him we know about Juan and how we found out. He's a careless fool. I'll tell Montague the same. I'll tell them that Faraday knows everything. I'll repeat the threat about going to the newspapers. Whatever they've got planned, we have to stop it."

Jerry nodded. "I'd still like to know about the baby. And whether another heir exists. *They* won't tell us, even if they do find out."

"You kept the key, didn't you?" Jamie said. "What's the problem, then?"

Leo, Kobi

42

'Southern Maid', March 1910

Nurse O'Halloran handed the infant to Violet Clarke, who clutched the small bundle and pressed it to her thin chest. "You must swear to me that you will make caring for this child your first concern from this day on, and that you will bring him up in our holy faith. You must swear it!"

"I do," Violet breathed. "Oh, I do swear it, and thank you. Thank you."

"Sure, it's a pig in a poke you're taking," the nurse said. "But chances to save a soul don't come along every day. I have to get back to the doctor. If he asks me I'll say the child died, but I doubt he will, heathen that he is."

Violet moved the swaddling cloth and looked at the small, puckered face. "The mother . . . ?"

"Will not last the day. If I can be of further help to you I will, but you and your husband will have to make shift for yourselves."

"Yes," Violet said. "Dennis is so clever. I'm sure he'll have some good ideas."

"Is he a good man? Strong in the faith?"

Violet nodded. She could not bear to think of the consequences if she told the nurse that her husband had merely gone reluctantly through some Roman Catholic instruction. Rusty had obliged her in this so that Violet could be married in the church attended by all her family.

It had been a lovely wedding, but Dennis was more interested in his stomach than his soul. He had grieved when the baby died, but then the inheritance had swept him up and he'd followed rubber prices in *The Times* and talked about something called copra. But he *had* grieved.

Grief was far from Rusty Clarke's mind at that time. Neither he nor Violet had been struck by the fever, and he counted that a good omen. He'd picked up a bit about New Guinea from some of the passengers and he was full of expectation. He sought Violet out to tell her the latest price for copra and was surprised to find her virtually hiding in their cabin, opening the door to him by only a few inches.

"I say, Violet, let a chap in. Damned hot on deck, and I've walked a few circuits. Need a good lie down. I must tell you how the jolly old copra's faring." Rusty was already affecting a slightly pukka manner and imagining himself walking around the plantation near sundown with his overseer—*Needs weeding there, old chap. Fence looks a bit shaky . . . Yes, Mr Clarke*.

Violet opened the door a few more inches and Rusty squeezed his bulk through. His wife held her fingers up to her lips. "Ssh," she whispered. "He's sleeping."

"Who is?" Rusty's mind filled with thoughts of adultery. Violet was a scrawny little thing, but not bad-looking in her way. She was forever reading romantic novels. Rusty had picked a few of them up and thrown them down in disgust after a line or two. He thought them corrupting, and wondered if she'd been corrupted. *Shipboard life. Notorious for it,* he thought. But Violet was bending over something in the bottom bunk. He saw it wriggle and heard a muffled sound.

"This is our son, Dennis. Yours and mine. It's a miracle."

"It bloody is," Rusty said. He was sweating in the stifling heat of the cabin. He wiped his red face and passed his hand over the thin, fair hair pasted to his skull by perspiration. "I don't understand, Violet."

She clutched his wet shirt and the words spilled from her. "I didn't tell you, darling, but after we lost our little boy the doctor told me I wouldn't be able to have any more children. Something went wrong inside. I was afraid to tell you. I was afraid you'd leave me."

Rusty took her hands and held them together in one of his big, meaty paws. For all his vanities and delusions, he was a kindly man who loved his wife and knew he was lucky to have her. "Never, Vi," he said softly. "Never."

"The nurse gave him to us. His mother's dead of the fever but he's alive . . ."

"We can't just . . . *take* a baby, Vi. What about the father?"

Violet Clarke pulled away and stood up to her full height, which was not much above five feet; Rusty towered a foot and an inch above her but at that moment he felt smaller. "He has four other children to care for," she said fiercely. "And we have none. What's more, he didn't even know his wife was carrying."

"Poor man," Rusty said.

"And he's a Protestant, or worse."

The baby emitted a mewing sound and Violet swooped down to the bunk. Rusty Clarke had little of it himself, but he knew determination when he saw it. He smiled and patted his wife's thin shoulder. "Righto, dear. Think I'll go and have a gin sling to toast the little feller's arrival."

"Nau, tain bipo, mi pikinin, nau mi stap long sip. Nau, bihain, mi lusim sip long bilum."*

Leo Clarke's story of how he was taken from the ship by his adopted parents was only one of the tales he used to fascinate the New Guinea highlanders among whom he grew up. He also told them about London and Sydney, the first of which he had never seen and in the second of which he had spent only days when he was a few weeks old. A description of the beard and nose of King George V were also in his repertoire, along with an eyewitness account of the KO of Tommy Burns by Jack Johnson at the

---

*"Now, a long time ago, when I was just a baby, I was on a ship. Now, afterwards, I left the ship in a shopping basket."

Rushcutters Bay Stadium. This happened in 1908, two years before Leo was born, but Leo never let a little thing like that interfere with a good story. He *did* say that he was very young at the time.

Leo Clarke was a liar. Violet Clarke's unremitting effort to bring him up with a respect for the truth—so much so that she had told him the circumstances of his birth and adoption as soon as he was old enough to comprehend them—had had no effect. Leo was not a reader—Violet had told him his real name, but this meant only that *Gulliver's Travels* was added to the list of books he had failed to complete. Rather than read the tales of others, Leo was led to weave inventions and fantasies around his own life. He started with the children of the labourers on Rusty Clarke's first plantation—the one Rusty had inherited and quickly bankrupted—and continued as Rusty moved around New Guinea, first as a plantation manager, then a bookkeeper, then an overseer, until he finally came to rest in Bougainville as the apparent owner of a number of trade stores on the island. Only Rusty, among the Europeans on Bougainville, knew that the stores were actually owned by a wealthy Hong Kong Chinese.

Leo's real life had been adventurous enough to support the embroidery.

"I was with Mick Leahy in '31 when we went into the highlands," he used to say. "First white men there and bloody nearly the first to die."

It was *almost* true. Leo had gone gold prospecting in the highlands eighteen months after the pioneers, and had indeed seen the warlike Kukukukus fire arrows in anger. Not at him though—at the *kiap*, the government patrol officer, and the native policemen he took care to travel with.

"Very hush-hush business, that coastwatching," Leo would say after 1945. "We all had to sign the British Official Secrets Act, so I can't say much about it."

Again, there was embellishment. Through all his years of transience in New Guinea, Rusty Clarke had endeavoured to provide Leo with an education. Violet, growing more and more gaunt and yellow as the climate took its toll, insisted that he be sent to prestigious Catholic schools in Australia. Leo attended a good many of them—a St Patrick's here, a St Michael's there, in the cities and larger provincial towns—but he quickly became homesick for New Guinea and pleaded for release. Violet and Rusty always relented, with the result that Leo's education was patchy. But as a white man and public schoolboy, fluent in pidgin and competent in Morse, he was able to be of some minor use to the coastwatchers who relayed information about the Japanese to the navy.

So Leo had a reasonable war in Bougainville and the British Solomons. Rusty had died within hours of hearing the news of the fall of Singapore, almost as if the fortress had been his own personal defence. Thirty years in New Guinea had intensified his Britishness as it had reinforced Violet's Roman Catholicism. Against all the odds they had been happy together and although disappointed in Leo (Violet had named him after a pope she mistakenly believed to have been canonized), they were comforted by the feeling that they had done their duty by him. Also, he had made them laugh with his stories and they had always been glad to see him when he lobbed in from one of his semi-successful ventures.

Violet died in an odour of sanctity in a hospital run by the Marists in Townsville, north Queensland. In her will she urged Leo to marry a good Catholic girl and raise all his children in the faith. She also left him a thousand pounds Australian. The money accumulated interest in the hands of a Townsville solicitor while Leo did his bit against the power of Nippon. After the war he went to Townsville and got the money. He spent a little in the fleshpots that had been established to service the US saviours, and took the rest back to Bougainville where he went into the business of salvaging and selling war surplus goods.

"I can get you a fleet of jeeps, well, three jeeps," Leo would tell a prospect in the Buka Club. "Barely used, spare tyres, spare battery."

"What's the petrol situation?" the prospect would ask if he was canny.

"Three bob a gallon at the bowser. I can let you have a few drums at a discount."

"Where'd you get it?"

Leo would rub the side of his nose and wink. From a puny, near stillborn infant, he had developed into a well-built man with thick, dark hair. Lean and hard in his youth, he was lately getting fleshy from spending more time closing deals over beers in the Buka Club than trudging along jungle trails. He approached life optimistically and seldom let sombre thoughts—such as what might have happened to the brothers and sister Violet had told him about—trouble him. He was making the transition from adventurer to salesman-businessman successfully.

"I suppose you could say I got the fuel from a grateful government." Leo held up two fingers to the native barman. "Did you know I was a coastwatcher?"

Leo was popular in the club and in the little town of Kieta, which was a dust bowl in the dry season and a swamp when the rains came. The Australians accepted him; the Chinese remembered his father as a reliable employee; the Marist missionaries remembered his mother as a devout woman. He had a lot of friends. Until he disgraced himself.

43

At thirty-six, Leo Clarke had had very little experience of sex. At home the subject was never discussed. Leo got the impression that Rusty and Violet had given it up for Lent at about the time he came along, and had never resumed. The priests and brothers at the schools he'd attended had disparaged it, of course. If there had been any homosexual activity at these schools Leo had never come across it. Later, out in the world which his teachers had described as sinful, he had found less sin than he'd hoped. Opportunities for sexual contact with white women were few in New Guinea and non-existent during his coastwatching period. A few quick, hot and unsatisfactory commercial transactions in Townsville and one drunken coupling on a Burns Philp island trader constituted Leo's entire sexual score sheet.

So he was entirely unprepared for the arrival of Lily Kobi Mong. Lily's genes were a compound of Chinese, European and Melanesian. One ancestor was a Scots blackbirder who'd raided the Solomons for labourers in the 1870s; another was one of the unwilling women the blackbirder had taken to a Queensland sugar plantation to work for three years at five pounds per year. Other predecessors were Chinese merchants, Australian seamen, Bougainvillean head-takers, one English missionary and one Polynesian girl—a child plucked from a beach on

Tikopia by Harry Kobi Hong, Lily's father, who was master of a rustbucket schooner, and never returned.

In looks, Lily favoured her mother—she had a broad face but surprisingly delicate features. Her skin was light brown and her hair was jet black and straight, like that of the Chinese. Her eyes were slanted but green, her body was strong and rounded. When she moved she gave the impression that she might suddenly do something acrobatic, such as a handstand or a cartwheel. She spoke English, trade store Chinese, pidgin and the language of the people of the central east coast of Bougainville, all in a loud voice that did not invite contradiction.

In 1946 Lily was twenty-three. She had done four years of school as a boarder in Brisbane and she could keep books, but she knew that there was no future for her in Australia. She spent the war years working for the American army as a filing clerk, handling the records of the 'coloured personnel'. As soon as she could, she returned to Bougainville. She would inherit her father's marginal trading business, some long-term leases he held and a little cash. Lily had it all worked out—Harry Kobi Hong had taken to opium in his old age to ease the pain from the multiple injuries he had sustained in his shortish but hard life. He had, Lily judged, less than a year to live. She needed a husband to give her credibility in the commercial world, and children, but she did not necessarily require him to accompany her through the whole of life's journey. Therefore an older man would be best. However, he had to be a sound one—not a drunk, not a coward, not a fool but not too clever (Lily tended to think of men in negatives), free of venereal disease, and white.

Leo Clarke was perfect for Lily's purposes. She arranged for one of the mining engineers, a breed that began sniffing around Bougainville as soon as the last shots of the war had been fired, to introduce her to Leo at the Kieta slipway, where she was supervising the refurbishing of one of her father's trading cutters. The bar of the club would have been better but Lily, as a coloured person, was barred. In preparation for the meeting she had stayed out of the sun for three weeks, applied a lightening makeup and wore a dark blue sharkskin suit.

The engineer had run up a debt in the Hong trade store and was therefore anxious to oblige Lily. "Mr. Clarke," he said, "I'd like you to meet Miss Lily Hong."

Leo saw slanted green eyes, a fine nose and lips and small white teeth. He smelt a perfume that took him away from the rotting kelp on the beach and the reek of stale, trapped seawater. "Miss Hong," he said.

Lily shook his hand. *Good grip*, she thought, *no broken blood vessels in the face*. "Mr. Clarke. Do you have a boat here?"

"Well, no, looking for one as a matter of fact. I've got a salvage job. Need a supply boat."

Lily's white-gloved hand rested on Leo's slightly grubby white linen sleeve. "Perhaps I can help you."

The engineer tipped his sun helmet to Lily and left them. She kept hold of Leo's arm and allowed him to walk her along the jetty to where the Hong cutter was being painted. It was close to midday in November and the sun was high and hot. Lily opened her sunshade and Leo instinctively moved closer to her underneath it.

"That's a good boat," Leo said, pointing at the cutter.

Lily smiled. "Perhaps we could come to an arrangement."

They discussed money and boats for a time, and then Leo invited Lily to have a drink with him at the club. As soon as he spoke the words he felt them turn to stones in his mouth. He stopped in mid-stride. Lily squeezed his arm.

"It's all right," she said. "I understand. We can have a drink at my father's place. There's a private room."

Leo knew the Hong Club, but had never been inside. He knew that some of the Americans left behind by the war, the mining chaps and an anthropologist fellow who'd passed through recently drank there. It wasn't *exactly* no place for a white man.

"Righto," he said.

Kieta did not exactly have a Chinatown. True, there were more Chinese trade stores in the short street where the Hong Club was situated than in other places, but there were commercial and government buildings too. And the whole place was changing fast. The Americans and the mining people talked big.

"They say Kieta could outstrip Moresby," Leo said over the first gin and tonic in the small courtyard behind the club. A fan stirred the air and moved the fronds of the potted palms Lily had moved into place that morning.

"It's exciting," Lily said. "Oil? Gold? A boom?"

Leo nodded. "Could be. Well, it'd soon pass a small operator like me by."

"Not necessarily." Lily refused Leo's offer of a Craven A, judging that he would prefer women not to smoke. In reality she smoked a packet a day. "You should be in a position to supply certain needs. Not all the operators'll have big money to start with. They'll need vehicles and equipment and be happy to take what they can get. You've got marsden matting?" This was the heavy metal sheeting the Americans had used to build roads, bridges and airstrips.

"Acres of it," Leo said.

Lily nodded and signalled to the boy for another drink. She was dying for a cigarette and feeling like other things too. Leo wasn't bad-looking, with his good teeth and strong chin. *A bit slow but he can see a joke,* she thought. She took off the jacket of her suit and draped it over the wicker chair. Under her silk blouse her breasts were full and heavy. She leaned forward as Leo lit another Craven A.

"Let me have a puff," she said. "Sometimes I like just to have a puff or two. You don't mind, do you, Leo?"

Lily had repressed the Oriental side of her nature in the furnishings of her flat. No paper blinds, silk coverings or brassware. Her furniture was as modern as a Myers catalogue and the regular Burns Philp shipping service from Australia could make it—paisley coverings in the sitting room, Wedgwood and Swedish stainless steel in the kitchen, walnut veneer in the bedroom. She steered Leo towards the walnut veneer, collapsed onto the bed with him and allowed him to kiss and handle her a little before she took over. She stripped off his jacket and shirt, pulled off his shoes, socks and pants and let him lie, hot and sweating, on top of the chenille bedspread while she shrugged off her jacket and let her skirt drop. Leo's eyes adjusted slowly to the dim light; he saw lace-edged silk and sheer nylon and heard the whisper of the fabrics as they glided against Lily's skin.

Leo's gin intake had been judged to a nicety by Lily. He was relaxed in mind and aroused in body. "God, Lily," he breathed. "You're beautiful."

"Yes," she said. She unbuttoned her blouse, bent forward over the bed, reached behind her back with both hands and unfastened her brassiere. Her large, round breasts seemed to tumble forward towards Leo's hands. Suddenly his palms and fingers were full of warm flesh; he trapped her big, brown nipples in the V between his thumbs and forefingers and squeezed hard on them. Lily moaned and strained away from him. The nipples extended and stretched like rubber. Leo let go and his mouth opened; Lily clasped her breasts together and pushed both nipples past his straining lips.

"Suck," she said, "suck hard."

Leo sucked. He felt her hands move inside his underpants. Lily freed his penis and worked on it with nails and fingers as the black sergeant from Tallahassee, Florida, had taught her in Brisbane. When Leo was fully erect she guided him inside her and clamped her thighs together, bringing every muscle she could control into play.

"Only *real* young pussy is tight pussy," the sergeant had said. "When a pussy passes eighteen, it's experience that counts."

Lily gave Leo the benefit of her experience, which amounted to six months with the sergeant, a shorter time with a white US officer and several flings, more or less alcohol-affected, with several other military personnel. An English nurse who'd learned a lot in boarding school was one of her more sober partners. Lily participated enthusiastically in all exercises and took care against becoming pregnant when appropriate.

"Oh! No!" Leo came mightily inside Lily's cream-and diaphragm-protected vagina. His hot, uncontrollable rush had been delayed just long enough to give him an intensity of pleasure he never imagined could exist.

Lily disengaged herself, pushed back the bedcovers and pulled a sheet over their sweating bodies. They shared a cigarette, Lily making sure to have one puff to his four. Leo was oddly embarrassed, which Lily found charming.

"You are a nice man, Leo," she said, handing back the Craven A. She kissed his mouth allowing just the tip of her tongue to pass between his lips.

"I'm mad about you, Lily," Leo said hoarsely. "I thought this sort of thing only happened in books. Not that I've read many of those sorts of books, or any books for that matter."

"What sort?"

"Well, you know—dirty."

Lily found this a promising line of talk. "D'you think what we just did was dirty, Leo?"

"God, no, it was wonderful."

"Even if I'm a nigger?"

"You're not! You're . . . God, who cares? I love you!"

Lily smiled. "We've talked business and had lunch and sex. Is that enough to say you love me?" Lily let the sheet slip as she spoke; one of her ripe breasts pushed against Leo's arm.

"Yes, why not? Love at first sight."

Lily tweaked her nipple so that it stood out, hard and quivering, from the puckered brown flesh around it.

"Let's do it again," she said.

They met the next day and the next. Leo was even more ardent when he was more sober, and Lily was convinced that she'd caught her fish. The tenth time he told her he loved her she moved away a little and took a drag on the shared cigarette. "Do you want to be rich?"

"I don't care," Leo said.

"Do you want to stay in Bougainville?"

"With you? Yes. Or anywhere else."

"Do you want children, Leo?"

Leo liked children. "Yes."

"Do you care what people think of you? What they say about you behind your back?"

Leo answered almost before she had stopped speaking. He had a sense that he was making a deeper commitment than he'd ever made before but he didn't flinch from it. "No, I don't give a damn."

Lily kissed him and probed his mouth with her tongue. She was surprised and pleased to find that she liked this simple, easy man. The nurse had told her that some people were excited by being abused; Lily found that she was excited by getting her own way. She stroked Leo's cock with her long lacquered nails. She'd been prepared to put it in her mouth if necessary but it seemed that she wouldn't have to. *He really does seem to be in love*, she thought.

Leo, masterfully easing her legs apart, was in no doubt at all.

Father Damien O'Connor married Leo Clarke and Lily Kobi Hong as a matter of duty. Leo had managed to stumble through enough of the rituals and observances in a preliminary interview to convince the priest that he had been raised in the faith, however imperfectly. Lily was delighted to discover that Leo was a nominal Catholic. She foresaw a measure of respectability in the church wedding and profit in business association with the missionaries. She took instruction and O'Connor found her an apt pupil, although he sensed that something other than piety motivated her.

As he performed the service in the small, hot, prefabricated church, Father O'Connor was struck by how few white faces were in the congregation—the mining engineer who had introduced the happy couple, two employees of Leo's, the anthropologist just back from a field work session in the bush and an American beachcomber, already drunk and hoping for more alcohol to follow. As well, there were several of Lily's siblings, half brothers and sisters with more or less mixtures of Melanesian and Chinese blood, several of their wives, husbands and children, and a blue-black young man from Buka who was hoping to enter the priesthood.

"God bless you," the priest said.

Leo kissed his bride enthusiastically. He was hot inside his stiff collar and dark suit, but Lily looked cool and demure in white. He hoped she would let him undress her; he wanted to undo the hooks and buttons that ran all the way up her slim, straight back, but he suspected that there were rituals involved in marriage that got in the way of such pleasures. As soon as he could he pressed a ten-pound note into Father O'Connor's moist hand.

"I hope you know what you're doing, my son."

For an answer Leo gave him a wink. He felt Lily's firm grip on his arm.

"We have to see my father first, dear," she said. "Then we can go to the reception."

The last word sobered Leo. "I tried for the club," he said, "but . . ."

"Never mind. At the Hong Club we have a better gramophone and Melbourne beer. We'll have a real party."

"Goodo," Leo said.

Harry Kobi Hong had suffered a stroke a few weeks before his daughter's wedding. He had never believed that the event would take place and was now probably barely capable of understanding it. But Lily needed him to understand. It would help her to keep a firm control over the business if her father could give her some sign of approval.

Still dressed in their wedding clothes, Leo and Lily entered the small bedroom behind the largest of the Hong trading stores. The smell of incense in the church had made Leo queasy and he was looking forward to a few head-clearing cold beers. The smell in the sickroom almost made him gag. The aromas of opium and ointments hung in the hot, dusty air, and dead insects crunched in the seagrass matting under Leo's feet. Lily touched his arm. "He is rotting," she whispered. "I'm sorry. Try to stand it. It's very important."

Leo swallowed, then tried to hold his breath. He did as Lily told him—shook the thin, grey claw of a hand and let the slanted eyes, clouded by cataracts, rest on his face.

Lily, shining like a pearl in her white dress, bent close to her father, kissed his cheek and whispered in his ear.

"What are you saying?" Leo asked. He had to breathe, he might as well speak.

"I'm telling him that you are an Englishman and my husband."

"Hardly English," Leo said. "I was born on a ship on the way out. Parents were English, though."

Lily nodded. "You must tell me about it." She bent and spoke again. A shiver seemed to run through the sick man. Lily called out sharply, and two of her brothers brushed aside the bead curtain and entered the room.

Harry Kobi Hong's twisted face contorted as he fought for speech. The sounds he made were like animal noises to Leo but Lily's brothers understood. They nodded, approached the bed and touched their father's hands. The sick man's eyes rolled back; he freed his hands and flapped them from his wrists like broken-winged birds. He made the noises again and drooled down his whiskery chin onto the sheet. Lily wiped his face. She twined his hands together and put them on the bedcover. She kissed his grey, furrowed cheek and signalled for Leo to move away from the bed.

When they were out of the room Lily reached up for Leo's puzzled face. She clasped it in her hands, forced it down and kissed him hard on the lips.

"Thank you. You were wonderful." Lily's passion was genuine; she had got her own way. "You'll get your reward later. And, darling, I *do* want to hear about the boat from England and your parents. Our children should know everything about their wonderful father."

44

Lily and Leo's first child was a boy, born nine months after their wedding. They named him John Gulliver Kobi Clarke but he was never called anything but Kobi. His birth was easy and the child grew quickly into a strong, graceful boy on whom the many gods in his racial background seemed to have smiled. Kobi was light-skinned, with European features that had an Oriental or Melanesian cast according to his mood and expression. When cheerful his eyes slanted slightly and something of Lily's calm came over his face; when angry his thick lips curled back from his strong white teeth and he needed only a breastplate and nosebone to complete the picture of the Bougainville raider.

Leo was ostracized by the Europeans after his marriage. As Lily was colour-barred from the club, Leo seldom went there and when his membership lapsed no one urged its renewal. In the aftermath of the war, the 'mastahs' were conscious that they were sitting on a powder keg. To the south, in the British Solomons, an indigenous nationalist movement known as Marching Rule was challenging authority and disrupting administration. The main islands of New Guinea and the Bismarck Archipelago were swept by cargo cults, some with a distinctly anti-colonial flavour.

"We must stick together," a planter would say in the club after his fourth drink. "Give 'em the right example. White an' superior in every way. That's the ticket."

This would draw nods from fellow-drinkers. The black barmen and waiters would mix drinks and serve them skilfully with their pink-nailed hands and say nothing. The whites were constantly on the watch for what they called 'cheek' from their employees, the punishment for which was the sack. Dismissal meant loss of income and prestige for the Melanesians. Few were 'cheeky' but they never conceded superiority. The better informed among them knew that these 'mastahs' were not the pick of the crop anyway.

Still, the whites were sticking together. What Leo had done by marrying a mongrel was to unstick himself. The stickers-together married white women from Australia or New Zealand or did not marry at all. Relationships with local women were kept secret, children went unacknowledged and irate kinsmen were bought off. Nothing was said to Leo, of course, but chaps with business in Kieta found occasion to take off their sunglasses and blink their eyes or stare into store windows when he was in view. Lily became 'Mrs Hong', rather than 'Mrs Clarke', to the whites who patronized her stores.

Lily was busy producing children and running the Hong enterprises that she had acquired when Harry Kobi Hong died within a month of her marriage. She had two daughters after Kobi and another son. Jenny, Sue and Harold seemed to be endowed with less vigour and personality than Kobi, but they were healthy, capable children who gave no trouble. Leo gloried in them, which was fortunate because his business languished from 1950 onwards. The supply of war materials dwindled in quality and quantity and some of the operations starting up in Bougainville demanded fresher goods.

"I'll be a rag and bone man the way things are going," Leo said to Lily, one night after she'd done a quick appraisal of his books.

"*Wonem, Papa?*" Jenny, who was eight, asked.

"Speak English," Lily snapped.

The girl's face crumpled and Leo bent to comfort her. They were in the living room of the big house, built of concrete bricks, to which they had moved after Sue's birth. Leo met the government charges and power bills but the Hong Company had paid for the house. Leo spent much of his time in the garden and Lily much of hers in the spare bedroom which she had furnished as a study. They still shared a bedroom but Leo often slept in one of his bush camps.

"Easy, love." Leo caressed his daughter's straight black hair. "She picks it up from the other kids. You know how it is."

"I do know," Lily said, "and I do not want my children growing up like kanakas."

"Right," Leo said. He still loved Lily, but had grown to fear her determination and persistence. He knew that he had given her an opening. "You're talking about their education."

Kobi, nine years of age, glowered in a corner of the room. Lily had used bribery and other forms of coercion to secure him a place in the Kieta school, the one attended by Europeans and the children of the most Anglicized Chinese. Though Kobi rapidly outstripped his contemporaries academically and was regularly beating boys years older than himself in athletic events, he was tolerated rather than accepted, and he was aware of it. Nevertheless, he did not want to leave Kieta and he knew that this was what his parents were coming around to discussing. His best friend was Mora, the son of a Buka man who worked as a labourer for his father, and a Vella Lavella mother. Mora was blacker than night and Kobi loved him and envied him his inky skin.

"Boarding school," Lily said firmly. "In Sydney if possible."

"Expensive," Leo murmured, "I was thinking about the schools in Moresby. They say . . ."

"No! Sydney for Kobi and Jenny at least. For Sue and Harry, well, we'll see." Lily had the Chinese habit of favouring the older children, regarding the others almost as understudies. Leo sensed a compromise and was willing to fall in with it. He certainly did not want all his children to leave.

"I don't want to go to Sydney," Kobi said quietly. "I want to stay here."

"The fact that you say that proves it's nearly time for you to go. There is nothing for you here, not yet. Anyhow, one day the business will be run from Sydney and this will be just one small part of it."

Leo nodded amiably although he regarded Lily's plans as fantasy. Knowing little of the Hong Company's financial dealings, he imagined them to be on no great scale. He hadn't married Lily for her money; no one could say that of him. He sometimes wondered about the quality of the furniture, the thickness of the carpets that kept the house hot and the cost of the fans that cooled it. But Leo wasn't one to worry for long about things not immediately apparent.

Kobi's face took on its stubborn Melanesian look. Jenny, precocious in her understanding of her family, knew the signs and stayed close to her father's solid legs. She had never seen her mother or brother give way on anything important and she sensed that an outright clash would come one day. This could be it.

Leo stroked his daughter's hair and lit a cigarette. He was singularly unable to pick up cues from people's behaviour and his insensitivity sometimes defused a situation. It did now. He got to his feet. "I'm going to surprise everyone and have a drink. Get you something, Lily?"

Lily smiled. She didn't want to fight Kobi until she had chosen and prepared her ground. "Yes, g'n't, please, dear. And give me a puff."

"Stunt your growth," Leo said, winking at his son. He knew that Kobi had tried smoking the strong twist tobacco rolled in newspaper, as favoured by the locals, having found Kobi vomiting behind a boatshed after the experiment. Kobi grinned at his father. Lily puffed smoke up towards the ceiling where the fan whirled it away. Jenny relaxed. Leo returned with the drinks and he and Lily chatted about a trip to Port Moresby to see 'the sights'.

"*Wonem* . . . what sights?" Jenny asked.

"Aeroplanes," Lily said quickly. She watched Kobi out of the corner of her eye. *All boys are interested in aeroplanes, surely*, she thought.

Kobi didn't react and Lily pressed. "You can fly to any part of the world from there—America, England, anywhere."

Leo had no inkling of Lily's strategy but he weighed in helpfully. "And ships," he said. "Big ships that sail all over the world."

"Like the one in Sydney?" Jenny said. "The one you were born on? The one with the *sista* who carried you in her *bilum?*"

"My mother carried me in the bag, but she wore the nurse's cloak wrapped around her and she pretended to be the nurse."

"Tell us the story again, Daddy."

Leo looked at Lily, who nodded, and at Kobi, who shrugged. He lifted his daughter into his lap. "There was a lot of sickness on the ship. Some people died. My mother and father *tru* died. No one was supposed to leave the ship, but they didn't even know I was alive. Except the nurse and my mother, not my real mother . . ."

"Mrs Violet Clarke," Lily said. "You've seen her name in Daddy's Bible."

Despite himself, Kobi acknowledged that with a nod. He'd read a good deal of the Bible and admired the copperplate writing on blank leaves at the back of the book. 'Violet Clarke *née* Sheehan dedicates this Holy Book to the life and soul of her adopted son, Leo Gulliver Clarke, baptised this day in St Matthew's Church, Woolloomooloo, New South Wales.' Kobi's retentive memory included the signatures: 'Mary O'Halloran, witness; Joseph Brady, BA, Dublin.'

"They took me off in the busiest time of the day," Leo continued. "And the hottest. I was sweating like a piglet . . ."

"Daddy!" Jenny shrieked. "You were only a baby. You can't remember."

"I remember," Leo said.

Kobi was squatting in the native way, comfortably with his weight evenly distributed. He plucked at the pile of the carpet in a way his mother found infuriating. It reminded her of the old dark men her father used to squat with; they peeled sticks, picked at sores, bored holes through shells and chuckled over ancient sexual conquests. Leo's voice was droning on. Lily looked away from Kobi's busy fingers and tried to calculate her margins on diesel fuel.

"Tell the truth," Kobi said suddenly.

"I don't know the truth, son," Leo said. "Only what my father told me."

"Mr Rusty Clarke," Jenny said.

Leo nodded and sipped his drink.

The corners of Leo's mouth turned down. "I wish I knew the truth," he said.

Lily was about to speak, to say something about writing to England to learn something about the Gulliver family, but Kobi spoke first. He'd bided his time to exact revenge for the talk of schooling in Sydney. He'd learned as much about his family from conversations with the islanders as from reading the Clarke Bible. "Tell us about your grandfather, Mum," he said. "The one who raided the west coast and killed the missionaries."

If Leo's business was in decline, the Hong Company was not. Lily had spent money on all aspects of the enterprise—refitting ships and stores, rebuilding jetties, hiring and training staff. She made it a point to discuss business with every outsider who came her way. She pumped them for information on products from outboard motors to battery-powered radios to laxative pills. She talked to a woman who had attended the Olympic Games in Melbourne and had been impressed by the rubber thong sandals worn by the Japanese swimmers. Lily had the first consignments of rubber thongs in the islands and she sold a great many at a heavily marked-up price. She also had the first chainsaws to be seen on Bougainville, and the first Polaroid sunglasses.

"Japan's the key to everything," she told Leo.

Leo was sceptical. "We beat 'em hollow," he said.

Lily smiled. "The Americans are pouring money in. They're afraid of Japan going communist. If we'd been on the Japs' side they'd be shovelling the money our way."

"Lily. Fight on *their* side?"

Lily was careful not to affront Leo's few principles too directly. "I'm joking, of course. But Japan's going to outperform everyone economically, mark my words."

"Australia'll see us right."

"Australia! Australia does what Britain and America tell her to do. The only time Australians show independence from Britain is when they play cricket."

Leo grinned. "And tennis. Beat the Yanks in the Davis Cup, didn't they?"

Lily wasn't listening. "Vehicles're the coming thing. I wonder if I could get the franchise for the Japanese four-wheel drives?"

"Old Land Rover's good enough for me," Leo said. "Never lets you down. The Japs can't make cars, can they?"

Lily smiled indulgently. "I think they can do anything, darling. And a clever person would be wise to follow along behind them for the crumbs."

"Don't like the sound of that much. I was wondering about planting. Your people've got some bits of land here 'n' there, haven't they? Think copra could make a comeback?"

Lily studied Leo over the top of her reading glasses. She had changed very little over the ten years since they married. Expenditure of physical and nervous energy kept her trim, and her Chinese genes gave her smooth, unlined features. She bought good clothes from Australia, ate and drank sparingly, and had never had a day's illness in her life. She was in her prime. Beer, gin and inactivity had thickened Leo considerably. He carried a paunch and moved slowly. Poor teeth made his breath rank and he snored when he slept. Lily was still fond of him; he was a patient and indulgent father and, in business matters the term 'silent partner' fitted him like a glove. Leo's name was on many of the documents—loans, leases, options, applications—that were the charters of Lily's commercial kingdom, but he signed everything that she put before him, and his will was in order.

"You never know," she said. "There's an island down the coast that could be right for planting. House on it, too.

The Gulliver Fortune 315

Do you fancy yourself as the ruler of an island kingdom, darling?"

Kobi was dismayed when he heard of the plans for his father to take up residence on Rabi Island. Leo had supported his resistance to Lily's plan that he should go to Australia for schooling. Now he was in his final year at the Kieta school and this change was brewing. Kobi knew his mother; he doubted that any coincidence was involved.

"She's too strong," he told Mora. "I'll have to go."

"*Nogat*," Mora said. "*Stap long hia. Yumi go long bus.*"*

Kobi shook his head. "She'd find us. She has people everywhere. Spies. People owe her money for motors and rice and tobacco and . . . everything."

Mora nodded. He took Kobi's hand and squeezed it. The boys squatted on the sand and looked at the peaceful water of their small inlet south of Kieta. It was *their* place. They took their outrigger to it whenever they could; they fished, swam, cooked their catch and slept on the beach. His friendship with Mora, and going to this place, were Kobi's major defiances of Lily. All the tensions he experienced at school and at home fell away from him here. He welcomed the sun that darkened his skin and he lapsed into the local language and pidgin as he shared the fun and work with Mora. He spoke the language now as he watched Mora roll a cigarette.

"What will you do, brother?"

Mora sighed. "I'm older than you, bigger and stronger too. Soon I'll be able to get work at the mine."

"I'll come back," Kobi said. "In the holidays and when school is finished."

Mora stirred the fire, took out a stick with a smouldering tip and lit his cigarette. A fish, wrapped in leaves, was baking in sand under the fire. "You'll change." Kobi grabbed Mora's big, black fist and wrapped his own smaller brown hands around it. "No, brother," he said fiercely. "I'll never change."

---

*"No. Stay here. We'll go into the bush."

45

Leo's last assertive act before he went into virtual seclusion on Rabi Island was to oppose Lily's wish for a Catholic education for Kobi. "Went to those places m'self," he said. "Terrible. Full of sadists and mumbo-jumbo. Send the boy somewhere else if he has to go away."

Lily reviewed the comparatively few options and decided on Newington College in Sydney. It was Methodist but liberal in outlook in all respects, except in regard to alcohol. Strict Rechabitism was written into its charter. In view of Leo's ever-increasing intake, Lily felt that some instruction in the evils of strong drink might be beneficial for his son. The Methodism was not a problem; the Clarkes' nominal Catholicism sat very lightly on Kobi. Lily did not fear spiritual confusion for him.

Kobi and Mora paddled to their beach one last time, baked fish and smoked cigarettes. They farewelled each other tearfully at the wharf. Lily and Kobi boarded the *Solomon Star*, a Hong vessel, with Jenny, who was also going to school in Sydney. The *Solomon Star* took them to Rabaul where they made a connection with the Burns Philp steamer.

Leo was on Rabi Island with Sue and Harold. He supervised the clearing and planting and worked his way through a case of beer every day. He was puzzled more than angry about the way his life had developed. His love for the children more than compensated him for the cold shoulders that were turned to him in Kieta. But after Harold's birth, Lily appeared to have no further sexual use for him. This saddened Leo and left him intermittently randy, but he knew so little of women that he imagined it to be normal. Certainly, in Leo's narrowly circumscribed world, it was normal for a man approaching fifty to have his first beer early in the morning before giving the *boss boi* his orders for the day. After that he had a beer almost hourly until sundown, when it was only reasonable to switch to something stronger and increase the pace.

Sue and Harry became accustomed to seeing their father dropping off to sleep earlier and earlier in the evening. Sometimes he slept on the verandah that overlooked the jungle-filled valley to the south of the plantation, sitting upright in a chair from late in the morning until sunset. They ran wild on the island, mostly defying the civilizing efforts of the young part-Chinese woman Lily had hired to act as their governess. After a time Miss Chan began to join Leo in his afternoon drinking, particularly after a frustrating morning session with the children. She played cards with Leo and laughed at his jokes.

"Up to the four times tables with 'em yet, Miss Chan?"

"I spent most of the morning arguing with Harold, Mr Clarke."

"What about? Care for an ale?"

"Just a small one, thank you. He insisted that six times six was sixty-six. I couldn't budge him."

"What about Suzie?"

Miss Chan sipped her beer and smiled. "She has learned bad habits from you, Mr. Clarke."

"How's that?"

"You know how you say to split the difference when there's an argument about money?"

Leo grinned and nodded.

"Suzie wanted us to split the difference between thirty-six and sixty-six."

Leo laughed. "Did she get the sum right?"

"Yes."

"You're doing a good job then. What're they doin' now?"

Miss Chan had no idea. "Sketching," she said.

"Good, good. Drink up. Lily, their mother, can draw a treat, did you know that?"

"No, Mr Clarke. I can draw too. I must show you some of my work sometime."

"Yes, yes, I'd like that." Through his beer haze Leo looked at Miss Chan. *Not a patch on Lily*, he thought, *but not bad-looking. Nice legs. And it's been so long and Lily's so far away. I wonder?* Leo poured more beer and touched the young woman's hand as he passed her the glass. "Where d'you keep your drawings, Miss Chan?"

Lily took a flat in Edgecliff for six months to be on hand while Kobi and Jenny settled in at school, although both were boarders. Jenny was attending a Catholic convent school in Neutral Bay and Lily saw her at the weekends. Kobi she saw less often; he threw himself into school activities—weekend science excursions, visits to the homes of school friends, sports meetings—so much that Lily suspected him of wanting to avoid her. Disparaging remarks she'd passed about Mora, she concluded, were the cause. She didn't care; she wanted an Australian gentleman and she would suffer some personal loss, if necessary, to get one.

Lily spent her time cultivating friendships among the business people of Sydney who were accessible to her and investigating marketing techniques and promising products. She put out feelers for contracts and franchises and made sure that the managing director of every Sydney firm with substantial Pacific interests received her card and at least one telephone call. This kept her busy. At first she performed the routine duties towards Jenny—trips to the zoo, the Botanic Gardens, Bondi beach. But after the second month she began to attend weekend business lunches and other functions. Jenny spent more and more time alone in the flat watching television. Eventually she told her mother that she'd rather stay at school.

"I'm sorry I'm so busy, darling," Lily said. "There's so much to do."

Jenny's eyes dropped to the deep pile carpet. "Like what, Mum?"

Lily waved her cigarette. "People to see. You want us to have lots of money and nice things, don't you?"

"I want to see Kobi."

Lily hugged her. "We'll have a big party before I go back . . . home. You and Kobi can invite all your friends."

Jenny could think of two possibles in her own case; her brother, she felt sure, would have *hundreds*. "When?" she said.

"Soon."

But first Lily had another party to throw. She prepared for it carefully, hiring the best caterers, getting the invitations out early and trying to select a night that didn't clash with any obviously important event. Her targets were leading figures in the Chinese business community—importers, restaurateurs, retailers and investors—and selected Australians who had connections with them. Lily's plans had grown. She envisaged shopping centres in the island capitals, office buildings, expansion of schools and other educational institutions, restaurants and clubs. All would need building and supplying. Lily felt equal to the task and hoped to convince others of her capacity—the men with the money.

The party began at eight p.m. on a Saturday night in March. It was a fine, mild night in a week that had seen business in Sydney buoyant after the usual post-Christmas and New Year slowdown. The forty-five guests, carefully selected by Lily as to age, marital status, competition and commercial arrangements, were in a good mood, ready for pleasure and for opportunities to consolidate their good fortune. They talked politics in a confident fashion—the conservative government, non-interventionist and complaisant, suited them and was firmly in control. Money was another major topic. Most thought that Australia's future still lay in minerals and other primary products; a few had an inkling of other opportunities, given the capital and right tax arrangements. Lily circulated, talking gaily, directing the waiters to top up the drinks and taking care not to outshine the wives. She hovered with groups that included some of the more adventurous thinkers. She put questions with an almost childlike candor and listened to the answers with a mind finely calibrated and totally engaged.

By ten-thirty p.m. Lily had found in Richard McGregor her perfect partner, her soulmate and banker.

Kobi's cricket match ended at five p.m. The plan for him to go to Phillip Hammersley's house for the night fell through at the last minute and in the confusion Kobi missed the bus back to school. He found himself in Ryde with money in his pocket and nothing expected of him. He had a pass for the night and most of the team members believed he was going to Hammersley's place in Epping where there was a swimming pool. No one would miss him. Kobi, at almost thirteen, was tall for his age and possessed a maturity that some of his contemporaries found daunting. Like Hammersley, his friends at school tended to be in the form above him.

He caught a bus into the city with the idea of going to King's Cross to look at the prostitutes he'd heard about from the boys at school. Then he'd have something to eat and go to the pictures. *Ben Hur* was showing. He imagined he'd finish up at his mother's flat eventually. As the bus crossed the Gladesville bridge he gazed down at the water and thought of home. Jenny might be at the flat and have news. *I wish Mora could write,* he thought.

Ben Hur was a long film, and Kobi felt like a walk afterwards.

He had things to think about. The prostitutes, with their shiny hair and tight skirts, had excited him. The purple dress one of them wore was cut so low he could see most of her bosom. Women's breasts were no novelty to him, but this was different. It was not just that most of the street women were white; their breasts were enticements, half-hidden, like secrets. One of the women had called out to him: "Hey, boy!"

He'd spun around to look at her because at home *boi* meant something else, possibly insulting. The short, wide blonde sidled across the pavement, swinging her massive hips. Her nipples poked out through her thin blouse and she smelled of perfume and cigarettes. Her red lips parted. "Gotta quid, sonny?"

"Yes," Kobi whispered.

The blonde reached for his arm. "Never too young t' start," she said.

Kobi had fled. The memory of the way she moved and smelt had stayed with him and distracted him through the early part of the film. Walking to Edgecliff and thinking about the encounter, he was aware of uncomfortable feelings in his groin. Erections were nothing new to him; he and Mora had had pissing contests and had touched each other until they grew hard. But this was different.

He could still hear the blonde's raucous laughter in his ears as he let himself into the flat with the key Lily had given him. It was well after midnight and Kobi was tired. He'd get a blanket from the cupboard in the hall and sleep on the couch, not disturb anyone. The door opened quietly and Kobi was surprised to find lights still on in the flat. He was about to call out when he heard a sound that froze him. It was a laugh, like the prostitute's, harsh and strident. He tiptoed forward and into the living room, which still bore the marks of the party, although the caterers had dealt with most of the debris. Cigarette smoke and liquor fumes still hung in the air. The laughter came again, and Kobi looked through the half-open door into his mother's bedroom.

Lily was sitting on top of a fat white man who lay on the bed. Lily laughed, pulled away, and the man's penis came out of her. It was red and distended. Lily squeezed it.

"Put it back," he said.

"It's lovely," Lily said. "I want to touch it."

"Put it in!"

Lily did; she dug her hand under his spread buttocks and probed. "Come on, Richard. Come on!"

The man convulsed, pushing Lily up like a buckjump rider. He shouted and Lily laughed again.

Kobi left the flat silently and caught a taxi back to Stanmore. He slept on top of some nets in a shed by the tennis courts and surprised the morning duty master by taking a seat for breakfast.

"Hullo, Clarke. Where did you spring from?"

"Just got back, sir."

"Fit for tennis after chapel?"

"Yes, sir."

"Goodoh. Get a proper breakfast into you."

46

The masters at Newington noticed a sudden change in Kobi Clarke. The quiet, friendly boy of the first few months was replaced by an aggressive, striving individual who won more respect than friendships. His interest in cricket and tennis lapsed, although he remained an excellent player of both games when he chose, in favour of water polo and football. He played with an equal mixture of skill and vigour and became a respected and feared competitor. In the classroom his work was consistently of a high standard. He excelled in mathematics and Latin, but was never below fifth or sixth place in the class in the other subjects.

His temper was uncertain. He rarely got into fights because the first one he had, towards the end of his second term, was over in a matter of seconds. His opponent's lip was pulped, two of his teeth were loosened and he nursed bruised ribs for ten days. 'Clarkey', a name signifying respect rather than affection, and earned in the swimming pool and on the football field, was not someone to pick on.

In his first two years in Sydney the softer side of Kobi was revealed only to his sister. Lily began to spend more time in Sydney than in Kieta; the ostensible reason was the welfare of the children, but in fact she seldom met them. Kobi saw her for as short a time and as irregularly as possible. Jenny was indifferent to her mother, happy at school and happy to meet Kobi on weekend afternoons to go for walks and to the pictures. Lily maintained the Edgecliff flat the year round, and the children sometimes spent time there in her absence.

On one such occasion Jenny opened a telegram they had found under the door.

"She'll be back next week."

"Shit!" Kobi thumped a pillow with his fist.

Jenny refolded the telegram and replaced it in the envelope. She was used to Kobi's fluctuating moods, which could run from hilarity to deep depression in a few seconds. She said nothing but looked at him.

"I hate her," Kobi said.

Jenny's smooth brow wrinkled. She looked very Chinese when she was puzzled. "Why?"

But Kobi would not tell her.

Towards the end of each term Kobi made an effort to be pleasant to one of his schoolfellows and he had no difficulty in securing an invitation to spend the holidays in his company. In this way he acquired a knowledge of eastern Australia. He stayed on farms in the Monaro, at houses on the Palm Beach peninsula and the south coast, and visited Melbourne, Canberra and Brisbane. Lily, foreseeing useful contacts in the Australian establishment, approved and was generous with money. She was unfailingly charming to the parents she met and it did not escape Kobi's notice that, on these occasions, her hair, clothes and makeup were designed to make her look as Occidental as possible.

For three years Kobi did not return to Bougainville. Jenny did and kept him up to date with developments there. Kobi was little interested in the expanding Hong businesses or the stagnation on Rabi Island. His question to his sister was always the same: "What's Mora doing?"

Jenny made a point of knowing. "Still at the mine," she said in her 1962 report, "but he wants to quit."

"Wish the bugger could write," Kobi muttered.

"I think he'd learn if you told him to," Jenny said.

* * *

Nothing had gone right on Rabi Island. The clearing was harder than it should have been, owing to outcrops of rock and the presence of ticks that put many of the labourers into the sick bay. Eventually planting got under way, but the trees failed to thrive. Many reasons were given—the soil, the wind, microscopic infestations, even the presence of spirits who did not want the white man to make money out of this bit of land. Leo battled the odds gamely, helped by a reasonable cash flow from the Hong company, but he knew he was losing.

Lily seldom visited him during her infrequent and short trips to Kieta. Sue and Harry played in the labour lines, often slept there and quickly became indistinguishable from the plantation workers' children. They were scrubbed up and presented to Lily on her visits. She was appalled by their shy, foot-twitching awkwardness.

"Leo, they're kanakas!" Lily exclaimed.

Sue and Harry turned and ran. Lily raged at her husband and Miss Chan. She wanted to dismiss the woman, but Leo dug in his heels.

"You frightened them, dear," he said. "They get on very well with Sally. They do their lessons . . . well, sometimes."

Lily could see which way the wind was blowing and she was wise enough to trim her sails to it. It suited her to have Leo semi-occupied and out of the way. There seemed to be no hope for Sue and Harry, with their sun-darkened faces, their shins scarred by mosquito bites, with scrub cuts and cropped hair. But she had Kobi and Jenny gaining in sophistication every day. She forced herself to be calm and accepted a tepid gin and tonic (Leo's kerosene refrigerator was giving trouble).

"I'm sorry, dear," she said. "I'm anxious about one thing and another. I'm sure the children are healthy and . . ."

"Should see Harry swim," Leo muttered. The beer he was drinking was his tenth for the day and it wasn't yet noon. News of Lily's surfside arrival had shaken him. "Like a bloody fish."

"I'm sure," Lily said. "And you're satisfied with Miss Chan, are you?"

Leo looked at her blearily. He was having trouble with his eyes lately, finding it hard to focus. And his bladder. He was thin, despite the amount of beer he consumed. These days, drink tended to make him belligerent. "Entirely," he said.

"Good." Lily drained her drink with a shudder. She was sure the water used to make the ice wasn't clean. "Perhaps I could just have a word with her before I go. I have to get back to town—some dreary thing in the administrator's office. Queen's birthday drinks, I think."

"Invited to that, are you?"

Lily smoothed the skirt of her white suit. "Times are changing, Leo."

"Goodoh," Leo said without much understanding of what she meant. "Well, you can pop in and see Sally. Her room's down the hall on the right."

Lily touched his unshaven cheek with her gloved hand before she left the room. She found Sally Chan's door open; the woman was sitting on her bed smoking a cigarette. She wore a white dress with a full pleated skirt and short sleeves. Lily noticed that her fingernails were long and painted bright red. Her toenails, visible in the high-heeled, open-toed sandals, were the same colour.

"Miss Chan, may I come in?"

Sally Chan waved the cigarette. "You've come to dismiss me."

"On the contrary." Lily entered the big room and noted and appraised the contents swiftly. *Likes nice things*, she thought. *Can't really afford them.* "How much are you being paid, Miss Chan?"

"Ten pounds a week, Mrs Clarke."

"I will pay you double, as of now, to keep Mr Clarke happy."

"Mrs Clarke?"

"Don't take me for a fool, girl. I can see what's going on. All right. It suits me. Can the children read and write?"

Sally Chan nodded.

Lily smiled. "Then you're doing an excellent job. I want to pay you twenty pounds a week and a bonus at the end of the year. I hope you're happy here?"

"Your husband is a good man, Mrs Clarke."

"I'm sure he is. We have an arrangement, then?"

"Yes."

"There is one more thing." Lily shifted on the bed to bring herself closer. She lowered her voice and spoke in Chinese. "If you become pregnant I will cut your heart out."

Sally Chan gasped and drew away. She had no doubt that Lily meant what she said, and the Hong influence among the Kieta Chinese was powerful enough for Lily to have such an act carried out. But she recovered quickly from the shock of the unveiled threat; she was safe.

"Do not worry, Mrs Clarke. I won't become pregnant. Mr Clarke is sick and he cannot make love."

"What do you do, then?" Lily had acquired an interest in unorthodox sex as a consequence of her relationship with Richard McGregor, who needed extra stimulation to perform satisfactorily.

Sally Chan stubbed out the cigarette that had burned unnoticed in her fingers. "I . . . make love to myself and Mr Clarke watches me."

"That's all?"

"Yes."

Lily got off the bed. "You say Leo's sick. In what way?"

"He makes water all the time and has a terrible thirst. He is losing weight. And he's impotent. I think he has cirrhosis."

"Does he know this?"

"I mentioned something once. He said that people with cirrhosis cannot drink and that he would rather be dead."

Lily sat down again and studied the young woman, looking for clues to her character. She detected intelligence and suspected greed, but what was the balance? *Risky, but worth the risk*, Lily thought. She opened her handbag and produced a chequebook. "Miss Chan," she said, "I think you should be paid your increased salary retrospectively for, let us say, six months. And I'm sure you have already earned a substantial bonus."

"Thank you, Mrs Clarke."

Lily scribbled with a gold pen. She tore out the cheque and put it on the bed. "I have a generous nature, you'll find, apart from being good to my employees. I think that people with serious illnesses should be . . . indulged, not upset. Don't you agree?"

Lily Chan looked down at the cheque. The amount was double what she had expected. She picked up the cheque and folded it. "Yes, Mrs Clarke," she said. "I do agree."

47

His father's death in 1962 brought Kobi, almost sixteen, back to New Guinea. Wearing a dark suit, collar and tie and his heavy black school shoes, he stood with his mother and brother and sisters in the sweltering heat of a tropical afternoon while Leo was buried in the Catholic section of the Kieta cemetery. Only Lily and Kobi were dry-eyed. Jenny had seen her father on holidays and loved him; for Sue and Harry he was the only parent they really knew. They stood a little apart from their mother, beside Sally Chan, who was slim and elegant in her black dress.

Kobi's feelings were mixed. He knew his father had been a kind man, but he wished he had been a stronger one. He was embarrased for him as a cuckold and hostile towards him as a European. He glanced at his mother, who touched her eyes with a lace-edged handkerchief which Kobi knew would be bone dry. *Probably a going-away gift from Richard McGregor,* he thought. He wondered whether his father had known of Lily's infidelity. When the priest had finished reading he closed the Bible and looked at Lily. She shook her head. The priest bent, took up some of the dark, sandy soil thrown up around the grave and dropped it onto the coffin.

The family moved away. Kobi heard his mother's firm, clear voice mention a headstone. The priest touched him on the shoulder.

"This was your father's, my son. You should have it." He handed Kobi the Bible with Violet Clarke's copperplate writing in the back. Kobi took it and muttered his thanks.

"Speak up," Lily said.

Kobi's look was pure hatred. Lily almost stopped in her tracks. The boy's eyes burned under his heavy brows and his nose seemed to flare. Kobi was almost six feet tall and well built. Lily suddenly realized that things had changed. With a strong flow of capital assured through the agency of Richard McGregor, she was in a position to expand rapidly in New Guinea and beyond. The prospect excited her but she realised that she was seeing not just the few years ahead, but the far future. Kobi's future. She had determined to put some energy into controlling and influencing her son. That beetling look he'd shot her was therefore disconcerting. *What did he know? And what did he care about?* Lily decided that her first task was to get to know him.

The drinking and eating back at the house—a still-bigger house now, high on the hill overlooking the town—were conducted quietly, but with no expense spared. Lily had invited certain members of the European community to attend and most of them, although Leo's choices in life had made them uncomfortable, found no difficulty in being polite about his exit. Lily circulated easily, talking generalities, and stopping occasionally in mid-sentence as if grief had cut in on her.

Kobi sneaked a beer and admired her performance. He was hot, sweating and tired, having arrived in Kieta just hours before the burial after rushed flights from Sydney and Port Moresby. He wanted to find Mora but he doubted that he could stay on his feet much longer. Especially after the third beer.

Sally Chan took Sue and Harry away after they had wordlessly met several of the guests and forced down some food. Kobi eyed her with interest. His approval was engaged by her kindness to his little sister and brother, but that soon changed to a different appreciation. Sally moved sinuously, with a sway to her lean hips that reminded him of the King's Cross whores, whom he'd often looked at but had not touched. Her hair was a glossy black and the fullness of her lips contrasted interestingly with her thin, slanting eyes.

Kobi watched her, and Lily watched him.

Sally Chan was naturally apprehensive after Leo's death. Her position on Rabi Island had been comfortable and agreeable to her. She was not of a sociable disposition, had something of the miser in her, and was inclined to be lazy about sex and other matters. She was not looking forward to the life of a schoolteacher which, she anticipated, was in store for her after Lily had given her her notice and, with luck, her last bonus. She sat apprehensively in Lily's study and was surprised to be granted a smile and a cigarette from Lily's gold case.

"I understand Leo resisted seeing a doctor until it was far too late?" Lily fitted a cigarette into an ebony holder.

"Yes, Mrs Clarke."

"Most unwise. I hope you are not thinking of leaving us."

Sally Chan puffed on her cigarette and said nothing. She was afraid of Lily's power and wondered whether, now that she could be of no further use, something worse than schoolteaching might await her.

"I want you to continue your work with Sue and Harold," Lily said. "They are most promising."

They were half wild, as both women knew. Sally Chan nodded. "There is room for improvement."

Lily nodded. "Always. I won't be in Kieta very much in the foreseeable future, and with my husband gone your responsibilities will increase. You will live here with everything paid for. I'm considering a raise in your salary."

If this was a bribe for her silence and inactivity over Leo's health, Sally Chan was very ready to accept it. "Thank you, Mrs Clarke."

"And bonuses as before, of course. There is something I want you to do to earn the first bonus."

Feeling more confident, Sally Chan stubbed the cigarette out in the ashtray on Lily's desk. She raised her eyebrows, which had been plucked to a fine line.

"You met my eldest son, Kobi. He's almost sixteen. I think he should know something about life apart from what he learns at school. Do you follow me?"

Sally Chan had found the tall, clean-featured boy attractive. "I think I do," she said.

"He is a nice boy, but secretive, and I suspect he harbours some resentment against me. I'd like you to get close to him and find out what he thinks. I'd like a regular report. Do you think you can manage that?"

Sally Chan reached across the desk for Lily's cigarette case, opened it and took one. "How close?" she said.

Sally Chan opened the door of her room in the new Kieta hotel to Kobi Clarke. She wore a white, tight-fitting cheong-sam slit to mid-thigh, with smoke-coloured stockings and white, spike-heeled shoes. Her hair hung thick and loose to her shoulders.

"Hello, Kobi." She put out her hand. When Kobi took it he noticed the long red fingernails and felt them scratch lightly against his palm.

"Hello, Miss Chan. You wanted to see me? Is it about Sue and Harry?"

"No." Sally Chan drew him into the room and pushed the door shut. "It's about you."

"Me?"

"Haven't you seen me looking at you? Didn't you wonder about it?"

Kobi had not seen. After the rituals, a genuine grief for his father's death came and preoccupied him for several days. Then he had set about getting to know his younger sister and brother again. More recently his thoughts were of Mora, who was due in Kieta in a few days on holiday from his job in a timber mill in Ysabel in the British Solomons. Kobi was too polite to say so to the woman, so he smiled and said nothing.

"How old are you, Kobi?" Sally Chan was backing away slowly towards the bed. It was natural for Kobi to move towards her.

"Nearly sixteen."

"Good." She stopped; Kobi stopped. She took a step towards him and put her arms around his neck. Even with her high heels she had to reach up. She kissed him, pressing her thick lips hard against his mouth. She moved her slim, firm body so that it pressed against his groin.

Several years of sexual longing rose up in Kobi. Clumsily he returned the kiss; the feeling of her lips on his sent thrills through his body. He put his hands on her buttocks and ground himself against her, feeling the hard bones and the softness between them.

"Oh, yes," she said. "What a big boy. What a man."

Her dress was fastened on one shoulder and she reached up and undid the hook. Kobi saw her smooth, ivory-coloured skin rise from the falling white silk. His groin was aching. She undid hooks below her arm, moved the top of the dress away and pulled it down. Things began to blur for Kobi. His mouth went dry. He felt her hands on him. She guided his hands as he touched her. His fingers went to the catch of her brassiere and slid under the band of her panties. She used him to undress herself slowly and then she worked his clothes off jerkily and impatiently.

He'd been swimming several times and was dark except where his trunks had covered him. Sally Chan took his penis in her hand and felt it slacken. Kobi looked at her with stricken eyes.

"First time?" she said.

Kobi nodded.

"Don't worry. Lie down."

They sank onto the bed and Sally put her mouth close to his ear. "The first time isn't easy," she said. "It's not like in the books. Girls go dry and boys go soft. It's normal."

Kobi nodded. He felt ashamed of his softness and wanted to run away. "I'm sorry," he said.

"Silly. Have you ever seen a woman's nipples go hard?"

Kobi shook his head.

"Look. Look closely. Touch."

Kobi did. His long fingers touched the taut, erect flesh. "Nice?"

Kobi nodded. Sally took his hand and guided it to her mouth; she kissed his fingers and made them wet with her saliva, then she put his hand between her legs and showed him how to stroke her. She moaned as his fingers moved and began to squeeze his penis gently. She took his free hand and put it on her breast. Kobi was entranced by the feel of her, the smoothness. Before he was aware of it he was hard again, and Sally Chan had spread herself and guided him inside her. "Try to hold it," she whispered. "Stop if you have to."

"I can't," Kobi gasped.

"Try, but if you can't . . . Oh! Yes. Yes. Go on. Yes!"

Afterwards she told him how wonderful it had been for her. Kobi wanted to do it again; he was sure he could last longer. Sally held him off and got him talking. He told her about Mora, although his friend was now a long way from his thoughts. Sally probed gently into his feelings for his family and for his mother in particular. Kobi was guarded. He was ardent, but Sally claimed she had things to do and that he'd have to wait until the evening. She sent him away feeling like a god or a worshipper, or both.

Kobi's meeting with Mora wasn't satisfactory. His head was full of thoughts of Sally's body and Mora was disappointed to find Kobi inattentive to his talk. He had worked throughout the Solomons in a variety of capacities and had met some of the Marching Rule leaders in the south. He was angry about the exploitation of his people.

"We work and get nothing. The white men don't work and get everything."

Kobi was rusty in the language and pidgin. He stumbled and made half-hearted responses. Mora had grown and wore a beard; he could drive a truck and had got drunk in Honiara and Gizo. He invited Kobi to drink with him in the hot room behind one of the Chinese stores, where the locals were served beer in paper cups.

"So we can't break the glasses when we fight," Mora said. "Also because they hold less than a proper glass, so the Chinese bastard makes more money."

The beer was warm and made Kobi feel sick. He refused a cigarette; he wanted to keep his breath sweet for Sally. "My father died," he said.

"I heard. I'm sorry. He was all right, for a white man."

Kobi was suddenly aware that Mora had disparaged the whites and the Chinese. That left only the Melanesians. Kobi wasn't feeling particularly close to his big, black friend at the moment. *I'm much darker than Sally*, he thought. *I wonder what she thinks.*

Mora came back with four cups. "How's your mother?"

Kobi looked at the beer and felt sick. The only thing he wanted to do was get between Sally's legs, but the question made him think. *Chinese like my mother. Maybe like me.* "She's all right," he said. "Getting richer."

Mora scowled and drank one of the cups in a long gulp. "It's all wrong," he said. "It's one of the things that's going to change around here."

Kobi spent every possible minute of the next three days and nights with Sally Chan, and it wasn't enough for him. They made love six times a night and he was ready for more in the morning. Sally enjoyed her assignment; after his initial clumsiness, Kobi proved to be a good and considerate lover and the intrigue involved added to the spice. She talked to the boy between bouts of lovemaking, and after swimming and eating; she had beer in her room and she loosened Kobi's tongue with it.

"I saw her with a white man in Sydney," Kobi told her. "Fat. Disgusting."

"Your father was sick," Sally said. "Women have needs."

"All she needs is money and power," Kobi said. "I hate her."

Sally's reports to Lily were edited. She was intelligent enough to know the threat to the messenger who brought bad news. She spoke of 'disaffection', 'feelings of confusion and desertion', and gave Lily the impression that Kobi's attitudes to her were adverse but not irreversible.

"He seems much less fierce than before," Sally said. "I think I'm a good influence on him."

Lily nodded. She regarded Sally Chan as a slut with a short-lived usefulness. "Try to find out what he sees himself doing, say, five years from now," she said.

One of Sally's sessions with Lily was overheard by Jenny, who had read all the signs accurately anyway. She had talked a lot with Sue and Harry and had pieced together from their guileless chatter a clear picture of Sally Chan's role in Lily Kobi Hong Clarke's grand plan.

"She's spying on you," Jenny told Kobi as they worked over some of the school exercises they had been set by the Sydney teachers. Both were going to miss the early weeks of the first term.

"Who?" Kobi said.

"Sally Chan."

Kobi blushed under his tan. "I don't know what you mean."

"It's time you learned something, Kobe," Jenny said. "Women have brains too, they're not just . . . cunts."

Kobi's head jerked up. He had never expected to hear such a word from his convent-educated sister. "Jenny, don't . . ."

"Bullshit, Kobe. Don't you think Mum has brains? Don't you think she can plan things out, try to get her own way?"

Kobi nodded. He pushed his exercise book away, sensing that Jenny was going to tell him something important. He was as hot for Sally as ever, but he *had* wondered about some of the questions she was asking him lately.

"I'm sorry, Kobe. I can see that you like her. But she's Mum's spy. I heard them talking. She reports to Mum on everything you say. And Mum gives her money."

Kobi's brain seized. He felt a blind rage that was directed towards his mother, Sally, even Jenny. He snapped three pencils and tore up every piece of paper within reach. Jenny got a bottle of beer from the fridge and opened it. Lily was in Lae talking business. Sue and Harry were asleep. The servants slept in separate quarters at the bottom of the garden. Jenny poured a glass of beer and handed it to Kobi.

"You're going to see her later tonight, aren't you?"

Kobi drank some beer and nodded.

"Harry says she stopped Dad from going to a doctor."

"Jesus," Kobi said. "You mean they killed him—Sally and Mum?"

Jenny poured herself a small glass of beer. "I think so. Sort of."

Kobi finished his beer and stood. His forehead was wrinkled with pain and concentration; his brows seemed to hang heavily over hooded, troubled eyes. He passed his hand over Jenny's sleek, straight hair and touched her cheek.

"What are you going to do?" Jenny said. His heavy, menacing look frightened her.

"Don't worry, Jen," he said. "Nothing silly. I'm going to see Mora."

48

Vila, Vanuatu, October 1986

Kobi Hong Clarke read again the letter he had received from Australia that morning.

Dear Dr Clarke
 I thought you might be interested in the enclosed items from the Australian press.
 You will recall that, when you so kindly granted me an interview last year, we reached an agreement that I would not publish the results of my researches into your antecedents. In return you were to place me in a privileged position in respect of any information I might seek with regard to movement for the independence of the Northern Solomons of which you are the leader.
 I hope you have found this a comfortable arrangement, as I have.
 However, Mr Cromwell's quest for descendants of John Gulliver appears to me to place things in a different light. From sources I am not at liberty to reveal, I have discovered that a great deal of money is involved. I imagine that you will wish to make a claim on the estate in order to secure funds for your Movement.
 This will involve you in certain revelations

which may not, at first sight, seem to be to your political advantage.

May I suggest, Dr Clarke, that my services as a Public Relations Officer might be of use to you at this time.

I await your reaction with interest while extending to you my very best wishes.

The letter was signed by Roderick Boon whom Kobi Clarke, in middle age and after more than twenty years in politics, regarded as one of the most oily characters he had met. He dropped the letter onto his desk and got up to pace about the room. His office was on the top floor of a building on Charles de Gaulle Avenue. From its large windows he could look down on Vila and observe politics, finance, history and race in action, Pacific style. He was an exile, a thousand miles from Bougainville, and he remembered every step on the path that had put him there.

After learning of his mother's machinations, Kobi sought out Mora and spent the next month with him. He travelled, talked to miners and boatmen, bushmen and plantation workers. He emerged from the month as a radical Bougainville nationalist. He was anti-European, anti-Chinese, anti-capitalist and very angry. At Mora's urging he made an apparent peace with Lily and went back to Australia to finish his education.

"We'll need men like you," Mora said. "After men like me throw the bastards out."

Kobi returned to school and channelled his anger. He was a sports star, a school prefect and captain of the debating team. He matriculated with honours in economics, mathematics and history. He documented every racial slur he suffered and he took a keen interest in his mother's burgeoning business affairs. Lily imagined he was preparing himself for an active role in the firm. Only Jenny knew that Kobi was planning to bankrupt her.

On Kobi's holiday visit to Bougainville at the end of his last school year Mora, now a forceful member of several subversive political organizations, managed finally to convince Kobi that Lily was too small a target. Kobi had his revenge on his mother by refusing to take up the scholarship he had won and the place he had earned in the law school of the University of Sydney. Instead, he went bush; he worked on boats around the islands, in the mines and in the massive timber felling and milling operations that proliferated in the 1960s. As a share-owning member of the Loloru Co-operative Society, he was bound in brotherhood to other Bougainvilleans who wanted an end to European commercial and political domination.

The Lolorus' ideas were eclectic. They borrowed from the Marching Rule movement, from Black power, from the John Frum cargo cult in the New Hebrides and from the writings of Marx and Mao. Kobi was one of the number of Lolorus who attended the University of Papua New Guinea in the late 1960s. By this time Lily was based in Sydney. She was spared the shame of seeing her son attending classes in quonset huts and wading through mud to hear lecturers who wore Hawaiian shirts and plastic sandals. Kobi was an activist on the new campus; he was frequently suspended for breaches of discipline, and took leaves of absence to work on village projects at home. It took him five years to gain his BA degree in economics but he was awarded first-class honours and his dissertation on the self-sufficiency of subsistence economies was accepted for publication in an influential Australian academic journal.

Kobi did not attend the graduation ceremony. He refused the tutorship he was offered by the Economics Department of the university. After consultation with Mora and other Loloru leaders, he joined the administration as a clerk in the Department of Finance. Kobi sweated in hot offices while his white counterparts lounged about with one-third of his workload, in air-conditioned comfort, at twice his salary. He remembered this as the most frustrating period of his life. He was learning daily how the system operated to the detriment of the local people and to the advantage of the expatriate residents and the foreign capitalists. He longed for action but Mora and Timothy Keriaka, a part-Tongan Bougainvillean who was one of the chief spokesman and policy formulators of Loloru, urged caution.

"You can't afford to get a police record," Keriaka said after he'd argued for hours with Kobi. Kobi had wanted to join in a demonstration in Port Moresby against the dispossession of some squatters from a shanty settlement.

"Why?" Kobi said.

"Independence is just around the corner," Keriaka said. "You know that."

"Independence!" Kobi blew smoke and sneered. "Exchanging white *mastas* for black."

"Maybe. But the independent parliament could be interesting. Loloru will need to be represented."

Kobi stared at the big, fleshy man. At five foot eleven Kobi was taller than most Bougainvilleans and a tall man in New Guinea generally. He had played football for the university team and that, plus his poor head for alcohol, had helped to keep him lean. Keriaka's Polynesian ancestry was displayed in his six-foot-two stature and eighteen-stone figure.

"Parliament is for pricks," Kobi said.

Keriaka nodded. "Pricks need watching."

The Lolorus' newsletter was written in pidgin, English and several island dialects, and widely distributed throughout Bougainville. In it the movement claimed that if one-tenth of the money that was conceded to foreign capitalist enterprises on Bougainville by the administration had been allotted directly to the people, the island would be prosperous and yield four times the present tax revenue. The formulas had been worked out by Kobi Clarke, who had submitted a thesis to the university on the topic in 1973 and had been awarded the degree of Doctor of Philosophy.

The Lolorus resisted independence, calling for a United Nations investigation of the injustice of the colonial carve-up of Melanesia. They burned the flags of Australia, Germany, Great Britain, the United States and Japan, in a ceremony on the waters of Empress Augusta Bay on the day independence was granted to Papua New Guinea. They boycotted the first election and burned Michael

Somare in effigy after he became the first Prime Minister of the new nation.

Jenny Clarke Sayers, now a graduate of the University of Queensland and married to an American law lecturer at the UPNG, took a job on the Prime Minister's staff, to her brother's disgust.

"He's a puppet," Kobi said. "The strings are pulled by Canberra and Washington."

They were sitting in the shady courtyard behind the comfortable Sayers house on the campus. "That's ridiculous," Jenny said. "You know nothing about it. He's a Niuguinian."

Kobi lifted his hands in a gesture of resignation. He had never learned to trust women; he had respect for their judgment but not for their motives. He would think over what Jenny had said. Meanwhile they chatted about Sue, who was happy working as the assistant manager of a Port Moresby hotel in which Lily had an interest, and Harry, who was setting up a fish-processing operation in Lae.

"They inherited the commercial instinct." Jenny refused a cigarette, although she had always been a keen smoker.

Kobi lit up. "What did we inherit?"

"The political instinct," Jenny said. She smiled at her brother who, she thought, looked older than his thirty years. *I wonder what he does for sex*, she thought. "I'm pregnant, Kobe. I hope I've inherited the maternal instinct from somewhere."

Kobi congratulated her and went away to think. He was staying with a Bougainvillean family in Hohola, resisting the pressures on him to apply for promotion within the administration, to buy a house, to marry. When Timothy Keriaka visited him the next day and revealed a plan, it seemed like an omen, a predestined course. He told Keriaka what Jenny had said. Keriaka was an enthusiastic watcher of Hollywood westerns, which were popular in local cinemas around the islands.

"More sheriffs got killed in the saloons than out in the street," he said.

Kobi nodded.

The Gulliver Fortune

Dr Clarke took his seat in the House of Assembly in 1977 as an independent member for South Bougainville, but no one with any knowledge of PNG affairs was unaware of his connection with Loloru.

Kobi turned away from the window and lit a cigarette. *How wrong Jenny was*, he thought. His political instinct was as uncertain as a rice harvest, as fragile as the shell money he had learned to make during a time in the Trobriands he now looked back on as idyllic. Everything had gone wrong and he was to blame.

The Loloru political programme was confused, to put it mildly. Some members believed passionately in Bougainville separatism, others in a Melanesian federation that would become a force in the Pacific. Arguments raged about the status of the inhabitants of the Polynesian outliers—Tikopia, Rennel and Bellona—within such a Melanesian bloc. And what of the Fijians, with their many ties to Tonga? Holders of these different views were united only in their opposition to the enemy—the European and Asian wielders of economic power.

It was the task of the educated Lolorus, Timothy Keriaka, Kobi Clarke and others, to resolve these questions, and they failed. Keriaka, himself part Polynesian, became heated when the racial and cultural questions came under discussion. Mora moved increasingly towards a militant, industrial-muscle position, claiming that, with the right funds and backing, he could bring capitalist enterprise in Melanesia to a halt. Kobi became enmeshed in parliamentary duties—committees, sub-committees. Increasingly he lost the feel for the grass roots politics that had inspired him. He found Mora crude and Keriaka insular.

As well he was beset by personal problems. After his treacherous introduction to the pleasures of the body by Sally Chan, Kobi had gone into a long sexual hibernation. He had tried prostitutes in Moresby and Honiara with lamentable results. A promising relationship with a woman of mixed European-Chinese and Melanesian ancestry failed when Kobi was hopelessly impotent with her. On a visit to

Sydney, ostensibly to attend his mother's wedding to Richard McGregor, Kobi conducted an experiment. He was incapable with Asian, Aboriginal and Maori prostitutes and randily rampant with their white counterparts.

The discovery devastated him as much as Lily's marriage disgusted him. His mother now lived in Point Piper, a blue chip Sydney suburb, with a swimming pool, servants and a twenty-four-hour limousine service. Kobi got drunk at the reception and insulted his stepfather. He singled out the blonde wife of an advertising executive and fucked her in one of the many spare rooms in Richard McGregor's mansion, which adjoined Lily's. The combined value of the real estate was more than two million dollars. Kobi called for a taxi and left twenty cents for his mother by the phone.

Back in New Guinea, Dr Clarke proved to be an unruly subject. His expertise and ability put him on various government committees, but his opinion was always dissenting and his behaviour usually disruptive. In the turbulence of economic and political change in the early 1980s, as Somare's fortunes rose and ebbed and the government wrestled with the problems of refugees from Irian Jaya, with international fishing disputes and urban crime, Kobi Clarke was merely an irritant. An effort to placate him with a minor ministry failed when he attempted to replace all expatriate officers in the department with locals. On an overseas tour he made statements in Britain about republicanism that embarrassed his leader in Port Moresby. On his return an increasingly conservative mood in Niuguini politics threatened to sideline Kobi and the Lolurus.

Then came the scandal and the running and the strikes that turned into battles as bloody as the old raids before the white men came.

Kobi picked up the telephone and spoke to the secretary whom the Vanuatu government had provided, along with this office and his comfortable apartment. He was under no illusions about the true loyalty of the secretary.

"Would you please send someone to my home to fetch the Bible from the bookshelf in the living room."

"The Bible, Dr Clarke?" The secretary had seen no signs of piety in Kobi; rather the reverse.

"The Bible," Kobi said. "The good book. There is only one."

He replaced the phone and thought back to the scandal and Josephine Timson. The whitest woman he had ever seen, Josephine was the wife of an Australian army officer on secondment to the PNG military as an adviser. She had white hair and eyes so pale it seemed unlikely that they could see. But they could, and they had fixed on Kobi Clarke the minute he had come into range. His passion for her long, pale body was like the craving for a drug. Their affair was blatant, unlike the discreet dalliances with European women Kobi had conducted hitherto. But there were other husbands with grievances who joined Arthur Timson the night he came to the Gateway Hotel with a gun.

Kobi still had nightmares about the shattering glass and the blood that spurted from Josephine's throat when the bullets hit her. He was wounded himself but he managed to get out of the house before the attackers set it on fire. After that it was running though the hot night, hiding in gardens and hasty phone calls. Then a night departure for Bougainville on a stinking copra boat, only to land in the middle of Mora's most extreme piece of adventurism. The Lolorus provoked a strike which divided the miners and resulted in bitter clashes between gangs of workers and strike-breakers hired by the management. Spending his days and nights in a haze of alcohol and guilt, Kobi fought alongside Mora without regard for his life or the welfare of the miners. Inevitably, it was a losing fight. The troops imposed control at the cost of a dozen lives, one of them Mora's. Kobi escaped into exile in Vanuatu.

Kobi shivered in the air-conditioned office. He'd been in Vanuatu for how long? A year? It seemed like ten. Mora was dead and Timothy Keriaka was in Libya. What was expected of him? Suicide had seemed like a viable option to him for some time. What was he? A politician without a constituency. An economic theorist without any faith in theory. And who was he? A black man who could have sex only with white women. Why? He knew the reason lay back in his adolescence, with his mother and Sally Chan, and he hated the knowledge. But in a way the bitterness of the past kept him going. He entertained a fantasy he could not shake. Sometimes it seemed more real to him than the world around him. In the fantasy, he was at the head of the Hong business empire. He had total power and was in the process of slowly turning each and every one of the profitable enterprises into co-operatives which would work for the benefit of Bougainvilleans.

A discreet knock came on the door and Kobi answered. The secretary, a handsome woman from Tana who was attracted to Dr Clarke and could not understand why he treated her like a piece of machinery, entered the room and put the Bible on his desk.

"Thank you," Kobi said.

The secretary nodded; her high-piled bushy black hair bobbed. She flashed her fine eyes at the tall man standing by the window. "You have a meeting with the Minister at twelve, Dr Clarke."

"Thank you."

The secretary could not understand how such an attractive man could be so boring. She had had practically nothing to report on him since she'd taken up her position. She would willingly have tried to alleviate his quite apparent sadness, and not just for the information she might gather.

Kobi watched the door close behind her slim back. He sat down at the desk and pulled Boon's letter, the newspaper cuttings and the Bible towards him. The letter had come to him privately and by hand. Roderick Boon was aware of how things worked for political exiles in Vanuatu. Kobi read the articles over carefully. Then he reacquainted himself with the entries written in copperplate on the blank leaves at the front of the book. He was in no doubt that he was John Gulliver's grandson and that

The Gulliver Fortune

he could prove it. He sat back and the fantasy filled his head. Enough money and luck could make it a reality. It had been a long time since Kobi Clarke felt that he could tap into a source of money and luck, but he had that feeling now.

'Harwich Seascape'

49

London, November 1986

Jerry had used the key to Montague Cromwell's house several times since her discovery of the letter from Amnesty International; Ben's sense of security did not improve. After she found the first of Kobi Clarke's telegrams, Jamie Martin telephoned Montague. He told him that he and Jerry knew about the Bolivian and New Guinean heirs and were determined to see fair dealing.

"Absolutely," Montague said. "Absolutely right. Everything should be perfectly above board."

"What does Ben say?"

"Haven't seen him for a few days," Montague said. He raised an eyebrow at Ben who was in the room with him, pouring an outsized Scotch. "But I think we're of one mind. By the way, would you like to meet this chap Faraday? He's arrived in London, you know."

"I would," Jamie said.

"Right. Well, Ms Gee and Dr Clarke are due in a couple of days, we'll all have a little pow-wow, shall we?"

Montague hung up. Ben advanced on him, holding his glass like a weapon. "Are you crazy? What did you do that for?"

"They know everything. You've been careless as usual. Your former bedmate's looked through your letters, it seems."

"Shit! She's got a key. I forgot to get it back."

Montague poured himself a more moderate measure of Scotch and lit a cigar. "Time for some thinking, Ben. Your brilliant idea of giving that interview really paid off. Now the cake has to be cut five times."

Ben drank and did the mental arithmetic. "I make it four times. Faraday hasn't got a direct interest."

"Correct, but I've had some bad news from the lawyers—it seems that they've had to make a settlement with some of the other Gullivers for the sake of keeping the peace and preventing any litigation. Five ways. And it gets worse. The lawyers are now saying that I have to extract my commission from consenting parties."

"What the fuck does that mean?"

"The Gullivers don't consent; Ms Gee and Juan La Vita do—tentatively, I may add. I doubt that the Russian and the gentleman from the Antipodes will. Say the painting fetches six million, we are now looking at at least ten per cent of two shares. Call it two hundred and fifty thousand, all up."

Ben sat down heavily. Some of the whisky slopped out of his glass onto his trousers. "I was hoping for a lot more than that."

"We *need* a lot more, laddie. I've spent money on this thing and I'm overextended in all directions."

"What d'you mean?"

Montague waved his cigar. "Business. I had expectations, so I thought. I . . . speculated."

"You got into hock."

Montague leaned down over Ben's chair. "Something has to be done. Two hundred and fifty thousand will be swallowed up like that." He snapped his fingers. "As things stand, there's *nothing* in this for me, and that means nothing for you!"

"Christ," Ben said. "You've really screwed it up."

"You bear part of the blame. Martin was the wrong man to hire and Jerry was the wrong girl to fuck. You should have had a policy of containment."

Ben finished what was left in his glass and stood up to get more. He brushed his father aside and laughed. "Containment. You don't know what you're talking about."

"Maybe not," Montague said. "I didn't have a rich father to pay for an expensive education."

"You paid bugger all. As often as not, Monique had to cover your cheques."

"The fact remains, you've got the education and you know what the words mean. Perhaps you understand bankruptcy, as well as spinelessness and alcoholism."

For an instant Montague thought Ben was going to throw the glass at him. He stood his ground, flinching inside. He knew he needed Ben for a deviousness and ruthlessness he did not possess himself. Ben fought for control. He knew he shouldn't have another drink. For one thing, it would confuse him about when to take his medication and when to eat. But he needed it. A small one. A judicious sip and he felt better. He faced Montague who was standing stock still with most of the colour drained from his face. "Don't worry, Dad. You've put too much into this to come out empty-handed. I'll think of something, I promise."

Montague Cromwell, Jerry and Jamie Martin were at Heathrow when the Qantas flight carrying Georgia Gee and Kobi Clarke got in. Lou Faraday said he would have *liked* to be there but he had to 'see a guy about a TV thing'.

Georgia and Kobi had met in Sydney and arranged to travel together. They interrupted their conversation only to pass through customs with their light luggage. They began talking intently again as soon as they were through the arrivals procedure. Montague, who had studied the photographs Georgia and Kobi had been asked to submit, strode towards the handsome, determined-looking woman and the man with the dark wavy hair, broad nose and slightly slanted eyes. His skin was no darker than an Englishman's after a holiday in Spain.

"Ms Gee," he said. "And Dr Clarke. Welcome."

Jerry and Jamie moved forward and there were handshakes and smiles all round. Jerry gazed with open admiration at Kobi Clarke, who wore a dark suit, discreetly striped shirt and a plain silk tie. He was freshly shaven and looked as if he had slept well, which wasn't likely after an economy class flight on Qantas. Jamie Martin found his penchant for commanding women gratified by Georgia Gee, whose loose trousers, shirt and jacket were crumpled and whose makeup had faded, revealing the lines of intelligence and humour around her eyes and mouth. *She's no fool*, Jamie thought. *If Montague and Ben have something sly in mind, it better be good.*

Kobi Clarke relieved Georgia of a bag as they walked towards the taxis. He said something in her ear and she smiled. Montague Cromwell was somewhat deflated by this display of colonial *sang froid*. After the bags were placed in the taxis Kobi Clarke arranged the distribution of the travellers in a way to which no one could object and which seemed logical. He would ride with Georgia and Jerry, leaving Montague and Jamie to follow in another car.

He's a politician, Jamie thought. *Manipulation of people is second nature to him.* His view was confirmed when Kobi approached Montague and placed a reassuring hand on his shoulder.

"Mr Cromwell," he said. "Be of good cheer. Georgia has removed all my doubts. I want to sell the bloody thing as much as you do."

Georgia Gee considered herself a professional judge of character with more than twenty years' experience. She made some rapid evaluations: Montague Cromwell—a deceiver, probably of himself as well as others; Jerry—an optimist trying not to be a clinger; Jamie Martin—spent too much time as one of life's deputies, wants to be a sheriff. About Kobi Clarke she had had longer to think, and the result was complete confusion. Her powerful attraction to him was cut across by forces she didn't understand. Was it race, consanguinity, her lifelong distrust of politicians? She was distracted by the warmth of his thigh pressing against hers but she began trying to work out the precise degree of their relationship and the term to cover it.

"You're my second cousin, Georgia," Kobi said suddenly. "I'm not quite sure what I am to you."

The Gulliver Fortune

Georgia jumped. *Christ, can he read minds too?* She nodded, looked out the window and absorbed not one detail of the landscape between Heathrow and Marble Arch.

Montague had booked Kobi and Georgia into the Cumberland Hotel. Both had been in London before and they quickly deflected Montague's inanities about seeing the sights.

"We're here on business, Mr Cromwell," Georgia said. "Let's . . ."

"Monty, please."

". . . see the picture, Monty."

"And meet your son, Monty," Kobi said.

"Out of town on business," Montague mumbled.

"And there's Mr Faraday," Kobi said. "I'm not quite clear about him, I must say. Does he have an interest?"

"Not exactly," Jamie said. He explained Faraday's concerns and hopes succinctly.

"I see," Kobi said. "Well, we'll have to think about that."

Kobi stroked the skin beside his right eyebrow and Georgia noticed a star, very small, faintly tattooed near the corner of the eye. She felt a thrill run through her and was suddenly very glad that their rooms were on different floors. *If he was next door,* she thought, *I'd be kicking a hole in the wall.*

"What's the media interest been like?" Georgia said, struggling to stay professional.

"Considerable," Montague said, "but I've kept them at bay. You don't want the tabloid stuff—'Lost Turner found in junkyard' and so on."

"Don't we?" Kobi said. "Why not?"

"Doesn't do. A Turner is a national treasure, it shouldn't be babbled about by hacks who wouldn't know a Constable from a Sargent." Montague smiled at the joke, which he'd made many times before. "No. I've lined up an interview for you with the art critic from *The Times*. Very knowledgeable chap."

Georgia had the working journalist's suspicion of experts. "But can he *write?*"

"Yes, indeed."

Kobi Clarke took Georgia's arm. "Right, well, lead on, Monty. Where d'you keep the Bentley?"

"Jag, actually," Montague said.

"That'll do nicely."

The party left the hotel lobby. Montague found himself ushering Kobi and Georgia through the door like royalty, but he moved swiftly to exit before Jamie and Jerry.

"Monty's not going to put anything over on *him*," Jerry said.

Jamie nodded. "Suddenly I feel a whole lot better about this. I think Montague and Ben are going to have to watch their steps very carefully with Dr Clarke."

50

'Harwich Seascape' was being kept under lock and key at a Belsize Park gallery in which Montague Cromwell had an interest. Kobi Clarke looked the building over carefully before he consented to go through the deserted display areas to the back room, which had an old fire door. Montague fiddled with a dial mounted on the door; after a time he managed to get a satisfactory click as the opening lever slid into a housing. The stiff hinges yielded to a hard push and the door opened. He reached through and flicked on a light. The only natural light in the room filtered in dimly through a barred window of reinforced glass. Montague cocked his ear.

"Hear that hum? Temperature-controlled. Very important."

"How was the temperature in the box room?" Georgia said.

Kobi smiled. "Can't say I think much of the door, but I'm more concerned about hands-on security. Watchmen, patrols and so forth."

Montague carefully extinguished his cigar before proceeding further into the room. "No problems here."

"Oh, come on!" Georgia said. "Let's see it."

Montague selected a key from a couple fastened to his watch chain and unlocked a large cabinet that occupied most of the space inside the room. He reached inside and carefully extracted a rectangular object wrapped in a grey cloth. "Wait a moment," he said. "Who's here?"

Jerry spoke from the doorway. "You, me, Dr Clarke and Ms Gee. Jamie's gone off to check on something."

"I wonder what," Kobi Clarke murmured. "Anyway, I'm glad to see you're security-conscious, Monty. Well, as Georgia says, let's see it."

Montague unwrapped the painting and set it on an easel at about eye level. The picture was about a metre square but gave an impression of much greater size. The details—waves and clouds, rocks and beach—were not insisted upon as separate things but seemed to be intimately related and harmonious. As Georgia looked at the canvas, the streaks of blue, cream and red that defined the sea, sky and sand seemed to draw and concentrate the light in the room.

"What wonderful colours," Jerry said.

Georgia had read up on Turner a little. She recalled now Kenneth Clark's remark that Turner's use of colour to define reality and reveal truth was a revolution in sensibility. 'Harwich Seascape', with its totally compelling combination of solidity and airiness, showed her what Clark had meant. She was stunned and felt herself drawn closer. The paint was thin and lightly textured, but the sky and sea had an impression of depth and immensity.

"A fine work," Montague Cromwell said pompously.

Kobi Clarke nodded. He had little feeling for European art. A finely carved death mask from Buka excited him more, but he could feel something for this.

Georgia sneezed. The room was dusty and there seemed to be a draught coming from one of the corners. She sneezed again, wiped her eyes and wasn't sure whether the sneezing or the painting had made her feel tearful. "It's beautiful," she said. "It shouldn't leave England."

Montague sniffed and brushed some dust from a corner of the simple frame. "That remains to be seen, my dear. If the custodians of the nation's heritage think it worth their while . . ."

Jerry was busily giving the painting literary associations—Coleridge, Wordsworth. She wished that Jamie could have been there to see it with her, but he'd rushed off almost as soon as they'd left the hotel. She wondered if she could ever write a novel good enough to deserve a reproduction of the painting on the dust jacket. She found herself saying, "It'd look wonderful on a book."

Kobi laughed. "We all have our dreams, eh, Ms Gallagher? What does Mr Cromwell the Younger think of the painting?"

"Oh, Ben's seen enough of it," Montague said. "He's photographed it, measured it, X-rayed it and so on."

"Why?" Jerry said.

"Insurance," Montague said. He rewrapped the picture reverentially and restored it to the inner recesses of the cabinet. "Back to bed," he said. "It won't be long now."

Over drinks in Montague's den in Cheyne Walk, Georgia and Kobi were given the details of the search for the Gullivers, shown the documents and presented with sheaves of legal papers to sign. Georgia leafed through the papers impatiently and accepted a second of Monty's large Scotches. Kobi worked his way slowly through the release forms, agreements and terms of sale necessary to the disposal of a multi-million-pound object. He sipped a weak Scotch and water slowly.

"Seems to be in order," he said finally. "I've got a legal chap calling around tomorrow morning to take a look. If he's happy, I'm happy. Georgia?"

Georgia shrugged. "I'll be guided by you. I'd like to meet Mr Faraday, though. I'm a journalist too, don't forget. I want to make sure he doesn't scoop the pool with this thing."

Montague Cromwell beamed. "Tonight," he said. "We all meet for dinner at a little place I know. I'm sure your legal adviser will be happy, Dr Clarke."

"Kobi."

Montague's smile widened. "Kobi. Excellent. All friends, eh? A wonderful story, isn't it? Tragic about John and Catherine Gulliver and poor Susannah, of course."

"Not so hot for Juan, either," Georgia said. She was wondering what plans Kobi might have for the remainder of the afternoon.

"No," Kobi said. "And Mikhail's in a ticklish spot, isn't he? They're my cousins, d'you realize? We might go on a lecture tour together one day. Revolutionaries and dissidents. What do you think, Monty?"

"I don't think the idea'd appeal to Lou Faraday," Montague said.

Kobi laughed. "We're a motley lot, to be sure. Russians and Yids, dagoes and niggers."

Montague Cromwell looked uncomfortable and offered more drinks.

Kobi refused and stood. "Georgia, want to share a cab to the hotel? Perhaps you could call one for us, Monty? And write down the name of your little place. Let me guess, Italian?"

Montague's broad smile was back in place. "Yes, Italian. Here, I've got their card. Are you sure you wouldn't like a lift back to the hotel?"

"Quite sure," Kobi said. "Georgia and I have lots of things to talk about in private."

Montague rinsed glasses and nibbled at the nuts and olives his guests had ignored. *Randy pair*, he thought. *Could hardly wait to get down to it.* Well, he'd done everything Ben had said to do and not put a foot wrong as far as he knew. He poured his fourth drink in an hour and sipped it. He'd always drawn the line at certain things—violence for one, blackmail for another. But he was uncomfortably aware that Ben's standards might not be his. *Where did Jamie Martin disappear to?*

Montague shifted uneasily. His collar and belt felt tight, although he'd been dieting lately. He had two disquieting thoughts as his digestion struggled to cope with the whisky, olives and nuts. One, he wished he knew what Ben was up to. Secondly, he felt that Kobi Clarke would be able to read Ben like a book. *Bloody savage*, he thought.

* * *

Georgia settled back beside Kobi in the taxi, glad of her warmly lined coat and the small glow the whisky had given her. "Kobi," she said, "I feel there's something fishy here."

"I feel it too. What would the right word be for Monty? Plausible?"

"That'd be kind. He's a transparent rogue. I wonder what the son's like?"

Kobi grunted. "I suppose we could find out privately, but there isn't a lot of time. Martin and Jerry Gallagher seemed altogether better types, didn't you think?"

"Yes, definitely. Before Jamie left he said he'd ring in the morning. There's something he wants to tell us. I have the feeling that it's about the Cromwells."

"Good," Kobi said.

"Well, let's not beat about the bush," Georgia said. "What are you going to do with the money? It's funny, but I feel I can ask you."

Kobi laughed. "Yes, you can. Do you know anything about the Loluru Society?"

"I've heard of it of course, but the Australian press reports are pretty garbled. I hesitate to use the words."

"Cargo cult?"

Georgia nodded.

"There's elements of that, I suppose, but it's really a much more sophisticated movement—part political party, part secret society, part church. Strictly speaking, I should turn all the money over to the movement."

"Ah. That's hard."

"It wouldn't have been a few years ago, but things have changed. I've become politically sceptical and personally insecure."

"You don't *seem* insecure."

One of Kobi's thick black eyebrows lifted. "I wouldn't want to bore you with the whole story. I want the money in order to give something back to people my mother's family have been exploiting for years. It's partly political, partly personal. I want it badly and the wanting makes me suspicious of our Mr Cromwell. I can feel he wants something too. Possibly we want the same money. Your turn now."

Georgia told him about the idea for the independent magazine in Sydney. She became heated on the subject of media monopolies. "So the money's important to me, too."

"Suddenly, it feels as if we're all a lot of pigs sticking our noses into a trough..."

"Come on," Georgia said. "It's not..."

Kobi put his hand on her arm. "I'm sorry. I didn't mean it to sound like that. We Melanesians don't feel the way you do about pigs. Wrong choice of words. Sorry."

That was when Georgia Gee was sure that she was in love with Kobi Clarke. She reached for his hand and squeezed it. He returned the pressure and they sat in silence while the taxi swished along the wet streets and crawled when it struck heavy traffic. Georgia glanced at his intent, clean-featured profile; she realised that she had a serious wish to touch his slanting eyes with her fingertips and pass her tongue between his slightly protuberant lips. She shivered and Kobi caught the movement.

"Cold?"

"No. I'd be happy to listen to the whole story, as you call it. I've been around; I know a few things. I've seen some people trying to climb down off the hook."

The taxi turned into Oxford Street and Kobi felt in his pocket for money. He hadn't much; some savings from his parliamentary salary and a few payments from the makers of TV political documentaries. Giving an interview on Vanuatu's neutral political stance in return for the airfare to Britain had been humiliating. He was glad that Montague Cromwell was footing the bill at the Cumberland. "I'm going to take you up on that," he said. "I'll talk your ear off if I start. Jet lag or no jet lag. D'you feel any jet lag, Georgia?"

"No," she said. "And I like to hear you talk."

"You'll have to talk, too. Something's eating you, will you tell me what it is?"

"Perhaps." *Loneliness is so banal,* she thought. *How*

can I say, 'I've always felt like an orphan'? I'll have to think up something more exotic.

Kobi paid the driver and held the door for her. Heavy rain was falling and they hurried for the Cumberland's stately Victorian entrance. When they reached it Georgia found herself pressed against him, ducking her head into his shoulder against a squally blast. He put his arm around her and they passed into the lobby locked together. Kobi fumbled in his pocket.

"I can't find the bloody card thing," he said. "I've probably put it in with the American Express and all that other rubbish by habit. I prefer a key."

Georgia flourished the light plastic oblong that opened the door to her room. "Don't be such a stick-in-the-mud. These are fun."

Kobi bent and kissed her. He tasted the rain on her lips and he felt her mouth open under the pressure. The marbled and tiled lobby of the Cumberland was busy with tourists checking in and departing, lodging valuables in safety boxes and booking cabs and theatre seats, but they didn't notice.

Georgia drew back a fraction; she saw the sweat on his upper lip and felt his excitement. "God," she said. "Let's use my card and go to bed. We can do all this bloody talking later."

51

A series of meetings with film and television people in New York and Los Angeles had changed Lou Faraday. His soft Californian accent had taken on an aggressive, east coast edge. Wealth and success were his for the taking. He had decided that 'indecision' was the worst word in the dictionary. He waved his fork. "This is great veal, Monty. You sure know how to look after yourself. Great little place too."

"Great," Rachel echoed. She had dressed up for the occasion; she wore a low-cut cloth-of-gold dress that fitted her spectacular shape exactly. A silk jacket in a tiger skin pattern hung over the back of her chair. Her hair was frizzed out in a giant Afro and she wore a pale lip gloss that made her mouth sharklike in her dark face.

Montague Cromwell inclined his head graciously. The dinner was a great success. Georgia and Kobi, who virtually reeked of sex, were easily entertained. Ben and Jamie, who might have lent an antagonistic note to the proceedings, were absent. Jerry was in green, looking Irish and imaginative. Lou Faraday's account of the Stanford writing programme had excited her, and he had some good tips on getting published in the *New Yorker*. To Montague's relief, Faraday hadn't clashed with either Georgia or Jerry over rights to the Gulliver story.

"There's plenty for everyone, right?" he'd said as Rachel had slipped off the tiger skin jacket.

"Right," Rachel said. "As long as you get in with the movie deal first."

Montague, watching the unveiling of chocolate-coloured skin, had scarcely heard the reply, but he'd felt the easing of tension.

"We don't have a problem with the Bolivia angle," Lou Faraday said as Monty poured more rosé. "In fact it's a big plus." He laughed and sipped some wine. "Great. I think they must've just plain forgotten about him down there. Anyway, Amnesty International's like motherhood, everyone believes in it."

"Not me," Rachel said. She was puzzled. *This big dude from cannibal land's got a lot of stuff*, she thought. But he was less interested in her than his bread stick. The woman regarded by Rachel as on the way to grandmotherhood had all his attention. She shrugged mentally. *So he likes crow's feet*.

"The Russian's a bit of a worry," Montague murmured.

"Why is that?" Kobi Clarke's voice cut cleanly through the restaurant hubbub.

Five pairs of eyes came to rest on Montague, who lit a cigar to buy himself time.

"I had every confidence in Ben and his helper, Mr Martin," Montague said, avoiding Jerry's eyes, "and in the good sense of Kobi and Georgia. I have to admit that I booked an auction date at Westerby's some time ago."

"When for?" Lou said.

"Two weeks from now. It's long enough to get the story in the papers and for Westerby's to do what they're good at. Which is spread the word among the well-heeled."

"You're my kinda guy," Rachel breathed.

Montague beamed and puffed his corona. "Thank you, my dear. As I say, though, the Russian could be a problem."

"Call him Mikhail," Jerry said.

Montague nodded. "As you wish. Mikhail, understandably, wants to remain anonymous. I gather the Soviet government wouldn't take kindly to one of its citizens inheriting a fortune in the West."

"Things are changing in Russia," Jerry said. "Surely . . ."

"I gather they haven't changed that much," Montague said.

Lou Faraday gulped some wine and frowned. "I don't get it. Is . . . Mikhail holding out on us in some way? Won't he agree to sell?"

"Oh, no, nothing like that." Montague held the waiter off with a motion of his hand. 'You don't think we'd be celebrating like this if there were *that* big a problem, do you? By the way, they do a wonderful apple crumble here. You all must . . .'

Jerry eyed Cromwell suspiciously. "Get on with it, Monty. What's the snag?"

"I want everything to be *nice*," Montague said. "Everybody happy, that's always been my motto."

"In a pig's ass," Rachel muttered. Faraday jabbed her in the ribs.

"There's a problem with Mikhail," Montague said.

Faraday snorted. "You figure he wants to get out."

Montague looked pained. "I imagine so, but I have no definite information. All I know is that he wants anonymity, whereas La Vita . . ."

"Shit," Rachel said, "what does *he* want?"

"He wants some publicity for his book," Montague said. "Some propaganda for his cause and his release. We've been useful there. I can show you the draft press statements."

"You'd better," Rachel said.

Montague, looking forward to his apple crumble and brandy, ignored her. "Dr Clarke has made no requests but, as he would know, a certain palm will have to be greased in due time. There were problems about his travel documents."

Kobi nodded.

"What about you, Georgia?" Lou Faraday said. "What's your angle?"

Georgia scarcely heard him. She was still thinking of making love with Kobi a few hours earlier. He'd admitted his hang-up about white women to her and proceeded to show her how potent he could be with one. She'd tried to remember how long it had been since she'd had two orgasms in a single session of lovemaking. She couldn't remember, but it was a hell of a long time. She had scarcely tasted the food and hadn't drunk much of the wine. "No angle," she said. "Everything's sweet."

Montague leaned towards her. "I'm sorry. Do you mean the wine or. . . ?"

Georgia laughed. "No, Monty, the wine's okay. We've got better in Australia, but that's not what I was talking about."

"She's sweet," Kobi said, in authentic educated Australian. "It means there are no problems."

"I'm relieved and glad," Montague said. "But it leaves the problem of Mikhail."

Lou Faraday looked at Rachel, who shrugged. The movement dropped the neck of her dress down close to the tops of her nipples but Montague didn't notice. He was intent on the reaction of Faraday, who appeared to be thinking.

Georgia felt the warmth of Kobi's leg against her own. She put her hand on his thigh and stroked towards his knee, although she wanted to move her hand in the other direction. She'd kissed the tattooed stars beside his eyes as he'd held her white breasts in his brown hands. *Mikhail is Kobi's cousin*, she thought. *I should be more interested in this*.

"I don't see a problem," Lou Faraday said. He winked at Georgia and Jerry. "Are we writers or what? Do we have imagination or do we have imagination?"

Jerry blinked. "I don't quite see . . ."

"We invent something, dummy."

Jerry paled and bright spots appeared in her cheeks. Lou grinned, threw up his hands suddenly and went into a broad Brooklyn accent. "Sorry, I'm sorry. It's justa way a' talking, ya know? I don' wanna offend nobody."

"Quit it, Lou," Rachel said.

"Okay. Here's what we can do." Lou drained his wineglass and looked at Montague. "We invent a story for the press, a story to cover Mikhail. Not hard. Just change it all to Chinese, say. Translate the name. Fix the details.

Who's to know? Chinese instead of Russian. Throws the Russians off the track, and if the Chinese want to set about finding their Gulliver, let 'em. How many people've they got now?"

Kobi's eyes were dark slits. "Over a billion," he said.

Lou smiled. "My point exactly. What d'you think, Monty?"

"Brilliant," Montague said. "You've got a brilliant mind, Mr Faraday, and you've set mine completely at rest. Let's move on to dessert, shall we?"

Lou Faraday was paying his own and Rachel's expenses. Their hotel at King's Cross had small, hot rooms, a noisy elevator and carpet that seemed to have retained smells from before World War I. The bed sagged in the middle so they put the mattress on the floor and upended the frame. Rachel used the legs to hang clothes on.

She looked up from the mattress at the cracked ceiling. A silk slip fell from the bed leg onto the pillow. She threw it at the window. "This place is like the goddamn Chelsea," she said.

Lou groaned. He had proved that good wine and brandy could give you as much of a hangover as bad stuff. "You were never in the Chelsea," he said. "You're from Queens."

"I looked at it," Rachel moved her head close to his and whispered. "You could write a whole book with the roach blood from a single room."

"Jesus, Rachel. You don't have to prove how Manhattan you are at two in the a.m."

"You always gotta prove it. Tough gotta be renewed. So if we're not goin' to sleep on account of you tying on a big one, and we're not goin' to have sex for the same reason, let's talk about the man."

Lou felt the beginning of indigestion and wondered if he had a Quick-Eze in his bag. "Monty?"

"Who else? You trust him, baby?"

"No, and I don't trust his son more."

"That's a relief. I thought you mighta bought all this British shit. So what you planning to do about it?"

Lou rolled onto his side. "What can I do? The paperwork for the movie and book rights is solid. I'll do fine out of that. The British lawyers won't find anything wrong there."

"I mean the sale, dummy."

"I'll look at the auction deal, the commissions and so on, but I haven't got any direct interest there."

"You got an interest in seein' that it sells for big bucks, haven't you?"

"Sure."

"Well, where do you think that kinda money is?"

"Oh, I get it," Lou said. "You mean I should make sure Monty's put the word out to the right people—the Texans and such?"

Rachel's Afro bobbed loosely. "I wouldn't exactly call them the right kind of people. But you got it—the *rich* honkies, baby."

That's amazing," Kobi said. "Really amazing. You mean she killed him?"

"Had him killed. I think so. That's how I understand it now, although I didn't take it in properly at the time."

Kobi and Georgia were lying close together in the single bed in her room. They'd made love after getting home from Monty's dinner, slept for several hours despite the lack of space, come awake together and made love again. Now they were relaxed and peaceful with light seeping in under the window blind. As they were sketching in their lives as new lovers do, Georgia had told Kobi something about her mother and grandmother. She felt him go rigid beside her and wondered whether she'd said the wrong thing.

"What, darling? What's wrong? It's an awfully long time ago. Women were chattels, I . . ."

Kobi stroked her dark, unruly hair. "It's all right. Nothing's wrong. It's just the familiarity of it all."

Georgia struggled up on the pillows. Kobi's long body seemed to stretch beyond the end of the bed. There was grey in his hair, about the same amount as in her own, and she noticed now something she hadn't seen before—a peculiar thickness to his wrists, as if they had an extra bone in them. Her father's wrist was the same in a photograph she'd looked at often and lost many years before. *Second cousins*, she thought. *I wonder whether it matters*. She touched his head and felt him relax. "Keep talking," she said. "I'm going to make a cup of tea."

She got out of bed and pulled on a long T-shirt. She belched slightly as she tugged the shirt down. "Sorry. I don't really like veal all that much, d' you? I don't think it agrees with me."

"Was it veal? I'm ignorant about food."

"It's overrated," Georgia said. She got the electric jug and the tea making things from a cupboard and moved to the handbasin. "I must tell you about my malnutrition phase. I don't think I ever completely recovered."

"I'm glad," Kobi said. "Probably accounts for the thin covering over those delicious bones."

Georgia filled the jug, put teabags in two cups and opened the foil tops of the little milk containers. "What did you mean when you said it was familiar—what my grandmother did?"

Kobi stirred in the bed uneasily. Naturally guarded and professionally reticent, he was surprised to find that he wanted to pour everything out, tell Georgia the smallest details of his life. Even the things he was ashamed of, like his conflicts with Mora. "My mother killed my father," he said. "I'm sure of it."

He felt tears well up in his eyes as he spoke. Through them he watched Georgia prepare the tea; she poured the water and lifted and dropped the bags, added the milk. He found the ritual comforting and soothing. Georgia brought the cups back to the bed and they balanced them on their palms, blowing on the liquid to cool it.

"Tell me," she said.

They sat in the bed and drank the tea as another grey London day began. Kobi told Georgia about Sally Chan and his father's life on Rabi Island, and what his sister had told him of their mother's machinations.

"She killed him," Kobi said, "as surely as if she'd knifed him in the back."

Georgia plucked at the hem of her T-shirt. "The Gulliver men don't have a lot of luck with women, do they?"

"Carl Gulliver did, in the end," Kobi said, "and Edward too, although they had their problems."

"It seems you Gullivers can't expect an easy passage."

"You're one too, don't forget." Kobi put his hand on the back of Georgia's neck and caressed the fine bones. "What about you? How's your life been?"

"I've done all right. This is the happiest I've felt since puberty, if it's of any interest to you."

"It is." Kobi moved his head forward and kissed her. "I'll have to go to Sydney to start buying up Hong Enterprises stock, white-anting it, or whatever they call it."

"I'll be there," Georgia said.

"Maybe we can help each other. I'm sure there's some skeletons in the Hong cupboard."

"Well, your mind-reading faculty could come in handy."

Kobi stared at her. "What?"

"I've sometimes felt that you could read my mind."

"That's just extreme compatibility, or maybe my Melanesian genes. There were some *men bilong poison* back there."

"What's that?"

"Sorcerers. How do you feel about that?"

Georgia reached for his cup and put it on the bedside table next to hers. She kissed him hard. "It looks like we've got each other. Now we need the money."

52

Tashkent, Uzbek, November 1986

Mikhail Bystryi knew that what he had been doing in recent days was very dangerous, but he didn't care. Since he had received the news of his inheritance—in the form of cryptic, almost coded letters from his mother—he had felt his ties to the Union of Soviet Socialist Republics drop away like a snake's discarded skin. Another letter, passed nervously to him by an English horticultural student, had given him more information and fired him still more. It was not the money.

"It's not the money," he told Sofya Vertova. "It's you and God and Jerusalem."

Sofya touched Mikhail's arm. They were in the park near the centre of the city. It was cold; snow covered the park and gathered in grey clumps in the branches of the trees. Still, the park was the best place to meet and talk in private. It was Sunday and there were a lot of people around. All walking, all talking. Sofya wanted to embrace Mikhail, to tell him that she understood and supported him, but public demonstrations of affection drew attention and comment.

"You are saying you want to leave," she said.

"I want *us* to leave. You, me and . . ."

"Your mother?"

"Yes. Of course, she will not go." Mikhail snorted so that a long plume of steam jetted from his closely wrapped face. He and Sofya wore heavy coats, hats and scarves. "She was born in 1920-something, but she says she remembers the cossacks and the Tsars. She wants us to go. She understands about love."

Sofya Vertova loved Mikhail deeply. She wanted him and his children. She wanted to raise a Jewish family in an atmosphere of certainty—precisely what she had not had— and she was prepared to do a great many things to achieve this goal. "She is very old, Mikhail. Surely they would not . . ."

"They might," Mikhail said. "They might do anything. There would be a great deal of publicity. You know what it is like in the West. Nothing excites them more than money. If the story of the money got out after we had left, they might punish her terribly."

Sofya nodded. She had visited Vitalia Bystryi in her small flat and knew how important each creature comfort was to an old woman, how badly the loss of one metre of space, one domestic appliance, could affect her. Sofya clasped Mikhail's arm and they walked on a few steps before she spoke. She was afraid of the idea forming in her mind. The right words from Mikhail now might head it off. "What are you thinking of doing, my darling?"

"I have been talking to some people," Mikhail whispered. He bent his head close to hers and she jerked away, forcing him to move into a less suspicious stance. "I'm sorry, Sophie. You're right. We must be cautious. I've tried to find out about the ways people use to get across the border. There are a hundred ways."

A *hundred ways to be killed*, Sofya thought. She struggled to keep her voice steady. "Yes? Your mother too?"

"Of course. There are ways to do it. You can *buy* documents. You can bribe people, if you have the money."

"Have you got the money, Mikhail?"

"No. Of course not. But if I can get some of it, some of the money from the sale of the painting, then I can do these things."

Sofya squeezed his arm encouragingly and they walked on. To her, the park seemed to grow colder around them and the looming buildings that flanked it seemed to draw nearer, to overhang the tram tracks and incline towards the trees above their heads. Sofya Vertova's family had been virtually eliminated by the earthquake that devastated Tashkent in 1966. She was at school in a newly developed area of the city, in a recently constructed building that withstood the upheaval. Her parents and siblings, in the old quarter, were killed. She had been raised by an aunt and uncle who lived on the outskirts of the city. Their values—religion and education—were at once limiting and liberating. Sofya derived certainty and confidence from one strand and ambition, with a certain amount of insight and ruthlessness, from the other.

"How can you make any use of English money?" Sofya bent and picked up a handful of snow. She bunched her gloved fist around it, but not long enough for it to harden. She flung it towards a tree and the snow fluttered and fell uselessly ten feet away. "Foreign money is like that."

"Not if you know the right people," Mikhail said. "I've talked to some men at the bazaar. Don't forget that my father dealt with the gypsies. He sent messages to my mother from the gulag."

God, a romantic, Sofya thought.

"A black market exists," Mikhail said. "For money, documents, train tickets—everything!"

"So I've heard," Sofya said coolly.

"Everything can be arranged."

Sofya pointed in the direction of a food stall; the brazier where the meat was roasted and the coffee was heated and the bread was toasted stood behind a series of low, wheeled and mounted partitions, which could be moved against the direction of the wind. "I want a coffee," she said.

Mikhail changed direction, stamping snow from his boots. He was relieved at Sofya's reaction so far, having expected violent opposition from her. "I *know* it's dangerous," he said, just before they moved behind the shelter of the partitions.

Sofya nodded and touched his cheek. She was fighting down an urge to scream at him. She wanted to condemn him for being criminally stupid in the eyes of God and man. Mikhail took out his money pouch and selected some notes. Sofya imagined the pouch stuffed with American dollars and the KGB man, tipped off by the bazaar tout, holding Mikhail by the throat as he examined the money.

Mikhail frowned at her pained expression. "What's wrong?"

"Nothing. Get the coffee, darling. I'll have a cigarette."

"You shouldn't smoke. It'll kill you."

Fool, she thought. *Your mutterings in rug shops are more likely to kill me*. She knew they could get out easily and safely as tourists if they were patient and made plans. But to propose taking along an old mother was a certain giveaway. Sofya smoked and struggled with her conflicting emotions—love, anger, hope and the dangerous idea that refused to go away.

Mikhail bought coffee and hot, spicy meatballs wrapped in crusty dough. They crouched below the level of the partition on the stools the vendor provided.

"Perhaps we should wait," Sofya said.

Mikhail sipped his coffee. "For what?"

Sofya bit back the words she wanted to say and said instead, "For the picture to be sold."

"Certainly," Mikhail said. "That must happen soon."

"Have you destroyed the communications you've had?"

"Of course, darling. I'm not a fool."

Sofya bit into the meat and tasted the fat it had been rolled in and the spices. She wondered if she would miss these things in Jerusalem or New York. She thought not.

The coffee was hot but bitter. Mikhail swallowed some and grimaced. "This is terrible. Do you want sugar?"

Sofya shook her head.

"You get better coffee in Moscow," Mikhail said. "I'll be going there soon, my love. I'll talk to mother and prepare."

"How will you persuade her?"

"I will tell her that you are pregnant and that we want the child to be born in Israel."

Sofya gulped some of the bitter coffee and made her decision. *He thinks this will work with a woman who bore a child at forty to a survivor of the gulag,* she thought. *Hopeless.* She risked frostbite by taking off her glove and caressing the beard on Mikhail's firm jaw. The hairs were stiffened by the cold. "We can make that true in a way, can't we, darling?"

Mikhail kissed her. "Yes," he said. "We can." He was relieved. He had expected a barrage of opposition. Sofya's lips were soft and almost warm. He kissed her hard.

Sofya felt her body and brain respond; she felt the tingle between her thighs and the firm, logical sequence in her mind. *This is right,* she thought. She would go to Moscow before Mikhail and she would take some morphine with her and she would pay Vitalia Bystryi a visit as a dutiful almost-daughter-in-law should.

53

Cochabamba prison, Bolivia, November 1986

Juan La Vita's hair and beard were white, although he was only in his middle forties. Prison food, frequent illness and long periods spent in solitary confinement for breaches of discipline had aged him. The guards called him 'El Chico' ironically but almost everyone in the prison had forgotten about Che Guevara and the time when he and his followers had sent soldiers trotting back into town naked and barefoot.

In recent years he had learned to keep his mouth closed and to stop his hands from forming fists. The publication of his journal brought him little international attention and that only briefly. Worse still was the indifference of the prison authorities. His punishment was three months in solitary, which was nothing and it showed they didn't care. His time on the chain gang, road building, was long past, as was the gruelling labour in the bean fields. Now he worked in the prison library. He nurtured the books like babies, smoothing their crumpled pages, repairing their covers, stiffening their cracked spines. Sometimes he typed out whole chapters and glued them into the books to replace pages that had become illegible from having coffee spilt on them or, in the case of legal and philosophical books, from being underscored and written on.

Quiet and scholarly, as well read as the prison library

system permitted him to be and outwardly acquiescent, he remained 'El Chico' in his heart.

"I am a revolutionary," he had lately told a young prisoner who was checking out a translation of Hemingway's *For Whom the Bell Tolls*.

"Me too, man," the young man replied. "When I get outa here I'm going up to Nicaragua and join the Contras. Kick out those Sandanista bastards."

Juan handed him the book sadly. "Be careful. Some of the pages are loose."

The prisoner winked. "Bet it's the pages where he screws the girl in the sleeping bag. I heard about it. That's what I wanna read."

"You don't have to borrow it to do that. You can do it right here in a minute or two."

Another wink. "I wanna read it at night, man. In bed. You understand?"

Juan understood. He had travelled the whole length of the prisoner's sexual road—from fierce celibacy to frantic masturbation, desperate homosexuality and final indifference. Now *los maricons* left him alone, respecting his grey hairs and his usefulness as a gaolhouse lawyer. Juan prepared appeals and parole applications; he petitioned officials and would-be employers; he wrote to wives, sweethearts and children. Some days he was so busy he forgot to eat and almost forgot that he was in prison.

He had the correspondence with Wade Phillips on his desk and he glanced through it again in between checking books.

> *Dear Señor La Vita* [Phillips had written]
> *Our investigations confirm Mr Cromwell's credentials and the authenticity of his story. Allow me to congratulate you on this good fortune after the hardships you have endured.*

Juan had responded by authorizing Montague Cromwell to dispose of the painting 'to the greatest advantage of the joint owners' and signifying his willingness to have funds lodged in his name in a bank of his choice. He had received several telegrams from Montague Cromwell, a letter from Georgia Gee and an options proposal from Lou Faraday. Ben Cromwell had written to him about Kobi Clarke, but Juan remained uncertain about Vanuatu, as no atlas or encyclopaedia in the library recorded the name. He noted suspiciously that all details of the Russian connection were vague in Cromwell's account. *These bloody capitalists are probably cutting the Russian out*, he thought, and he wrote making it a condition of his agreement that the proceeds were to be divided four ways. Montague Cromwell's reassurance was endorsed by Wade Phillips.

The flock of correspondence had occasioned a summons to an audience with the prison governor. "What's all this?" Raoul Hoja was a lazy, impatient man nearing retirement. He wanted peace and quiet in his gaol and no black marks on his record.

Juan shrugged. He had never learned respect for authority, which had caused him trouble in his youth but was now regarded as an eccentricity. "A small inheritance," he said. "Nothing."

"A painting, *ingles*?"

"A religious work." All the correspondence had been worded cryptically and Juan doubted that the prison boasted a person of sufficient education to discover its true import.

Hoja waved an envelope bearing the Amnesty International sign. "And this? You are a terrorist, not a prisoner of conscience, whatever that is."

Juan shrugged again. "Definitions vary, *jefe*."

"Not in my prison. No trouble, you understand? No inspections, no Red Cross, no television."

Juan nodded. He had difficulty in keeping a smile from his face. Lou Faraday's memo had suggested that he stay in prison long enough 'to maximize the emotion generated by incarceration', but he kept a straight face; signs of amusement in prisoners generated fury in officials. "No trouble," he said. "They ask me if I want to get out and I say yes. What else can I say?"

It was Hoja's turn to shrug. "Your papers say you will never get out." He studied the man standing in the middle of the room. *There is something here*, he thought.

Something to be careful of. Raoul Hoja had not survived thirty years in the Bolivian bureaucracy through luck. He knew himself to be shrewd. He waved at a chair beside the desk. "Sit down, La Vita. Cigar?" He moved the box across the desk.

Juan sat. "Thanks." He took a cigar and put it in the pocket of his denim shirt. "I don't smoke, but thanks."

Hoja frowned. "What do you do with your tobacco ration?"

"I give it away."

Hoja smiled. "Ah, yes, of course. You are a communist."

"I was," Juan said.

"No more?"

"When I get out I'll see."

Hoja shook his head. "It's not smart to be a communist in Bolivia," he said. "It has never been smart."

"I know," Juan said.

The governor flicked his fingers at the door. "Back to your duties, La Vita. You are restricted to sending two letters per month."

That's enough, Juan thought.

Since then he had received another letter from Phillips. It told him of the moves to secure his release, of the approaches made to the Bolivian authorities, of their wish to avoid adverse publicity when the story of the Gulliver fortune broke.

> *Provided you make certain undertakings, our negotiators expect no difficulties in securing your release in the very near future. Technicalities remain to be resolved and the wheels turn slowly, but events in London are progressing satisfactorily . . .*

Juan checked out *The Adventures of Huckleberry Finn* to a man who had tied his landlord to a chair in the flat he rented from him, doused the room in petrol and thrown a match in through the front door.

"Thanks, Juan," the man said. "Are there any fires in this book?"

"I'm not sure. It's a long time since I read it."

"I hope there's some fires."

Juan gave the man the governor's cigar. His eye fell on Phillips's letter: 'make certain undertakings'. Well, he knew they would be made. He would play a different game from Nelson Mandela. He would renounce violence as a means of achieving political change. He would swear it on the Bible and his mother's grave. Then he would be free and very rich. He wondered just how many guns the money would buy.

54

London, December 1986

"The painting's not insured," Jamie Martin said.

Lou Faraday's eyes popped. "What! You're kidding!"

"I'm serious." Jamie looked at Kobi Clarke and Georgia Gee, who were sitting close together on the couch in Jerry's flat. Jerry stood by the window. Rachel rose from the floor where she'd been sitting with her legs crossed. Anger seemed to loosen her limbs and she flowed upwards to tower over Faraday. She shook her fist at Jamie.

"I knew there was some kinda scam going down here, you bastard. Don't . . ."

"Shut up, Rachel," Kobi said quietly. "If there is something dirty going on, Jamie and Jerry aren't behind it."

Rachel stood in front of Faraday with her legs apart and her hands on her hips. "You hear that? You going to let him talk to me like that?"

Faraday gazed at the solid, impassive figure of Kobi Clarke. "Yes," he said. "The man's talking sense. Shut up, Rachel. What do you think he got us together for? It's the Cromwells, right, Mr Martin?"

Jamie nodded. "I checked every possible insurance company. There aren't that many of them and there aren't many qualified assessors. No attempt to insure 'Harwich Seascape' has been made."

"Montague said Ben had arranged the insurance," Jerry said. "Remember?"

Georgia nodded. "Yes, that's right." Something in Jerry's voice and manner told her that there were undercurrents here. *Jerry and Ben Cromwell?* she thought. *This is going to be tricky if old wounds are still open.*

"I need a drink," Lou Faraday said.

It was eleven a.m. and the only alcohol Jerry had in the flat was a bottle of Algerian red. She opened it and poured six glasses. Faraday drank half of his measure and stared at the wall.

Kobi Clarke sipped the wine and shuddered. "God, get me back to Sydney. Well, it's pretty obvious what they've got in mind."

"Is it?" Rachel said.

Kobi put his glass down out of reach. "They're going to steal the painting and dispose of it some way beneficial to them and non-beneficial to us."

"How do you figure that?" Lou said.

Georgia looked at Jerry, who was staring miserably out of the window. "We've been naive. Those security arrangements were only so-so. If the painting had been properly insured the insurers would've insisted on much tighter security."

"Yes," Jamie said. "And now, if the picture's stolen, there's no insurance investigation to contend with. No awkward questions. The Cromwells look careless, incompetent even, but no multi-million-pound insurance company is out of pocket and on their backs."

"No story," Rachel said. "Who wants a story with no ending? We're the only ones . . . whadidya call it, outa pocket?"

"Don't forget Mikhail and Juan," Jerry said. She drank her wine without tasting it. "Jamie and I knew that they . . . Montague and Ben, were up to something. Montague wanted to close the investigation down before it reached you, Kobi. They've never been interested in seeing justice done, or the truth, or whatever."

Georgia stood and moved to the window beside Jerry. "I haven't met Ben Cromwell," she said. "But the way you say his name suggests you knew him pretty well. Is he capable of this—defrauding everybody?"

Jerry thought about Ben's perpetual air of grievance, the half-truths, the drinking, the deceptions. "Yes," she said miserably. "Yes, I think so."

Georgia put her hand on Jerry's shoulder. "Don't worry. It won't happen. Kobi?"

Rachel watched Kobi Clarke respond to Georgia's voice. *I could show him shaved pussy with a bow and he wouldn't notice*, she thought. The large man in the immaculate dark suit, discreetly striped shirt and plain tie looked like one of the diplomats she'd seen around the UN building on First Avenue. Now he got up from his chair and moved to the centre of the room. He looked intently at Lou Faraday, smiled at Georgia and Jerry and favoured Jamie Martin with an appreciative nod. "Thank you for this, Jamie," he said. "I take it the Cromwells don't know of your suspicions?"

"No," Jamie said.

"Then we have an advantage."

Faraday sounded weary. "Should we go to the cops?"

Kobi shook his head. "I don't think so. The safe thing to do would be to arrange to insure the painting. But it would be very slow and costly. The Cromwells might try to frustrate us. I doubt we could arrange a sale for . . ."

"A year, possibly," Jerry said. "Once the lawyers and insurance people got into it. Montague *has* arranged an auction for the end of the month. I've seen the brochures—they're flashy and a bit vulgar, but . . ."

"Nothing wrong with that," Lou Faraday said. "Money's the vulgarest thing there is. I don't like the sound of a year wait. Too long. Who knows what stories could break in a year? Billy Graham might get AIDS. You got anything in mind, ah . . . Kobi?"

"Jamie?" Kobi said.

"I thought we might try to steal the painting ourselves, but that's about as far as I got."

"Great for the story," Faraday said.

Georgia laughed. "And substitute a copy."

"Hey," Rachel said, "not bad. What's the thing look like? I can paint. I've done some great stuff on subway carriages."

Everyone laughed and the tension in the room eased. Jerry described how she'd used the key to enter Montague's house and keep tabs on the progress of the investigation. She undertook to go into the house again.

"With me along," Jamie said.

Kobi Clarke made notes on one of Jerry's writing pads. "The auction house must have some insurance arrangements," he said. "Maybe we can find a way to move the cover forward discreetly. It'd also help if we could find out why the Cromwells are playing fast and loose. Any ideas, Jerry?"

Jerry shrugged. "Money for Montague, I suppose. He doesn't care about anything else much, except . . . appearances. With Ben, I don't know. Ben hates the world."

Kobi made a note. "Now, has anybody got any money? I mean several hundred pounds, perhaps a thousand."

Jerry and Jamie said they might have about half that between them.

"You look like *you* got money," Rachel said.

Kobi smiled. "Thank you, but I haven't. If I don't eat in the hotel where Monty's paying the bill I don't eat at all."

"I've got some," Georgia said, "why d'we need it?"

Kobi tore the top sheet from the pad. "To hire help. We have to start guarding the bloody picture ourselves. Round the clock. Night and day."

55

Three nights later Jamie Martin got an urgent call from one of the private detectives he had hired to watch the gallery where 'Harwich Seascape' was stored. He immediately phoned Kobi Clarke. The two men met the detective, a sharp-featured Scot named Livingstone, in a doorway across the street from the gallery.

"What's going on?" Jamie said.

Livingstone pulled his coat collar up against the sharp wind. "It's a wee bit difficult to figure out. There's someone on the roof and there's another couple of laddies around the back. The watchman on this shift likes a drop and he's had a few too many. He's sitting in his bloody car, half asleep."

"How many ways are there down from the roof?" Kobi said.

Livingstone admired a man who could ask the right question. He pointed to the corner of the building. "Just the one," he said. "See there, where you can get from the fence up onto that low section of the roof? It's thirty-foot drops everywhere else. I checked."

"Other buildings?" Kobi said.

Livingstone shook his head. "No way. Carl Lewis couldn't make the jumps. That's where he went up and that's where he's got to come down. There's a skylight on the next stage of the roof."

Jamie clenched his fists inside his overcoat pockets. Like many scholars, he dreamed of being a man of action but, now that the moment had seemingly arrived, he was apprehensive. "What are the other two doing?"

"We'll know in a minute," Livingstone said. "Young Charlie Bow'll be along to give us the drum."

A chunky man in a quilted jacket and wearing a knitted cap appeared from nowhere. His trainers had made no sound on the footpath.

"Charlie," Livingstone said. "These're the gaffers. What can you tell us?"

"It's a torch job, man," Charlie said. His accent was London—West Indian. "Looks like they're waitin' for the geezer on the roof to come down and then—zappo! They've got the gear to blow the wiring and boost the heat."

Jamie was puzzled. "What?"

"Electrical fire," Livingstone said. "It's the modern way. What d'we do, gents?"

A car swished quietly past on the wet street, then another. A few lights showed in the surrounding buildings, but it was two a.m. and the district was quiet. Kobi surveyed the street carefully. A truck was parked close to where the roof climber would have to descend. Once down he had three choices—left or right along the street, or down the lane that ran beside the gallery.

Livingstone appeared to read Kobi's mind. "He'll go right. He's got a vehicle down there."

Charlie rubbed his hands together and jammed them into the pockets of his jacket. "He can signal the other geezers from the footpath. They're at the end of the lane. A whistle maybe, or a flashlight."

"He'll be carrying something," Kobi said. "A whistle's the best bet. Okay, Charlie, you and me'll be over by the truck. We'll grab him as soon as he comes down."

"What about us?" Jamie said.

Kobi's teeth flashed in the darkness. "He may have a gun. If he does you'll have to improvise. You in, Charlie?"

Charlie Bow didn't know what to make of the geezer with the dark skin and crinkly hair who talked like a professor but looked as if he could kick heads. He nodded. "In, man," he said.

Livingstone gripped the sleeve of Kobi's coat. "The important item is what the man on the roof's carrying, right?"

Kobi thought of Mikhail and Juan La Vita, and Georgia. He looked at Jamie who nodded. "Right," Kobi said. "Keep your eye on it but don't interfere unless you have to."

Kobi and Charlie scuttled across the road and crouched behind the truck. After a few minutes Kobi heard a scraping on the roof and a man appeared, briefly silhouetted against the sky. He dropped down onto the low part of the roof. He was carrying something under his arm. Kobi's gestures left Charlie in no doubt as to what they were going to do. The man crept cautiously across the roof, turned and settled himself on its edge. He waited until he was satisfied about his balance, then took a long step onto the top of the fence, pushed off hard and prepared to make what was really a broken leap to the pavement. Charlie and Kobi moved as the man committed himself to the jump. He hit the footpath, nicely bent at the knees and with his bundle safe under his arm.

Kobi's arm locked around the man's neck and cut off his wind. He dropped the bundle and Charlie scooped it up. Kobi forced the man's arms up behind his back and drove him hard into the wall. He yelped as his nose hit the cement. Kobi held him against the wall with one hand and, reaching around, gripped his scrotum with the other.

"What's the signal?" he hissed. "Quickly and don't piss me around or I'll turn your balls to soup." He squeezed hard.

The man's voice was a squeal of terror. "I whistle twice when I get down."

"Do it!"

"Hey, man," Charlie whispered, "they'll torch the whole place."

"I know," Kobi said. He squeezed again. "Whistle, and make it loud."

The man whistled, his fear producing two solid rushes of sound. Kobi hustled him across the street to the doorway. Charlie handed the bundle to Jamie. "What now?" Jamie said.

Kobi kept his prisoner's face pressed against the brick wall. "Watch," he said.

They waited. A light filled one of the windows in the gallery; then it seemed to spread to other windows and a roaring sound followed which blew glass out in all directions. Flames leapt from the building and cascades of sparks sputtered up into the dark sky.

Kobi turned his man around and let him see the blaze. "Your name is?"

"Where do you get off . . ."

Kobi hit him in the stomach.

"Blake," the man said. "Blake."

"Where was the painting going, Mr Blake?"

Blake didn't speak.

"Do you want to be here when the police come?"

Blake shook his head. "I've got a motor down the street. I was to pick him up in Earl's Court and give him the picture."

"Good idea," Kobi said. "Let's do that. What does Ben Cromwell look like, Jamie?"

Jamie described Ben, but Blake shook his head. "Phone job," he said. "I've never seen the man who set it up."

Kobi pushed Blake out onto the footpath. "Hang onto the picture, Jamie. Would you and Mr Livingstone and Charlie care to follow us?"

The sirens were wailing as Blake pulled the blue Ford Escort away from the kerb. Kobi checked that Livingstone was behind them in his Datsun as they drove through the quiet steets.

"Paid up front, were you?" Kobi said.

Blake shook a cigarette out as he waited for a roundabout to clear. "Half."

"Think yourself lucky."

Blake lit the cigarette and drove, following the signs south to SW5. He drove cautiously, nervously aware of the big man who sat silent and menacing beside him. The Escort turned into Old Brompton Road. Blake said, "He's supposed to be on the corner there, by the Wimpy. He's got the make and number of the car. I circle the block until he flags me. Christ, why don't you just drive the fucking car and let me go?"

Kobi didn't reply. After slowing and passing the corner with no result, he told Blake to stop. He took the keys from the ignition and stood by the driver's door while the Datsun drew abreast. Kobi told Livingstone what was happening. The detective nodded and waited while Kobi got into the back seat of the Escort. He passed the keys to Blake and hunched down in the darkness. "Just play the game out, Blake. Don't do anything silly."

The traffic was light and after three circuits Kobi wondered whether the Escort and Datsun had a suspicious appearance of travelling in tandem. He risked a glance through the rear window and saw that Livingstone was holding his car well back and driving tentatively, encouraging other cars to pass him. The fifth time the Escort approached the corner a tall, dark-haired man stepped from the kerb and raised his hand.

"This is it," Blake said.

Kobi hissed, "Stop, reach over and open the door. Don't say a word."

Blake complied. The interior light came on, revealing the man's dark hair and eyes, well-defined features and expression of arrogant hostility. He sat in the passenger seat and slammed the door clumsily. "You're late. Where is it?"

Blake didn't speak. He engaged first gear and inched the car forward.

"Where's the bloody painting?"

Kobi sat up and depressed the knob that locked the front passenger seat door. "Good evening, Mr Cromwell," he said. "My name is Kobi Clarke."

Ben's head whipped around. He stared at the impassive dark face and expelled a long breath, heavily flavoured with whisky. Blake hit the brakes and jumped from the car, but the Datsun was already alongside and Charlie Bow was out on the road and blocking Blake before he took a step. Jamie Martin got out of the Datsun and stood, caught in the Escort's headlights. The rolled bundle under his arm was plainly visible.

"Jesus Christ." Ben Cromwell's voice was a shocked, booze-blurred mumble.

"We've got a lot of talking to do, Mr Cromwell," Kobi said. "I think we'd better go and see Monty, don't you?"

56

The auction rooms of Westerby International Ltd were in an imposing building in the Strand, a block from Australia House and close to other embassies and consulates. The marble steps and granite pillars promised solidity and respectability, the thick pile carpets suggested discretion. A touch of opulence was given by the brocade curtains over the windows and fringing the stage on which the items for sale were to be displayed. On the night of the auctioning of 'Harwich Seascape', a traditional glass of champagne was served in the anteroom to all of those present by invitation. For the press, the TV crew, several art students and the security men, there was orange juice.

A hundred and fifty people packed into the small auditorium, in which the seating was arranged with an eye to protocol and practicality. The best view and sight of the auctioneer was afforded by seats to his right, where two men and a woman sat at desks equipped with sophisticated telephone hookups. They would receive bids from principals in Europe, America and Hong Kong. The group, which the press had dubbed 'Cromwell's army'—Montague and Ben, Jerry Gallagher, Jamie Martin, Kobi Clarke, Georgia Gee, Lou Faraday and Rachel Hattie Brown—sat in the front row on a level with the auctioneer's knees.

Harvey Peel was an art addict; the greatest moment in his life so far had been when he'd lowered his hammer, almost reverentially, on the sale of a Gauguin for eight million pounds. He was proud of his profession—he thought art was the most important thing in the world and believed in securing top prices for it. "No other measurement counts," he once told an interviewer. "I expect to live to see a Van Gogh fetch a billion dollars." This attitude appealed mightily to the firms that handled the sales of paintings, and to vendors. Harvey Peel was in demand as a consultant, valuer, go-between and auctioneer. He was incorruptible and he charged moderate fees for his work.

The sound of conversation in the room steadied to a low hum; there was a smell of expensive tobacco and wine in the air, but it came from the bodies of the people—smoking, drinking and eating were strictly banned in the auction room out of deference to the works on display. Harvey Peel had been known to frown at persistent coughers as though their microbes might nibble at the surface of a Gainsborough. The Westerby directors had heeded his injunction to keep the TV cameras at the furthest possible distance. For this, Harvey Peel had two reasons. One, he was a vain man and knew that his tall, spare figure looked best in long shot. His hair was combed carefully to conceal a bald patch. Secondly, he still thought of cameras in terms of men ducking under black hoods and igniting flares. He feared fire, the great enemy of art, and he loathed photography for its pretensions.

The auction got under way with a number of noteworthy items—a Corot, two Turner drawings, a pleasant Roscoe landscape—attracting polite interest and attractive bids.

"Preliminaries to the main event," Lou Faraday whispered to Kobi Clarke. Ever since Kobi had told him about thwarting Ben Cromwell's plan to steal the painting, he had been an open-mouthed admirer of Kobi's.

Kobi nodded. He noticed that Faraday had a film of sweat on his upper lip. The American was the only one in their party wearing a dinner suit, but even the stiff shirt, waistcoat and jacket shouldn't have made him sweat in the cool room. "What's wrong?" he said.

Faraday's hands twisted the gold-edged auction catalogue out of shape. "What do you mean?"

"You're nervous." Kobi glanced at Rachel who was wearing the cloth-of-gold dress again. The dress was somewhat crumpled and Rachel had apparently managed more than one glass of champagne. Her eyes, under gold-dusted lids, sparkled hectically.

"I'm bidding," Faraday said. "You'd be nervous."

"I'd be petrified. How can you bid?"

"Shh." Georgia, sitting next to Kobi, waved her catalogue.

In the pause after the Corot had fetched a handsome price and the organizers were preparing the next item, Faraday beckoned to Jamie Martin to step out to the room set aside for smokers. Jamie's eyes watered when he entered the stark, foggy room which seemed to be furnished with ashtrays. Several men and women stood around puffing nervously.

Faraday drew Jamie away from a man who was craning towards them as he lit a cigarette from the butt of another. He dropped his voice. "I'm bidding. I'm acting for Dahlia Raymond."

"What's that?"

"Not that. She! She's only the hottest producer in Hollywood right now and she's *personally* going to produce *The Gullivers*."

"The film?"

"Right, and maybe a TV series later. Who knows? Dahlia thinks the painting'd be a great investment the way art prices're going. Plus we can use it in the picture. You can't beat authentic."

"You can get it," Jamie said, "if you've got the money."

"I know you Britishers think we're weird. You're right. We are. So's everyone. I live in the richest country in the world and you wouldn't believe how hard it is to make a buck. Anyway, are you sure that asshole Cromwell hasn't got some trick up his sleeve? This auction's the real McCoy?"

Jamie recalled the three a.m. meeting at Montague Cromwell's house—the recriminations, the humiliation of

Ben Cromwell, the deal struck. "Yes," he said. "It's a genuine auction."

"Good. Now, what's the Turner going to bring?"

"I haven't the faintest idea."

"Christ! There's no one I can cut a deal with?"

Jamie laughed and turned away.

Faraday came after him, babbling, "Look, this is important. The producer reckons to get the budget of the movie back from selling the painting later. The budget's like twenty-five million above the line."

"So how much can you *bid*?"

"I don't know. I gotta use my judgment."

"What if the film's a flop? It could actually *devalue* the picture. Have you thought of that?"

"Dahlia's a gambler, you've got to understand. That's the way it is. If the movie rates she cleans up, if it doesn't she's down the toilet, but not all the way down maybe, if she's got the picture."

Jamie was suddenly weary of the whole thing. The tight, strained looks on the faces of Montague and Ben Cromwell, as they sat like prisoners awaiting sentence, oppressed him. He wanted to go somewhere with Jerry. Somewhere clean—on the water or amid the trees.

"I'm working for peanuts," Faraday said. "I'm on points. If we make it big I'm on easy street, if not . . ."

"You're down the toilet?"

"Yeah. I'll be comfortable around the five-million mark."

"It depends who's here, Lou."

"I don't like the look of those phones. Who's on the other end, some sheik?"

"That's the way it is, Lou."

"Yeah," Faraday said.

Kobi Clarke felt Georgia's fingers intertwine with his own as 'Harwich Seascape' was lifted onto the easel. He glanced away from the picture at her fine, firm profile; his eye travelled down her body, taking in the swell of her breasts under a grey silk blouse and the easy elegance of her loose black trousers and calf-high boots. The warring, disparate elements in his nature—the political calculation and personal recklessness, the suspicion and the need to be loved—seemed to fuse and find harmony when he was with her.

"You own all the sky in the right quadrant," Georgia whispered.

"What about you?"

"I own the sea underneath it."

"Okay, I wouldn't mind the boat, though."

"That's Mikhail's. And Juan's got the cliffs."

"Right." Kobi lifted her hand and kissed it. "Here we go."

Montague Cromwell shook his head. "This should have been a triumph," he said. "Instead, it's a disaster."

Ben Cromwell, present and sober as part of the deal struck with Kobi Clarke, said nothing.

"I can't believe it," Jerry said. "Lou Faraday's really going to bid?"

Jamie grinned. "He's wearing a dinner jacket, isn't he?"

Georgia, sitting on Jerry's right, whispered in her ear, "I've heard one of the Australian billionaires is interested."

"You mean Murdoch?"

"He's American now."

"Oh, yes. Of course he is. Well, I hope it stays in England."

Jamie pointed to the telephones. "I don't think that's Maggie Thatcher ringing," he said.

"Go to it, baby!" Rachel dug her fingers into Lou Faraday's thigh.

"That hurts!"

"Not as much as you'll hurt if you don't get that picture. My instinct tells me the deal hangs on it."

"Christ," Faraday said. "Thanks a lot."

"This is the big time, Lou. You cut it here or you don't cut it."

Lou glanced at the men and women further along in the front row. He felt overdressed. A man in a denim suit with no tie was casually doodling on the catalogue. Lou envied his calm. A woman in the second row was working a pocket calculator with intense concentration. She looked up and Faraday was convinced that she caught the eye of the woman manning one of the telephones. *Shit, this is a tough game,* he thought.

Rachel's fingers dug in again. "Give me the proxy if you're worried. I'll bid their balls off."

"Shut the fuck up, Rachel," Faraday said.

"Ladies and gentlemen," Harvey Peel's voice, firm and resonant, came through the sound system. "Acting on behalf of the executors of the estate of the late John Gulliver, through the agency of Montague Cromwell Esquire, Westerby International offers for sale 'Harwich Seascape', by the most notable of all British landscape artists, Joseph Mallord William Turner. As many of you will know, the painting, executed in the second last year of the artist's life, is mentioned by Ruskin, and a photograph of the work by William Fox Talbot forms part of the collection of the Royal Photographic Society.

"I will not dwell on the merits of the work. They are self-evident. All of the techniques and understandings of light and form for which Turner is justly renowned are on display in the painting before you."

Peel had taken up a place in which he tantalizingly obscured the left half of the painting which, in a handsome gilt frame, sat on a sturdy easel in front of a black velvet backcloth. Now he stepped aside and allowed the audience an unobstructed view. Glancing around, Kobi Clarke saw spectacles adjusted and moustaches stroked. Georgia stifled a yawn.

"I'm not getting enough sleep," she said.

"An historic work, ladies and gentlemen, with a fascinating history. I invite your bids."

Lou Faraday tucked his thumb firmly into his palm and held up the hand with the fingers extended.

Peel's tiny nod turned all eyes on Faraday.

"Four million pounds," he said.

"A respectable opening," Peel said. "In view of it I will accept bids in lots of one quarter of one million pounds."

The woman with the calculator nodded twice.

"Four and one half million pounds."

The man in the denim suit nodded.

"Four million seven hundred and fifty thousand pounds."

Faraday released his thumb and held up his hand.

"Five million pounds."

The price crept up from a scattering of bidders around the room. After the woman with the calculator had communicated by a signal with one of the telephone operators and bid seven and a half million pounds, Peel received slips of paper from a Westerby employee who had circulated discreetly among the bidders. Lou nodded.

"Eight million pounds." Peel glanced at a slip.

The man in the denim suit tapped his catalogue against his knee.

"Eight million two hundred and fifty pounds."

A signal from the woman on the telephone.

"Eight and one half million pounds."

"Go for it, baby," Rachel hissed.

Lou nodded twice.

"Nine million pounds, ladies and gentlemen. The bid is nine million pounds." The tiny nod again, this time to the woman with the calculator. "Against you, madam. The bid is nine million pounds."

A stillness came over the room. Two of the telephones were replaced quietly in their cradles and the sounds of breaths being slowly expelled and joints clicking told Harvey Peel what he needed to know. "Going once at nine million pounds. Going twice. Are you done, silent, finished?" He raised a small wooden mallet from a post on the lectern where his microphone was mounted and tapped it on the wood. A sharp popping sound came through the loudspeaker and Peel glanced quickly at his slip of paper. "Sold to Mr L. Faraday for the sum of nine million pounds. Congratulations, sir. Thank you, ladies and gentlemen."

Epilogue

57

Kobi Clarke and Georgia Gee were married in Amsterdam in March 1987. As a sideline to their European honeymoon, they located members of the Riebe family in that city, some of whom acted as witnesses to their marriage and toasted them in schnapps afterwards.

In November 1988, the first issue of the independent magazine *Inside Out*, co-edited by Georgia Gee Clarke, appeared in Sydney. It contained an article by Kobi Clarke critical of the financial operations of certain Pacific trading companies, especially Hong Enterprises. The company's stock lost value on the Sydney Exchange and Kobi Clarke was an energetic buyer.

In April of the same year Mikhail Bystryi and Sofya Vertova arrived separately in Basle, Switzerland. Each travelled under an assumed name, using documents that had cost Mikhail a great deal of money. He paid the bulk of the price in Basle after gaining access to the funds lodged for him there. After spending a few days in Switzerland, Mikhail and Sofya travelled together to Israel. Carefully concealed in Mikhail's luggage was a small box that contained the ashes of his mother.

Juan Gulliver La Vita was released from prison in April 1987. He had signed a statement renouncing violence as a means to achieving political ends and had been restored to full citizenship rights in Bolivia. Immediately on his release he was contacted by Wade Phillips of Amnesty International. Juan flew to the United States with Phillips and met members of the committees that had petitioned for his release. In May he signified his intention to apply for United States citizenship declaring assets in excess of several million dollars. In his statement he described himself as 'a fulltime, voluntary research officer for Amnesty International'.

One of Jerry Gallagher's stories, entitled 'The Orphans', was published in *Writing Now* (1), 1987. Jamie Martin was appointed to a lectureship in social history at the University of Devonshire. They spend weekends together in Exeter and London along with a portable word processor—Jerry is writing a novel and Jamie is preparing his thesis for publication.

In May 1987, Benjamin Cromwell was sentenced to three years' imprisonment for issuing a false company prospectus, misuse of Her Majesty's mails and conspiracy to commit fraud. In the same month, Montague Cromwell was declared bankrupt in his absence, having failed to respond to legal summonses. The court was informed that he appeared to have left the country and the machinery was put in motion to dispose of his assets in the favour of his creditors.

Lou Faraday's edition of his uncle's novel was submitted to the University of South Arkansas Press in June 1987. His script *The Gullivers* went through five drafts under the supervision of Dahlia Raymond, who announced in August 1987 that the project was 'on hold'. Rachel Hattie Brown became Ms Raymond's personal assistant and live-in companion, with special responsibility for New York office liaison.

In December 1987 'Harwich Seascape' was stolen from a safe in the office of Dahlia Raymond, head of

Albion Pictures, located in Glendale, Los Angeles, California. After an extensive investigation, the police were unable to bring any charges. In January 1988, a man who had been identified by 'a reliable source' to the London *Daily Mail*'s correspondent in Mexico City as Montague Ireton Cromwell, gave the journalist an interview. The man, who was heavily bearded, wore dark glasses and appeared to be affluent, refused to confirm or deny that he was Montague Cromwell. On the theft of 'Harwich Seascape' he commented: "I know, from my long experience with the art world, that these things are done. Almost certainly, that beautiful painting now hangs in some Texas billionaire's mansion and he goes to look at it after swimming in his pool and drinking martinis. It's absolutely deplorable."